D1042263

DAUGHTER
OF THE
CENTAURS

DAUGHTER
OF THE
CENTAURS

CENTAURIAD BOOK I

Kate Klimo

RANDOM HOUSE   NEW YORK

Text copyright © 2012 by Kate Klimo
Jacket art copyright © 2012. Front cover: picturegarden. Back cover and p. xi: Nick Sokoloff.

All rights reserved. Published in the United States by Random House Children's Books, a division of Random House, Inc., New York.

Random House and the colophon are registered trademarks of Random House, Inc.

Visit us on the Web! randomhouse.com/teens

Educators and librarians, for a variety of teaching tools, visit us at randomhouse.com/teachers

Library of Congress Cataloging-in-Publication Data
Klimo, Kate.
Daughter of the centaurs / Kate Klimo. — 1st ed.
p. cm. — (Centauriad ; bk. 1)
Summary: Alone after her village is destroyed by Leatherwings, young Malora and her father's horse, Sky, survive on their own with a herd of wild horses until she finds a new home with a civilization of centaurs.
ISBN 978-0-375-86975-4 (trade) — ISBN 978-0-375-96975-1 (lib. bdg.) — ISBN 978-0-375-87137-5 (trade pbk.) — ISBN 978-0-375-98542-3 (ebook)
[1. Survival—Fiction. 2. Horses—Fiction. 3. Centaurs—Fiction. 4. Fantasy.] I. Title.
PZ7.R719693 Dau 2012 [Fic]—dc22 2010052503

Printed in the United States of America
10 9 8 7 6 5 4 3 2 1
First Edition

For Bob Jeffreys, master horseman.
And for Mallory, who wanted a story about centaurs.

Contents

Haven't you sometimes seen a cloud
that looked like a centaur?
—*The Clouds,* by Aristophanes

There appeared a chariot of fire, and horses of fire,
and parted them both asunder; and Elijah went up
by a whirlwind to heaven.
—Second book of Kings, 2:11

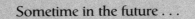

Sometime in the future . . .

CHAPTER I

Jayke's Rope

For as long as she can remember, Malora has dreamed of dancing with horses.

"Daughter of the Mountains," Malora's mother calls her, for her skin and hair are the dusky red-brown of the rocks, and her upturned eyes—so like her father's—are the vivid blue-green of the nuggets of malachite that dot the streams running down from the peaks. But when Malora hears herself so called, she frowns. "No!" she insists. "Not the mountains! I am the Daughter of the *Plains*."

For the horses come from the plains.

These are the days when the People occupy the Settlement, a mere one hundred men, women, and children living together in a canyon in the shadow of the mountains that rear up over the plains running to the north. From this canyon, the men ride out on horseback every dawn to hunt, leaving the women to keep the houses and raise the children. Like all the women, Malora's mother has a secondary job, and hers is healer. She expects her daughter to follow in her footsteps, as she has in those of her own mother, and so on, as far back as any of them can remember, to the time of the Grandparents. Malora is an only child, as well as the sole survivor of a juvenile epidemic that wiped out all the children born within three years of her. Many in the Settlement believe that it was her mother's skill at healing that saved Malora and, while no one can prove it, her mother's witchery that killed all the others. Malora knows this to be ridiculous, but it has discouraged her from pursuing the healing arts.

Malora's father, Jayke, is a master horseman, and what she wants, more than anything, is to ride and hunt as he does, wheeling about and charging off, bow and arrows strapped to her back. As fond and indulgent as he is of Malora, Jayke does his best, without being unkind, to discourage this ambition in her. No one knows better than he how dangerous horses and hunting can be. His broad-shouldered, rangy body, with its white scrawl of scars writ large, its litany of broken bones, and its nearly constant complaint of aching joints that only his wife's herbal liniment can satisfy, is testimony to this fact. Malora likes to point to each scar and get him to tell her the story behind it; the stories, after many tellings, are pared down to a kind of point-and-response game:

"Horse kick."

"Boar gore."

"Bull elephant tusk."

"Rhino charge."

Malora, a sturdy and independent eleven years old, tags along behind Jayke like a barn cat as he inspects the horses for ticks. "Run along and grind herbs with your mother. Do you want to end up like the Simple One?" he asks her.

The Simple One is Aron, whose horse, spooked by an asp, bucked him when he was a child, cracking his skull like an ostrich egg against a sharp rock. Ever since, Aron has been as simple as a five-year-old, though he has retained enough sense to be an adequate stable boy and an oddly fitting companion to Malora. While their actual age difference is fifteen years, she has outsmarted him since she was three. Yet there are things about horses he can still teach her. Things like: "Never feed a horse at the same time every day, Malora. If the horse knows the food is coming, her stomach will start a-boiling and bubbling, and before long she's burned a big hole in it. If she doesn't know when the food is coming, her stomach simmers down and she waits."

Or: "Never come up on a horse you don't know when he is at his feed. He'll think you're trying to take it away from him, and he might attack you."

Or: "Never try to catch a horse who is all stirred up. Ignore her for a while and pretty soon she'll walk right up to you."

"I wouldn't mind being like Aron," Malora says to her father. "He gets to sleep with the horses."

"What about Stumpy Eld?" Jayke asks. Stumpy Eld lost the tips of the fingers on one hand to the gnashing teeth of an angry stallion.

"He came at the stallion with an open palm," Malora says. "How many times have you told him never to do that?"

And then there is Gar, Jayke's best friend, whose limp is the result of the lightning-quick kick of a feisty mare.

"Horses kick," Malora says with a world-weary sigh worthy of Jayke.

"My point exactly! You can never be too careful around horses," Jayke says, "and no one can be careful *all* the time."

"I can be at least as careful as you," Malora says, indicating with her little finger the head of a tick he has missed.

All else having failed, Jayke says, "Look at these brutes," pointing to the two long rows of bobbing horse heads facing into the stable aisle. As if to illustrate his point, one of them lands a thunderous kick on the side of the stall. "And look at you. How do you expect them to pay you any mind when you're no bigger than a rabbit?"

Malora has seen rabbits streak across the paddock and send the horses into a tail-whipping tizzy until Jayke goes among them and gentles them with his low, steady voice and his large, rough hands with their blunt-tipped fingers. Only Jayke can enter the paddock when they are riled, because he has made himself one of them. He is, in a manner of speaking, the lead horse. One day, the horses will follow her lead the way they do her father's. Meanwhile, Malora, side by side with Aron, peers through the slats in the training-pen fence and watches Jayke work.

Jayke works each horse every day in a ring made from upright trunks of ironwood saplings pounded into the earth. He has but one training tool: a long, tightly braided black-and-white rope with one frayed end. Attaching the opposite end to the rope halter, he then runs the horse in a circle around him, three turns in one direction, followed by three in the other. Spinning the horse, he calls it. When spinning, he moves very little, remaining at the center of the circle and turning slowly in place. To change the direction of the horse's movement, he has only to reverse the position of his hands on the rope and step to the other side of the horse's nose. To set the horse to spinning again takes only the pointing finger, then the pressure of his glance, first on the horse's neck and then on its rump. He has a way of inviting the horse to move that can be as subtle as a single brow raised in expectation or as dramatic as a flapping of both arms. To make the horse stop, Jayke stops and the horse turns to face him. Other times, a head cocked at the hindquarters can cause the horse to shift its back legs and halt.

When horses are reluctant to be Jayke's partner, Jayke's eyes turn as hard as a stallion's chasing yearlings off his hay. He will bray at them and crack the frayed end of the rope like a whip. But with most of them, all Jayke has to do is lift a hand. With a few, he can dispense with the rope altogether and merely point to get the horse spinning. To make the horse back up, he frowns and waggles an imaginary rope; to bring the horse forward, he hauls the "rope" in with a warm and welcoming smile.

On his own horse, Sky, a majestic stallion with a coat of sleek black and eyes of an unsettling shade of blue, Jayke rides without a bridle and reins, keeping his hands free to work his bow. He looks with his whole body in the direction he wishes to go, then squeezes the horse's sides with his calves and pushes with his seat to urge him forward. The great beast picks up his hindquarters and goes wherever Jayke's eyes are focused.

Every night, before sleep, Malora lies in her bed and imagines herself as the steadily turning hub of some horse's rolling wheel. When the wheel is spinning smoothly, first in one direction and then the other, she urges the horse to break out and follow her in an elaborate dance of zigzags and spirals and loops and wide, graceful arcs. When she steps, the horse steps. Wherever she goes, the horse comes along. And all the time, the horse's ears swivel to follow her, eyes looking to her for the next move, the invisible link between them powerful and forged from love and trust and day after day of working together.

"One day I'll ride Sky alone," Malora boasts to Aron. Malora rides Sky with her father all the time, one of his arms wrapped around her waist while she clutches the saddle horn with both hands, her legs as widely splayed as if she were mounted on an elephant.

When Jayke and six other men dragged Sky in off the plains, furious and snorting, everyone told Jayke that Sky was too much horse, even for him—but Jayke proved them all wrong.

Aron tells Malora, "Sky is not too much horse for you, either, Malora Thora-Jayke. You're Jayke's daughter, and Sky knows it."

By the time Malora is twelve years old, Thora and Jayke have resigned themselves to their daughter's dreams, but have told her that her formal training can begin only when she can no longer walk under Sky's high belly without ducking. One evening, Malora goes into Sky's stall while Jayke is grooming him, polishing his ebony hide with a chamois-skin cloth. Malora loves the stable when it is lantern-lit. With its mingled scents of horse and leather, dung and hay and sweat, it is home.

"Good evening, big fellow," she says to Sky, and then ducks down to pass beneath his stomach. With a happy grin, she greets her father on the other side. "I'm bigger than a rabbit now, Papa!"

"Very well," Jayke says, his daughter's enthusiasm warming his malachite eyes. "We'll begin training tomorrow, when I return from the hunt."

The next day, Jayke and the others ride out before dawn, as they always do. Malora busies herself helping her mother arrange herbs on a wooden drying rack and grind roots in the big red stone mortar and pestle. But Malora is too distracted to participate in small talk, a thing her mother loves to do as they work, so Thora shoos her away. Trotting off to the stable, Malora grabs the black-and-white braided rope from its hook and loops it over one shoulder, just like Jayke.

"I'm going up to the nest to watch for Papa. Want to come?" she asks Aron.

Pausing to lean on his shovel, Aron says, "I can't, Malora. Jayke counts on me, you know. You go on and have fun."

"I'm going to. Do you want to watch me spin later today?"

"Yes, Malora, I really do," says Aron.

Malora jogs along the main road, out the city gates, and through the narrow canyon path. Halfway down the path, she scrambles up a grand natural staircase of boulders leading to the nest, her favorite perch high in the cliffs overlooking the plains. There, she settles in to wait, and excited as she is, she begins to doze in the cliff's shadow. It is because she is up there waiting for her father, and not down in the city, that she is the only human witness to what follows.

She awakes to a low, throbbing hum, like a swarm of angry bees. Sitting up, she looks out over the plains and sees the red cloud of dust that signals the hunting party's return. She gives a yelp of joy and is just about to leap to her feet and wave to them, when she happens to look up.

The creatures at first appear to be a gathering of vultures, drawn, Malora guesses, by the fresh kill lashed to the cantles of the hunters' saddles. Then the few are soon joined by many more, and before long, the sky is black with them, the hum having risen to an ear-numbing drone. As they drop down closer to the earth, Malora sees that the creatures aren't vultures at all. They are bigger than vultures, bigger than eagles, bigger than fully grown men, with black leathery wings that beat the air like giant fans and waft toward Malora an unpleasant odor, reminiscent, on a magnified scale, of rodents nesting in the stone walls of her home. Though small compared to their bodies, the creatures' round heads have an eerie mannishness, with tufts of dusty brown fur and sharp fangs protruding from thin black lips. Their outstretched arms, trapped in the wings' sleek leather casing, end in talons, and their taloned legs stretch straight out behind them like the gawky legs of riverine divers.

"Leatherwings!" Malora whispers to herself.

There have been tales of Leatherwings, told around the fire, handed down through the generations, but no one believes them. They are tales told to tighten the arms of young men around their mates, to tame misbehaving children. But as Malora now sees with her own eyes, the Leatherwings are real.

Malora wants to warn her father, but she knows her voice

will be lost in the din. Besides, the dogs already know, freezing on their haunches, teeth bared and fur bristling. The horses know, too. They wheel beneath their riders, unbalanced by terror and the carcasses lashed to their backs. As for the hunters, they are simply too dumbfounded to fit arrows to their bows. Gimpy Gar is plucked from his saddle and borne off in the sickled talons of a Leatherwing. His horse, white-eyed, spins in circles as another Leatherwing alights on its back. A second joins it, and the two, working in tandem, make off with the madly squealing, wildly kicking horse.

After that, all Malora sees is a roiling chaos of black leather. She is aware of a deafening roar, beneath which she can barely make out the shouting of the men, the howling of the dogs, and the screaming of the horses as they are plucked up and borne off, one by one. By the time the red dust has settled and the last Leatherwings have been swallowed up by the innocent pale blue of the late-afternoon sky, there remains not a single living thing on the plains except for Sky. His saddle is askew, his exposed back raked and bloody. He runs this way and that, as if trapped by an invisible fence, pausing now and then to give off a heartrending, almost foal-like whinny as he calls out to the others, who are no longer there. With a stony numbness that will never quite leave her, Malora understands that her father—and all the menfolk and every horse except Sky—is gone forever.

Sliding and stumbling down the cliff side, Malora runs out onto the plains. At the sight of her, Sky rolls his eyes and rears, his powerful hooves churning the air, flecks of pink foam flying from his mouth. Malora shrinks back, her heart pounding, as she makes calming motions with her arms, the way she has seen her father do with a badly spooked horse. She speaks to him in a rasping whisper. "It's okay, Sky. It's okay, boy."

Grunting, the horse gradually rocks back onto the ground, his ears flicking forward. She continues to talk to him, a combination of nonsense and information: "There's a good, big boy. There, now. The bad Leatherwings have gone away, and now it's just you and me, Sky. Just you and me, yes, that's right, Sky, so we have to stick together and take care of each other, don't we?"

Sky lets out a wheezy neigh of agreement. Then he rears again, but this time Malora isn't afraid. She knows he is only trying to shake off the shock of the attack.

"I know, I saw it all from my nest, Sky, and it was horrible," Malora says, her voice soothing despite her shaking hands. "You were so brave! You were too big for them to lift, but they tried, didn't they? That's how you got all those scratches on your back. What a beautiful back you have. It's all scratched up, but we'll fix that. I'll take you to Thora, my mother. She has special healing salves."

Sky licks and smacks his lips to show that he is willing to go along with her plan. Finally, he heaves a great gusty sigh.

By now, Malora is right up next to his massive bulk. His tail is twitching, but his feet are planted. She stands where he can see her with one large, pale eye and holds up her arms slowly, the one with the rope and the other one, too. "See, Sky? No weapons, no fangs, no talons, nothing but this rope. I'll tell you what I'm going to do. I'm going to undo your saddle the rest of the way, okay?" Malora reaches up to Sky's ribs, where the cinch has shifted, and unfastens it slowly, one set of ties at a time, so he can get used to her hands on him. She releases the last tie, letting the saddle, which is far too heavy for her to hold, slough off to the ground with a *thump*. Sky slews, slamming into her body and knocking her off her feet.

For a moment, Malora sees nothing but a bright-white light shot through with swirling spirals of color. She gasps and blinks and clears her vision to find herself on her hind end staring up at the matted vault of Sky's belly. He stands over her, ribs heaving, legs splayed, as if aware that a single hoof will crush her. She whispers up at him, "Sorry, big boy, but that saddle was too heavy for me. We'll just have to leave it here and let Aron pick it up."

Malora climbs carefully onto her hands and knees and crawls out from beneath Sky's belly, rising shakily to her feet where he can see her, the rope still looped around her shoulder. "And now I'm going to take this rope. See it? This is Jayke's rope. Feel it?" She rubs the rope along his flanks. "Smell it?" She places it beneath his nose. He dips his muzzle and sniffs at it, then bobs his head as if confirming its provenance. Malora brings the coiled rope beneath her own nose. "I smell him, too."

She smells the sweat of her father's hands, the musky scent of the oil he used to soften tack, the ghost of the wild onion grass he chewed. The mingled scents bring him briefly back to life: a dusky-skinned giant of a man with weedy, wild red hair trapped in a horse tail by a leather thong. She remembers how it feels to ride Sky with Jayke's long arm wrapped around her middle, the calloused fingers of his other hand scraping, like bars of sandstone, the tender skin at the back of her neck. Slowly, she brings the rope to her breast and lets the tears spill out. She weeps as much for the loss of her father as in gratitude that this rope, like this magnificent animal, both once his, are now hers. She weeps as if she were emptying her head and her heart of tears. And while she does, she feels herself, with one hand, letting go of her father and, with the other, reaching out for Sky.

Malora smiles up at the horse through the haze of her tears. He peers down at her and grunts, nudging her with his nose.

"I know. It's a bad idea for us to stand out here in the open, isn't it?" She wipes her eyes and looks up at the sky.

Red streaks of dusk now remind her of smears of blood. Never again will she see the sky in quite the same way. From now on, even on the finest days, the sky will always hold a hint of menace. "Okay," she says, "I'm tying this rope around your neck. I know it's insulting to your dignity, but I can't risk losing you. Let's go home, big boy."

Having looped one end of the rope around Sky's neck, she stands just behind his left shoulder and points toward the Settlement gates. She makes a kissing sound. Sky hesitates, and her heart lurches. This really *is* too much horse for her, she thinks. Then Malora remembers her father's words: "If the lighter cue doesn't work, add more to it." She waves the frayed end of the rope at Sky's haunch. When Sky stays rooted, she points ahead, waves the rope, and then throws in the kissing sound. He gathers up his mighty hindquarters and, ears swiveling back to her, moves off exactly the way he would have done for Jayke. Malora feels the exhilaration surging through her.

The dance is beginning.

CHAPTER 2

Rain of Bones

Malora tethers Sky to a post and then goes to the gong that stands in front of the Hall of the People in the Settlement's main square. She bangs it long and loud, bringing the women and children pouring forth. When they have all gathered around her, Malora begins, with clear eyes and a steady voice. As she speaks, she turns in a slow circle, as if she were a hub. Instead of spinning a horse, she is spinning the tale of what happened out on the plains. When she stops, a bleak silence descends.

Aron is the first to react. He screams and covers his head with his arms. As if invisible Leatherwings were pursuing him, he runs off to the stable, where they can hear him baying like an abandoned hound for its master.

Thora holds the polished malachite stone she wears on a thong around her neck, a gift from Jayke on mating day. Her eyes glitter with tears. "They are with the Grandparents now," she says.

Felise, the potter, steps forward and spits in the dust. "Malora Thora-Jayke lies. Grown men being taken away kicking and screaming by giant bats?" she hisses. Her four small children cling to her, their eyes wide and scared.

Betts, the basket weaver, joins in. "It's the part about the horses being carried off that I don't believe. I can see an owl lifting a rabbit, a hawk lifting a pup, perhaps. But how could any air-bound creature be big enough to carry off a full-grown horse?"

Frustrated, Malora fights her way through the crowd and comes back, leading Sky into their midst.

The women gasp when they see the wounds on the stallion's back. The scratches are deeper and wider and more vicious-looking than those on the flanks of a horse whose rider was dragged off into the bushes by a lion. That horse later died of his wounds; all that remained of the rider was a bloody foot retrieved by one of the hunting dogs.

A few of the women break down and begin wailing. To those who still disbelieve her, Malora gives directions to the site. Thora, taking charge, sends Aron and some of the women out to investigate.

Meanwhile, Malora leads Sky to the stable, where Thora sees to his injuries. Malora holds Sky's head and croons to him while Thora cleans the wounds, applies a salve, and then packs the wounds with a poultice. "To draw off toxins," she explains to Malora, ever hopeful that her daughter will take a practical interest in the healing arts. But all Malora says now is, "Will the wounds leave scars?"

"To be sure," Thora says. "The wounds are deep and the hair will never grow back."

When Malora turns pale, Thora says, "Think of the scars on your papa's body. A body without scars has no character. A body without scars hasn't really lived. Scars tell the story of your life and how you have lived it. From now on, Sky will have a big story to tell."

Aron returns lugging the saddle, with the women close at his heels. They report seeing no sign of man or horse, but there is a vast black pool of blood clotting the sand near the place where they found the saddle. Darting reproachful looks at Malora, they shuffle off to comfort their children.

"You might as well get used to it now," Thora says to her daughter. "They'll never forgive you for being the bearer of this news."

"But it wasn't my fault!" Malora says. Anger bubbles up in her, melting her grief.

"Better to be spurred by anger than hobbled by sadness," Thora tells her. "I learned that a long time ago."

"I *hate* them!" says Malora.

"Don't hate them," Thora says. "Hate the Leatherwings. The Settlement has been dealt a mortal blow. For these women, blaming someone helps ease the pain."

In the days to come, the women castigate Malora for not crying.

"She's a stonyhearted one, that Malora Thora-Jayke," they mutter behind her back just loud enough for her to hear.

"It's unnatural," they say.

"I do feel sad," Malora says one night while Thora combs out her daughter's long red hair, "but I can't *make* the tears fall. I have cried, and now I'm like a streambed in a drought."

"That's just as well. Too many tears will only addle you,"

her mother says. "It's important to keep your head clear, given the circumstances."

The dead cannot be officially consigned to the Grandparents because there are no bodies to bury. So every evening, the women kneel beside the canyon wall and keen, sending their voices soaring out over the rooftops. Their children, left at home, cry and fret and whine. Thora and Malora, wringing cold, wet cloths over Sky to quell his fever, continue to speak over the eerie lamentations of the women.

"I wish they'd stop," Malora says. "They're so loud I'm afraid the Leatherwings will hear them. Mama, I don't know what to do. I'm afraid all the time."

"Fear is good. Fear can keep you alive. Only fools don't fear," Thora tells her. "And you're right to want them to stop. Crying is an indulgence we can ill afford right now."

"Do you think the Leatherwings will return?" Malora asks.

"Of course they'll return," Thora says. "They've gotten a taste of the People and they'll want more."

At the weekly meeting in the Hall of the People, Thora—who has become the leader of the women, as Jayke had been the leader of men—forbids anyone from leaving the city. Better to survive without the bounty of the plains, she says, than to be part of it. Within the city gates, there are gardens: corn and yams and other root vegetables growing year-round. There are chickens and some cows, sheep for wool, and a small herd of goats to give milk and cheese. This will suffice. But the women and children complain of hunger.

Thora and Malora go about the canyon setting snares for rabbits and snakes and squirrels and partridges. Then mother and daughter go from door to door, delivering braces of small game. The women receive these gifts with sullen gratitude. Spoiled by years of the hunters' big-game kill, they are used to serving sizzling ostrich roasts stuffed with doves, slabs of eland and kudu meat that the older ones can sink their teeth into while the little ones teethe on the bones. The women curl their lips at the idea of rabbit and snake stew, but Thora tells them they are lucky to have it.

Ten days pass, and then the bones start falling, more every day, picked clean and scattered here and there, pelting down from the heavens.

It is raining bones.

With only one horse to care for, Aron is free to serve the women. He feels important, needed. Malora thinks the women treat Aron worse than a dog. She is outraged on his behalf, and yet he seems inordinately happy, his life filled with purpose as never before.

"I am so busy," he tells Malora. "These women keep me working harder than Jayke ever did."

The women, squeamish about the bones, order Aron to retrieve them. The bones are horse and hound and human. Aron digs a big hole near the Hall of the People. He claims to know which bones belong to whom, which are horse and hound and which are human, but only Malora and her mother believe him.

"The very young and the simpleminded have insights the rest of us have lost," Thora says.

The women want Aron to dig a second hole for the animal bones, but Aron refuses.

"It isn't right. They died together, they lie together," he says stubbornly.

The women tire of arguing, so into the big hole all the bones are lovingly placed, one by one, by Aron. He leaves the hole open. The women ask him to fill it in so the dead can be consigned to the care of the Grandparents. But Aron says, "Not yet."

Over the next few days, more bones rain down. Only when Aron announces that the last bone has landed does he fill in the hole. Felise makes a clay tablet into which she incises the family mark for each man. Malora wants marks for the horses to be inscribed there, too. Her father has marked the hide of each horse with a sign that matches the marking on its tack. Thora tells her daughter not to be unreasonable. Most of the horses didn't even have names. While this is true, Malora finds it sad, even in the midst of all this unspeakable sadness.

"When I have my own herd of horses," she vows to Aron, "I'll name every one of them."

"Can I help you name them?" Aron asks eagerly. "Let's name one Tenacity and another one Veracity," he says.

"Tenacity and veracity," as Jayke had repeated tirelessly to Malora and Aron, "are the two most important requirements for a good horse trainer." Tenacity, because every new thing, in order to sink in to a horse's head, bears patient repeating hundreds of times. Veracity, because you must always tell a horse the truth. A horse knows when you are lying.

"I had a dream about them last night," Aron says on the morning of the consignment. "Tenacity and Veracity were twins, and they both looked just like you. They were so beautiful! One had red hair like you, and the other had silver hair."

Hearing this fills Malora with longing and loneliness, imagining these twins in the world somewhere. As she does often these days, she shakes off the feeling. Standing beside the grave, she must shake off, too, the pictures in her mind of the Leatherwings swooping down upon the Settlement and making off with Sky and her mother and Aron. She tries to imagine, instead, Jayke and Gar and Eld and all the others, on horseback, riding to join the Grandparents in a place where there is plenty of game to hunt but no Leatherwings.

Thanks to Sky's robust constitution—and Thora's salves—the wounds have begun to scab over and heal in long pinkish-white stripes radiating back from his shoulders to his haunches, in perfect symmetry, as if they had been painted on by someone with great dramatic flair. Malora catches Aron one day trying to color in the pink stripes with wet charcoal. "Don't be simple, Aron," she tells him.

"His back was so beautiful, but now it's ugly," Aron whines.

"It's even more beautiful for the scars," Malora says. "His back has great character and tells a story."

"It is the story of the Leatherwings, and I *hate* them," Aron says bitterly, his face crumpling. "They have ruined *everything*."

Aron cries all the time, about Jayke, about the horses, about the loathsome Leatherwings.

"I hate them, too," Malora says soothingly, rubbing his broad back as he blubbers into his hands like a small child. After a while, he lifts his face, streaked with snot and tears.

"There, now. Do you feel better?" Malora asks.

Aron nods and smiles beatifically. "Leatherwings are

going to get me next," he says, stretching his arms toward the sky as if he can't wait for the day.

"Don't say that!" Malora scolds him, pulling his arms back to his sides because they seem to be offering such an open invitation. She wonders what's gotten into him. When she asks her mother, Thora says that she thinks Aron has spent too much time handling the bones of the dead; it has made him morbid. Malora's efforts to cheer Aron are unflagging, even though they begin to weigh upon her. "The women depend upon you, Aron. What would they do without you?"

"*Die!*" he says as he grabs the shovel. "Leatherwings going to get them, too. Malora! Leatherwings going to get everybody here! Everybody except you and Sky!"

Malora shakes this thought from her head. She tries to stay busy. Every day, she goes to the stable and leads Sky to the training pen. Aron and the children line up along the fence posts and peer through the chinks. Day after day, she spins Sky every which way at the end of Jayke's rope until she unfastens the rope and tosses it aside. Now she mimes the use of it. When the miming is reduced from broad gestures to subtle movements of head—mere flickers of her eyelashes— Malora knows it is time for her to mount up. Aron helps her bridle Sky and then boosts her onto his back. She will ride him bareback until his scars have healed.

Aron stands back and stares up at her admiringly. "See? He's not too much horse for you."

The fact is, Sky *is* too much horse for her, but Sky is sensitive to this in a protective way. His ears are cocked, listening for her cues. As her legs squeeze him into a walk, she remembers Jayke's words: "You must have a clear idea of what you want the horse to do. If you aren't clear in your own mind, the horse won't be able to read your intention."

Without her father's arm to brace her, it is such a long way down to the ground. For all her bravery, Malora gets flustered. Her clear intentions fly from her head, or else crowd in upon her in contradictory profusion. *Stop. No, go. Go right. No, left. Back up. Trot. Stop. I mean go, and go faster!*

Sky strains to interpret her muddled meaning, to sort through her garbled cues. He does everything he can to keep his body beneath hers. Over days and weeks, she calms her mind and clears it, learning to present one discrete intention at a time and, finally, the two of them begin working together in earnest. She rides him in circles, one way and then the other, first at a walk, then at a trot, and finally at a big, lolloping canter. The training ring is too small to contain them.

"Sky and I are getting dizzy riding in circles," Malora tells Thora one night while Thora brushes her hair. "Can I take him out on the plains and let him gallop?"

"Absolutely not," her mother says.

"But it's been weeks since the Leatherwings attacked," Malora says. Working with Sky every day has made her forget not just her grief, but her fear as well.

"It's only a matter of time before they come back," Thora says. "And Sky might not be so lucky next time."

In her frustration and boredom, Malora teaches Sky tricks. She trains him to count by pawing his hoof in the dust, to untie knots with his teeth, to bow, to rear, and to prance prettily in place. She teaches herself how to run and vault onto his back, how to dismount by sliding off his hindquarters and then slip off each side, all while Sky is in motion.

She learns how to ride standing with her bare feet planted on either side of his spine, holding an ironwood pole to keep her balance.

The children, whose spirits the Leatherwings have sapped, revive at the sight of her antics. They whoop and cheer and run along the outside of the pen, goading her to perform ever more daring feats.

More weeks pass, and the sky mocks them with its clarity and mildness. Every few days, Thora rings the gong in the Hall of the People and conducts drills. In the event of a Leatherwing attack, Sky will be put in his stall and Aron will stay with him, Thora having forbidden Malora from doing so. Malora will stay with her mother in the root cellar beneath their house.

"But the Leatherwings are noisy," Malora says, "and Aron hates noise. It makes him scream."

"I'll make him lambs' wool plugs for his ears to block out the noise," Thora says.

Aron takes to wearing the plugs all the time, and Malora often has to pluck them out so she can talk to him.

"You won't hear them coming if you wear these silly things all the time," Malora warns him as, together, they groom Sky.

Aron stares at the ground and scuffs the red dust. "I wear them because I don't like what the women are saying."

"What are they saying?" Malora asks, ducking under Sky's belly and coming face to face with Aron.

"I can't tell you," Aron says, his face reddening. He turns away and bursts into tears.

Sky heaves a horsey sigh, as if to say, *Not again!*

Malora goes to Thora. "The women are saying things that are upsetting Aron."

Thora is pouring ground herbs into jars. She sets her mouth in a hard line. "I'm sorry he's upset."

"What are the women saying? If I know what they are saying, I can convince Aron that they're wrong."

Her mother says, "They say that you and Aron should mate."

Malora is baffled at first, then incensed. "Like you and Jayke? But Aron is a boy, and he will always be a boy. He is my friend, but he will never, ever be my mate."

Her mother's eyes are soft with regret. "It is our most immediate hope for the People's survival. You are the eldest woman child, and he is a boy in a man's body. It will not happen until you are older, and by then you will understand. For purposes of propagation, this will have to do."

Malora says airily, "It will not do for me."

Later, Malora finds Aron crouched in an empty stall, weeping almost hysterically. "I heard what you said to Thora," he sobs, his chest heaving, his nose gummy with snot.

"I'm so sorry, Aron," she says, moved to pity by the sight of him. "I didn't mean it. I will be your mate one day." She will say anything to stanch his tears.

The next day, Malora hears the hum of angry bees just as she and Aron are oiling Jayke's saddle. Thora rings the gong. Aron plugs up his ears and leads Sky into his stall. Malora runs home to join her mother in the root cellar. The others barricade their windows and doors.

Afterward, they learn what happened from Betts, whose need to see the Leatherwings with her own eyes drew her to a chink in the window barricade. Betts tells them that Aron ran out of the stable into the open and held out his arms like a small child begging to be carried off. Betts screamed at him to take cover, but Aron wouldn't listen. He seemed fearless.

"Only a fool has no fear," Thora says, wagging her head as she listens to Betts's report.

Malora takes this in, wide-eyed and dry-mouthed, understanding that this is exactly what Aron had said would happen. Would all his other predictions also come to pass? Would she and Sky, alone of everyone in the Settlement, survive? And would she one day give birth to two girls named Tenacity and Veracity? If so, who would be their father now that Aron has been taken?

Aron isn't the only casualty of the latest raid. The women soon discover that the Leatherwings broke through the thatching on Felise's roof and made off with her and all four children.

While the women can't blame Malora for this, they do hold her responsible for the loss of Aron.

"She should have stood watch over her own precious horse," they mutter darkly among themselves.

"Look at her," they say. "Her best friend, and not one tear does she shed for the poor simple lad."

Malora retreats from the Settlement into Sky's stall. She has few words for anyone, including her mother. But the women are wrong. She does weep for Aron. Yet even while she weeps, another part of her is secretly relieved that she won't have to keep her promise to mate with him.

"Next time the Leatherwings come," Malora informs her mother tersely, "I'll stay in the stall with Sky."

"You will not," Thora says, for she has a plan.

She moves Malora into her own bedroom and quarters Sky in Malora's room. Malora's room proves to be a surprisingly satisfactory stall for Sky. Malora takes some cheer from hearing the *clop-clop* of Sky's hooves on the stone floors and seeing the place where she and Aron once sat and played with their dolls now covered with hay and horse piss and dung, which it is her daily job to shovel out the window into the yard. Malora secretly likes that the house now smells of stable instead of her mother's herbs.

Each night, in the bed she once shared with Jayke, Thora tries to bring Malora out, to get her to talk.

"I have no more time for small talk," Malora says, turning away from her mother.

"There is always time, especially now, for there is great solace in small talk."

Night after night, Thora talks. At first, Malora listens in silence, her back turned to her mother, curled in upon herself. Mostly, Thora talks about her life with Jayke. One night, she tells about the time they rode up into the mountains and swam in a crystal-clear lake so cold they had to build a fire on the banks to warm themselves. The wood of the fire gave off green-blue sparks, the color of Jayke's eyes, the color of the eyes of the child they would conceive that same night.

"How do you know it happened that night?" Malora asks, turning around at last to face her mother.

"A woman knows these things," Thora says dreamily.

"Will I one day know such things?" Malora asks.

Thora brings Malora's head to her breast. "Yes!" she says, raking her fingers through Malora's hair.

But Malora doesn't see how this can be. Where will *her* mate come from when the Settlement holds the last of the People? After this night, Malora rejoins the small talk. The silence of the Settlement swallows their voices. Felise and her brood were a loud, brawling lot, and the remaining children are as quiet as an abandoned nest of baby mice. The second shower of bones falls—and such tiny bones they are, too—and another wave of the dead are consigned. Immediately afterward, Thora orders the women to dismantle the training pen and sharpen the ironwood sticks. The women climb onto the roofs and plant the wooden pikes in the thatching.

The next time the Leatherwings attack, the pikes prevent them from breaking into any of the houses. They go away hungry, their thwarted cries echoing off the canyon walls as they wheel away over the mountains in search of easier prey.

CHAPTER 3

Daughter of the Plains

Thora has taken to conducting daily morning walks for the purpose of teaching Malora plant lore. It is the only reason Thora can think of to risk venturing out of the Settlement onto the plains. Malora hears a new urgency in her mother's voice these days. Every morning they pass beneath the gates, walk down the canyon corridor, and step out onto the open plains. There, they are greeted by the familiar three-beat call of the ring-tailed dove.

"Do you hear that?" Thora says. "She's talking to you: 'Ma-lo-ra! Ma-lo-ra! Ma-lo-ra!' She wants you to listen carefully to everything I have to tell you. And this is *not* small talk. This is important. Hear me, please, O Daughter of the Mountains!"

"I hate the mountains more than ever!" Malora says with a deep scowl at the towering wall of red rock at their backs. "The Leatherwings come from the mountains, and the mountains reek of them. I am the Daughter of the *Plains*!"

"Very well, Daughter of the Plains, listen to what I tell you of the bounty of the plains."

Malora, exasperated, says, "You can talk forever, but I'll never remember the names of the plants and flowers the way you do."

"That doesn't matter," Thora says, "so long as you know them by sight and remember how to use them."

Sometimes it will take them all morning to go only a few steps, so numerous are the plants that grow along the way, so infinite their uses.

"The fruit of the poison apple bush soothes a bad tooth."

"The roots and leaves of the velvet bush willow treat bites from ticks and snakes."

"The lavender fever berry's bark, when pulverized, is a stomach purgative."

"A branch of the puzzle bush works as a twirling stick, against a rubbing stick cut from the silver bush, to make fire."

"A branch from the wait-a-minute bush makes a good snare."

"The marilla tree's fruits, when eaten fresh, are tasty. A little tart perhaps, but most refreshing on a hot day. The stones are nuts. The bark, boiled in water and made into a tea, treats fever."

"The violet tree's bark makes cloth and also fishing nets."

"The leaves of the wild camphor bush, when dried, make a sedative."

"The fruits of the russet bush willow are edible, but beware the seeds, for they are poisonous. The powdered bark of the silver cluster leaf neutralizes the poison, but you must catch it in time, within the day. Are you listening to me, Malora?"

Malora's head swims. "I *am* listening, but what I really want is Jayke's bow and quiver. It's all very well to heal, but I must learn to kill."

Jayke's spare bow and quiver still sit in the corner by the front door, like the ghost of their owner standing sentry over his family.

Thora says, "That? That bow's not for you."

Discouraged, Malora barely listens to the rest of the plant talk. When they return to the Settlement after their walk, Malora follows her mother to the shed behind their house. Thora brings forth a bow Malora has never seen. It is smaller than Jayke's but beautifully made.

"Whose is this?" Malora asks. It is almost too beautiful to touch.

"It was mine," Thora says. "And now it is yours."

"You never told me you shot a bow," Malora says.

"You don't know a lot of things about me," Thora says, the faintest trace of a smile on her lips.

The bow, made from golden wood, has a graceful shape. The quiver, which is packed with arrows, is made from impala skin. With one foot bracing the bottom of the bow, the muscles in her arms bunching, Thora bends the bow and strings it. "Your father made this for me before we mated. He taught me how to shoot, and I will teach you."

The skin on Malora's face is tight and hot as she holds the bow for the first time. She is conscious of the gift's worth. Like her rope, anything that was made by her father now has a sacred value. Malora plucks the string, which gives off a deep *twang,* like the call of a winged predator, poised to launch itself at its prey in a single swift shot. She fears this power; something in her wants to fling the bow away and never lay hands on it again. And yet something else even stronger wants to master it, to harness its force to do her bidding.

"Before you were born," Thora says, "your father and I used to go hunting every day. We had such fun together."

Malora imagines a day long ago when her parents were a young and laughing couple.

Thora is saying, "The bowstring is made from silk. The sinew of animals will work but it will eventually crack and break. Better to use the stuff of the silkworm, if you are able to obtain it. The nock of each arrow is reinforced by a sliver of horn from a kudu. The glue is cooked down from the hooves of the wildebeest."

Thora removes each arrow from the quiver and sights along it, setting aside the two that are crooked. "A crooked arrow is as useless as a wandering eye. To get the arrows straight, lay them over a pot of steaming water and weight them with flat rocks. The tip is sharpened slate. It will pierce the hide of an impala or a small lion."

"Or a Leatherwing?" Malora asks.

"Only if you aim for their vile little potbellies," her mother says, her voice grimly matter-of-fact, her eyes not meeting Malora's.

Each arrow is fledged with the dark blue feathers of Malora's favorite bird, the lilac-breasted roller. First, Thora shows Malora how to lay the arrow across the bow stave, trap the arrow with her left thumb, and stretch the cord with her right thumb until it engages the small nock at the arrow's fledged end. To demonstrate, Thora hauls back the cord with a single finger. As Malora watches her mother pull back the string, she sees this woman through new eyes. She is no longer Thora the Healer. She is Thora the Huntress.

Now it is Malora's turn. It requires all the fingers on her right hand to pull back the string. Sweat beads on her upper lip, and her entire arm trembles as she draws the cord all the way to her right ear, the way she has seen Thora do it with the one finger. She looses the arrow, not when she is ready to but when her arm gives out on her. She tracks the bright feathers of the escaped arrow, watching as the shaft speeds toward the tree trunk she has chosen as a target. It misses! She frowns. Her shoulders sag, and she groans in discouragement. Put the bow back in the shed, Malora tells herself. You are not meant to be Malora the Huntress. You are neither healer nor huntress. You are nothing.

Thora is neither surprised nor disappointed. "Remember always to look at what you are aiming at, never at the arrow," Thora instructs her. "Burn a hole with your eye into the target and the arrow will seek it."

Malora practices that afternoon and for weeks thereafter, until her arm is strong enough to hold the string to her ear without trembling and her eye can direct the arrow directly to the target every time.

Another gift follows the bow and arrow, this one small and wrapped in a leather wallet. Unwinding the leather tie, Malora finds a shiny little knife with a very sharp blade, as she discovers when she runs her finger along it. It draws blood and yet she feels no pain! She sticks her finger in her mouth and sucks the salty blood.

"Where did you get it?" Malora asks. "And what is it made of?"

"It is a material called metal. It is taken from the earth. The knife was made in a forge long ago when the People, the Grandparents, lived in a grand city north of here."

"What is a forge?" Malora asks.

"It is a place where metal is heated by fire until it is soft, and then pounded with a hammer into useful shapes," Thora says. "Your grandfather, many generations back, made this in his own forge. Now most of our knives are chiseled from stone. They serve well enough, but they are nowhere near as sharp as this one. Cherish this knife. One day, it will save your life."

It is only a few days later when, in the dead of night, Thora shakes Malora roughly awake. Sitting up, Malora sees reflected in her mother's dark eyes two bright, dancing flames.

"Get up, Malora!" Thora says in an urgent whisper. "Get up this instant."

Malora knows right away that something is wrong. "What is it? What's happening, Mama?"

"The Leatherwings have set fire to the thatching," Thora says, clenching the malachite stone. "You have no time to lose."

"Me? What about you?"

Without replying, Thora bundles Malora into a robe and boots and hooded cape, then leads her down the hall and out the front door, where Sky stands, restless and already saddled. Malora realizes that her mother tacked up Sky while Malora was still fast asleep.

"It's time for you to ride away from here," Thora says.

"By myself?" Malora asks in a tremulous voice. "There's lots of room for you on Sky's back. Jayke and I rode on Sky together all the time. Now *you* can ride with me."

"No, I cannot," says Thora wearily. "I'm the only leader the People have." She bends and makes a stirrup of her hands. "Come now. I'll hoist you up."

Malora obeys, and her mother lifts her high into Jayke's great saddle. Thora, looking small from where Malora sits, grasps her feet firmly and fits them into Jayke's stirrups. "Keep your toes pointed up," she says, working Malora's feet to show her how.

"When will I see you?"

Thora's face closes like a flower at dusk. For the first time, Malora takes a good look around her. Screaming women and crying children run everywhere, seeking shelter from the Leatherwings.

"If I leave, they die. I'm their only chance of survival," Thora says, eyes glittering, her hand squeezing Malora's calf so hard that it hurts. "You must go and never return here. Promise me," she says, her eyes fierce, "that you will never return."

"I promise," Malora says sadly, when all she wants to do is climb off Sky, crawl back into their cozy bed, and lie in her mother's arms. She watches Thora lash the bow and arrow to the cantle and knows she will never again lie in bed with her mother and make small talk. This knowledge brings on a torrent of tears.

"Won't you need the bow?" Malora asks, swabbing her face on the sleeve of her cloak.

"You keep it," Thora says. "I have your father's."

Next, she hands up Jayke's rope. Malora slips it automatically over her shoulder.

"Ride north," Thora says. "Follow the river, but go no farther north than the place where the two rivers run together into one."

"Why?" Malora is confused.

"Because our old enemy lies to the north," her mother says.

"More Leatherwings?" she asks.

Thora sighs and shakes her head. "Not Leatherwings. An older enemy. The ones who stole the Grandparents' homeland and drove them here. I meant to tell you the story one day, but now there's no time and you'll just have to take my word for it. Stay to the south."

Thora leads Sky down to the road. Along the way, she picks up one of the sharpened pikes and walks with it, lethal end pointed at the swarming sky.

"Don't look up," Thora says. "If you look up, so will Sky, and he may panic. Lie low in the saddle and give him his head. He will outrun the Leatherwings and keep you safe. But just in case, use this to fend them off."

She hands the wooden pike to Malora. "Mind you keep the point away from yourself. I've dipped the end in a poison serum."

"From the seeds of the russet bush willow," Malora says.

Thora's face lights up. "You were paying attention after all!"

Malora nods and holds tight to the reins with one hand, to the pike with the other, as Sky prances in place. Overhead, giant wings flap. The air is acrid with smoke, and the droning of the Leatherwings is pierced by the screams of the People. For all the deadly commotion, Malora feels as if she and Thora are sealed in a dreamlike bubble of their own.

Thora leads Sky over to a large rock. For a moment, Malora's heart lifts, thinking her mother has decided to join them after all. But instead, Thora climbs up on the rock and embraces Malora, then kisses her three times—lips, nose, and forehead. She holds Malora's face in her hands. For some days after this, Malora will feel on the sides of her face the imprint of her mother's fingertips.

"I love you, Daughter. Always remember that. Now run for your life, and whatever you do, don't look up and don't look back! At nightfall, find the biggest machatu tree and camp beneath it. Dig a hole for yourself to sleep in beneath the blanket I've packed for you. If the Leatherwings find you, cut Sky loose. He can take care of himself. Whatever happens, you must promise me never to return to these mountains. Prove to me once and for all that you truly are now the Daughter of the Plains."

Thora steps down from the rock. "Let me hear you promise!"

The tone of her mother's voice frightens Malora more than the sight of the burning roofs and the sound of screaming People and Leatherwings combined. She nods and whispers, "I promise I'll never come back."

Malora leans down for a last hug, but Thora smacks Sky's flank and he shoots forward. Malora clings to the pommel, and beneath the heavy saddle, she feels the muscles of the great animal coil and extend as he lunges through the city gates and gallops down the canyon corridor, hooves grinding against the soft red stone, carrying her away from her mother, away from the grave where her father's bones lie, away from the life she has always known, and off into the night.

Sky carries her steadily northward. At night, they pitch camp beneath the biggest machatu tree in sight. Beneath the tree, she digs a burrow with the pickax and spends the night with the scorpions and the dung beetles rattling in her ears. She continues doing this long after it becomes apparent that the range of the Leatherwings does not extend any farther than a day's ride from the mountains. It occurs to her that, had the People known this, they might have escaped as she has. Malora is half-tempted to ride back and tell them, but she has made a promise, so she keeps riding.

CHAPTER 4

Finding Shadow

At first, Sky is the dominant one. It is as if all the training she and Jayke have invested in him over the years has been blown clean out of his head by the wild air of the plains. They trot when he wants to trot, gallop when he feels the urge, and stop to graze wherever and whenever he wishes to. Malora has no say in the matter. She is simply a passenger.

Then one night when they have stopped to make camp, she smells something wilder than usual in the air. It is a smell that makes her stop what she is doing and quiet her breathing. She swivels her head, nostrils twitching. It is a smell like raw meat and fresh dung and damp fur ruffled by a thousand different winds bearing a thousand different seeds and spores.

Malora has never seen a live one before, only a carcass brought back from a long-ago hunt. But when it slinks out from behind the trunk of the tree, she knows it is a leopard. A female, as beautiful as she is terrifying to behold. Malora is in the midst of setting a circle of rocks for their fire, but she moves ever so slowly—slowly enough, she hopes, not to trigger an attack—to stand behind Sky.

"Smash her with your hooves, Sky," Malora whispers to him. "Show her how fierce and mighty you are."

Sky, who moments ago had been avidly cropping the grass at his feet, seems to have been turned to stone by the leopard's hungry gaze. The leopard has no interest in Malora. The leopard wants fresh horse meat.

"Oh no you don't!" Malora growls.

With one of the rocks still clutched in her hand, Malora comes out from behind Sky and steals toward the leopard, like a hunting dog bearing down on a snake. She growls low in her throat and makes herself as big as she can as she closes in on her mark. Every hair on her body stands on end, and her eyes blaze with ferocity. She waits until she is close enough to see the flecks of black in the leopard's huge amber eyes, and then she flings the rock with all her might at the creature's head. She clips an ear, and the leopard ducks her head and turns tail. But Malora doesn't want merely to discourage the leopard. She wants to drive her off so that she will never return, so that her cubs waiting for their meal back in the den don't return, either. Picking up more rocks as she goes, Malora chases after the leopard, pelting her with rock after rock after rock until the muscles of her arms burn and her throat is raw from growling.

Afterward, she stays up all night, feeding the fire, hunkered down next to a big pile of rocks, waiting for the leopard to return, but she never does.

The next morning, as horse and rider set out, Sky responds willingly to the cues Malora gives him with her legs and feet and hands and voice. Exhausted as she is, she is giddy with the discovery that she is the leader now, the way Jayke had been the leader of the horses, the way her mother had become the leader of the women.

One day not long after this, while riding across a land of rocky outcroppings and grass-tufted hillocks, Malora hears a sudden loud snort. She swings around, thinking it might be a zebra colt strayed from the herd. But it isn't a zebra. It is another horse, a beautiful filly, with a coat as lustrously black as Sky's. The mare stands on a hillock, eyeing Sky, tossing her wild black mane.

"Hello!" Malora hails her.

To Sky, she says, "I think someone wants to be your friend."

Sky, having given the mare a cursory glance, turns his back and flips his tail at her.

"Don't you want a friend, Sky?" Malora asks. "If one of the People suddenly showed up and wanted to join us, I'd say, 'Welcome!' Even if it was that old basket-weaving biddy, Betts."

After many days of being shadowed by the filly, Sky finally deigns to circle around and jog over to her, rubbing his velvety nostrils up the length of her muzzle and down again.

"Good work, Sky!" Malora crows.

She names the newest member of their small band Shadow. It is not long before Shadow's belly bulges. In the spring, she drops twins. And so the herd begins to expand.

True to her vow to leave no horse nameless, Malora names each one as it slips out of its dam and into the world. First come Coal and Lightning. Then Silky and Raven and

Blacky and Posy. These horses, in various combinations over time, produce Charcoal, Ember, Smoke, Fancy, Streak, and Stormy.

She hears Aron's voice ask her, "Why aren't you naming two of them Veracity and Tenacity like in my dream?"

And Malora answers him aloud, "Because they are neither red-coated nor silver, are they?"

Although they are all as black as the depths of a moonless night, Malora knows each one as an individual. Coal is sullen and balky with small, bright eyes. Lightning is nearly as big as Sky. With teeth and lips as clever as her sire's, she can untie any knot. Silky has a small, shy head and a tendency to wander off by herself. Raven has lopsided nostrils and likes to pull pranks, like stealing Jayke's rope and dumping out Malora's elephant-foot water bucket. Blacky has a scar on his neck where Posy bit him. Posy has a bite mark on her rump where Blacky bit her back. Blacky and Posy are inseparable. Charcoal has a beard of white whiskers. Ember has reddish eyes, while the whites of Smoke's are as yellow as the yolk of an egg. Fancy has long legs and small, delicate feet with hooves that have a tendency to crack. Streak has a long hank of white hair sprouting from the center of his mane, and Stormy more than lives up to her name.

By the third spring—Malora's fifteenth year—there are fifteen horses in Malora's care, including Sky and Shadow. But this doesn't count the twelve horses they have rescued from other herds or found wandering alone. These, too, are black: Oil, Flame, Ivory, Star, Butte, Sassy, Thunder, Cloud, Light Rain, Beast, and Mist. And then there is Max.

While she sometimes mixes up the horses she has rescued, Malora would know Max anywhere by his swayback covered with sores and buzzing with flies, and his huge, limpid, infinitely grateful eyes. She rescued the starving Max from a band of wild painted dogs. Max, she explains to the others—who are reluctant at first to accept the homely, half-dead bay—is the horse of her heart.

The boys and girls, she calls the horses in her herd, both the young and the old. They are in so many ways the brothers and sisters she never had. Taking care of the herd lends a comforting and relentless routine to her days. She finds herself remembering Felise, the harried mother of four. No wonder Felise was so cross all the time! Malora even catches herself sounding like Felise sometimes: "How would you boys and girls get along without me?"

Malora picks off burs and ticks, and files their hooves with sandstone; she oils their hooves with sable tallow when they split or grow ragged; she curries their coats with her own hairbrush, treats them for snakebite with the velvet bush willow, nurses them through tick-bite fever, and assists the foaling.

"You're a poor, defenseless bunch, you are," Malora says, for it is she who keeps her head when the predators come sidling up, hungry for horse meat. The plains swarm with predators. There are giant snakes that strangle foals, lions that maul, and teams of leopards and packs of wild painted dogs that harry and terrorize those who wander off. Her ability to defend the horses from these predators improves over time as her arsenal of weapons expands. With the little knife Thora gave her, she whittles wood to fashion weapons: spears and slings to fling rocks, clubs and daggers and ever larger and more powerful bows with which to shoot ever sharper and surer and swifter arrows. Thora was right. The little knife has saved her life, and the horses', too.

"You ungrateful boys and girls never give me a moment's peace, do you!" Malora carps at them on bad days. But the boys and girls forgive her these moods. They have their ways of showing their gratitude, with the warmth of their bodies and their honest, steadfast companionship. As she leads her herd from one grazing ground to another, from one watering hole to the next, she keeps up a running patter with them. They respond to her with knowing bobs of their heads and skeptical sidelong looks, with interested flicks of their ears and contrary whips of their tails, with defiant tossing of their manes and stubborn stomping of their hooves, with a vast and intricate vocabulary of nickers and whinnies and licks and neighs and snorts and nibbles and nips. But never, of course, with words.

In the end, it is the words—the small talk with Thora, in particular—that Malora craves the most. She longs for it with a ferocity that sometimes strikes her dumb, lasting for days until Max comes up to her and places his slightly rank head directly over her heart. This gesture of sympathy always makes her burst into the kind of tears the mothers of the Settlement would have lauded. A good, loud squall always brings an end to the sulks, and Malora feels much better afterward, at least for a while.

Every night, as she lies in her great warm nest of slumbering horses, her thoughts return to Thora. In her mind, her mother praises her for the job she is doing, keeping safe, keeping the horses safe, staying away from the mountains to the south and the enemy to the north. Even Jayke, from his hole of bones, speaks to Malora, advising her how to make the best traps and snares and nets and stews, how to skin and cure and fashion leather into clothing and shoes and bags for storage and water. She breaks her shoulder when Shadow bolts beneath her during a thunderstorm, and it is the voice of her father that instructs her to tear her old hooded robe into strips and bind her shoulder to her body. It is the voice of her mother that guides her to the place where the healing plant called bone knit grows.

In the third spring of her wanderings, when Malora's shoulder is free of the binding but still stiff, she decides that she can fend off any number of Leatherwings for the chance to see and hear her mother again. On that day—a day when the earth lies stunned beneath shimmering waves of heat—she turns Sky and the herd southwest and makes her way back to the mountains, back to the Settlement, against her mother's wishes but somehow helpless to do otherwise.

As Malora rides, she wonders with rising excitement what her mother will say when she sees her. Two of the mares, Silky and Posy, will foal soon, and Malora will be able to show Thora how she has learned to midwife the birthing. And won't Thora be amazed at how tall she has grown? Malora now measures up to the middle of Sky's neck. The red robes and tunics have all been torn up and used for bandages and rags and fishnets and water filters. She wears a short tunic made from a leopard she slew, skinned, cured, and stitched together with reebok sinew. Her hair hangs in a long, snarled tail. Her mother will not approve of this, but who has time to brush hair when there is a herd of horsehide and manes and tails to groom and tend? Under the circumstances, Malora thinks that her mother will forgive her. And, if not, then Thora at least will have the satisfaction of once more running a brush through her daughter's hair as they sit and make small talk far into the night.

As Malora leads the herd loping toward the rising mountains, then trotting single file down the narrow canyon path to the Settlement, she knows something is amiss when Sky pulls up at the gates and refuses to go any farther. Malora sits stock-still in the saddle and listens.

She hears nothing but the ticking of the red dust blowing against the canyon walls. If anything, the canyon is hotter than the plains, a vast red oven rippling with heat. It is time for the evening meal and yet there are none of the familiar welcoming smells of stew.

Malora slips off Sky's back and leaves the horses to graze on a small patch of grass that has grown in the middle of the road, itself an indication that something is wrong. As she walks down the empty road, she tries to tell herself that the People must have left and gone somewhere cooler, but in her heart she knows different. She sees shards of pots lying scattered about. The Settlement cats, gone feral, stare at her from the shadows and snarl. Then, against the canyon walls, she sees something that pulls her up short.

There are mounds of ruined flesh banked in the shadow of the canyon: long, jagged bones and desiccated black leather. She veers off the road to take a closer look, her heart hammering in her breast. At closer range, she sees that each pile of Leatherwing bones is matched with a set of human ones.

"What happened here?" she says aloud, her voice bouncing off the canyon wall, sounding small and lost.

Had the People battled the Leatherwings, she wonders, and both sides somehow perished in the struggle? She takes a stick and walks along, poking at the piles but uncovering no spears, no bows, no arrows, no knives, no clubs, no weapons of any description. Just stacks and stacks of bones, both Leatherwing and human, the latter with clothed flesh still clinging to them. Why, she asks herself, did no one bury the human dead or, at the very least, drag the Leatherwing corpses out onto the plains for the scavengers to dispense with? And, given that the Settlement seems deserted, why have no scavengers ventured inside the gates to get at the remains?

Backing away from the bones, she heads to the main square and finds the rest of them near the Hall of the People, in a neat circle. As was the case with the other remains, the dried sinew and flesh are still attaching bone to bone, with the rock-red clothing clinging to their shrunken forms.

She walks slowly around the outside of the circle and stops when she comes to the bright malachite stone that is sunken into the chest of one of the bodies. She bends down and gently untangles the leather thong from the ribs, placing it around her neck. Then she sits down with her mother's skull cradled in her lap.

She looks around and blinks. The air sparkles like mica with her unshed tears. In the middle of the circle, her eyes settle on the object that holds the answer to all her questions. It is Thora's red stone mortar and pestle. In the hollow of the pestle lies a large pile of small black seeds: the deadly poisonous russet bush willow.

Thora's plan comes to Malora as clearly as if Thora herself had whispered it in her ear with her last breath. Thora had known that the People were ultimately helpless to save themselves from the Leatherwings. And so, as Aron had done before her, Thora offered herself up—along with everyone else. But this was no simple sacrifice. Thora had poisoned the People so that the Leatherwings, having tasted their deadly flesh, would perish along with them.

No dead Leatherwings lie in the vicinity of Thora's circle. Either all the Leatherwings had already been poisoned or the survivors had flown away. In either case, it seems that Thora and these others have needlessly sacrificed themselves.

And then it dawns upon Malora: Thora acted to protect her. Her mother had known all along that Malora would, sooner or later, in spite of her promise, return. And when she did, Thora wanted to make sure that Malora was safe from the Leatherwings.

Malora is tempted to tip the contents of the mortar into her mouth, to lie down here and let the poison take her and the sun slowly sear the flesh from her bones along with all the others. But this, she knows, she cannot do. If she did, Thora's spirit would never rest and the Grandparents would renounce her.

Gently, Malora sets down her mother's skull and goes to the stable to get Aron's shovel. Her mending shoulder aches as she digs, breaking into the old grave. When the grave is laid bare, Malora drags the remaining bodies over to the hole and rolls them on top of the others, taking cold comfort from the knowledge that at least now her parents lie together.

But where, Malora wonders as the tears begin to fall, does that leave her?

CHAPTER 5

The Horse Hunters

Orion Silvermane feels as if he is trapped in a fever dream. The Ironbound Mountains are aptly named, he thinks, for their towering red rocks radiate a forgelike heat from which there seems to be no escape, not even in the dead of night. Orion is hopeful that today will be their last in this infernal place, for after three weeks of hunting and tracking, it seems they have finally found what they have come here for: a herd of Ironbound Furies.

Orion watches as the herd of horses comes thundering across the high plains, like black ink spreading across red parchment. Bringing up the rear, the Twani march in a ragged line, pounding their drums to hasten the herd onward. Diminutive and short-legged, their fine coating of body hair rimed in red dust and bristling with tension, another line of the Twani stands off to the side with polished squares of metal that reflect the sun into the horses' eyes, steering them into captivity.

At seventeen, Orion is the youngest son of the noble House of Silvermane. He, too, has completed what he has set out to do on this expedition. The others might be here courting adventure in the bush and hunting horses, but he has come in search of flowers and wood and resin and twigs to add to his alchemical cupboard. The specimens he has gathered over the last weeks are packed away in a trunk, some suspended in jars of water, others wrapped in oilcloth. He hopes they will survive the journey home. The sooner they finish with this business and are on their way, the better.

Directly below him, the wrangler in chief, a Twan known as Gift, leans out from a rocky cliff dangling a long pole with a loop tied to the end of it. Just behind him are Orion's elder brother, Theon, and their cousins, other youthful members of the House of Silvermane. They stand in a circle, bright squares of cloth saturated in scent pressed to their noses. Above the cloths, their eyes are weary and bloodshot, and their skin is burned from the sun. They want to finish with this and head home as much as he does. They are all here at the behest of Medon, Orion and Theon's father, the Apex of Kheiron.

It is Medon who wants the horses. Not just any horses will do. They have to be fast horses, racehorses, capable of winning trophies and showering the House of Silvermane in glory, ending the Highlanders' forty-year losing streak. Horse racing has always struck Orion as a foolish endeavor, but it is not Orion's place to question, at least out loud, his father's obsessions and amusements. And it is not as if the Apex's interests do not reflect those of the centaurs he leads, both Highlanders and Flatlanders.

Orion's Twan reaches up and, with a small broom, whisks the red dust off his master's shoulders. He is called West, an approximation of his Twanian name, which means "where the sun sets."

"Thank you, West," Orion says, grinning, "futile though the gesture may be."

Like the other centaurs, Orion holds a cloth to his nose. The fabric has been saturated in a mixture of juniper berry, rose oil, and neroli. It is his own mixture: the juniper braces him, the rose oil soothes him, and the neroli masks the musk of his sweat. Beneath the simple cotton wrap that passes over one shoulder and modestly drapes his horse half, perspiration trickles off his flanks in an unending stream.

Below, Gift backs away from the edge of the cliff, cursing and holding the empty loop aloft.

"Not again!" Orion says with a disappointed sigh. Will they never return home? Over the fragrance of the cloth pressed to his nose, Orion swears he can smell his own flesh simmering.

"He's a demon, that blue-eyed one," West murmurs, stifling a wide yawn behind his short-fingered hand, shaking his head vigorously to stay awake.

"My father will not take it well if we fail," Orion says.

Just then, the centaurs below cry out and point.

"There he is!"

"Do you see him?"

The centaurs draw nearer to the edge of the bluff. They are all fascinated by what they take to be the herd's leader. One of the Twani has gotten close enough to see that the lead stallion actually has blue eyes. This exotic, monumentally proportioned specimen has made the hunt for horses—after days of tedious tracking and standing around in the sweltering heat—lively and very nearly as entertaining as the sport of racing them.

"If they fail, I don't see your father settling for a brace of Lapithian nags," West says.

"He'll never win the Golden Horse that way. The Apex wants *Furies*," Orion says. "What do you suppose will happen now?"

"They'll keep at it. They've got to catch Blue Eyes. Once they do that, the rest of the herd will follow along."

"If they don't, we'll be purchasing horseflesh off the traders in the market at Kahiro," Orion says.

"You know what they say about the market at Kahiro," West says. "Anything you want, you can get."

"Except Furies," Orion says.

"True enough," West concurs. "No one's ever seen a Fury in the market at Kahiro." West pauses, then adds, "You know what I think?"

Orion turns to look at West. West stares back at him with his huge feline eyes, the pupils contracted to black pinpoints against the bright sunlight. He blinks slowly and raises his shiny pink palms. "Perhaps the Furies are uncatchable."

"Perhaps," Orion says as he returns his gaze to the scene below. "But let us hope not."

This particular breed of horse seems to be limited to this remote segment of the bush, the high plains bordering the Ironbound Mountains. The herd comes about, as if undergoing a tidal shift. Orion catches sight of something that makes the hairs on the back of his neck go up.

"Look!" he says, pointing to the horses as they move in a red cloud of dust down below.

West says, "An impressive sight, all right."

"No!" Orion shouts, jabbing his finger at the heart of the herd. "Can't you see her?"

It is a vision from out of a dream—running with the horses, Orion sees a lithe and powerful female centaur with long, streaming red hair and dusky red skin, a creature who seems to have sprung full-bodied from the rocks of the Ironbounds.

"All I see is black horses kicking up red dust," West says, cracking a wide yawn.

Orion has already lost sight of her. Perhaps she was only a product of his heat-stricken brain.

The centaurs below have trotted over to Gift to discuss their next strategy. "They won't be trying that again," West mutters. "Blue Eyes is on to them."

As if taunting them, the stallion leads the herd only a short distance away to a patch of cloud grass. He dips his great black head to tear at the grass, and the others follow suit, their heads all dropped in the same direction, facing away and directly into the wind, their long tails twitching to the same mysterious, internal, uniquely equine rhythm.

Orion scans the grazing herd for the creature of his vision, but the dust is everywhere and the sun and his own sweat conspire to blind him.

Gift drops to all fours—as Twani do when they need to move fast—and pounces down the rocky escarpment onto the plain. Regaining his full height, Gift begins strutting about, bellowing orders. All around him, the other Twani spring into action and start to gather sticks and branches and logs, dragging and rolling them toward the canyon.

From the promontory, Orion has a clear view of the mouth of the canyon and the narrow corridor leading into it, bounded on both sides by high walls of red rock.

In the commotion, unnoticed by the horses, a lone Twan slinks through the high grass toward the far side of the herd.

"What's that Twan over there up to?" Orion asks.

"He's doing what he has to do to ensure a successful outcome," West says, his small lips pursed with disapproval. "That's a box canyon at our backs. There's only one way out of it. The wranglers will drive the herd into the canyon, bottle them up, and stick a plug in its neck."

"What good will trapping the horses in the canyon do?" Orion asks.

"Not much good for the horses, that's for sure," West says with a barely suppressed snarl. His sharp pink tongue darts out to lick the hair on the back of his hand, which he then uses to wash his face, a compulsive habit as much as it is an attempt to clean off the red dust.

The single Twan comes slinking back and joins the others just as the grass on the far side of the herd goes up in flames, soon forming a fiery wall that the wind banks toward the herd. The horses lift their heads, ears pinned, winding in circles, squealing. Then they head in the only safe direction, toward the canyon. Orion can spot neither the blue-eyed stallion nor the red-haired centaur maiden anywhere in the desperate surge away from the fire.

The other centaurs gather to watch the horses gallop past. When the tail of the last horse disappears into the canyon, the centaurs lower the scent cloths from their faces and burst into cheers and rowdy applause.

Below, the Twani set about inserting the cork, quickly wedging brush and branches into the mouth of the canyon, piling it so high that not even the most desperate horse would be able to clear it.

"And now," West says grimly, "we wait."

Almost immediately, Orion hears the restless snorting and muttering of the horses echoing in the canyon behind them. He imagines them milling about, in search of a way out, baffled but still hopeful, raring to be on their wild way.

"The floor of the canyon is littered with boulders. The walls go straight up, but that won't keep them from trying to climb out of there," West says bitterly.

"Won't they hurt themselves?" Orion asks. "What good will wounded horses be to my father?"

"Some of them will break their legs and necks, for sure. Others will be trampled to death. But eventually, the fight will go out of them. Then the ones still alive will be meek as a centaurean maiden's prayer and ready to race their hearts out for the Apex's glory."

Over the howling and shrieking of the horses and the harsh scraping of their hooves against the canyon rock, Orion hears an ominous rumbling sound. Can there be a second herd of Furies on the way? Then he feels a sudden downdraft of icy-cold air on the back of his neck. Before he can appreciate how refreshing this feels, he looks up.

A vast and unfathomable purple-blackness has moved in from the south, boiling over the mountains, seething with moisture and bristling with needles of lightning. A deafening clap of thunder draws exclamations of alarm from the other centaurs.

"Hurry, Excellence!" West runs alongside Orion, bounding on all fours as he herds Orion downhill, slipping and sliding. "Brace yourself. Here it comes!"

The next moment, freezing-cold rain bursts from the sky. Soaking wet, Orion and West arrive under the overhang seconds after the others have also taken refuge. Stomping their boots, the centaurs brush the rain from their hair and tails and wraps. The Twani shake themselves from head to toe, expelling fine clouds of mist. Then, pink tongues unfurled, they begin grooming with their usual thoroughness. Water sluices down the overhang and makes it seem as if they are standing behind a wide waterfall. Suddenly, the group—centaur and Twan alike—goes silent and still, staring into the watery blur before them. Over the roar of the storm, Orion can make out the shrieks of the wild horses as they fight for their lives in the canyon.

Then the rain stops, as abruptly as it began. The sun comes out, striking the rocks with a slick glaze the color of henna. Orion shivers. The rain has drastically cooled the air. West scampers out into the mud and looks up at the sky, then all around him. He nods and beckons to the others.

"Watch your footing in the muck, Your Fine Excellences," he tells them, licking the back of his hand and running it over his face, first one side and then the other, to wash away the mud splash.

Gingerly, the centaurs splash out from beneath the overhang. From the direction of the canyon, Orion hears a bleak, hollow dripping sound. The horses are silent. He feels an overwhelming sadness, that all that power and beauty should be stilled and silenced so quickly. Then there comes a sloshing sound, followed moments later by a mighty crack. Water bulges monstrously out of the canyon and crashes over the barricade.

West throws back his head and screams at the sky, "Flash flood! Head for higher ground!"

Frantically, everyone scrambles uphill, all except for Orion. He has to find her. Vaguely aware of West calling out to him, he heads downhill, toward the foaming red river that teems with the bodies of horses. He sees that some are dead, floating sideways like abandoned rafts. Others, stiff-necked and white-eyed with terror, come flailing out of the canyon.

Then he sees her, with her long red hair streaming with water as she races along on the current.

Orion looks around for a stick and sees that a wrangler's long pole has washed downhill. He grabs it and holds the loop out over the river just as the female centaur shoots past. Snagging the loop over her neck and around her shoulders, he braces his hooves and pulls with all his strength.

Back straining against the current, he feels the weight of her, surprisingly light, lift clear of the water and swing toward him, like cargo in the net of a ship's boom. Losing his footing, he falls backward, smashing his tailbone and rendering himself momentarily senseless with pain.

When the agony subsides, he gapes at what lies on the muddy bank before him.

CHAPTER 6

Pussemboos

Having struggled for so long to hold her head above the floodwaters, Malora suddenly realizes that she is no longer in the water at all, and that it is her own sopping hair, plastered across her face, that is smothering her. Lifting her arm, she clears the hair from her face and looks around. At first, she thinks she is surrounded by a crowd of the People on horseback. Men! They sit astride compact but beautifully conformed horses. She opens her mouth to hail them, and then realizes with a visceral jolt that these are not the People! They are something else altogether, something she has never seen or heard of before, some sublime and unearthly combination of human and horse.

Her next thought, irrational though she knows it to be, is that the bones of the horses and the bones of the People have sprung from their mass grave in the Settlement and become these splendid creatures. With their proud human heads and muscular torsos merging with the powerful yet shapely equine forelegs and body, surely they are made up of the best features of human and horse. And yet, unlike the horses in her herd, these creatures have hides of all colors, some gray, some black, some golden, some white with brown splotches, with as much variety in the color of their human skin and hair.

One of them, with a hide of dappled gray and a head of black wiry hair, steps forward. He holds a cloth of pale green to his nose and stares at Malora with a look of withering contempt. Then he opens his mouth and out comes a loud, braying voice: "By the Blessed Hand! It's a *human being*!"

Malora scowls at him, dislike seeping through her like the poison from a puff adder.

"Yes! It's one of the People," another of them whispers in a voice filled with something—awe, perhaps? "What a remarkable specimen. Honus will be *thrilled*." He stares at Malora with blue eyes as clear and startling as a splash of cold water. His skin is sun-burnished, and both his hair and hide are a lustrous black. If Sky were to become part-human, wouldn't he look like this creature? But this creature seems younger than Sky and smaller and more compact, with a face that still holds some of the roundness of a child. "I am truly impressed!"

Malora is about to open her mouth and thank him when the donkey-toned one says, "Impressed! How can you say that, little brother? The Apex will be *disgusted*. Just look at her, Orion. She's wild and filthy. No wonder we killed them all off."

The little brother replies in a cold voice, "Well, obviously, and quite possibly fortunately, we did not altogether succeed."

"That's quite all right," the older brother says with a wolfish grin. "We can address that unfortunate omission here and now."

Malora is outraged. Then, as she listens to the exchange between brothers, understanding slowly begins to dawn. These creatures are the ancient enemy, the ones living to the north that her mother warned her against—and here she is, surrounded by them!

"Look at her," says the brayer, his lip curling. "Not so much as a glimmer of refinement in those cold, dead eyes of hers."

My eyes are *not* dead, Malora thinks. They are full of life, the same color as my father's, and they are beautiful. Hadn't Thora always said so? How dare he insult her and her father? Malora rises up from the mud and goes at him with fists and feet, clawing and kicking.

The one named Orion stands clear of the fray and says in a bemused fashion, "My, she's quite strong, isn't she, Theon? And *angry*. It's almost as if she understands what you said and is taking issue with you."

Suddenly, Malora feels many hands on her, needle-clawed, pulling her off the brayer. She needs her little knife. Where is her knife? With a sinking feeling, she realizes she has no knife. Her knife is in her saddlebag. Her saddlebag is on Sky. And where is Sky? She hadn't been riding Sky when they fell into the trap. She had been riding Lightning, stretched out across the mare's back, exhausted and in a sort of grief-stricken swoon. This would never have happened if she and Sky had been acting together. But now she is in the clutches of the enemy. It is then that Malora notices that the needle-clawed hands holding her belong to yet another strange order of being she has never seen.

Coming up no higher than her waist, they have short legs encased in knee-high boots and bodies clad in belted tunics. While they appear at first to be miniature men, their faces are flatter, their bodies (what she can see of them) are covered with pale, almost translucent fur, and their eyes are not at all the eyes of men. They are the eyes of cats. Tame cats, Malora thinks. But are even domesticated cats really tame?

She stops struggling and stares down at them, fascinated in spite of herself. She remembers that in the Hall of the People, beneath the floor, was a large chest containing vast treasures: the Grandparents' Box. Aron had first shown the chest to her when she was little and, over the years, they returned to it often to marvel at its wonders. The chest overflowed with mysterious objects whose function they could only guess at, with strange little black boxes, with precious jewels and fabrics, and with a number of mold-ridden items that Aron called books. The most interesting of these books had colored pictures in it, showing a tall, handsome man and a cat who stood on its hind legs, wearing a wide-brimmed, plumed hat and high boots. Aron's grandmother had told him the cat's name. It was Pussemboos. These little cat-men call to Malora's mind Pussemboos, except that they have human ears and no tails and—save for their short, bandy legs—human bodies. There are four of these pussemboos, two clinging to each arm. As her eye travels from one to the next, they return her gaze, calm and unblinking. She swears she can hear, escaping through the neat little purses of their lips, a rumbling, rattling purr.

The high whinny of a horse distracts her. She looks up to see the other cat-men, five or six to a rope, hauling the horses out of the river and leading them over to a pen. The cat-men treat the horses gently and with skill. She remembers the cats in the Settlement and how, when they came to the barn to hunt the mice, they would wind their lithe bodies around the horses' legs, fearless and oddly compatible with much larger animals capable of crushing them with a single hoof. She is about to say something to the cat-men but decides instead to hold her tongue.

Meanwhile, the two brothers are still arguing over Malora's fate. Finally, the younger one throws up his arms. "I will engage no further with you, Theon!" he shouts. "There will be no slaying. Enough life has been lost today. We will keep her."

Keep her? Who is he to *keep* her, Malora fumes. She is no one's pet!

"Bind her up, just to be safe," he says to the cat-men holding her.

While she could easily swing these pussemboos over her head and dash them against the tree, Malora allows them to tie her arms behind her back and bind her to the base of the machatu tree. She overhears their talk and understands that they mean her no harm. They are only following the orders of the horse-men, who are obviously their masters. Although they speak with an odd inflection, both the cat-men and the horse-men speak the language of the People. Had the horse-men, Malora wonders, when they defeated the People and drove them into the wilderness, stolen their language as well as their homeland?

Sky is gone. Malora knows this much. Had he been close at hand, he would have come crashing into their midst, untied the knots, and set her free. He is alive, somewhere. She senses him running free, even as she watches the little cat-men straining to drag off the bodies of Streak and Smoke and Mist and either Sassy or Butte—she can't tell from this distance. Somewhere far off, she knows that Sky's legs are churning, carrying him away even as the pussemboos, one by one, round up the surviving horses and herd them into a pen made out of a circle of ironwood tree trunks pounded into the earth.

Malora is struck by the irony, for it is one of her father's pens. His pens, the wood silvery with age, dot these canyons like the ruins of other lost civilizations hereabout. How unhappy it would make Jayke to know that one of his pens is now being used to trap Malora's herd. The herd isn't particularly happy about it, either. Without Sky or Malora, they mill about, ears pinned, nipping at each other's flanks.

Bound to the base of the tree, Malora watches her captors from behind the thicket of her hair. Close to the pen, the pussemboos pitch camp for the horse-men, who lounge about in the grass on their haunches, twirling wildflowers in their fingers, laughing and talking.

"That storm," one of the horse-men says, "saved us. It brought us the horses, and it took away the heat."

"The human brings us good fortune," Orion, the blue-eyed centaur, says. The others pelt him with pebbles, but Malora can tell it is meant in fun.

The pussemboos erect a wide half circle of pretty silken

tents striped blue and white. As the tents billow in the late-afternoon breeze, they give off a spicy perfume.

Malora surveys the camp as it gradually takes shape before her. One of the tents appears to be meant for bathing. A line of horse-men proceeds into the tent while, from above, one of the pussemboos stands on a ladder and directs a spray of steaming water down on them. The horse-men emerge from the other side of the tent, rosy-skinned and wrapped in fleece. From there, they disappear into other tents and emerge dressed some time later.

Malora has to keep her jaw from dropping, for their fashion of dress is splendid. The horse-men wrap their bodies in a shimmering fabric that drapes over one shoulder, leaving the other bare, and winds around their bodies clear down to their horse tails and hiding their private parts. Malora can tell that the garments are made from one piece of cloth, beautifully woven. She wonders how they avoid soiling the fabric when they need to relieve themselves. Around their necks, arms, and waists are bands and chains of silver and gold studded with precious stones.

Other than what was preserved in the Grandparents' Box, the People never knew fine fabrics but dressed in simple clothing, coarsely woven wools dyed red to help them blend in with the canyon. The People's precious silver and gold was also kept in the box. Surely, flaunting all their finery in the open like this, these horse-men must be powerful princes, like the human companion of Pussemboos.

Malora finds herself longing to wash off the mud and douse herself in spicy scents and wrap her body in shimmering finery and gold. These lush trappings of civilization draw her, like a wild animal to a hearth. She toys with the idea of making peace with these creatures and going north, she and the horses, to live among them. But how can she win them over now that she has started things off so badly? She needs a plan worthy of Thora, and right now she is too hungry to think straight, much less form a plan.

Delicious smells waft from a plain brown tent pitched a ways off from the others. The pussemboos set up a long table, drape it with a crisp white cloth, and arrange beautiful embroidered cushions around it. The horse-men come to the table and recline on the cushions, sitting on their haunches with their front legs neatly folded beneath them. Soon afterward, the cat-men bring platter after platter piled high with colorful mounds of cooked food. Malora's mouth waters at the sights and smells. The horse-men bend over the table and eat with care, using shining implements and drinking from goblets. They are making merry!

Malora feels strangely left out. The sound of their voices, so human in spite of their bodies, and the longing for things she didn't even know she wanted make her feel like crying. But tears, she tells herself in Thora's voice, are an indulgence she cannot afford. They will only addle her.

"To the Apex and Herself!" the horse-men call out in one voice. They lift their goblets and drink.

"To the Golden Horse!" Theon adds, and they all chime in.

Pussemboos go around the table refilling goblets.

"The finest, fleetest, most handsome horses in the world,"

another horse-man calls out. Once again, the goblets are hoisted and clinked. "To the Ironbound Furies!" they shout.

Ironbound Furies. Is this their name for her horses? Malora wonders. It is a strong name, a good name. Malora feels a powerful surge of pride. Over in the pen, the boys and girls have settled down and are munching on their feed and slurping up water. They are being fed and watered and protected from predators without any help from her. Isn't this a good thing? she asks herself. The horse-men's way of capturing the band was cruel and even murderous, but perhaps now the kindness and respect of the pussemboos will prevail. *The finest, fleetest, most handsome horses in the world.*

Malora's defender rises from the table. He takes a spot only a short distance away and stares openly at her, a blue cloth that matches his eyes covering his mouth and nose. He approaches her and appears to be studying her from all angles, the way her mother studied a new botanical specimen.

He speaks at last, to himself. "The feet are so exotic! How delicate and how unlike our hooves—much more like fingers, only shorter and plumper. I wonder if they are as dexterous as hands. Kheiron, in his wisdom, says that it is our hands, and our ability with those hands to fashion objects of use and of beauty, that set the centaurs above the wild beasts. But here we have a creature in possession of two such sets of appendages. What does this mean when compared to us centaurs?"

Centaurs! Malora seizes upon the word. So *that* is what they call themselves. And now this centaur draws closer. She peers warily at him through her hair. A sweet scent engulfs her, of flowers and fruit and fragrant wood smoke. The smell seems to emanate from the blue cloth he holds beneath his nose. Lurking not far beneath the sweet aroma, she detects the far more earthy and familiar scent of horse. She wonders if the centaurs hide from their horse halves behind these scent-laden pieces of cloth. How strange! She likes the sweet scent well enough, but she much prefers the honest smell of horse.

Malora flinches as he reaches out and touches the malachite stone around her neck. "Humble yet strangely beautiful." Her arms are still bound; otherwise, instinct would have prompted her to strike out at him for touching her. He doesn't even know her! He has no right to touch her. A horse would have bitten him for less. "Is this object of religious significance, I wonder?"

Then his hands move to her hair. He brushes a few strands away from her eyes. "I'm sorry!" he says in a low voice. "You'll have to forgive me. I've never seen so much hair. Centaurean maidens, when they reach a certain age, stuff their hair up into caps. The Seventh Edict. Your hair's all matted with mud, of course, but I can imagine how lovely it will be when it's clean and combed."

He parts her hair with a finger and peers at her face. Emboldened, he gathers up more of her hair and rearranges it with care over her shoulders, then says, "I can see your whole face now. And I'm sure it must be more pleasant for you, as well!" He stands back, cloth to nose, head tilted to one side. "That's better," he says softly. Lowering the cloth, he smiles. His teeth are white and straight, with no pointed ones like those she has in her own mouth for tearing meat. His teeth are more horselike. She wonders if centaurs graze. Lifting her chin, she looks right back at him, meeting his unsettling blue gaze.

He nods and appears to reach a private conclusion. "It's a very good face," he declares. "An honest face. It's moments like these when I regret I did not take on drawing as my Hand. You'd make a fine subject." He frowns, rocking ever so slightly on his hooves, which are sheathed in heavy cloth boots that lace up the backs of his legs. "What are these white marks, I wonder?" He points to the faint tracings of scars on her arms and legs, where horses have nipped her in friendly, and sometimes not so friendly, fashion; where insects and snakes and small mammals have bitten her; where sparks from the fire have burned her.

"Except for these odd white marks and your extraordinary eyes, you're all the same tone—a sort of warm Iron-bound red. An artist would have to sketch with chalk mined from these mountains to get it right. But I'm not an artist, so all I can do is perhaps attempt to concoct a scent in honor of you. Let's see. What shall I call it? Ironbound? Or perhaps Fury." He stops, and suspicion darkens his eyes. "There is such a look of intelligence on your face, I could swear that you can understand every word I'm saying." His eyes narrow. "Can you?"

Malora, tempted to reply, remains silent. She knows much more useful information will be forthcoming from the centaurs and their feline underlings if they go on thinking she doesn't understand a word they are saying.

CHAPTER 7

Small Talk

Plains and mountains both are cloaked in silence, as if every living wild thing lies stunned in the wake of the storm and flood. A half-moon, like a shard from a shattered pot, has swung to the top of the rain-scoured sky. Malora wriggles free from the second set of knots. Three pussemboos sleep in a pile near the tree, the ones who, she supposes, are meant to guard her. She skirts them and heads toward the scullery tent, making her way past the blue-and-white-striped tents where the centaurs slumber. She stops at the entrance to one tent.

A lantern hangs from a hook on the tent pole, burning dimly. Malora peers further into the tent, curious to see how the centaurs sleep, and sees that this one, at least, sleeps on a low, wide bed, stretched out on his side, much the way she has seen horses sometimes sleep in the safety of their stalls. The centaur clutches a light woven coverlet to his bearded chin. A table near his bed holds the copper bangles he wore at dinner. She eyes with envy the assortment of silver-backed brushes of different shapes and sizes. Wouldn't they be useful, she thinks, to curry the hides of horses, especially after the winter when their hair comes off in tufts big enough to line the nests of a hundred buffalo weaver birds.

Next to the brushes sits a green glass bottle. Perhaps it contains water, she thinks, her mouth dry enough to choke her. She takes another step into the tent and waits. The centaur sleeps on. She sees no weapons. Had she been in his place, Malora reflects, she would have been up on her feet and holding a knife to the throat of the trespasser. But then again, she means no real harm, and perhaps the centaur, even in his sleep, senses this.

Malora steals over to the table and uncorks the green bottle. Lifting it to her nose, she inhales a rich floral aroma. In her mind, she sees the centaur who sleeps nearby. He is standing in a field of flowers kissing a female centaur wearing an odd-looking hat. Malora shrugs and shakes her head, then replugs the bottle of scent and sets it down. She picks up a silver-backed looking glass and stares at herself in the dim light. The looking glass shows all too clearly how matted and wild she has become. No wonder Theon fears her! Compared to these elegant centaurs, she is a fright, more baboon than person—and at least baboons groom themselves. Hastily, she sets the mirror facedown and makes her way out of the tent.

Malora enters the cooking tent and finds sacks hanging on hooks from the tent frame. She sniffs around until she finds something redolent of mint and wild onion. She brings the bag down and eats everything inside so quickly that she gets a violent case of the hiccups. She wipes her mouth, looks around for water, and finds none. Smothering the hiccups in her fist, she heads out of the camp.

The receding floodwater has gathered in a gully near the mouth of the canyon, making a pool that is bigger than a puddle but smaller than a pond. Malora drops to her knees at its edge and drinks deeply. By noon tomorrow, Malora knows the pool will be shrunk to half its current size, surrounded by the tracks and scat of a dozen animals, and bugs and tadpoles will already be hatching in it. But right now, it is pristine, cool and fresh from the sky, as good as water gets on the plains. When Malora has drunk her fill, she slides all the way into the pool and immerses her body. She shivers, but her hiccups eventually subside. Sitting in water that comes up to her chin, she grabs handfuls of sand to rub into her skin and scalp.

When her hair is rinsed and her skin is raw and tingling, Malora lies on her back and floats, listening to her breath, moving in and out of her body as she gazes up at the stars. Now that she is fed and watered, perhaps she can come up with a plan. It would be so easy to go to the pen and simply free the horses while the centaurs and the pussemboos sleep. But without Sky, she isn't eager to return to what she already thinks of as her life before the centaurs. Without Sky, she has no interest in leading a herd. She is happy that Sky is free, but she realizes suddenly that she doesn't want to leave the centaurs. Freedom on the plains has been such hard work and so lonely. Her mother's death has left her feeling ungrounded. It is as if she has been surviving all this time only because she might one day go home to her mother. Without her mother, Malora's life has lost its purpose. She knows she needs something different, and the centaurs and the pussem-boos are certainly that.

Then, through the water, the nearby yelp of a jackal brings her surging to her feet. Splashing out of the gully, she dashes onto the plains. She pulls up short and gasps. There they are, lying everywhere, like great dark boulders stranded in the moonlight.

"Oh, my boys and girls! What have they done to you?" she whispers.

The bodies of Blacky and Mist and Streak lie in a matted mound where the cat-men have dragged them. She walks past them and sees that there are other bodies as well, strewn about, belonging to horses she believed to have escaped. She sees Oil. And then she sees, off by herself as she often was in life, the moody and solitary mare, Silky.

"Oh, my sweet, shy Silky! Look at you!" Malora falls to her knees and throws herself over the body. "I'm so sorry, my dear," she whispers to the mare's lifeless head. "Your girls, Fancy and Stormy, are in the pen. They're safe and sound." And then, like the afternoon's cloudburst, something inside of her breaks loose and comes pouring out in a torrent of tears, her loneliness and her grief. Just knowing that her mother was somewhere, going about her life, had made Malora eager and willing to go on with her own life. Now that willingness is drained from her, replaced by a great weariness.

Malora doesn't know how long she lies there with her head buried in Silky's side. When she finally looks up, she is too spent to do anything but stare at the centaur who stands over her holding a lantern. She wipes her face on Silky's mane, smooths back her hair, and stands up.

She thinks she sees tears pooling in the centaur's startlingly blue eyes, but perhaps this is just the moon's reflection.

"Theon is wrong," Orion says to her softly. "He said you were vicious and wild. But if you are capable of feeling grief, then it stands to reason that you must possess other civilized traits." He ventures a tentative smile.

Malora returns his smile, realizing with a slight uneasiness that her tears have weakened her resolve not to speak. The sound of his voice is a balm to her sadness. He goes on talking as he stares out over the plain of dead horses. "I realized this afternoon, after I fished you out of those floodwaters, that I had dreamed once, years ago, that I met a human girl by a river. In the dream, we walked along the riverbank and we spoke and it was the most enjoyable conversation. I wonder if you dream." He turns to scrutinize her. "But that's just as absurd, I realize, as my having the feeling that you understand every word I say, when how could that possibly be?"

"It's true!" she says before her sense gets the better of her. "I do talk . . . and I do dream."

His jaw drops and he backs away from her, as if she has just burst into flames.

"But I couldn't speak, don't you see? We're ancient enemies," she says, moving toward him slowly so as not to spook him. "Theon said so. I needed to learn as much about you as I could. If I had spoken up, you wouldn't have carried on so openly in my presence. You wouldn't have said certain things. I wouldn't have learned nearly as much about you."

His eyes dart about, as he seeks to recall what was said.

Hesitantly, he asks, "What was it exactly that you learned about us?"

She hides a smile. "I learned that centaurs are a princely race who like to lounge around in the grass plucking wildflowers while the poor pussemboos do all the work."

He stares at her in puzzlement. "The poor *what?*" he asks.

Malora says, "Pussemboos. You know . . . those little cat-like men you travel with. The slaves who do your bidding."

He tosses his head back and howls with laughter.

Malora feels her face heating up. She does not like being the butt of a joke she doesn't understand.

Recovering at last, he wipes the tears of mirth from his eyes and says, "Pussemboos! Is it *Puss in Boots* that you mean to say?"

Malora bristles. "I do not. I said *pussemboos* and I mean *pussemboos.*"

"The ancient tale of the clever cat who wears high boots and assists his human master is, I do believe, entitled *Puss in Boots.*" He wags his head.

Is it possible, Malora wonders, that Aron's grandmother was as simple as her grandson? She should have known this to be the case.

Orion says, "Actually, now that you point it out, the Twani do bear a rather remarkable resemblance to Puss in Boots. I wonder why I never thought of that."

"The Twani?" Malora asks. "Is that what you call them?"

"It's what they call themselves. And they are no more our slaves than you are my enemy." He flashes her a smile that is full of warmth.

"Really?" she asks, very much wanting to believe both of these things.

"It's true. We rescued the Twani from an erupting volcano ages ago, and they came to live with us. They have taken care of us ever since because they owe us a debt of gratitude for saving their lives. As for the centaurs and the People, we might have been enemies ages ago, when the People outnumbered the centaurs, but as far as I can tell"—he looks over her shoulder as if the human dead stood massed behind her—"there's only one of you left."

Malora sighs. "It's true. I just buried the last of the People in the Settlement. I think I went a little mad from grief or maybe the heat. I ran the herd all night, and that's why we fell into the trap your pussemboo—er, Twani—set for us." She realizes as she says these things that while they are sad and unpleasant, she is happy to be saying them aloud, rather than keeping everything to herself.

"You're quite sure all of the People are dead?" he asks hesitantly.

She nods.

Orion's face floods with relief, and she feels the need to point out, "Including my own mother."

He looks stricken. "I'm so sorry! That was very thoughtless of me. When I lose my lady mother, I'm sure I'll grieve for the rest of my days."

"This was my mother's," she says, holding up the malachite stone to share something of hers, but also to lessen the sudden onslaught of sadness. "I took it from her before I buried her."

The centaur looks so genuinely distraught that she thinks

he has had next to no experience of hardship, let alone death. His arms and face and chest are smooth and free of scars. She wonders whether he has any stories to tell, or whether they still lie in wait for him.

"The stone is beautiful, and it's good that you have something of hers," he says softly.

"Yes, I have my mother's stone and my father's rope. The rope!" Malora cries, clapping a hand over her mouth. It is one thing to lose the knife, but she cannot lose the rope, especially now that she has lost Sky. "I have to find it," she says, spinning around and heading toward the dark maw of the canyon.

"Wait!" Orion calls after her. "Can't you look for it in the morning?"

"No, I can't," she says. "I need to find it now . . . before some greedy raptor finds it and uses it to line his nest."

"Then let me come with you. This lantern will help," he says. When she doesn't slow down, he adds, "I'll be happy to accompany you if only you'll wait up. You move very quickly for a two-legger."

Malora is about to say that he moves very slowly for a four-legger, but she doesn't want to hurt his feelings.

"I just realized," he says, trotting up alongside her, "I don't even know your name."

She stops suddenly. "Malora."

He smiles. "Very pretty. We'll call you Malora Ironbound, which is most suitable. My name is Orion Silvermane."

"I know," she says.

"That's right! Of course!" Orion says.

Malora wonders whether to correct him about her last

name, and then decides not to. She thinks Malora Ironbound sounds better than Malora Thora-Jayke. If she carries the dead in her heart, she reasons, why should she need to carry them in her name as well? This is more of the *something different* that she so badly needs right now.

"It's very nice to meet you, Malora Ironbound," he says, placing his right hand over his heart, and then raising it palm out to her. He looks at her expectantly. "You're supposed to do what I'm doing."

"Why?" she asks. She has gone back to looking for the rope, eyes scanning the ground.

"It's the centaurs' salutation," he says.

She smiles and says, "But I'm not a centaur." Just then, the familiar black-and-white shape of the rope materializes out of the darkness of the canyon corridor. It has snagged on a gnarled tree limb growing out of the canyon wall. Malora lunges for it, glad she has been saved a trip all the way back into the box canyon, that place of desperation and suffering.

"True enough. But you will be coming to live among centaurs," Orion says with a disarming smile. "You're going to return with me to Mount Kheiron, in triumph, leading those beautiful horses."

Malora frowns as she untangles the rope from the limb. She says, as much to herself as to him, "I guess I am."

"Good! It's settled, then. After all, you're the last human, and the last human can't very well go wandering about in the bush by herself," he says. "You might get eaten by a hippo."

She laughs shortly. "Hippos don't eat humans," she says, looping the rope. "I swim with hippos all the time, and they've never taken even a small bite out of me."

"They eat centaurs," Orion says. The lantern swinging back and forth makes the canyon floor appear to be rocking. "At least twenty centaurs disappear every year, and hippos are the culprits. I ought to know. My brother Athen was one of them."

"Well, Athen must have come too near a cow with calves. Hippo mothers will do *anything* to protect their young," she says, adding silently, *like my mother.* Then she dislodges the lump in her throat with a joke. "It's too bad the hippos didn't eat Theon instead."

Orion laughs. "Oh, Theon's all right. He has a slight tendency toward hysteria. I keep pressing him to accept a lavender-based scent called Serenity to calm his nerves, but he claims it dampens his spirit. I assure you, the centaurs back home will be charmed to make your acquaintance. Like me, they've never seen a living human being before."

She stops and catches his hand. "They have seen *dead* ones?"

Looking flustered, Orion says, "Not exactly. But there is a mass grave of the People on the flats below Mount Kheiron. It is very old, and there is a mural on the side of the monument marking the burial place. It depicts . . . well, People who look very much like you."

"Really?" Her pulse quickens. "I would like to see this monument."

Orion's look of discomfort deepens. "I'm not really all that sure that you would."

"Why not?"

"Well, the painting is called the Massacre of Kamaria. It shows centaurs . . . well . . . *slaughtering* the People," he says.

"Oh." She blows air out between her lips.

He looks startled. "You sound just like a horse!"

Malora glances at him briefly, and then grins. The grim moment passes. "I'm probably more of a horse than you are." Not waiting for a response, she asks, not entirely in jest, "So, can I take it that it is not your intention to slaughter me?"

"Never!" Orion says, aghast, then hastens to add, "It would be in direct violation of the Fourteenth Edict. The Apex and Herself would never allow it."

"The Apex is the leader of your herd?" she asks.

Orion looks mortified. "He is leader of our *nation-state,*" he says. "He is also my father."

"And Herself is . . . ?"

"My lady mother," he says, "Hylonome Silvermane. But everyone calls her Herself."

"The Apex and Herself rule together?" Malora asks. She likes the sound of this. She sometimes wonders whether the People would have lasted longer had the men and women not divided the labor quite so strictly.

"He is first among equals," he says. "And Herself, well, she rules him."

Understanding dawns upon Malora. "Like the lead stallion and mare of a herd."

"You might put it that way," he says, his teeth glinting in the lantern light. "But I don't suggest you do so. Centaurs, as a rule, prefer to overlook their horse halves."

Malora nods slowly. This confirms her theory about the scented cloths they hold to their noses. "That's an awfully big part of yourselves to overlook," she says.

Smiling, Orion puts his finger to his lips. "Shhh," he says, "it's a secret. You mustn't tell."

CHAPTER 8

The First Whiff

Malora feels a laugh bubbling in her throat. It is good to appreciate a joke, other than one of her own.

Girl and centaur walk together back to the camp. Malora notices that their heads are of equal height. "How old are you?" she asks.

"Seventeen."

"I am fifteen," she says. "I think."

"You seem both older . . . and younger," he says. Then he grabs her hand and squeezes, his voice excited. "Look there, Malora! One of the horses is still alive!"

Malora breaks away from Orion and runs toward the horse, then staggers to a halt. Stomach churning, she backs off. This is no horse struggling to stand, but a horse, quite dead, being ripped open by a scavenger. It is pulling the horse's entrails up and out of the body, unraveling them like a long, gory ribbon.

She takes a deep breath and roars. "Be off!"

It stops tugging and stares at her, its eyes alight with ancient grudges and insatiable greed.

Malora hears Orion gasp. "It's one of them! A scavenger!"

"A hyena," she says, wiping the spittle from her mouth. She knows the animal serves a function in the natural scheme, but that doesn't mean she has to like anything about it.

"I have heard of them but have never seen one at work," Orion says.

"Then you are lucky," Malora says, her voice dead. "Usually they don't come slinking around until the bodies start to bloat and stink. By tomorrow night, the plain will be crawling with them."

She loathes the sight of the hyena, with its small ears cropped close to its knobby skull and its body swarming with spots. The hyena's eyes go on challenging her, devoid of fear or shame. It is the look of death, and there has been too much death in her life. Although she knows it is a futile—even ridiculous—act, Malora picks up a fallen tree branch and swings it at the hyena's head. It flinches, drops the string of horse guts, and slinks off.

"What a despicable creature," Orion says, staring after it. "Still, Honus will be tickled to learn we saw one. I don't believe he's ever seen a hyena, either. I wish I had some souvenir of it I could bring back for his collection."

Malora sighs. "Hyenas aren't so bad . . . unless they happen to be feeding on someone you once loved. They serve their purpose. The hyenas come first, then the jackals and the painted dogs, then the vultures and the bustards and the crows, and, finally, the insects, until all that's left is bones. Very little goes to waste here."

"You know so much about the bush," he says admiringly.

Malora wonders what this *bush* is he keeps speaking of. It isn't until this moment that she realizes she has been caught up in the first real talking she has had since leaving the Settlement. This feels like something even better than small talk. She wants the talk to go on, but they have come to the horse pen.

Malora leaves Orion and steals past the gate where the Twani snore in a pile. Inside the pen, the horses sleep, standing in groups of five or six, arranged head to tail. At her approach, a nearby cluster wakens with startled snorts, lifting their heads and swinging their noses toward her. Whinnying softly, they trot over to where a series of shorter uprights create a low spot in the fence.

Malora boosts herself up and lowers herself into the pen. The horses offer their long black heads, which she holds in her arms and strokes, breathing into their nostrils as they breathe into hers, butting her head softly against theirs. She nickers at them, and they nicker back. The others soon wake up and come to take their turns. She wades deeper into the herd, the animals slipping around her as she passes from one to another like a swimmer in a flowing river of horses.

Malora counts twenty-two heads and does what little she can in the darkness to take stock of them, running her hands up and down their legs to detect the heat that might mean a break or a sprain, checking their hooves for splits and their hides for open wounds or tears in the flesh, damage wrought by the flood or the capture.

In the far corner of the pen, Malora comes upon Lightning, standing next to Posy, who has just foaled. The mare nudges the bloody lump with her nose, trying to breathe life into it. Sometimes some stubborn instinct in the mare makes her keep up this futile effort for days following a stillbirth, until the tiny dead horse is just a rolled-up ball of flesh lying in the dust. But the knowledge of her loss is already weighing heavily upon her. Her tail hangs lank, her ears are limp, and the light is gone from her eyes. Malora approaches with care and starts to stroke her side, speaking to her in soothing tones. "It's okay, Posy. You'll have another chance, you'll see. Everything's going to be all right."

Lightning erupts in a loud snort. She paws the earth, ears flattened to her skull, nostrils steaming.

"Easy, big girl!" Malora says, placing a calming hand on her neck. "What's the trouble?"

Malora follows the mare's baleful look and sees, through the low section in the fence, Orion looking on. In his wide blue eyes, pale as milk in the darkness, she thinks she has found a kind of consolation for what is past, and a hope for things to come.

"It's okay, girl," Malora tells Lightning. "He's a friend."

She awakes in the morning to the smell of molasses and grain. The Twan who has come into the pen, waddling beneath the weight of the feed buckets hooked over his shoulders, nods warily at her.

"Orion Silvermane knows I'm here," Malora tells him, rising hastily from her bed of cloud grass and dusting herself off.

"He came by first thing and explained how things are,"

the Twan says. His voice is high-pitched, a little sharp and whiny, the way Malora would expect a talking cat to sound.

"Oh?"

"You are no longer our prisoner. You are a guest," the Twan says, his catlike lips pursed in disapproval.

"And this is not to your liking," she says.

"What I like doesn't matter. My concern is the horses," he says.

The horses, meanwhile, smell the feed. They are poking their heads under his arms and into the buckets. Malora pushes their noses gently but firmly away. She dips her own nose into one of the buckets and sniffs, then tastes and chews a few grains. "Go back and rework the portions. Give them only half as much," she tells the Twan. "They're not used to such rich food."

"Begging your pardon," the Twan says, "but I'm in charge—"

"Actually, *I'm* in charge," Orion says, his head looming suddenly over the top of the fence. "And I would like you to do as she says, Gift."

Gift stiffens, his flat face unreadable. His large eyes blink once slowly. "Very well, Master Orion," he says. "But the Apex—"

"The Apex will be happy to have Furies who are not felled by colic owing to a too-rich diet," Orion says curtly. "Come along to breakfast, Malora, unless you intend to eat what's in the buckets."

Malora hesitates, wanting to stay and see the horses properly fed, but Orion has a look on his face this morning that brooks no disagreement—from either Twan or human. Malora hurries out of the pen to join Orion, saying to Gift over her shoulder, "After they've eaten, can you check them for gashes and sprains?"

"As if I wouldn't do that without being told by the likes of you," Gift mutters.

"His name is Gift?" Malora whispers as they move away from the pen.

"That's a dandy irony for you, isn't it?" Orion says. "He's my father's newest hire. He's wrangler in chief."

Malora halts, frowning deeply. "He's the one who tricked the horses into the canyon."

Orion nods. "In fairness to him, however, he couldn't very well *not* deliver Furies to my father."

Malora walks on. "I *knew* there was something about him I didn't like."

"He has, however, a reputation for success," Orion says.

Malora wants to hear more about this reputation of Gift's, but they have arrived at the table. The centaurs are eating and laughing and bantering, much the way they had been at last night's meal. At her approach, they set down their spoons and fall silent. Their finery and jewels packed away, the centaurs are dressed for travel in tan wraps and brown leather boots.

"Brother and cousins," says Orion, "please welcome to our table Malora Ironbound."

On either side of the table, the centaurs rise and regard Malora from under hooded eyes, as proud as two rows of stallions presenting themselves for inspection. Orion draws Malora closer to them.

"My brother Theon, you already know," Orion says, his voice even.

"Hello," Malora says in a bold and friendly fashion, determined to make a new start with the braying centaur who not so long ago lobbied for her execution.

Theon picks up the lavender cloth beside his plate and sniffs at it with a gusty snort. Malora assumes that Theon has finally accepted his brother's offer of Serenity, although Theon seems more sullen than serene this morning. Over the cloth, Theon's gray eyes slide away from her like melting chips of ice.

"This is my cousin Mather," Orion goes on. Mather directs his haughty gaze over Malora's head. Malora smiles to herself. It was into Mather's tent that she crept last night. In the daylight, she sees that his flanks, a glossy nut brown, match his neatly trimmed beard.

Orion introduces more cousins—Devan and Brandle and March and Felton and Marsh and Elmon. Marsh and Elmon are also brothers; she can tell by the shape of their heads and the color of their flanks, a rich, tawny golden. They remind Malora of a pair of very well-groomed lions. The tightly curled hair on their heads and their bushy tails is nearly white. A horse with this coloration would be splendid, she thinks, wondering, fleetingly, whether a centaur would ever let her ride on his back.

None of the centaurs, Malora is interested to note, treats her to the centaur salutation. Orion may have spoken to them, but they are resentful about her new status, that much is clear to her.

"Please, sit down and eat," Orion says to Malora, pointing to the pile of cushions next to his.

Malora sits, startled by the softness of the cushions. A Twan appears and sets down a bowl of steaming mush before her. The centaurs, having resumed their places at the table, push at the mush in their bowls and mutter to one another. Unlike Orion, who takes pains to draw her into conversation, they exclude her from their talk. She notices that Theon hasn't touched his mush. He keeps looking at her with an expression of mingled contempt and terror. When she smiles at him, he dives for the lavender cloth and buries his face in it.

"The Serenity may take a few days to reach its full effectiveness," Orion whispers to Malora with a sly wink.

"You could always double the dose," she says. Orion leans into her and chuckles.

The Twani go back and forth from the cook tent to the table, refilling goblets and fussing over the centaurs. Malora notes that each of them seems to serve a specific centaur. The Twan who serves her is the same one who serves Orion. The mush is not all that much different from what the horses are eating, except that it is cooked. It is also mixed with berries and honey and goats' milk. It is a welcome change from the strips of dried kudu she gnaws upon most mornings. The food she scrounged last night in the cook tent was also grain. Malora wonders again whether the centaurs have flat teeth because, like horses, they are meant to eat grass and grain.

When the Twan comes to take away her empty bowl, she sits back on the cushions and says, "That was delicious."

The Twan's pale pink mouth curls into a neat bow. His large eyes close slowly and then open, the pupils wide and black. Malora thinks that she hears the rumble of a purr. He places a hand lightly on hers. The fingers are short, the backs of his hands covered with fur. The palms of his hands are pink and shiny and hairless. She smells the morning sun on him, a scent that is fresh and clean and pleasing.

"I'm glad that you liked it, Malora. My name is West. If there's anything you need, you'll just let West know."

West's voice is deeper, less whiny, and more sibilant than Gift's. As he leaves, Malora swears that she feels him lightly brush up against her back. But when she turns, West has already disappeared into the cook tent.

Orion says, "He likes you."

"I like him, too," Malora says. "So far, I like all the Twani—"

"Except for Gift," Orion says with a knowing smile.

"Except for Gift," Malora says.

"I think I will have a word with Gift," Orion says, and excuses himself, leaving Malora alone with the other centaurs. The moment Orion leaves, the centaurs resume talking, their voices loud and jolly. Malora feels distinctly unwelcome.

When, at last, the centaurs set down their spoons, Malora is relieved to see the Twani swoop in and clear the table. The centaurs rise slowly from their places, stretching and patting their stomachs. They amble off into the grass and collapse as if they had been toiling since before dawn. Malora squats at the foot of the machatu tree and watches, fascinated by the efficiency with which the Twani gather the cushions and the table. No sooner do some of the Twani remove chests and cots and tables and lanterns from the tents than others are collapsing the tents and rolling them up. Everything gets carefully stowed into the beds of two long wagons, to which teams of stout ponies have been hitched.

When Orion rejoins her, Malora says, "Your Twani are making fast work of the camp."

"Yes," Orion says. "They are very efficient fellows."

"You say they aren't slaves. Do you mean to say that they *willingly* work this hard?" Malora asks.

Orion, watching the flurry of Twanian activity, says, "I often wonder about that myself, but this is how they are. They still feel the obligation to serve us, even though the debt has long ago been paid in full. Occasionally, some up-start Flatlander will foment to free the Twani, but the Twani will have no part in it. Their place is with us. From the day we are born, we have our own Twan to look after us. They are with us until they die. Twani live nowhere near as long as centaurs."

"Why is that?" Malora asks, thinking, in spite of what Orion has just said, that the centaurs must work the Twani to death.

Orion shrugs. "That's just the way it is. A single centaur can go through at least three Twani before he or she dies."

"What do the mother centaurs do if they don't take care of their own young?" she asks.

"They enjoy the society of other centaurs."

"Do none of you ever learn to do for yourselves, then?"

Orion says, "I do *some* things for myself. I comb my own hair and shave my own face. I prefer to wash myself, but no centaur can really do an effective job of grooming his other half. Although," he adds, "my little sister, Zephele, tries her best. She likes to keep her Twan busy with utterly meaning-less tasks while she looks after herself."

"I think I might like your sister," Malora says.

"She is sixteen and has taken care of herself since she was quite small. Sunshine, her Twan, would try to dress her, but our Zephie would stamp her little hoof and insist upon doing it herself, even if she wound up looking like an unmade bed. Nowadays, she looks quite presentable. Still, the whole situation is highly unusual, and sometimes Herself fears it will affect her prospects. Zephele doesn't seem to care."

He turns to her. "We'll let the others get underway, and then we'll follow with the horses. I persuaded Gift to let you handle the herd, at least for now."

"Thank you," she says.

The centaur cousins, walking in a group, take the lead, followed by the two wagons. One Twan is at the reins of each wagon, while the rest drape themselves across the cargo, curl up, and fall fast asleep. Traveling just far enough behind not to be tasting the dust of the wagon wheels, Malora rides Lightning, abreast of Orion, with the herd at their heels. Glancing back at them, Malora can tell from the way they carry themselves, with heads low and tails lank, that they are exhausted from yesterday's ordeal. It's just as well that the centaurs and wagons ahead of them are moving at a tortoise's pace.

But Malora feels far from exhausted. She feels a tingling sense of anticipation. She has made up her mind that she is going to a new place where she will meet more centaurs, ideally all of them just like Orion. Malora thinks that her life, razed to the ground by her mother's death, is perhaps starting to build itself back up again. She is hopeful in a way she hasn't been since the morning the men rode out on their last hunt.

Orion lifts the cloth to his nose again and sniffs.

Curious, Malora asks, "What does that smell like?"

He hands the cloth up to her. She places it beneath her nose, as she has seen the centaurs do, and inhales deeply from it.

CHAPTER 9

The Otherian

A picture enters Malora's mind and comes into such sharp and sudden focus that it almost hurts. She sees a room with a vaulted ceiling sparkling with golden tiles, an orange sun flaming at its center. Beneath the sun, there is a big bed draped with a decorative canopy of dark blue. The canopy is sprinkled with golden stars forming pictures that shift and change as a gentle breeze blows in through an arched window at the foot of the bed and ripples the fabric.

Looking through the window, she sees the most beautiful garden. The flowers are bigger and brighter than any that blossom on the plains. Small, colorful birds flit about in fruit trees whose crowns are perfectly spherical and dotted with ripe fruits. Malora hears the sound of running water. She looks back into the room and sees her father's black-and-white rope hanging in a coil on the wall by the bed.

Malora shivers with pleasure and a strange feeling of relief as she lowers the cloth and holds it to her breast.

"Are you quite all right?" Orion asks her.

With an effort, Malora blinks and shakes her head. As she hands the scented cloth back to him, the picture fades from her mind like a dream upon wakening. "What *is* that?"

"This? Let's see: sweet almond oil, Rosa damascena, hectorite . . ." He itemizes on his fingers. "Clover leaf extract, Althaea officinalis root, citronellal, benzoate resin as a fixative, but it carries its own scent—burnt honey, I'd say. Raspberry seed oil, and, let me see, what else . . . oh, yes! Kalanchoe extract! I call it Homeward Bound. Do you like it?"

Malora nods dumbly. Then, because Orion is looking at her so eagerly and because she feels she has to say *something*, she says, "Homeward Bound smells good."

It *does* smell good, she thinks, but it is a good deal more than a pleasant scent. Nevertheless, Malora keeps her thoughts to herself.

"I would very much like to mix you a scent of your own," Orion says earnestly.

Experiencing the scent has unsettled Malora. "I don't think so," she says, raising her hand. "Thank you very much, but I need to keep my head clear . . . to smell predators."

Orion lowers the cloth from his nose and looks worried. "Oh?" he says. Hastily, he tucks the cloth away in his wrap and shakes his head with vigor, imitating her. She wonders if, even with a cleared head, he would know the smell of lion if he were sitting on top of one.

"Why didn't you have a scented cloth with you last night?" Malora asks.

He frowns. "I never use them at night. I find the scents of the night—particularly out here in the bush—are ravishing enough as they are. The very early morning is fragrant as well, before the sun bakes the essence from the plants and the trees," he says. "It has something to do with the way the earth cools after the sun sets, and then in the morning, before it rises high. It's similar to the process that occurs in the distillery. Honus calls it evaporation."

Malora has no idea what he is talking about. "Who is this Honus you keep mentioning?" she asks.

"He is the Otherian who taught me and my brothers and who now teaches my little sister."

"What is an *Otherian*?"

Orion pauses in his stride to pick a pebble from the boot on his right foreleg. "An Otherian," he explains, "is someone who is not of us; therefore, an *other* and hence, an Otherian."

Malora's mind races. "You mean Honus is one of the People?"

"No, no," he says hastily. "I mean that he isn't a centaur."

"What is he, then, if not of the People and not a centaur?" she asks.

"He calls himself a cloven-hoofed polymath, but, technically, he is of the faun hibe," Orion says.

"What is a polymath?" Malora asks. She finds the complexity of Orion's vocabulary both frustrating and fascinating.

"Someone who knows something of everything. He is very wise. This faun is wiser than all the centaurs in Mount Kheiron."

Faun sounds to Malora like some sort of animal, an impala, perhaps. Do the animals where they are going speak? she wonders. What will an entire city of centaurs be like? In this brief time, she has seen enough of the centaurs to know that while they might be part horse, they are much closer to humans. They have four hoofed feet and fur-covered flanks and tails. But, unlike horses, they don't relieve themselves where they stand. They go off into the bushes and modestly attend to their needs. They eat with tools and drape their private parts and have complex thoughts and ideas, which they express in words rather than snorts and nickers and neighs.

Malora has lived with horses for so long that, in some ways, she had begun to think like them. In order to live among the centaurs, will she have to start thinking like a centaur? Then a new thought occurs to her. "Are Twani considered Otherians?" she asks.

"No. They are considered . . . Twani."

Malora nods, oddly satisfied with Orion's cryptic reply. "Tell me more about Mount Kheiron," she requests.

"It is the Home of Beauty and Enlightenment," says Orion.

Malora finds this description unhelpful, more of Orion's fancy words for which she has no context. "Does this mean you all dress in finery? I, too, would very much like to be draped in finery."

He glances at her leopard-skin tunic and then quickly looks away. "I imagine my mother and father will insist on your dressing appropriately."

"What does this mean?" she asks.

He looks flustered and confused. "Like a centaur maiden, of course."

Malora snorts. "Not unless I grow another set of legs."

He laughs, enjoying her joke. "Honus is a two-legger, and our tailors and cobblers have managed to keep him sartorially satisfied. I imagine they can cut and stitch clothing to the contours of your body. And, of course, you'll have to wear your hair in a cap, although I do hope you won't have to cut it."

"Why would I have to do that?"

"It's an Edict. The Seventh Edict, guarding against inflammatory public displays. Females over twelve baring their heads in public amounts to what is known as an inflammatory display. This is solved by pinning the hair under a cap or covering of some sort. Among the Highlander maidens and ladies, the caps can be quite stylish, with feathers and beads and whatnot."

In the brief silence that follows, Malora cocks her head at the sky; she tries to picture herself wearing a cap and fails. When they pause to watch a family of giraffes lope across the path, Malora asks, "And what of the horses? What will happen to them? Will they have to wear caps, too?"

Orion laughs, even though she has posed her question in all seriousness. "Only bridles and carriage harnesses. They will be treated exceedingly well, I should think. My father has the finest stable in all of Mount Kheiron."

"Will they have water to drink and grass to eat?" Malora asks.

"The freshest water and the finest oats," Orion answers. "And jobs to do as well. Everyone in Mount Kheiron has a job to do, including the horses."

"And your job is . . . ?"

"I am an alchemist," he explains.

Malora repeats the word silently. "What does an alchemist do?"

Orion smiles. "It's complicated. But basically, I create scents in my distillery," he says.

"So it was you who concocted Homeward Bound?"

"And Theon's Serenity and Mather's Bower and all the scents my cousins use. I mix essences together to create scents to inhale or burn or sprinkle. I distill the essences from fruits and seeds and plants and flowers and bits of wood and bark. I studied under Kheiron's master alchemist, who has, unfortunately, passed away."

Compared to hunting or healing or even basket weaving, Orion's seems like a frivolous job to Malora. And yet there was nothing frivolous about the vivid picture the scent spawned in her mind. "Is being an alchemist an important job?"

"Anything centaurs do with our hands is considered important. Properly mixed and prepared, scents establish the very tone of society. They control emotions and set moods. I've seen them bring about radical transformations. They can make a drowsy soul feel lively and an overly excited one find peace. They can attract mates and repel enemies and bring forth dormant emotions and suppress unwanted ones. They can make for happy, lively, gracious households. A home without scents is a cold cell. I'm proud to have chosen alchemy as my Hand."

"What is this hand you speak of?" Malora asks. "Apart from these things sticking out at the end of our arms?"

Each new question of Malora's seems to make Orion happier. "The Hand," he explains, "according to our Patron and Founder, Kheiron the Wise, is what sets us apart from the beasts. A Hand entails the making of things, like jubilation or paintings or tapestry or sculpture. Or it can be that which you can't see, like law or religion or philosophy."

"Or scents!" she says.

"Indeed." He nods. "Boys and girls at age twelve choose a Hand and study it until age sixteen, when we begin to practice."

This doesn't sound all that different from the way life went in the Settlement, Malora thinks, except that jobs there were far more dull and practical. Entertainment and beauty were extras, fit in around more important things like survival. Women in the Settlement took pride in the pots they molded, the fabrics and baskets they wove—and some of these objects were even beautiful—but function was more important than form. Had she told her mother she wanted to study jubilation—whatever that was—Thora would have thought she had gotten into the monkey weed. A job was practical, and most children had no choice but to follow their parents. Life in Mount Kheiron sounded altogether freer and easier.

"Will I, when I come to stay among the centaurs, be able to choose a Hand?" Malora asks.

Orion's brow creases. "That's a very interesting question. At fifteen, you're coming to it rather late in life."

"Then I will simply choose horse training for my Hand," she says airily.

"Oh, horse training is not a Hand," Orion says.

"Then how do your horses get trained?"

"The Twani—like our fine friend Gift—train our horses

for us. The Flatlanders train horses, too, in their own stables, but Flatlanders don't choose a Hand."

"What are Flatlanders?" she asks. "Another hibe?"

"No. They are centaurs, like me and my cousins, except that they are born down on the floodplains surrounding Mount Kheiron. The centaurs born up on Mount Kheiron are called Highlanders. Flatlanders are—in many ways, as you will see—a breed apart from Highlanders. They don't have Twani, and they don't have Hands, and they don't have representatives who sit in our Salient, which is the ruling body headed by my father. Flatlanders serve Highlanders by doing practical tasks, like farming and carpentry and, like my old friend Neal, serving on the Peacekeeping Force."

"Flatlanders sound like the People," Malora murmurs.

Human and centaur lapse into silence. She enjoys their silences almost as much as their talk. This morning, the talk feels bubbly and light, fortifying and refreshing, as if she has been riding down a stream, tripping and dashing and splash-ing and sparkling in the sunlight.

Orion strides along jauntily in his khaki boots. His wrap, flapping in the hot wind, has begun to turn blotchy with sweat. He looks around and, taking a deep breath, says, "The bush is beautiful today, is it not?"

Malora looks where he looked. "Where is this bush you keep speaking of?" There are thousands of bushes and thou-sands of trees and boulders and scrub stretching out for as far as the eye can see in all directions.

Orion shakes his head and laughs softly. "Oh, Malora, you have no idea what delightful company you make. The bush is what we call the lands extending from Mount Kheiron to the Ironbound Mountains in the south and, to the north of us, all the way to the coast where Kahiro—capitol of the Kingdom of the Ka—lies. We refer to all wild, uncivilized areas as the bush."

Malora smiles and wonders, Does this now make me the Daughter of the Bush? But no, that makes her sound like some wild thing that crouches in a thicket and skulks out at night to gobble up stray goats and little children.

They are, as it happens, traveling through a particularly lush and densely populated area of the "bush." Shade trees and clumps of bushes—actual bushes, she thinks—dot the landscape. Herds of wildebeests gambol in their comical way, while impalas leap above the downy cloud grass. Rhinoceroses graze placidly in the middle distance, as still as gray boulders. Flocks of tiny yellow butterflies flit and skim back and forth across the tasseled tops of the high grass. The bush *is* beautiful today, Malora sees, but, as always, it holds the potential for violence. Any moment now, a predator could slink from behind some tree and send all of these creatures, including them, running for their lives. It occurs to her again that she is unarmed. "Where do you keep your weapons?"

"The centaurs have no weapons. The Twani keep theirs in the wagons," Orion says.

Malora laughs shortly. "I hope you don't expect the Twani to defend us. They are so small and, from what I have seen, not at all fierce. Why do centaurs have no weapons?"

Orion dips his chin. "As a rule, we travel with an escort of Peacekeepers—Flatlanders authorized by the Apex to carry arms—but they have all gone off to Kahiro on a special mission. Father was impatient to have his horses now, so we braved the bush with only our stalwart band of Twani to protect us."

"Isn't self-defense considered a Hand?" she asks.

Orion wags his head. "Highlanders are forbidden to own or use weapons of any kind. No weapons are permitted in Mount Kheiron. The Third Edict."

Malora is shocked. She cannot imagine living without weapons. "So I, too, will have to follow the Third Edict?" Malora asks.

"Naturally, as you must follow all fourteen," he says. "If you are to live among us, you must be bound by the same Edicts that bind us. That is the way of it."

"What happens if someone refuses to follow the Edicts?"

"They are turned out," Orion says bluntly, as if the subject were unpleasant to him.

Turned out is an expression her father used when he set the horses loose from the stable to run in the paddock. The horses were always happy to be turned out. "That doesn't sound so bad to me," she says.

"Oh, but it is very dire, indeed. To be turned out is to be banished from Mount Kheiron," Orion says. "Sent into the wild with nothing, not even the wrap on your back."

Malora reflects that her mother had turned her out of the Settlement, even if it had been for her own good. Except that Malora had been sent off fully clothed on Sky, with saddlebags bulging and with weapons and tools. Would she have survived naked and unarmed? "Are many centaurs turned out?" she asks.

"Very few," Orion says. "It is the fear of being turned

out that makes most Highlanders hew quite closely to the Edicts."

"The Edicts are the cue, and fear of being turned out is the motivator," she says, using terms she understands.

Orion regards her narrowly. "That sounds interesting. Tell me what you mean."

"When you are training a horse to go faster, you might urge him with a kissing sound. That is a cue," Malora explains. "If the horse doesn't listen, you add a more insistent cue—a kick in the ribs, perhaps. If he still doesn't go, you might whack his rump with a stick. The horse goes faster because the stick has motivated him, but after a while, you can take away the stick—and even the kick—because the horse will speed up with the kissing sound alone. That's because the horse would just as soon not be kicked or swatted. The kiss is the cue; the memory—or you might say the fear—of the kick and the stick are the motivators."

"Yes," Orion agrees, "the threat of being turned out is a very sharp whack with the stick."

Malora grins. "Then I will make a point of following the Edicts." She makes a kissing sound, and Lightning instantly picks up a trot.

Orion, a little breathlessly, trots to catch up. "You certainly don't have to use a stick to get *me* going," he says.

CHAPTER 10

Lion Country

"Have I described to you yet the Founders' Day fest?" Orion asks.

Two days on, they are progressing northward, talking nearly every step of the way. When Malora doesn't answer the third time Orion puts the question to her, he glances over and sees that, in the heat of the midday sun, she has dropped off to sleep on Lightning's back. Her eyes are shut, her back relaxed, the black-and-white rope looped over one shoulder like some sort of bush-inspired fashion accessory. The movements of the horse beneath her ripple up through her body. Her hand is entwined in the horse's mane, her legs are draped around the creature's ebony barrel, her hips rock, right-left-right, just as the horse's hips move, her shoulders moving in time with its front legs. They are two separate creatures moving as one. Orion sees how like the most graceful centaur the combination of Malora and Lightning are, as natural together as he is in his own skin—perhaps even more so.

Orion feels oddly abandoned by his new friend, but then thinks guiltily that she probably needs her sleep. How restful can her night's slumber really have been, he muses, curled up on a mound of cloud grass in the horse pen? He wishes he could sleep while he walks, but that's impossible. Unlike the combination of Malora and Lightning, Orion is a single creature who can do only one thing at a time.

He wants her to wake up and tell him more names of the plants they pass on the way. In his short time with Malora, he has already learned so much. He has slung a pouch over his shoulder for collecting specimens. Even more than the lore of the plants, he savors their names: lavender fever berry, puzzle bush, wait-a-minute bush, silver bush, violet tree, russet bush willow. He likes Honus's more mysterious and complex words for plants: *Tanacetum parthenium, Chamomilla recutita, Lavandula angustifolia.* But Malora's words sound so much more sensible and grounded, which seems only appropriate for the names of things that spring from the soil. The prospect of introducing these new plants into his distillery excites him. Who knows what exotic scents he will derive from them?

Suddenly, Malora wakens and sits up tall. Her nostrils flare as she scans the bush, her head turning slowly. "I smell lion," she says. Then, incongruously, she yawns and stretches with her fingers linked high above her head.

"Really?" Orion says, his eyes shifting nervously.

"Yes," says Malora, lowering her arms languorously and smiling sweetly. "I'll ride ahead and alert the others. You should be fine. Stay with the herd." She makes the kissing sound and off she gallops on Lightning.

Orion looks around nervously. The bush looks as it always does to him. He can't *see* any lions. Then again, with its tawny bushes, rocks, grass, and hills, the entire bush is lion-colored, so he wonders whether he would be able to see lions even if they were here. Earlier, the bush was teeming with impalas and kudus and zebras and baboons and even elephants, but now they all seem to have vanished. Orion wonders whether they have gone off somewhere to hide from the lions. Where would he hide, he wonders, to keep himself safe? Orion shivers. Malora is right: the air *does* smell different, rank and damp and strangely *meaty*. Since centaurs—at least the Highlanders—eat no meat, this scent is not a familiar one, nor is it pleasant. It makes him think of his own body reduced to the raw meat of someone else's meal. It takes all of his self-control not to abandon the herd and dash after Malora in a cold-blooded panic. But he doesn't want to appear cowardly in her eyes, so he masters himself and walks on.

It is just before dusk when they come to the horse camp on the banks of the River Lapith, whose course they will follow until it merges with the Upper Neelah. They will follow the Upper Neelah until they reach Mount Kheiron. They have left behind the circles of ironwood saplings built by Malora's father, the master horseman. This camp has two sturdy paddocks, built by Flatlanders who have gone on previous horse hunts. They are made of posts and rails, with high grass growing inside so that the horses can graze protected, wild horses in one, domesticated in the other.

The Twani herd the wild horses to the river to water them. Other Twani unhitch the domesticated horses and lead them to their own section of the river. Whenever a horse from the domesticated group gets close to a wild one, ears go back and lips pull away from teeth. Gift bawls at the Twani to keep them separated.

Gift makes his way down the riverbank and says to Malora, "That swaybacked one over there, you can't tell me he's a Fury."

"No, he is not," she says. "He is Max."

"Well, if it's all right with you, miss, I'm going to cull him from the herd when we get to Mount Kheiron."

"Max stays with the herd."

Gift looks to Orion, who shrugs and says, "The nag stays. That is the way of it, Gift."

"As you wish," Gift says. But Orion can tell from the gnashing of Gift's sharp little teeth that he is not happy. Orion actually understands. Gift wants to make the best possible impression on the Apex. The flea-bitten, swaybacked Max will ruin the otherwise flawless presentation.

"Max may be no beauty," Malora says as Gift slinks off, "but he is honest, and he is a good horse. I rescued him from certain death. That horse would do anything for me."

"As well he should," Orion says absently. "Tell me, do you happen to still smell lion?"

"Can't tell," she says, pointing to the dancing branches of the trees. "The breeze is carrying the scent away."

Lions or no lions, Orion is relieved that they have finally come to the river. It means they are that much closer to home. And the breeze, while not conducive to detecting scents, is wonderfully refreshing. While he stands on the bank enjoying it, Theon sidles up to him.

"The others want to wade and wash off the dust of the

bush," he whispers in Orion's ear. "Ask her if there are hippos in the water."

"Ask her yourself," Orion says.

"You're the one who jabbers with her incessantly. You ask," Theon says, and wheels around to join the rest farther down the bank, where the tame horses are. The wild horses make Theon and the cousins nearly as uneasy as the human does.

Malora wades into the water, her long red hair swaying behind her. She wears it bound in the back like a horse's tail. It is nearly as long as his own tail, only not as carefully groomed. She keeps her clothes on in the water. She doesn't ever take off the leopard-skin pelt because, as she has explained, she has sewn it onto her body. She will wear it until it is too tight, and then she will rip it off and sew on a new piece of hide. What an extraordinary relationship to have with one's clothing, Orion thinks, more second skin than aesthetic display.

"Do you think there are hippos in this water?" Orion asks.

Malora shakes her head, her tail of hair whipping behind her.

"What makes you so sure?" he asks, reluctant to follow her into the water all the same.

She gestures up and down the river. "No river grass. The hippos eat river grass," she says.

The wild horses follow her into the river, snuffing and splashing, chasing each other into the deeper water and immersing their entire bodies. Others buckle their forelegs and roll on the muddy banks. Orion takes their frolicking as confirmation of Malora's assessment that the river is, for the time being at least, free from the predators that killed his brother.

West helps Orion unlace his boots and he wades in up to his shanks, enjoying the icy sensation of the water on his aching hooves and legs. The horses all around him drink deeply, their mouths making a steady sucking sound as they pull in great drafts of water from the river. He resists the urge to dip his face into the water and drink like a horse. It probably wouldn't work, his face being snoutless.

West and the other Twani stand along the bank and, as if responding to some silent cue, all commence to lick themselves clean. They are careful to stay clear of the water. West once explained to Orion that soaking in water dries out the oils in the Twanian skin and hair and makes them itch.

When West is finished washing himself, he hands Orion a skin of water he has previously boiled. "Drink up. You're parched from the bush."

"Come on in!" Malora shouts to Orion as she treads water in the middle of the river, but Orion demurs. Centaurs are as leery of water as the Twani, although for different reasons. Centaurs feel awkward and vulnerable in the water. They are not built to move gracefully in it. He envies her the lithe, simple body that lets her do so many things that his ungainly horse half will not permit. She climbs out of the water and shakes herself, then casually dries off against the shoulders and haunches of a horse that has remained onshore.

When the breeze dies down abruptly not long afterward, the scent of lion falls heavily upon them, like something rancid is burning. The Twani scurry to set up the tents and light a fire. The fire is for safety rather than for heat or cooking. Their evening meal will be cold leftovers, for tonight the Twani will be otherwise occupied. Gift now walks among his fellows carrying a sack of leaves that Malora introduced him to and helped him gather. Each Twan reaches in for one and then chews it. The leaf, Malora tells them, is a stimulant that will keep the Twani from succumbing to their natural inclination to nap. They will patrol the perimeter of their camp all night.

"I hope the dear little Twani can protect us from their tawny cousins," Malora says before she goes to check on the horses.

Orion finds it strange that Malora isn't anxious. On the contrary, she seems to find the situation a source of some amusement.

Just after dark, the centaurs sit down at the long table by the fire to a meal of dark bread, creamy goat cheese, and a pitcher of honeyed lemon tea. Orion has invited Malora to join them, but she prefers to eat with the horses.

The animals that have been hiding from the lion earlier seem to have reemerged under cover of darkness and are making a racket: elephants trumpeting, painted dogs howling, hooligan baboons hollering, owls screeching, and a whole mob of insects shrieking away, the likes of which he never hears back in Mount Kheiron. Over the noise, Orion can still make out the softer sounds of the horses in the nearby paddocks as they blow out and munch grass, and the urgent whispers of the Twani as they orbit the camp, swinging their lanterns, crossbows strapped to their backs. Theon and the others are laughing and joking nervously. They have all gone without their evening shower and still wear the same dusty wraps they traveled in all day. The fire burns low, but no one volunteers to venture off to get the wood to feed it.

"Why don't you ask *Malora* to fetch us some wood? I'm sure *Malora's* very good at that," Theon drawls. "Perhaps we should add *wood gathering* to the list of the Hand."

Orion is in the process of telling his brother to use his precious *tail* to fuel the fire when they hear the first roar.

Every other creature in the bush is struck silent. It isn't that the sound is loud so much as it is deep and mighty enough to vibrate the plates on the table and bring tears to the eyes. The cousins bound to their feet, mouths agape.

"Lions!" Mather says.

"Won't they go for the horses first?" Theon whispers.

No one answers him.

Around them, the Twani shout to each other as they stumble and crash through the bushes, either to get away from the lion or to discover where it is.

Orion's heart thumps in his chest as the thought hits him: Malora is in the pen with the horses.

The centaurs make sudden desperate lunges for the lanterns, each swiping one from the table and somehow leaving none for Orion. Before he can protest, they have scattered to their tents, leaving Orion alone in the dying firelight. He stands there for a moment, listening to the sound of his breath rasping, and arrives at a decision. Lions are not going to make him run like a scared rabbit. The lions might very well eat him tonight, but he is not going to give in to his fear. Determined to maintain his dignity, Orion makes his way slowly to his tent.

He hears the other centaurs calling out to each other, fumbling to fasten the flaps on their tents, like tortoises retracting into their shells. Orion makes another decision. He will keep the flaps on his tent wide open. If a lion is coming for him, Orion wants a clear view of it through the tent's flimsy mesh. His childhood friend Neal Featherhoof, a Flatlander, wears around his neck the claw of a lion he has slain. It is as long as Orion's middle finger and three times as thick, sickle-shaped and razor-sharp. A lion could enter his tent, he reasons, with no more than the swipe of a single paw. That being the case, Orion would rather see the lion coming than be taken unaware by the harsh sound of ripping cloth.

Suddenly, he thinks, Serenity! Just the thing to calm my nerves! But he gave Theon the last vial of the scent just this morning. "Are you *drinking* the stuff?" Orion asked his brother. Theon has gone through three vials in less than five days. "I can't help it," Theon said in his own defense. "The bush *riles* me."

Thoroughly riled himself now, Orion settles onto his camp bed and watches the lanterns of the Twani shuttle this way and that, their voices calmer now. Perhaps the lions are just passing through.

Let the lions take me while I'm asleep, Orion thinks, as exhaustion overtakes anxiety and his eyes grow heavy.

He awakes to a sound like heavy fabric being ripped by a powerful hand. Opening his eyes, he blinks. The air in the tent is sweltering even though the flaps are wide open. The sound he hears, he realizes, is that of a very large cat purring. The three-quarter moon has risen, and through the netting at the front of his tent, Orion sees an enormous male lion padding down the path, his shaggy head swinging back and forth, his great haunches swaying and shifting.

Orion has never seen a lion this close-up before. He has seen them as mere dots on the horizon, no bigger than the nail on his small finger. As the lion's tail thumps the side of Orion's tent, he smells damp fur and raw meat and hot breath scalding the night air. He wishes he had an entire bucket of Serenity to pour over his head to wash away the musk and soothe his nerves. He wishes Neal Featherhoof were there with his spear and his bow and arrow. Orion actually thinks he hears the juices in the lion's great belly gurgling, digesting his previous meal or preparing to receive the next one.

Then he sees West standing gamely in the lion's path with a crossbow loaded and the arrow pointed at the lion. Orion sits up. "West!" he whispers. "Don't do it!" But the Twan doesn't seem to hear and, besides, West seems determined to stand his ground, the fine hairs on his body bristling as he bares his sharp little fangs in an effort to make himself as ferocious-looking as possible. Orion watches the Twan fumble with the crossbow as the lion pads almost casually toward him. Panicked and frustrated, West flings the whole apparatus at the lion's head and turns to make a run for it. The lion leaps at him. West lets out a shrill cry as the lion clamps its huge jaws around his head and begins to drag him off into the bushes.

Orion looks around the tent in vain for something, anything, to use as a weapon against the lion. Never in his life has he felt so helpless and inadequate. He curses the Edict that forbids Highlanders from owning weapons.

Then he sees Malora. He wants to call out, to warn her

about the lion, but then he realizes that she is striding with purpose directly toward the lion. She holds a stout stick that is taller than she is and sharpened to a point. Coming to a halt not five paces away from the lion, she pounds the dull end on the ground.

The lion rumbles querulously, his mouth full, and shakes West back and forth like a doll.

"Don't you dare make me skewer you!" Malora growls at a pitch to match the lion's. She takes two paces closer and draws the stick over one shoulder, sighting the beast's head down its length.

The lion's jaws open wide, spilling West onto the ground. West rolls away from the lion, then goes on rolling, under his own power, toward Malora's feet.

Malora keeps the spear trained on the lion's head. As if daring him to move, she heaves up the spear and jams it spike-first into the ground. With little more gentleness than the lion showed, she shakes West by the scruff and empties him out of his tunic. Wadding up the garment, she tosses it at the lion's head.

"There, Grandfather," she says. "Take your prize and go. Consider yourself lucky I didn't run your bony old carcass through with this fence rail."

The lion catches up the tunic in his teeth, gives it a sound shaking, and then pads off into the night with it.

West lies whimpering.

Malora catches sight of Orion through the tent's mesh. Shrugging as if what she has just done were nothing, she flashes him a smile that is full of sisterly tenderness and says, "Run like an impala, get eaten like an impala."

Homeward Bound

Lanterns swinging, the centaurs pour out of their tents. It is the middle of the night and yet they seem wide-awake as they clap and cheer and chatter among themselves. While the Twani bear West off to see to his wounds, the centaurs crowd around Malora.

"You were magnificent!" Theon tells her, his gray eyes brimming.

"Truly valorous!" Mather says.

"I have never seen anything like it," Devan crows.

"Wait till they hear about this back home!" Theon says.

"Did you see how she faced down the lion?" Marsh says to Elmon.

"I will remember it for the rest of my days," vows Elmon to Marsh.

"We will tell our children," says March.

Theon bows before Malora. "Take my tent, please. You have earned it with your brave act tonight."

Malora laughs lightly. "I don't want your tent. And I really wasn't all that brave."

Mather protests, "You are too modest!"

Malora says, "I am just being honest. The lion was *old.*"

Theon rolls his eyes. "The lion was *ferocious.* Did you not hear his growl? Did you not smell his feral stench? And what about West's poor ravaged face!"

"He had just enough teeth in his head to bite a Twan, but he never could have choked down a whole centaur," Malora says.

The others all speak at once, begging, with all due respect, to differ with her.

"I am afraid you will just have to accept the fact that you are our heroine," Orion says in her ear. "And I must insist that you sleep in *my* tent tonight. I will stay with Theon."

"He will, indeed!" says Theon, as if sharing a tent with his brother were a rare honor.

"But I don't *want* to sleep in your tent," Malora tells Orion. "I'd rather stay with the boys and girls." Then she looks at the gathering of centaurs. They appear so eager, so thrilled, so touchingly grateful—and so very much more friendly than they have been—that she hates to disappoint. "All right," she concedes, "just for tonight."

At first, Malora finds the bed in Orion's tent so comfortable it is difficult to fall asleep. She wants to stay awake so she can revel in it like a horse wriggling on its back in a fine dust wallow. The mattress is big and soft, and her body sinks into it and hangs suspended. The blanket covering her is as soft as down and sweetly scented, smelling faintly of roses. In the lantern light, the Twani keep darting in to set small gifts on the blanket for her: tiny bags of dried fruit and a square of deliciously moist cake with nuts in it; small bouquets of khaki flowers tied with ribbon; and a cup of tea that tastes the way dew-drenched wildflowers smell at dawn.

Gorged on cake and quenched by tea, Malora eventually drifts off and sleeps more deeply than in recent memory, awakening to the morning sunlight beating down upon the blue-and-white tent over her head. Her first thought is, How in the world will I be able to go back to sleeping on the ground with the horses? She stretches. She notices that there is a small pale blue crystal flask on the camp table next to the bed. She reaches over and lifts the stopper, bringing it to her nose and inhaling deeply.

Her mind fills with a picture of a much younger Orion. He is laughing and playing a game using black-and-white stones with a much younger Theon. They are arguing in a good-natured fashion. A third centaur with wild black curly hair charges into the room and seems to be shouting something at them, something Malora cannot hear. Orion, his face white, says something, a retort perhaps. More angered still, the wild-haired centaur fastens his beefy hands around Orion's throat and starts to squeeze. Orion's face turns red, the blue veins in his forehead bulging, and he crumples to the floor while Theon beats the larger centaur on the back with his fists. The large centaur laughs at him while Theon weeps. It is all Malora can do not to weep along with him. Her heart aches for the two little centaur boys.

With a small sob, Malora quickly replaces the stopper and returns the crystal flask to the table. Moments later, West ducks into the tent. He is carrying a tray.

West falls still. He seems to be staring hard at something invisible in the tent. "Are you all right?" he asks at length. The lion has left a double ridge of red teeth marks running beneath his eyes from cheek to cheek.

"I'm fine," Malora says, though she is anything but. "Are you all right?"

West nods slowly. "I am."

West's quality of stillness calms Malora and chases away the disturbing picture. "West, what is in this blue flask?"

"That would be Orion's Heart, the master's personal scent. You really do look pale, miss. Perhaps you are having a delayed reaction to that grim encounter with the lion?"

"The old snaggletooth was nothing," she says.

"You may see it that way," West says gravely. "But to you I owe my life. Please eat and fortify yourself. I gave you extra berries and a large dollop of honey."

Malora sits up in bed and takes the tray onto her lap. While West looks on, she digs in with her spoon. The mush is sweet and the berries are tart, and the combination is delicious. She thinks of the dried kudu meat Sky ran off with in his saddlebags and says, "Do the centaurs ever eat meat, or do their flat teeth prevent them?"

"Their teeth are filed straight across as soon as their adult set grows in," West says.

Malora puts down her spoon and stares at him. "Filed? Who does the filing?"

"The household Twani. It is a simple matter, and it doesn't hurt. Mind you, I wouldn't want anyone doing it to me," he says, flashing his own two sharp rows of fangs.

"Why do they do it?" Malora asks.

West shrugs and licks the back of his hand, then runs it quickly over the scruff of his neck. "To make their faces look handsome and comely, I suppose. But probably to keep them from eating meat. Eating meat is against at least two of the Edicts . . . don't ask me which ones."

The Edicts again. But it makes sense, Malora supposes. If you don't hunt animals, you certainly don't need weapons to kill them or sharp teeth to chew them. "Why is eating meat against the Edicts?" she asks.

"It has to do with Kheiron the Wise's dictates," West says. "He believed the eating of red meat incited bloodlust in the centaurs, causing them to go on the rampage and be a public menace."

"A menace to the People?" Malora asks.

"And to other hibes. They raped and plundered and slaughtered indiscriminately, from what I'm told. Hard to believe, looking at them now, but they say it once was true."

"Do the Twani not eat meat as well?" Malora asks.

"Oh, we eat whatever's at hand," West says vaguely, staring at the air above Malora's head.

She fixes him with a suspicious look. "Grains and berries?" She knows of no cat, including those in the Settlement, that does not have a penchant for catching and killing prey.

He smiles slyly and says, "Even Puss in Boots indulged in the occasional mouse."

Malora grins. "Orion told you."

"Orion tells me most things," West says. "The Twani are furtive in our hunting practices, out of respect for the centaurs."

"And their Edicts," Malora puts in.

"Their Edicts and their squeamishness," he says. "Although I'm not sure mice and rats and the occasional fat moth constitute a violation. Eat up, Miss Malora. You overslept, and it's time we were packing up."

Malora cocks an ear, suddenly aware of the sound of the camp being dismantled around her. "It's this bed," she says. "It's far too comfortable. I could lie in it all day and not mind a bit."

"You'll get used to it in time. There's nothing *but* comfort to be had in Mount Kheiron, the Home of Beauty and Enlightenment. And I am afraid you must get used to me as well, because now that I owe my life to you, West will be at your elbow, serving your every need."

"Please don't," says Malora. She finds the notion of being served by anyone highly unsettling.

West looks momentarily taken aback, almost wounded.

"Really," she says as gently as she can. "That arrangement would not make me comfortable. It's not you. It's just that I'm used to taking care of myself."

"I will do my best to refrain from attending to your needs," he says carefully. "But it will be difficult. We are compelled to serve those to whom we owe our lives."

"So I hear," Malora says with a sigh. "Why don't we leave it that you will go on serving Orion, and I'll just ask you for the occasional favor."

"Very good," West says. "But the favors will have to be substantial."

"I hope one day that you will let me get you a hat with a

wide brim and a big, feathered plume—like the one Puss in Boots wore," Malora says with a smile.

"That, miss, would be a very big favor, indeed."

Two days later, the centaurs all ride with Malora as she leads the horses on the last leg of the journey. The Silvermane cousins are proud and eager to point out to her the signs that the bush is giving way to their homeland. There are now squat stone farmhouses rising up on both sides of the road. There are neatly fenced-in pastures holding sheep and goats and cows, and lushly cultivated fields that make the small patches of garden scratched out by the People in the Settlement seem by comparison shabby and barren.

Orion points to a field covered with a hazy carpet of delicate blue flowers and says, "That's flax." He reaches out, plucks a stalk, and hands it to her. "We harvest it and make our scent cloths from it, among other things."

Malora nods, twirling the big blue flower between her fingers.

"We're coming down onto the floodplains now," Orion explains. "Mount Kheiron is surrounded by floodplains."

"The Flatlands," she says.

"Just so," he says. They trot through fields tidily divided into a patchwork of squares, each square planted with a different crop. Some of the squares are rich black dirt. Others are blooming with flowers with big fat blossoms. "Anytime now," he tells her, "we'll be seeing Mount Kheiron."

Malora keeps her eyes trained on the horizon and feels a nervous fluttering in her stomach. Why so nervous? she asks herself, and wonders whether the three nights she slept in Orion's tent have already begun to make her soft. The road takes them through a grove of silver-trunked trees as stunted-looking as any in the bush.

"Olive trees," Orion says. "They say the oldest groves were planted by your ancestors. The Grandparents, as I believe you say."

"Planted by the People?" she says, peering about as if to see their ghosts flitting through the gnarled trunks, twisted branches, and silvery-green leaves. How much more comfortable life must have been for the People here. There is a kind of justice in her returning to claim these comforts as her own.

"We eat the olives and make oil from them," Orion explains. "I use the oil in my distillery, too."

Malora nods absently. There is a rich look to the earth here, as if the dirt itself were edible, like the crumbs from the moist cakes West brings her every night before bed. The olive groves give way to orchards, their branches festooned with great white and yellow blossoms. In the shade of the trees, fat sleek goats and fluffy sheep browse.

"Oranges and lemons will grow where these blossoms now are," Orion says, breaking off a sprig and presenting it to her.

Malora sniffs the fragrant petals. The scent is heady. She turns around to find the horses chewing on the branches. "Stop it!" she scolds.

The horses stare at her blandly, chewing the blossoms, their quivering lips reaching out to pull off more. Then she turns around to find Lightning doing the same. She cuffs her on the side of the head, and Lightning stops with an irate stomp.

"These boys and girls have very bad manners," she says.

"That's all right," Orion says easily. "I'm sure the blossoms taste delicious. The cheese made from the milk of the sheep and goats who browse here is faintly perfumed. Nothing in the world tastes so good, except perhaps for the oranges when they come in, which are very nearly as big as your head."

Malora doesn't know what an orange is but recognizes it by name as being one of his ingredients. "Do you make your scents from these same oranges?" she asks.

"No, those groves are closer to Mount Kheiron. The oranges there are small and very sweet, but too oily and riddled with bitter pits to eat."

It is midafternoon when Orion points to the ridge of a nearby field and says, "There it is, the Home of Beauty and Enlightenment."

"Isn't it beautiful!" Marsh says.

"And bathed in enlightenment!" Elmon concurs.

"How I missed all this!" Mather says.

Malora sits back, and Lightning rocks to a halt beneath her. She takes it all in. It is like a city out of a dream, materializing out of thin air, mysterious and shimmering with promise. If the Settlement had cowered beneath the mountain ledge, Mount Kheiron boasts its existence to the world. As if it had been crafted entirely by hand, it rises up above the Flatlands, teeming with multicolored roofs stacked one on top of the other, bristling with arches and spires and statues and towers, with a great dome at its summit shining like a competing sun. She sees the figures of centaurs and Twani going up and down steep roads, like termites swarming in a mound made of gold dust. A golden aura rises from it. The whole mountain hums with excitement, with activity, with life.

"That golden dome is the temple of Kheiron," Orion says. "The House of Silvermane, my home, is just down the Mane Way from it."

"Ah!" is all Malora can manage to say. Her glance drops to the high stone wall ringing the base of the mountain, gapping only at the river, where a row of colorful roofs crowds the riverbank. "What is that?" She points.

"That's the Port of Kheiron," he says. "From there, the Lower River Neelah flows northward to the Kingdom of the Ka and its great port city, Kahiro, which is even more splendid and exotic than Mount Kheiron."

That there exist even more splendid and exotic kingdoms than this one fills Malora with a sense of infinite possibilities. How happy Thora would be, to know that her daughter has all this stretching out before her.

"Can we go to Kahiro someday?" she asks.

Malora's question seems to delight Orion. "You sound like my sister. She has never left Mount Kheiron. Perhaps one day my parents will permit her to travel, and then you can go along to guard her from the fearsome predators along the way. But in the meantime, you'll just have to settle for poor shabby little Mount Kheiron."

They proceed onward, their steps hastening toward the mountain of the Highlander centaurs. The stone farmhouses of the Flatlanders grow more plentiful and more colorful, with roofs painted bright blue and decorated with bold pictures of clouds and suns, moons and stars, birds and butterflies and flowers. Teams of horses, driven by centaurs, harrow the fields or haul wagonloads of crops. These centaurs are different from the princely ones who are her companions. Their human halves are clad in plain, tattered, sleeveless shirts, and their horse halves are covered with what look like backward aprons with ragged fringe that conceals their private parts.

"Flatlanders?" Malora asks.

"Flatlanders," all the centaurs confirm in a happy chorus.

"Good old Flatlanders," says Elmon.

"I'm even happy to see *them*," Mather says.

"Yes, it's good to leave the bush behind us," says Theon.

The Flatlanders tip their ragged straw hats as the noble party passes. They place their right hands over their hearts and then raise their hands, palms out. The Highlanders respond in kind. When the Flatlanders smile, Malora sees that their mouths have their sharp incisors intact, like hers. She wonders if, correspondingly, they eat meat. She hasn't eaten any meat since the night before joining the centaurs, and she has been craving it.

She catches her first sight of women centaurs among the crowd. They are more finely built than the males, and their heads are wrapped in colorful cloth.

"No caps?" Malora asks Orion.

"Flatlander females are not obligated, but many are modest enough to cover their hair in public," Orion explains.

One of the Flatlander women calls out lustily, "Congratulations, Your Lordships! Mighty handsome horses you got there! But they don't look fast enough to beat our Athaban-shees."

"What's an Athabanshee?" Malora asks Orion.

"A very fast breed of horse," Orion says. "Faster, some say, than Furies."

Malora calls out to the female centaur, "Bring me your fleetest Athabanshee and I'll beat it fair and square mounted on any of these Furies."

The centaur woman cries out when she sees Malora and buries her face in her hands.

Orion gives Malora a stern look. "What did we discuss?"

Malora replies in a small voice, "The need for me not to call undue attention to myself when I am among the cen-taurs."

"Because . . . ," he prompts her.

"Because the centaurs might be fearful of me at first."

Again, he prompts: "Because . . ."

"They've never seen one of the People before."

"They may fear you, just as you feared us when you first laid eyes on us in the flooded canyon."

When she first saw the centaurs, she felt not a jot of fear. She was delighted, for they were the Perfect Beings. But it is obvious that centaurs don't feel the same way about her.

A little boy and girl centaur, their horse halves as small and leggy as colts, trot alongside their party. The girl calls out to Orion, "What happened to that lady centaur?"

"Did a lion gnaw off her wrong end?" the boy asks.

Far from finding her a Perfect Being, the centaurs see her as a mauled centaur!

Orion tells them, "She has no wrong end. She's not a centaur at all. She's one of the People."

Their eyes darken with fear and their little faces turn ashen, and they stumble off to tell their parents.

Malora watches the parents receive the children's report with expressions of fear. The males sweep off their hats and work the brims with nervous fingers. The children then gallop forward and tell the centaurs waiting ahead. Malora can literally see the word travel up the line. It isn't long before the roads are thronged with spectators waiting to catch sight of Malora. She isn't used to this many eyes focused on her. The kernel of nervousness inside her begins to swell. Lightning, sensing this, starts to dance beneath her.

Orion, also sensing her unease, says, "Don't worry. It's just that they can't believe their eyes. They'll get used to the idea of you in time. If Theon and my cousins can do it, the rest of them can."

But the crowd's reaction to her seems more substantial than a simple fear of the unknown and the different. "I can't possibly be all that frightening to them."

"You're not," Orion says, "but the stories that have been passed down to us are."

"What kinds of stories?" Malora asks.

"Stories of People with magical boxes and transforming potions and powerful sticks of fire," Orion says.

However powerful those boxes and potions and sticks of fire might have been, Malora reflects sadly, they weren't sufficient to keep the centaurs from slaughtering nearly every last one of the People. Shouldn't such a victory have made the centaurs fearless and confident instead of cowering and fearful? But then she remembers how she has felt in the past, sitting beside the fire on a night after she has killed something big and splendid, like a lion or an eland. She never felt fearless or proud. She felt terrified and humbled by her act. It is terrifying to take a life. Perhaps the terror of killing hundreds—maybe thousands—of the People lies dormant in the hearts of these centaurs, and seeing Malora brings it back to life.

The smaller road soon shunts them into a larger road that is paved with white stone. This white road leads to Mount Kheiron. The horses' hooves *clip-clop* along the white stones. More Flatlanders gather on the grassy verges.

Orion teases her. "You needn't think they have gathered just to gape at you. It's market day."

But Malora isn't fooled. The centaurs have indeed gathered to gape at her as the party passes. Their handcarts and wagons carry bags and wooden crates, coils of rope and skeins of thread, pots and pans, bolts of cloth, and heaps of tanned hides.

"And this," says Orion, "is the Great Gate of Kheiron."

Up ahead, springing from a high stone wall, looms an elaborate gate. Atop the gate is a golden arch engraved with a picture of a massive, noble-headed centaur standing on a raised hill holding a tablet, with other, smaller centaurs crowded around him.

"That's our Wise Patron, the first Apex, Kheiron of Melea," Orion explains. "Here you see him delivering the Edicts to the Melean refugees."

The centaurean refugees, their legs folded beneath them,

crouch like children at the feet of the mighty Kheiron. Above the gate, a vast square of cloth tied to a pole ripples and snaps in the breeze. The picture embroidered on the cloth shows a big golden hand on a field of blue, with a red-and-black eye staring out of the palm.

"It's our nation's symbol," Orion explains. "On the flag is the Hand of Kheiron, with his Ever-Watchful Eye on its palm."

Malora has never heard of a flag, but the sight of the eye on the hand makes her slightly uneasy, like staring down an aggressive stallion or a really rude mare. She looks away.

Their procession halts next to a house painted the same blue as the flag. It is big enough to fit one centaur, who clambers out the door at their approach. Hand over heart, he then raises his palm to them. Theon, doing the same, advances and confers with the gatekeeper, who, draped in white and red, appears to be wearing a version of the flag.

Orion goes on explaining to Malora: "We have been authorized by my parents to bring wild horses within municipal limits. There are five stables at the foot of the mountain belonging to five of the first families, so presenting wild horses at the gate is not unusual."

Malora levels a look at him. "These horses aren't wild," she says. "They stop and start on command, walk, trot, canter, and gallop. They move away from the pressure of my hand or my foot. I can make the best of them move with no more than the force of my glance. These horses are not wild . . . any more than I am wild."

"Of course not," Orion says, bowing. "I beg your pardon."

The Twani pile their clubs and crossbows by the gate.

"Have you any concealed weapons on you?" the guard asks, staring pointedly at Malora.

Malora leans down to Orion and asks, "How is it the guard can keep a weapon but none of the rest of us can?" There is a spear propped up by the gatehouse door, encrusted with gems and feathers and other trinkets.

"That's largely decorative. He's a bureaucrat. I'd be surprised if he even knows how to use it."

Malora, straightening, stares at the guard.

The guard stares back. "So this is the human being," he says.

"Yes, and she's ours," Theon says merrily.

"Actually, she's *mine*," Orion calls out.

Malora mutters under her breath, "I'm nobody's but my own."

Hearing this, Orion catches her eye and frowns. "I'm sorry, but you can be no such thing. You are an Otherian. You must be sponsored and monitored at all times." Orion says to the guard, "I will vouch for this Otherian. I will be delivering her directly to the Apex."

CHAPTER 12

Mount Kheiron

Monitored at all times. The words ringing in her head, Malora considers swinging Lightning around and leading the herd galloping away from this place. Lightning paws the ground as if to say, "Make up your mind."

A steady jumble of noise pours down off Mount Kheiron, more cacophonous than anything Malora has ever heard. She feels she could easily leave all this behind and return to the familiarity of the plains. Then she thinks of the pleasures she has discovered in the past few days. The mattress that cradles her body, the delicious meals served to her on a tray, the lively companionship of centaurs and Twani, the conversations with Orion and West. And finally, she hears Thora's voice in her head: "Better to be an Otherian, sponsored and monitored, than a lone human wandering forever in the wild."

Orion, at her elbow, says, "Malora, are you ready to take the horses to the stable?"

Malora sees that the other centaurs and both wagons have already passed through the gate and are disappearing up a cobbled road, into the shadows of the towering buildings. She wants to see up close what is on this mountain. But first, she knows she must tend to the horses. They are bunched up, noses to tails, alert, ears swiveling every which way. "I'm ready," she tells him.

West stays at the gate to see if he can hail what he calls a lorry to give them a ride up the mountain after their business at the stable is finished. Malora and Orion follow Gift along a dirt road that banks around the base of the mountain and then begins to ramp upward. Over the next rise, the mouth of an enormous cave yawns before them.

Malora pulls up short, the herd skittering to a halt behind her. "What is this place?" she asks.

Orion says, "This is the Silvermane Stable."

Malora stares at him in disbelief. "The Silvermane Stable, the finest equine facility in all of Mount Kheiron, is a *cave*?" She dismounts and holds up one finger to signal Lightning to stay.

Lightning snorts and stomps but remains in place, as do the rest of the herd, who drop their heads and graze on the bright green grass carpeting the mountain on the downhill side of the dusty road. Malora follows Gift.

Outside the mouth of the cave there are at least forty empty railed enclosures, big enough to hold one horse each. Malora ventures into the cave, where it is much cooler and smells sweetly of hay. Gift makes a hissing sound, and Twanian wranglers, dozing in the shadows, leap to their feet and brush the hay dust off their tunics. Torches on the wall burn brightly, illuminating a series of delicate one-seated, two-wheeled vehicles hanging from the ceiling.

To one side, the cave is honeycombed with sturdy wooden stalls. The cave echoes with the sound of horses banging their buckets against the stalls as they nose their feed, their eyes shifting only briefly to Malora before they return to eating. There are horses here that look like none she has ever seen: horses with gracefully curved necks and manes that cascade down their backs in a riot of curls, bull-necked horses with crestlike manes like the stiff bristles of brushes, and some that are nearly as big as Sky but with long, knobby, gangling legs. They all look healthy, well fed, and groomed.

On the other side of the cave, harnesses, cleaned and oiled, hang on pegs. A series of deep stone troughs hold crystal-clear water, with not so much as a stick of hay or a dead fly floating in it. There are no flies anywhere that Malora can see or hear. Aron slaved to keep the Settlement stable clean, but it had still been plagued by stinging flies that left itchy red bumps the size of a barn swallow's eggs. At the sound of a horse releasing a load of droppings, a Twan rushes to the stall and rakes them up. This stable holds at least fifty horses and is cleaner and altogether better organized than Jayke's. Although it is a cave, it is a surprisingly pleasant one. Her herd will take time to settle in, of course, but eventually, they will be content here. They will be well cared for, well fed, and protected from predators. And if they have to work in exchange for such luxurious room and board, it seems fair. Best of all, they are behind the high city walls and Malora won't have to worry about them every day, all day, day after day.

"Very good," she says, turning to Gift. "But my horses won't tolerate being cooped up. At least not at first. Put them in the outdoor pens, two to each. Let them get used to being in a new place before you put them in the cave."

Gift seems reluctant but he looks to Orion, who nods firmly. "If that's the way the human wants it," Gift says in a snide tone, "that's the way it will be."

While Malora has been inspecting the stable, the herd has straggled and spread out on the hillside, some wandering down into the shadow of the city wall. It is as if their steadily clicking, pulling, munching teeth have become attached to the grass.

Twanian wranglers go to round them up, but Malora says, "Give them more time. I don't think they've ever had grass this green and juicy."

Gift clenches his fists, waiting for Malora to say when the horses have had enough. Then Malora and the Twanian wranglers lead the horses, two by two, to their little paddocks, while Malora introduces each of them by name. There are buckets for feed and water in every pen. "You'll have to double up on the buckets so they won't fight. Put the buckets at opposite ends of the enclosure.

"If Lightning gets out, don't worry," she goes on. "She can untie knots, so I'm sure latches won't hold her if she wants at that grass. Raven's a prankster. And Stormy has a temper, but only if you come at her too fast. . . ."

Orion reads the worry in her voice. "I think the boys and girls will be fine here, don't you?" he says.

Malora nods uncertainly.

"I think it's time we left the Twani to get to know the horses on their own, don't you?" he asks.

Malora nods again, reluctant still.

She remembers something else. She catches Gift's eye. "Oh, yes, and you might think it's a good idea to keep the stallions away from the mares, but it's not. Mares have a calming effect on stallions. Let them mingle now and then. You know the ones who get along. You saw how they grouped themselves in the camps."

Gift nods. "I did."

"Right," Malora says, looking around.

Orion catches her eye. "Right?" he says, eyebrows raised.

"Right," she says again with a resigned sigh.

While Orion looks on, Malora goes around saying good night to the herd, stroking their necks and untangling their forelocks and rubbing her nose with theirs. She saves Lightning for last. "Keep an eye on the boys and girls," she whispers to the big mare. "I'm leaving you in charge." But all Lightning cares about right now is her feed.

As Malora walks away, she feels as if she has forgotten something, and then she realizes what it is: it's the horses! This is the first time she will be separated from them—from many, since they were born; from others, since she rescued them. She feels a squeezing sensation in her chest. She will be on the top of the mountain and they will be at the foot, and that, as Orion would say, is the way of it. Without Lightning beneath her, her two legs feel stubby and insubstantial as Orion walks her back toward the gate. They round the bend and are blinded temporarily by the rays of the lowering sun.

West calls out to them from the high front seat of a long, many-wheeled wagon loaded with smooth, square stones. West sits beside the driver, another Twan. The wagon is hitched to a team of six horses as big as the Furies but stockier, with huge, shaggy hooves.

"Such giants!" Malora exclaims as she walks among the horses, scratching ears, stroking noses.

"Beltanian draft horses," Orion explains. "They do the heavy hauling in Mount Kheiron."

The lorry driver alights and pulls a ramp down from the rear of the wagon. "For Your Excellence's convenience in boarding," he says.

"Come, Malora!" Orion says. "I want to show you the city before it's dark."

Malora pulls herself away from the team and follows Orion up the ramp into the back of the lorry.

The Twan slides the ramp into the wagon and then climbs into the front seat next to West. He clicks his tongue. Malora and Orion hang on to the slatted wooden side of the lorry as, heads bobbing, the team begins its plodding uphill progress, dragging stones and passengers.

"Where is this Twan's centaur?" Malora asks, gesturing to their driver.

"Not every Twan has a centaur. There are more Twani than there are Highlanders. Many of the Twani simply have jobs and, in that way, satisfy their sense of obligation. This is the market," Orion explains. "It is quite the plainest, most businesslike section of our city."

Surrounded on three sides by vaulted stone arches and

colonnades, it doesn't look plain to Malora. It looks like the central square of the Settlement, only grander.

"Who built this?" she asks.

"This part of Mount Kheiron dates from the olden days," Orion says. "The People—the Grandparents—built it."

Malora nods, pleased that she recognized it.

Flatlanders, packing up their wares, stop as the lorry passes and stare up at Malora, fear and wonderment mingled in their eyes. The lorry rolls on, and Malora takes in the sights. Buildings tower on all sides, sparkling in the last rays of the sun. The buildings are covered with countless tiny gems that form pictures: of centaurs and animals, of mountains and pools and waterfalls and flowers and trees and birds and insects and suns and moons. Malora is entranced by the sparkling images.

"We call these mosaics," Orion explains. "It is an ancient art that uses materials placed together to create a unified whole. The materials used are stone, gems, mirrors, glass, even shells from far-off Kahiro."

Malora notices that there are mosaics and paintings on nearly every structure in sight, towers and arches alike. Almost nothing looks like a humble home. It is a city made up almost entirely of palaces, and everything she sees, every pillar and every post, is decorated. When it isn't portraits or scenes, it is patterns: leaves and feathers and fish scales and stripes and rainbows and colorful spiraling patterns like those she sees when she closes her eyes and presses her fingers to her eyelids, which she feels like doing right now.

"My eyes hurt!" she says with a helpless little laugh.

"That's not surprising," Orion says. "You are accustomed to seeing the world stripped to its primal essence. I've been in the bush long enough that I can understand a little of how you must feel right now, blinded by all this. Surrounded as you have been by natural beauty, this must seem almost garish by comparison."

"If you mean it's ugly, no," she says. "It's beautiful. Is all of this beauty the work of centaur hands?"

"It is," he says proudly.

Malora's eyes dart about. Even the paving stones beneath the lorry's iron wheels have been glazed or individually painted with intricate designs. "I don't know where to look," she says.

"Yes," he says thoughtfully. "I see what you're saying. Out in the bush, one's eyes do, in fact, know where to look, because nature doesn't overplay her own hand. It occurs to me for the first time that there might be something just a little arrogant about our need to express ourselves on every available surface. It's as if we were attempting to outdo nature rather than pay tribute to it."

Malora has no idea what he's talking about. All she knows is that it will take her days, maybe years, to visit each mosaic and really look at it. Impervious to all this glorious workmanship, West has fallen fast asleep, head resting on the driver's shoulder. When the hill can get no steeper, the driver swings the wagon into a sharp turn and proceeds down a street that is level but bumpy and narrow and hugs the mountainside.

"We're on a service road," Orion says. "Rest your eyes."

Malora is astonished to see that even the backs of the

buildings are decorated, less lavishly perhaps but still amply adorned.

The lorry finally grinds to a halt before a blue-and-white canopy that calls to mind the centaurs' tents. They have arrived at the House of Silvermane. Two Twani in blue-and-white tunics push themselves away from a blue-striped pillar.

"There she is, all right," one of them says, gawking up at Malora.

"There she is, indeed," the other one says.

"Allow me to present Rain and Lemon, keepers of the rear gates. Rain and Lemon, this is Malora Ironbound."

Malora nods to them, smiling. Just this morning, she saw her first lemons, ripening in a grove on their way into Mount Kheiron. Malora is guessing which Twan is Lemon by his halo of yellow hair.

Lemon tears his eyes away from Malora to say, "Welcome home, Your Fine Excellence. Rounded up more than just horses on your expedition, didn't you now?"

"Is the Apex at home?" Orion asks.

"Yes, Your Young Excellence," says Rain, licking a hand and lifting it to wash the hair on his head, which is sleek and white. "He and Herself have just returned from a jubilation of the Hand."

"Whose?" he asks.

Rain pauses in his washing to think. "Your cousin Brea has achieved recognition for painting."

"Would you like us to request an audience?" Lemon asks.

"I can take care of that myself, thank you." Orion clatters down the ramp and reaches up to shake West gently awake.

Rain and Lemon stare up at West's face in fascination. "So the rumors must be true," they whisper to each other.

West stirs and wakens. He slips down from the lorry bench and shakes himself vigorously awake. "Come along, master, let's get you bathed," he says.

"I can see to myself tonight, West," Orion says, turning to Rain and Lemon. "I'd like you to take West in hand and make sure his wounds are healing properly."

"We clean our own wounds," Rain says, with a flick of his pink tongue.

"Nevertheless," Orion says, "I'd like to look after him this night. He has had a challenging time in the bush."

"Don't worry about me, master," West says. "Rain is right. I can see to myself."

"As can I this evening. Do this for me, West," Orion says.

West blinks once very slowly. The long hairs of his eyebrows twitch. "As you say, master."

As Lemon and Rain drape their arms around his shoulders, West begins to tell his story: "It was a sweltering night in the bush, deep in the heart of lion country. . . ." The Twani guards disappear with West into a small side door as they listen avidly to his tale.

"Very distractible, those two." Orion says to Malora with a grin. "And that's why they are on the *back* door and not on the *front*. Come, please."

Malora follows him beneath the awning and through a set of wide double doors painted blue with ivory handles. She stares hard at the door as it opens, trying to figure out how it works. In the Settlement, animal skins on screens served as doors.

The floors inside the house are paved in polished amber. She is conscious of how dirty her feet are as they pad alongside Orion down the gleaming, golden hallway.

"This is very grand," she whispers, leery of her voice echoing off the walls.

"This?" He laughs. "This is only the servants' quarters. Up front it's *much* grander."

At the end of the hallway is another door, this one green with simpler handles. "I can't wait to see the look on Honus's face," he says as he knocks.

"Come!" a mild voice calls out from within.

Orion positions Malora to the side of the door and mimes for her to keep silent. He peers around the door, and she puts her eye to the chink. Inside the room, he sees a small man with a pointed beard and curly brown hair through which two small horns protrude. He is seated in a plush chair, and his legs, encased in brown leather, are crossed at his furry ankles. His feet, she sees, are delicately cloven like a goat's. This, then, is the faun called Honus, half goat, half human being, the so-called cloven-hoofed polymath.

Honus is speaking to someone beyond the range of her vision. "We'll continue this later, my dear," he says, and then his eyes shift to Orion.

"Back from the bush at last, are we?" He removes a pair of gold-rimmed spectacles. There is a pair much like these in the Grandparents' Box in the Hall of the People. The table next to Honus is a chaos of books and quills and scrolls, all items Malora has also seen in the box. She presses closer to the crack in the door and sees more books than she can count crammed onto shelves lining the walls. Mixed in with the books are rocks and crystals and skulls and other objects of great mystery, jeweled statues of birds and lizards and monkeys. Honus must be a powerful Otherian to be trusted to flaunt such treasures.

"Come in, my boy," Honus says, "and tell us all about it."

"Yes, do!" A small graceful centaur ambles into view. She has a round, beautiful face with eyes the same startling splash of blue as Orion's and a pronounced dimple in her little chin. Her soft, pale blue wrap, pinned at her shoulder with a jeweled butterfly brooch, is filmy and swirls around her compact equine form like mist. Her shiny black curls escape from an oddly shaped cap that has a design of purple flowers on it. She throws her arms around Orion and cries in a musical voice, "Welcome home, Orrie, dearest! We missed you!" Then she backs off, her little nose twitching. "Orion Silvermane, shame on you, of all centaurs. You smell like a horse! And look at you! What happened? You look like you've been mauled by lions."

"I was, actually," he says with a modest smile.

"No!" she gasps.

Orion shrugs. "Well, West was, at least. And I was witness."

"It sounds to me as if you have had yourself quite an adventure," Honus says with an eyebrow raised. His face is dominated by a broad, smooth forehead that looks exactly as Orion described it to Malora during one of their talks in the bush: "the vault containing most of the knowledge and intelligence in Mount Kheiron."

"Do please stay to sup and tell us all about it," the keeper of the vault says.

"*After* you've gone to your rooms and showered," Zephele stipulates, arms akimbo, tapping a hoof in its bright red boot.

"First, I have something special to show you," Orion says.

Zephele claps her hands together. "A souvenir of the bush? Oh, bliss! What is it? Rocks? Feathers? Bones? Some cunning fossil specimen to add to our darling Honus's collection?"

Orion reaches out and reels in Malora from her hiding place behind the door. "Her name," Orion says proudly, "is Malora Ironbound. I found her running with the wild horses in those self-same red-rocked mountains. She's half wild herself and very brave. She saved West from the predations of a lion." He turns to Malora. "Malora, this is my sister, Zephele. And our teacher, Honus. Both of whom you have heard me speak."

Malora is embarrassed by Orion's introduction. "Except that I am *not* half wild," she says with what she hopes is a very civilized smile.

Honus strokes his pointy little beard and says, "Of course not. You are something much more valuable. You are the survivor, the living artifact of a bygone age. I believe that I am looking at a genuine *Homo sapiens* who, with her first utterance, offers proof that my theory was correct all along, young Silvermanes. Centaurs did indeed adapt the tongue of the People during the years before the Great Massacre!"

Orion turns to Malora. "Didn't I tell you that his head is replete with brainy theories?"

Malora nods slowly, understanding too that Orion and, to a lesser degree, his sister have copied the inflections of their tutor. She looks down upon the faun, who is a head shorter than she is. "You are the cloven-hoofed polymath," she says, then, turning to Zephele, "and you are the centaur maiden who likes to do things for yourself. Where is Sunshine?"

Zephele blushes. "She is off washing all of my brushes for the third time this week. Did you keep *nothing* secret from the Otherian?" She punches her brother's arm affectionately and smiles, her dimple deepening in her chin.

Malora finds herself enchanted by this female centaur and envious of the relationship between the siblings. Her envy is offset by the feeling that these two, whether out of natural kindness or curiosity to learn more about her, are offering her a place in their sibling circle.

Orion says, "Oh, Zephie, I daresay you'll have a few secrets of your own to reveal to Malora, once you get to know her."

Zephele's pretty face flushes anew. "Oh, my Hands! Can she really stay with us, Orrie? I hope so! What will everyone say when they see her? They'll surely want one of their own. Are there more where she comes from? What is that she's wearing? Is it fur? Was it once alive? It looks filthy and crawling with bugs. Didn't any of my dandy cousins even *think* to offer you one of their wraps? Oh, you must let me dress you! I know just how to do it! And your hair! It's a beautiful color, and I know it will look gorgeous once it's clean. But if you have to stuff it up into a cap, I'll just die. Let's get you into a hot bath. Honus happens to have the only bathing tub in all of Mount Kheiron, don't you, Honus? Honus won't mind if you use his tub, will you, darling Honus? I promise I'll have Sunshine scrub it clean, for she's sure to leave a rather large and grubby ring in it. Half the dirt of the bush, from the looks of her, plus twigs and burs and ticks and who knows what other hideous crawling organisms are in that thatch. If Father doesn't let her stay, I shall be very vexed with the old grumble guts." Zephele stops speaking only because she has run out of breath.

CHAPTER 13

The Hall of Mirrors

Malora turns to Orion with a worried look. Until now, she has assumed that there will be no question that she will be allowed to stay. Avoiding meeting her eyes, Orion says, "I must deliver her to them without delay."

Zephele wags her head. "But won't they be adversely influenced by her stunning lack of hygiene?"

"I think it will be more than her cleanliness that will determine their decision," Orion says.

"That's all right," Malora says helpfully. "I bathed in the river only yesterday."

Zephele shudders. "In the Upper Neelah? Oh, but you mustn't. Our eldest brother was eaten by a hippo, you know. He went down to the river to bathe one hot day, they say, and no one ever saw him again. They found his wrap downriver, bloodied and torn. So you must stay out of the river. Promise me that you will."

"As Orion knows," Malora says, "I have been bathing in hippo waters my whole life and I am still alive."

"You're right, Orrie!" Zephele says to Orion, her eyes glittering. "She *is* half wild."

"And that's why I'm going to need you," Orion says to Honus, "to take her under your tutelage and civilize her."

"I will endeavor to do my best," Honus says. Malora thinks he looks pleased at the prospect. "But I suspect it is *we* who have much to learn from *her.* Nevertheless, I am happy to offer her my hospitality and my humble pedagogical skills."

"Thank you, Honus. I knew I could count on you."

With a modest lift of his narrow shoulders, Honus says, "'If a man be gracious and courteous to strangers, it shows he is a citizen of the world, and that his heart is no island cut off from other lands, but a continent that joins to them.' "

Orion pauses at the door. "Francis Bacon?" he says.

Honus beams with pride. "That's my boy!"

Orion steers Malora out of the room and leaves her standing in the hall. "Wait just a minute," he tells her as he returns to the room. She hears them speaking in lowered voices and wonders what it is they can't say in front of her. Orion is back soon enough with an apologetic smile, steering her down the long golden hall away from Honus's room. Malora would have preferred to stay and curl up to sleep in a corner. All these crowds, all this noise, all this excitement has made her suddenly very sleepy. She likes the talk, but it would be nice if the centaurs stopped talking now and then. Her ears feel hot, as if wild dogs have been licking them.

"I hope my parents have not already retired to their evening meal," Orion says. "My father doesn't give audiences while he's eating. He says it gives him the colic."

"What if they don't let me stay?" Malora asks gloomily, fatigue making her drag her feet.

"They'll let you stay," he says with confidence. "My father wants to win the Golden Horse that badly."

"The Golden Horse?" Malora has heard mention of this.

"It is a prize," Orion says carefully. "No Highlander has won the Golden Horse in forty years. Medon desperately wants to win, particularly against a barley farmer, a Flatlander named Anders Thunderheart, who runs the championship stable. He raises Athabanshees who are maddeningly fleet-footed."

"Ah, yes, the Athabanshees!" Malora says, remembering the lady centaur on the road to Mount Kheiron. Talk of horses perks her up.

"There are five racing stables run by Highlanders and five run by Flatlanders, and they all compete every year for the Golden Horse."

"When is this competition?" Malora asks.

"In three months' time," Orion says. "On Founders' Day."

"If it is a prize your father wants, then I think I can ask my horses to run to win."

"That's just it," Orion says, with a guilty hunch of his shoulders. "My father will most likely not want you involved. You see, he lured Gift away from the Thunderheart Stable. Gift has a reputation for training winners."

"Why didn't you tell me all this before?" Malora asks.

"Because I know you think ill of Gift," Orion says.

Anger seizes hold of Malora as Orion pushes open the door in front of them. He nudges her gently through it, and she gasps, her anger forgotten.

"This is the lower gallery," Orion says. "For receiving. The upper gallery is the jubilation floor."

The lower gallery is a long room without furniture. Its soaring vaulted ceilings seem to drip with gold. There are gold-framed paintings of centaurs romping through fields of wildflowers. And above the heads of the centaurs flitting through the puffy clouds is something new: a flock of fat little pink babies with white wings.

"What are they?" she asks, pointing.

"They are putti," Orion says.

"Putti!" she exclaims. "Do they live here, too?"

He laughs. "No, they are imaginary beings."

"Really?"

"They are figments of the imagination of the artist whose Hand wrought them," he says.

"I see. They are just stories," she says, looking to him for confirmation.

"Yes," he says, "stories told in pictures."

Malora cranes at them and wonders why the artist wasted so much effort, when to enjoy the work properly one would have to lie down flat on the floor. From the center of each golden vault, bunches of green and purple and golden grapes dangle down. Candles twinkle among the grapes, making colored lights dance on the walls.

"What are they made of?" she asks, pointing at the grapes.

Orion says, "Colored glass. Our glassblowers are quite

clever. They symbolize the grapes on the vines of the Silver-mane Vineyard, the source of the house's wealth."

On the walls, green- and blue-tinted water spouts from the mouths of leaping fishes carved from blue and pink stone. Malora sniffs. The air is delicately scented.

"The very finest rose water," Orion says, splashing his fingers in the fountain, "distilled by me at my lady mother's request."

Beneath Malora's dirty feet, there are pictures on the floor made from a multitude of tiny sparkling tiles, pictures of wreaths and vines bearing fruits and vegetables so tantalizing she wants to bend down and pick them.

"Do you ever stumble and fall on your face just looking?" she asks, her voice echoing off the walls, as if they had entered into a magical cavern. "It's glorious!" she adds, lowering her voice to a whisper to avoid the echo.

"I'm glad you like it," he whispers back. "Come along."

At the end of the hallway, a Twan dozes against a massive set of doors, painted white and blue with golden handles in the likeness of lions' claws.

"This is Ash," Orion explains. "He is my father's Twan, and my mother's, too, since his mate Bella died of tick-bite fever. Ash, say hello to Malora."

Nearly as round as he is tall, Ash has a face as wrinkled as a dried nut, and fine white hair that stands up around his head as if permanently lightning-struck.

"Ash is the oldest living Twan," Orion says.

The ancient one peers up at Malora through a little round glass he wears on a black string around his neck. One dark eye bulges at her through the magnified glass as he murmurs, "They say the Ka have taken to counterfeiting People for their houses of ill repute."

"What is counterfeiting?" Malora asks.

"They fix up the female Ka, the SheKa, to look like humans," Ash explains, continuing to examine her. "But she looks genuine to me."

Malora stares back at him, challenging him to address her directly and not through Orion.

The Twan drops the glass from his eye and says to Orion, "Take my advice, my young buck, and guard your pet closely. Highlanders will be suspicious, and Flatlanders will resent her for living in luxury under this roof. What's more, if word carries beyond our boundaries, we will be besieged by Otherians looking to get their hands on—" Ash freezes, having switched his focus to Orion. He fumbles for the glass and brings it to his eye once again. "What in the name of the Blessed Centaur's Hand happened to *you*?"

"You see the results of four weeks in the bush," Orion says with a grin. He turns and lifts his hand to knock on the door, three swift knocks in a row, pause, then a fourth. On the other side, a voice bellows, "It's about time!"

A softer, female voice, says, "Enter, dearest one!"

Orion squares his shoulders and gives Malora a look of mock severity. She meets his eyes and says, "I'll try not to frighten them."

He smiles, eyes twinkling at some secret joke as, holding her hand, he leads her into the room.

For a moment, Malora thinks one of the People is marching forward to meet her on the arm of yet another handsome dark-haired centaur. Fatigue drains away as she prepares to greet these on-comers with enthusiasm. Then she stops short, realizing that she is looking at her own reflection and Orion's in a vast, crystal-clear mirror that covers an entire wall. She looks to the wall on her right and is met by another vast, crystal-clear mirror and herself and Orion in profile. She swivels her head and sees that all four walls are covered in mirrors. She is surrounded on four sides . . . by herself!

"Is this some sort of trick?" she whispers to Orion.

"Not really. It used to be a ballroom," he whispers back.

Try as she might, Malora cannot take her eyes off her many reflections. There is no way to escape them. She has seen herself only in very small, very speckled shards of mirror in the Settlement, in the wavering surfaces of pools and rivers and puddles, in the centaur's hand mirror by lantern light, but she has never taken in the sight of her entire body. Is this dark-skinned, rangy girl with broad shoulders and the tangle of russet hair really her? She looks like a smaller, more feminine version of her father, with her mother's sharp chin and high cheekbones.

Orion rouses her with a whisper: "I know nothing is more fascinating to you at this moment than your magnificent reflection, but try to remember why we're here."

He takes her by the shoulders and directs her attention toward what has to be the world's biggest centaur, big enough to blot out both her reflection and Orion's. His horse half makes Sky look like a pony. And his human half, with its bulging biceps and barrel chest, is bigger than any of the People, including Malora's father, who had been a giant of a man. Size alone would make this centaur the leader. Malora resists the impulse to fall to her knees and bow. But he isn't a king, as Orion has explained to her. He is the Apex, *chosen* by the centaurs to lead them.

"Malora Ironbound," Orion says, "permit me to present you to Medon Silvermane, the Apex of Kheiron, and his consort, the Lady Hylonome, Herself."

Malora cannot tear her eyes away from the sight of this splendid centaur. He is as gray as a bull elephant, flanks and hair and beard, with bristly gray brows that stand out in an unruly array above his fierce gray eyes. He is clad in a silvery woven wrap that is cinched at the waist with a silver-buckled belt, slung with a small pouch made of silver mesh. Two lone spots of color in his cheeks are as pink as the ostrich quill he clutches in his fist. She mutters to Orion through bared teeth, "You didn't tell me your father was a *god.*"

Orion whispers, "The God of Paperwork, you mean."

The Apex presides over a table on which towering stacks of paper vie with piles of scrolls. To judge by the flush in his cheeks and the fierce look in his eyes, he does not especially enjoy this work. Malora makes herself return his gaze until finally she seeks refuge in the sanctuary of Herself.

Standing on the other side of the table, the Lady Hylonome is as small and delicate as her mate is huge and hulking. She sports the same fashionable cap Malora has seen on Zephele. Made of rich purple stuff that has the texture of mountain moss, it looks much like an overturned bucket. Beneath the cap, her hair is white and her face is pale, and her eyes are a faded blue in which Malora can read deep sadness.

The silence draws out and Malora knows it isn't her place to break it. She drops her eyes and studies the floor, where the stone beneath the table is well worn from the scraping of hooves. Worn, too, is the path leading from the door to the table. Into this room every day, Orion has explained to Malora, dozens of centaurs from the city and the Flatlands file to plead their cases, air their grievances, and get permission to do everything from choosing a Hand to building a new fence to taking on a mate.

The Apex finally breaks the silence. "So!" he says in a voice that vibrates Malora's breastbone. "The report I received is accurate. Orion, bring the Otherian closer and let us get a better look at her."

Malora takes two steps toward the Apex. Orion moves with her and stations himself just behind her left ear. She feels his hand on her left elbow, warm and slightly moist, and the smell of him—human sweat and horse and rose water—calms her.

"Tell me about her," Medon says, his eyes still on Malora. His teeth have the same chiseled straight line as the other centaurs of the House of Silvermane. With sharp incisors, he would be truly terrifying, Malora thinks.

"We found her running with a band of Furies and—" Orion begins.

Medon cuts in. "Were there others? Humans, I mean. Or was this the only one you captured?" he asks.

Orion hesitates, then says, "She is the only one."

Medon thumps the table with his fist and topples one of the paper towers. "Thank Kheiron!" he says with visible relief.

Malora feels her hackles rise. Why does everyone view it as such a blessing that all the other People are dead? Are they that afraid of retribution?

Orion goes on. "She was separated for several years from a lone settlement of the People. When she went to rejoin them, she found only bones. She believes that the People, save her, have all perished."

"Better still," says Medon.

Malora feels the lump rise in her throat. She has had many distractions in the past few days, but her grief for Thora comes back to her now, fresh and raw, aggravated by this hulking, heartless-seeming centaur.

Malora feels her eyes welling up with tears.

As oblivious to Malora's pain as an elephant to a buzzing fly, Medon continues: "The last thing we need is some lost tribe of the People swarming up from the bush to avenge the Massacre of Kamaria."

Orion squeezes Malora's elbow gently. "Malora has no wish to avenge any ancient wrongdoing and holds nothing against us personally." Orion leans closer to her ear. "Isn't that true, Malora?" he says, prompting her with his eyes.

Malora blinks away the tears and nods, not entirely sure she means it at this moment.

"She seems to understand you," Medon comments.

"Oh, she understands everything," Orion says emphatically. "She's most intelligent."

"Really?" Herself speaks up in a voice that is soft and musical like her daughter's. "She understands everything? Then perhaps she can assist us in resolving the latest Highlander-Flatlander clash." She turns good-humored eyes on her son.

"Tell us, Orion, what in the name of Kheiron's Ever-Watchful Eye happened to you? You look quite . . . undone."

"I've been sleeping out of doors," he says. "I gave my tent to Malora."

"Was that wise?" Herself asks.

"Theon volunteered his tent, but I offered mine instead."

"Theon tells us that the trip was not without its dramatic highlights," Herself says, her eyes shifting meaningfully to Malora.

"We are told that the human attacked a full-grown lion with her bare hands," the Apex says.

Malora blurts out, "I was armed and it was an old lion, past his prime. I didn't kill him. I shooed him away before he could further harm poor West."

"She sounds quite fearless to me," Herself comments.

"Only fools are fearless," Malora says. "I am more than capable of feeling fear. For instance, at this very moment, I fear that you will not let me stay here among you, that you will turn me out."

This statement seems to unsettle the two older centaurs, who exchange a look across the table. Veracity, Malora says to herself, is probably as important in dealing with centaurs as in dealing with horses. And, besides, why not tell the truth? She has nothing to hide from the centaurs.

"Father, please, you have to let me keep her!" Orion says. "She is meant to be among us."

Medon glares at him. "Meant? *Meant?* Don't talk rubbish."

Chastened, Orion says, "I promise you she won't be any trouble, you'll see. She can stay here with us."

"Under the roof of the Apex?" Medon thunders in a voice that combines wonder with outrage.

"Honus has room to spare in his suite. He says he is looking forward to civilizing her."

Medon glances at Malora. "I will consider this petition only on condition that there be no further violence nor use of arms of any kind. This is a civil society. We do not square off against each other like animals. The Edicts must be adhered to in Mount Kheiron, even by Otherians."

Malora looks quickly away. In the mirrored wall, she sees herself standing hunched and looking not in the least bit civil. She quickly straightens her shoulders and turns to deliver what she hopes is a harmless smile to the Apex. That this colossal leader of centaurs might be in some degree afraid of her is unbelievable. She finds herself thinking of rabbits in the paddock.

Orion is saying, "Malora understands and respects the Edicts, Father."

"I wonder . . . ," the Apex mutters, staring hard at Malora.

Malora wishes she knew what he is thinking.

Orion says, "And Honus will school her, along with Zephele."

"Is that advisable?" the Apex asks. "For all we know, the Otherian might exert an adverse influence on your sister."

Herself laughs shortly. "Knowing our Zephie, I rather think it's the other way around."

"How true," says Orion. "But, Father"—he clasps his hands to signal a change of subject—"wait till you see the Furies!"

Medon suddenly lights up with more enthusiasm than Malora has yet seen in him. "Both Gift and Theon have been here to sing the praises of these horses. I intend to go down to the stable first thing tomorrow and inspect them. Gift tells me he has never seen such healthy horses. No burs, no ticks, no diseases, and none of the usual infirmities caused by living in the wild."

Malora speaks up. "That's because they *aren't* wild."

Orion elbows her.

"It's the truth," she whispers to him.

"I beg your pardon?" Medon says, with that same ferocious look in his eyes. Malora is coming to the conclusion that *ferocious* is simply the way he looks. Its source is the wild gray eyebrows, perhaps, or the sheer enormity of him, or the commanding voice that keeps the other centaurs in line.

"I have known most of these horses since they were born," Malora says. "I have cared for them and trained them to respond to my hand or foot or glance."

"Ah, but are they trained to *race*?" Medon says smugly.

"They can outrun predators, if that's what you mean," Malora says.

"But can they run fast . . . *around a track*?" Medon makes his four meaty fingers gallop in the air.

Malora remembers the days of monotonous running around the pen. Forbidden from riding out on the plains, she and Sky had been relegated to relentless circling. What a foolish thing to do if you don't have to, like chasing your tail. "If that's what you want them to do," she says tactfully, "they can do that, too."

"There is little time to lose. Gift will begin the training at once, culling out the slow ones and concentrating on the very fastest," Medon says. "The fastest of the fast will be entered into the competition. And we will win. Do you hear me?" He draws himself up and menaces his own reflection behind them. "We will win! And winning will help subdue the upstart Flatlanders that are rising on all sides of us."

"Yes, of course," Orion says softly. "Does that mean you will let Malora stay? You can't very well take her horses and not take her. It wouldn't be fair."

"Let me make this clear," Medon says in a quiet, exacting voice. "They are no longer *her* horses. They are the property of the House of Silvermane. Is that understood?"

Malora's eyes narrow. The Apex can say anything he likes, but the horses will always be hers. She nods almost imperceptibly, to minimize the lie, and feels Veracity taking a tumble.

"The Otherian can stay on a probationary basis," Medon says.

"But, Father—" Orion protests.

Malora interrupts. "The Apex is right, Orion. I must first prove that I can live peacefully and civilly among the centaurs. That is fair."

Orion looks relieved that they have managed to settle the matter.

"You must understand this, my son," Medon says. "If her presence here causes either a local stir or, worse yet, interest or curiosity beyond our boundaries, I will cease to look so favorably on her continuing to stay among us."

"What do you mean?" Orion asks.

"As you said yourself, she is the last of the People." Medon speaks carefully and clearly, pointedly *not* looking at Malora.

"Who knows what purposes those of the Otherian nations may wish to put her to? She is a living symbol, and symbols can be useful scientifically, politically, strategically. She may be a source of contention, and we centaurs pride ourselves on avoiding confrontation of any kind for any reason."

"Then let us make good use of her while she is with us," Orion says. "Honus has declared her a living artifact. He says there is much we can learn from her."

"Then may I make a suggestion, dear one?" Herself puts in. "Go and bathe the artifact—and yourself—rather thoroughly. You bring shame upon your Hand coming in here, the two of you, reeking of the bush as you do."

"Yes, Mother," Orion says with a humble bow. "Good night to you both, and thank you for your consideration." He turns Malora around and sweeps her toward the door. "That went *very* well," he whispers.

Catching a final glimpse of herself in the mirror, Malora sees a less than triumphant look on her face. Giving her horses over to some surly trainer? Lying to the Apex to get her way? Agreeing to go without weapons and to follow the other Edicts, whatever they are? Is all of this really worth the price of a soft bed, good food, fine clothes, and lively talk?

Malora certainly hopes so.

CHAPTER 14

Zephele Silvermane

Zephele takes Honus's shaving blade to Malora's leopard tunic and, with surprising strength, saws it up the front.

Hooking the pelt over one finger, Zephele trots it over to the door, her black braided tail swinging saucily behind her. She has shapely legs of tawny brown encased in bright red leather boots with shiny black buttons running up the sides. She sings out, "Honus darling, West dear, anybody! Can somebody please come and take this *abomination* away and burn it?"

Having divested herself and brushed her hands clean, Zephele comes trotting back to stare at Malora in frank fascination. She reaches to take off the malachite stone, and Malora holds fast to it, shaking her head.

"You wish to bathe with this item of crude jewelry?" Zephele asks, wide-eyed. "Very well. It makes you seem slightly less bare naked, I suppose. Tell me, do you scrape the rest of your fur off, or have the rigors of the bush rendered you quite bald?"

Malora looks down at her naked body, feeling suddenly self-conscious. "No, this is just the way I am made."

"You don't say! Imagine, having so little hair on one's body," Zephele says. "In that case, I don't understand why you can't keep it clean. But we'll take care of that."

Honus's washing place, which Zephele calls the marble convenience, is a big square room tiled in pale green stone just off the sitting room. In one corner stands a cloth screen, painted with flowers and purple salamanders. Behind the screen, Zephele shows Malora a stone grate in the floor. She instructs Malora to do her business, then pull one cord that sends a stream of water to wash the waste away and a second cord that sprays scented water on her parts.

When Malora asks her to repeat the instructions, Zephele says, "You mean to say you didn't have a similar facility where you come from?"

"In the Settlement," Malora explains through the screen, "we all did our business in a single building. It was a long board with holes in it, hanging out over a reeking hole swarming with flies and poisonous snakes."

Zephele peers around the screen with a look of horror on her pretty face. "Great Hands! I'm sure my bowels would turn to stone. Come with me, you poor darling." Zephele leads Malora over to large green trough. "You're lucky. Honus has the only bathing tub in all of Mount Kheiron. And I daresay you're going to need it."

"How do you centaurs bathe?" Malora asks.

"We take showers," Zephele says. "Usually twice a day.

Otherwise," she whispers behind her hand, "we start to smell like horses. Honus *loathes* our custom of showering. He is very sensitive about temperature since he was recovered from the frozen north. He says showering is like getting pelted by a downpour. This tub is his pride and joy. It's made of green onyx," she says, patting it fondly, "carved from a single piece of rock, imported from Suidea, I think. Honus adores precious and semiprecious stones. He is the Apex's pet, you see, and that's why he got the tub he asked for."

"Honus is Medon's pet?" Malora asks. This is yet another detail Orion has neglected to tell her.

"Oh, yes. Just like you are Orion's pet. Orion is truly following in the footsteps of the Apex, bringing you home. So you must be sure and ask the world of Orion and see if he can deliver," she says with an impish grin.

Malora asks, "Did Medon journey to the frozen north to recover Honus?"

"Hands, no! No centaur has ever gone there that I know of. It is very cold and slippery, I'm told. No, Father obtained Honus once he was quite thawed out, in Kahiro. Everyone in Mount Kheiron knows the story. Long before he was Apex, when he was not much older than Theon, my father purchased Honus for a pretty nub at the bazaar in Kahiro. Anything on earth you desire," Zephele says, heaving a dreamy sigh, "you can purchase at the bazaar in Kahiro."

"So Orion has said."

"And so is it true. Honus was on display in an exhibition run by a Dromadi proprietor of exotic creatures from the far corners of the known earth. Let me see if I can remember what my father says was there." Zephele pauses, squinting at the ceiling, as she begins to recite: "An ophiotarus, that's half bull and half serpent; a griffin with clipped wings; an al-mi raj, which I believe is a one-horned rabbit; a blue-maned wolf from the west; and an asp-headed leopard called a sta. The family is endlessly grateful, every time we hear this story, that Medon chose Honus and not something else. Imagine, being schooled by a sta! I'm not even sure stas know how to read, much less do figures and recite poetry and dance and pipe, and Honus can do all of those things and more." Zephele catches herself. "Listen to me, babbling on while you stand around bald as a baby bird tumbled from its nest. Orion would never forgive me if he knew, so please don't tell him."

Zephele leans over the bathing tub and indicates two golden spigots, shaped like a lion's and lioness's head. For a race that seems to be petrified of lions, Malora thinks, the centaurs seem extremely fond of decorating with them.

"The male gives you cold water, and the female hot. I suppose that's very true of hibes and beasts alike, isn't it?" Zephele smacks her hand over her mouth. "I'm too bold, aren't I? Herself hates when I go on like this. You mustn't tell her. Let's make sure you get plenty of hot water."

For Malora, hot water is for boiling meat too tough to roast. She has never used it for bathing. Even in the Settlement, the People dunked themselves in the icy-cold cistern first thing every morning. "Is there a fire burning underneath the bathing tub?" she asks, getting down on all fours to look.

Zephele blinks in surprise. "A fire, my goodness, no! What a primitive notion. The water is heated by the sun in great vats on the roof," she explains, turning on the taps and flooding the tub.

As the steam rises, Zephele hands Malora two chalky cakes. Malora is just beginning to wonder if she is meant to eat them, when Zephele says, "This one is lavender, and this one lime pumice. Use the lime to scrub your body and the lavender for your hair."

Malora continues to look uncertain.

Zephele's hand returns to her mouth. "Oh, Hands. Don't tell me you've never even used soap before?"

The soap Malora's mother cooked up from animal fat and herbs is a distant memory. "We weren't allowed to use it in the cisterns because we drank that water," she says, dragging the recollection up. "We only used soap when we bathed in the river."

Zephele shudders. "There you go again with that river bathing. It's a wonder you haven't lost an arm—or a leg—and it's not as if you had all that many to spare! Still, you must tell me all about this Settlement of yours, and all about the bush as well. I think the bush quite agrees with Orion, don't you? He looks wonderfully handsome and rugged, all scratched up and scabby and brown from the sun, and I think he may even have developed a few muscles. The only muscles he gets from distilling essences are in his nose."

"Properly mixed and prepared, scents establish the very tone of society," Malora says dutifully.

Zephele rolls her eyes. "And did my darling brother also give you that business about scents making drowsy souls feel lively and overly excited ones find peace?"

Malora nods. Zephele sighs. "I'm sure alchemy is as old as the Hills of Melea, but the fact is that Orion is its only practitioner. It's not even remotely popular, although certainly everyone seems to like the scents he distills, so I suppose he will be kept busy. Still, it's too bad that he couldn't have declared something more *physical,* like sculpting or dancing. Of course, no Hand is as physical as being on the Peacekeeping Force, like Neal Featherhoof. But Peacekeeping is not a Hand, nor are Highlanders permitted in the Force."

Malora dips a foot into the water. Scalded, she quickly pulls back.

"Did you burn yourself?" Zephele leans over the tub to adjust the temperature, then swishes her hand in the water to mix the hot with the cold. "Try it now," she says. "Orion hardly sees Neal anymore, now that they're grown. It's a pity, really, because that means I hardly ever see Neal anymore, and I do so adore seeing him." She eyes the ceiling. "I'm quite sure, however, that he doesn't know I exist. Alas, poor little invisible Zephie!"

Malora follows her foot with the rest of her body until she is immersed in water up to her chest. The heat makes her shiver pleasantly. She hopes no one will make her get out anytime soon. Here is yet another wonderful experience to savor. Beds, blankets, food, and now baths. What next?

Zephele prattles on. "Neal's father runs the vineyard that has been owned by the House of Silvermane for eons. He's blissfully strapping and handsome—Neal Featherhoof, that is—and as strong as a team of Beltanians. You and he will have a great deal in common, for he has hunted lions."

"Is that what the Peacekeeping Force does, hunt? Isn't that against one of the Edicts?" Malora asks. Maybe, she thinks as she slips farther beneath the warm blanket of water, she could join this force.

"Hands, no. Neal hunts for sport, and Flatlanders aren't held to the Edicts the way we are up here. The Peacekeepers are an army that's supposed to keep the peace, but it's really sort of silly because all we ever have around here is peace." Zephele settles gracefully on the floor beside the tub. "Then again, if all we have is peace, then I guess one might conclude that they do a fearfully good job. Mostly, they escort Highlanders to Kahiro, which must be great fun, but they also turn out those who have violated the Edicts, which can't be much fun at all."

Malora glances over at Zephele, whose chin is nestled on her hands, which are resting on the rim of the tub. "You know," Malora says, "from where I am right now, you look like one of the People."

"Do I?" Zephele's eyes ignite, then quickly dim. "Of course, as soon as I stand up the illusion will be dashed, so I shall endeavor to remain here as long as possible to sustain for you what is undoubtedly a comforting illusion. Now, where was I?" She taps her pursed lips, eyes searching the ceiling for her lost thought. "Ah, yes! The Peacekeepers! The Peacekeepers are a joke, when I really think about it, because no one ever attacks us and we attack no one. So the Peacekeepers all bash each other about in practice, and that's just about that. It would be far more exciting if we had an actual war to fight. About the most interesting thing that happens around here is the race for the Golden Horse on Founders' Day. We bet on it and brawl about it and it's almost like war, although I really wouldn't know, would I? None of us would know. There hasn't been a war here since the Great Massacre." She clamps her jaws shut and speaks from the corner of her mouth. "I don't suppose they've told you about that particular unpleasantness. Oh, dear, there I go again!"

Malora says, "Don't worry. They told me. Every last human being was slaughtered."

"Except for your lucky forebears, my darling dearest, who must have escaped!" Zephele says with a fresh burst of good cheer. Then she catches her lower lip in her perfectly straight teeth, her brow creased. "Orion said you have recently buried your own dear mama. He told me in his Stern Voice not to speak of it, but then why, pray tell, did he mention it in the first place if he didn't want me to speak of it? My brother can be most exasperating. Are you upset that I'm speaking of it? If you are, please don't tell my brother. He'd be very cross with me, indeed. First there is his Hurt Look, then comes his Stern Look. Following that is the Cross Look. Don't even ask what comes next, because you don't want to know. Orion has more than a bit of the Apex in him. Will it make you feel better to tell me about your mama?" Zephele asks. "Or will it make you feel infinitely sadder? When I lost my dear pet squirrel Johnnyboy to one of Neal's hunting dogs, I wept for days but found that it helped to talk about it."

Malora says, "Her name was Thora. She was very wise. She knew the uses and lore of all the plants. She was a healer. In the end, she sacrificed herself to save my life."

"Healers are frightfully serious," Zephele says, brows knit. "Whereas I am unerringly frivolous. Do go on."

"She was also, before I was born, a huntress. My father made her a beautiful bow, and they used to hunt together."

"That's sounds most romantic," Zephele says, "apart

from the killing animals part. I shouldn't like to kill anything, particularly not some dear, helpless wild animal."

Malora thinks many wild animals are far from helpless. "Sometimes you have to kill animals in order to live."

Zephele makes a face. "I can't imagine it. Apart from the fact that it's in defiance of the Third Edict and most definitely the Fifth, it's really quite thoroughly revolting. Tell me about your father . . . who is also no longer living, I presume?"

"Jayke was a master horseman," Malora says, the heat of pride burning in her cheeks.

Zephele's mouth drops open. *"Your father was a centaur?"*

CHAPTER 15

Shimmering Finery

Malora's laugh explodes as her head rears out of the water. "No, he trained and rode horses. Horse. Man."

Zephele sags with relief. "You cannot possibly imagine what was running through this head of mine when I heard you say that. I see—so what you mean to say is that your father was an accomplished horseback-riding human who taught you everything you know about horses, which Orion seems to feel is an infinite amount. More than Gift, I imagine. Gift is exceedingly cross, as Twani go, but that's because he is under a great deal of pressure to win the Golden Horse for our father. Plus which, he is being paid for his efforts, and that almost never happens with the Twani. I maintain that Twani are much happier when not being paid. But to return to the far more fascinating subject of your father, did you bury him along with your poor dear dead mother?"

"No, he died earlier. The Leatherwings got him."

"What are the Leatherwings?" Zephele quickly holds up

a hand and, looking pained, averts her eyes. "Never mind, don't tell me. I'm sure I don't want to know. But you poor dear darling, what a tragic life you've led!" Then, with determination, she adds, "Well, there will be no more of that gloomy business now. Here you will find only beauty and enlightenment. Would you like me to wash your hair? I wash my own, so I'm as good as any Twan at doing it."

Malora nods. "My mother used to wash my hair and brush it."

Zephele gathers up Malora's hair in her hands. "That must have been quite a challenge. We keep our hair short or else pinned up. Because of the caps. I had long hair when I was little, but I cut it when I took the cap, as most of us do. Why bother if it's going to be hidden away?"

"Why do you all have to wear caps?" Malora asks. "Orion explained it, but it's still a bit unclear to me."

"We're told they are a concession to modesty. It has something to do with not inflaming the bucks. Everyone wants the young to marry, but no one wants anyone falling in love. Marriage is a practical contract. Herself and Father feel that I've been adversely influenced by reading far too many books about love. Ancients like Charlotte Brontë and Jane Austen and Victoria Roberts and Danielle Steele and Nico Simonette and Shakespeare and Stephenie Meyer. The characters in these stories follow no Edicts. But Edicts, however vexing, are made to protect us. I must constantly remind myself of this."

Zephele scrubs Malora's scalp, working the soap up into a fragrant lather that drips into the water. "Oh, dear, I do hope it won't be too boring for you to be with us. After the drama of the bush, I'm afraid you might find life among the centaurs tame and rather stifling."

Malora enjoys the sensation of Zephele's fingers massaging her scalp. "So far, I like it here. It's nice to have people to talk to." She catches herself. "Centaurs, that is."

"And then of course, when you get fed up with centaurs, there's always Honus. Honus is an absolute darling," Zephele goes on. "He's very wise and kind. All those books out there in the big room? He's read every one of them once and some of them twice or even three times! Do you read?"

Malora shakes her head. "The Grandparents did," she says, "but none of the People knew how. They say the Grandparents had great halls filled with nothing but books."

Zephele's hands falter and grow still. "Oh, dear, I'm afraid we stole all those books from you. *My* ancestors, that is, from your poor unfortunate ones. They needn't have bothered, if you ask me. Your average centaur would just as soon stare at a fruit bowl as sit down and read an entire book, although we've all learned how. It's—"

"The Edicts," Malora finishes for her.

"Number Twelve, to be exact, and that's the way of it! You'll have to learn how to read, too, if you stay with us."

"I *want* to learn," Malora says.

"Really?" Zephele sounds surprised. "Imagine that! Well, good for you, because it's fiendishly difficult, and that means Honus will be so busy teaching you that he'll ignore me. Now *that* will be my idea of bliss! Dunk your head and rinse out the soap now. Your hair will smell like a whole field of lavender, which will be a vast improvement over the way it smelled before."

Malora slides under the water until only her nose, like a reed poking above a river's surface, connects her to the air. The water foams fragrantly around her. A huge sigh escapes her as her clean hair fans out like a lily pad. Above the waterline, Zephele's voice murmurs on. It doesn't really matter that Malora can't hear exactly what the centaur maiden is saying. The cadence of her voice alone is a comfort. In Mount Kheiron, she thinks, she will be surrounded by the constant babble of voices.

After the bath, Zephele wraps Malora in a big fleecy cloth and seats her on a stool before a looking glass to comb out her hair. Delicious smells waft from the next room, making Malora's stomach gurgle. Closer in, Zephele's scent, even more than the lavender and the lime, tantalizes her. It is a warm, horsey fragrance combined with something more complex and spicy. "What is your scent?" she asks.

"Wild jasmine. Isn't it divine? We don't cultivate jasmine here, so we must obtain precious vials of the essence from the market at Kahiro. Then Orion mixes it with water and a little olive oil. He hates that I want just the single scent and not some fearfully complex concoction he can cook up in the cauldron of his distillery. He says single-scent aromas lack lyricism and potency. I put it behind my ears and on the insides of my wrists and brush it into my coat and tail. The essence comes from the far west, borne to Kahiro by Dromadi caravans. Don't you love the sound of that?" Her voice lowers to a dramatic pitch as she intones, "*Borne to Kahiro by Dromadi caravans.* One day, I shall journey to Kahiro in a caravan of my own and roam the bazaar to my heart's content. Well, not exactly *by myself,* of course—I'll have scads of bodyguards, for everyone knows that young females aren't safe on the streets of Kahiro, and the only daughter of the Apex of Kheiron even less so. Imagine being someplace that's not safe. How *exhilarating!*"

Zephele stops combing Malora's hair and flaps her arms. "Now I know how the Twani feel. This is hard work!"

Malora loves the sensation of Zephele's hands in her hair and hopes she won't stop. Still, she feels guilty being taken care of and says, "I *can* comb my own hair, you know."

"Can you really? There are so many snarls in here, I was thinking your hair might never before have made the formal acquaintance of either comb or brush. I'm almost done. Ah, Sunshine, there you are, my darling little Twan!"

The female Twan looks much the same as the males Malora has seen, except she has a long, furry tail trailing down between her legs. The Twan edges into the marble convenience, carrying a big reed-woven pack on her back. Malora sees how the Twan has come by her name. Sunshine's hair is bright reddish-orange and stands out around her face like the rays of a miniature sun, in the center of which her big golden eyes are glum and lifeless.

"Whatever's the matter, Sunshine?" Zephele asks.

"Your lady mother came to your rooms to find you," Sunshine whispers. "She questioned why I would be working so hard to clean brushes that were already spanking clean, miss."

"Oh, Hands! And did you tell her I had ordered you to do so?" Zephele asks, pausing only briefly in her combing.

"I did, miss, and she told me I must be more insistent about not getting caught up in useless tasks. I must stay with you," Sunshine says, wringing her hands, "and protect you."

"What from? Squirrels?" Zephele asks with a frown.

"But don't worry. Even though it was Herself who did the asking, I would never presume to insist," she says.

"Thank you, Sunshine, I do appreciate your kind consideration. Now go curl up on a cushion and get yourself some sleep. I'll wake you when I'm ready to leave. And thank you for bringing such an abundance of wraps. Did you bring the belts and brooches and the other things I asked for?"

The Twan nods and sets down the big pack, then departs.

"Poor Sunshine!" Zephele sighs at the ceiling. "It's not easy being the Twan of Zephele Silvermane."

"The Twani seem to like to sleep," Malora says.

"Oh, it isn't that they *like* to sleep, darling. They *need* to sleep. Honus thinks the reason they all die so young—they don't live much longer than twenty-five years, poor dears—is that they don't let themselves sleep as much as they need to, so intent are they on serving us. Honus told me this fact when I was three, and Sunshine, who was a mere kit of one and a half years at the time, had just come to me. I determined from that day forth that I would not be responsible for the early death of my Twan. I let her sleep whenever she likes. Sometimes I even stand over her and *order* her to sleep. At the rate she is going, she will outlast me! Would you like me to plait your hair? I know how. Sunshine plaits my tail, but Herself used to let me plait hers all the time before it got all white and straggly. Oh, I hope I never grow old, don't you? The old can't possibly enjoy their lives as much as the young and vital do."

Thinking of her careworn mother, Malora is inclined to agree. "How long do centaurs live?" she asks.

"They say Kheiron the Wise lived two hundred years, but I think he must have been different from the rest of us, because most centaurs expire when we are sixty or seventy years of age, unless fever or snakebite or disease takes us. Centaurs have very sensitive stomachs. The Apex before Father died of colic at the Golden Horse banquet table. It was considered quite portentous because it was the last time an Apex won the Horse. Everyone thinks my father frightfully brave for being so bent on winning the Horse because what if he were to drop dead at the banquet table just like his successor? There!" Zephele holds up a hand mirror so Malora can see her hair from behind. Zephele has plaited Malora's hair into a single long braid and tied it with a blue ribbon. "Do you like it? I think it looks cunning! You can wear it down the center of your back, or you can flip it over your shoulder like this."

It looks just like Zephele's tail! Malora is charmed.

Zephele takes the mirror back and stares at her reflection in dismay. "I wish I could grow my hair like yours and show it. If they make you wear a cap, I'll throw a tantrum. We'll just have to make up some excuse." She squints as she conjures one up. "Let's see. We'll say that hats give humans brain fever. Would that be a violation of the Edict against the telling of falsehoods? Oh, well! Now, let's see about dressing you. Tell me when you see something you like."

Zephele lifts the pieces of fabric from the basket and flaps them out, then drapes them across the table before Malora. "I'm more than happy to give these to you. I told West to tell Sunshine to bring anything with blue or green in it because we want to bring out the color of your eyes. You have such remarkable eyes. The centaurs' eyes are round, but yours tilt upward. Did all of the People have slanted eyes?"

"My father did," Malora says.

"He must have been very handsome . . . for a human, at any rate."

"All the women thought so, but he had eyes only for Thora."

"See? That's romance for you. Centaurs could do with a little more romance."

Malora points to one that is blue with green and gold threads. It has a watery sheen to it. "I like this."

"Oh, Hands! The human has taste." Zephele drapes the fabric over Malora's right shoulder, leaving her left shoulder bare in the centaurean style. Then she wraps the fabric around Malora's body and stands back to study the effect through narrowed eyes. She shakes her head and frowns. She wraps and rewraps Malora's body several times while Malora stands patiently with her arms held away from her sides. She feels like a giant doll in the hands of a commanding child. "Did all the People have this lovely skin color? Some of us are as black as coal, some as yellow as saffron, others as pale as chalk, but none of us is quite this divine color. As red as a clay pot. It's very pretty, indeed, and we want to show just enough of it to intrigue but not so much as to violate the immodesty Edict. What a shame there isn't some handsome young human to properly savor your beauty."

Malora stares down at her feet. Whenever this thought occurs to her, she feels wistful and sad. How wonderful would it be to come across another human, a male human, handsome and kind and good with horses like Aron, only younger and with his wits intact.

Zephele misinterprets. "You needn't worry about your toes. I had a quick conference with Orion earlier. We discussed having Cylas Longshanks, the cobbler, make some covering for your feet. Your toes are delightfully unique but so very vulnerable-looking, and we don't want any clumsy-hoofed centaurs smashing them flat. It's bad enough for us maidens dodging them on the jubilation dance floor, but you, with those tiny little things wiggling out there in the open, why, they'd be trampled like the grapes of the Silver-mane Vineyard. There, now. Walk across the room and turn to face me."

The fabric is wrapped so tightly around her that Malora is reduced to small, mincing steps. She is sure that the mirrors in the Apex's receiving room will confirm that she looks like a large silkworm in a blue-green cocoon. "It will be difficult to run. And I won't be able to ride."

"Oh, there's no need to run in Mount Kheiron. There are far too many hills, and besides, it isn't done," Zephele says dismissively. "And riding, well, not even the two-legged Twani ride horses. Horses pull carriages and plows."

Malora teeters. "I don't think I can even *walk*. Can we perhaps cut the cloth in half and wrap me slightly less snugly and only down to my knees?"

Zephele nods slowly, tapping her pretty little chin. She takes Honus's shaving blade and slices the fabric in half. Then she rewraps Malora as requested. Zephele fishes a handful of sashes and belts out of the pack. She wraps a wide purple sash around Malora's waist and ties it. "Perfection!"

"What do you wear for warmth?" Malora asks.

"Heavier wraps. Brocades and wools and velvets. And sometimes fur capes. I have the most heavenly sable cape. If you ask him nicely, Orion will get you a sable cape. Ask him for two, why don't you?"

Out in the bush, the sable, with its distinctive sickle-shaped horns, was almost pitifully easy to kill. "I can get my own sable," Malora says.

"By running the poor creature to ground and killing it?" Zephele says. "No, no, no, you'll do no such thing. Listen to me, my dear little Otherian, you have to get all of this hunting and killing business out of your head now that you're here. It simply won't do. Not only is it against at least four Edicts, it's unspeakably disgusting and I'll not hear one more word about it."

CHAPTER 16

Portarum Curator

In a daze, Malora follows her bossy new centaur friend out into the larger room, where Honus stands at the massive stone hearth stirring something in a big black pot over a fire. She wonders what the pot is made of. It doesn't look like clay. More such pots sit warming to the sides.

"May I present to you the new Malora Ironbound!" Zephele announces.

Freshly showered, in a blue wrap that matches his eyes, Orion looks up from the table, where a book lies open. The table, which was cluttered earlier, has been cleared, moved out into the middle of the room, and covered with a white cloth. West is setting down plates and goblets and an impressive array of eating implements.

"She looks very fine, indeed," Orion says, closing the book and setting it aside, "and I have no doubt is ravenous, for all the time you've taken in the convenience. Come on, you two beauties, let's sit down and eat."

West pulls out a chair and offers it to Malora. "Very pretty wrap, miss. I guess we've seen the last of the leopard skin?" He brushes against her shoulder, and she finds herself releasing a held breath.

Zephele says, "I forbid anyone to mention that vile thing while we're eating. Or ever again, for that matter."

Honus brings over a pot from the hearth and sets it down in the middle of the table. "You catch me ill-prepared for two-legged visitors," he tells Malora. "I have but two chairs. One for my desk and an easy chair for my terrace. I will let you have my easy chair."

With its soft, dark red cushions, the chair is aptly named. Honus serves Malora from the pot. "This is one of my specialties. I call it Barley Surprise."

Malora glances around to see what the others are doing. The centaurs on the trail ate with large silver spoons. At this table, the implements sit beside their bowls in a baffling row. The implements her tablemates hold look remarkably like miniature silver hay forks to her. She picks up hers and turns it slowly in her hand, then pokes it into the Barley Surprise, about which there is little to surprise her. It is a meatless stew with carrots and root vegetables and onion and bits of fungus, which she eats while trying not to impale her tongue on the hay fork. The others don't seem to be having any difficulty. They talk easily as they eat. While Malora concentrates on mastering the implement, Orion recounts the lion story. Honus and Zephele listen, their implements arrested halfway to their mouths.

"The lion was old," Malora breaks in, but none of them pays her the least mind. Their eyes are wide as they take in Orion's tale.

Later on, while Malora finishes the Surprise, she breaks in on Orion again to say, "It wasn't a spear. It was a fence post and far too dull to have ever penetrated the lion's tough old hide. This thing would have served me better," she adds, brandishing the miniature hay fork.

West removes the fork from her upheld hand and takes her empty bowl. "I'm glad you enjoyed it, miss." He sets down a bigger bowl filled with a thick, fragrant orange soup with chunks of black bread. "You'll like this, too," he says.

"And then there was the asp that visited us on our last night in the bush." Orion dips a large spoon into his soup.

"The asp," Malora quickly explains, taking up her happily familiar spoon, "was attracted to the heat of our campfire."

"There we were," Orion says, his eyes alight with the memory, "sitting around the campfire, enjoying a hot cup of tea before we trundled off to our tents, when this small, harmless-seeming snake comes slithering out of the darkness into our midst. It comes up between me and Theon.

"'That snake is deadly poisonous,' Malora announces in the most unimaginably casual way. 'Stay where you are and don't move.' Theon, poor fellow, freezes like the temple statue of Kheiron, sweat popping out all over his brow. Before any of us moves, Malora Ironbound leaps up and grabs the snake by the tail, whips it around over her head, and flings it into the flames. Sizzle! Pop! No more snake! Now that," Orion says, "is what I call *style*."

"It was a very small asp," Malora says, the talk making her self-conscious.

Orion rears back from his bowl. "And what would you have done had it been a much younger lion and a far longer snake?" he asks, one black eyebrow cocked.

Malora shrugs and admits, "The same thing."

"My point exactly," he says to the others. "She's simply the most fearless creature on two legs or four."

After the soup, West comes along with what he calls pood. It is as red as berries and escapes the smaller spoon Malora attempts to scoop it into. She is chasing the pood all around the bowl when Orion asks, "And how have things been here in Mount Kheiron?"

"*Achingly* boring," Zephele says with a languid stretch. "We've been preparing for the Midsummer Jubilation."

"What will this year's theme be?" Orion asks.

"Death by Boredom," Zephele says with a sigh. "Actually, I'm desperately in need of inspiration. Perhaps now that the cousins are back, they will help me."

"Come, come, Zephie, my dear," Honus says. "How can you say you have been bored, when you have been reading one of the great tragedies, *Romeo and Juliet*?"

Zephele rolls her eyes. "Those two lovers were so completely *pinheaded*, I find it difficult to summon even the slightest bit of sympathy for them. And that nurse! What an impossible busybody! Not to mention that friar person— well, anyone who fell for his line of talk deserved to be turned out. If William Shakespeare were alive today, do you know what I'd do? I'd demand that he write his play over so that Romeo and Juliet ignored everybody's advice and lived happily ever after."

"It wouldn't be much of a tragedy if that happened," Honus points out with a wry smile.

"Then let it be a comedy!" Zephele says righteously. "How much more entertaining are Shakespeare's comedies! Give me the antics of *Twelfth Night* any day over that miserable, bloody *Titus Andronicus.*"

"And what news of the Peacekeepers?" Orion asks.

"They returned late last night," Honus says. "Neal Featherhoof came here this morning to confer."

"So *that's* why you sent me out on that silly errand," Zephele says, eyes narrowed, hoof tapping.

Honus's face is grave. "This must not leave this room, as Featherhoof has yet to report to the Apex, but Neal tells me that a band of wild centaurs is rumored to be menacing the trade routes to Kahiro."

Malora's head snaps up from her pood. *Wild centaurs?*

"How thrilling!" Zephele says with a shiver.

"They have been attacking Dromadi trade caravans en route from the west to Kahiro," Honus says. "They've lost three caravans in less than nine weeks."

"Were there any survivors?" Orion asks.

"Neal says none, ever," Honus replies.

Zephele says in an undertone, "How beastly. I wonder if they were after my essence of wild jasmine?"

"Zephie, don't be shallow," Orion tells her. Turning back to Honus, he says, "If there are no survivors, how do we know that wild centaurs are to blame?"

"The culprits left clear hoof marks in the sand," Honus says.

"I wonder . . ." Malora abandons her pood and speaks

up. "Could they be hoof marks left by men riding on horse-back instead of centaurs?"

They all stare at her in puzzlement.

"The tracks of horses and those of centaurs are identical. Perhaps instead of wild centaurs, they are the tracks of People mounted on horseback," Malora says, looking around with growing excitement.

"But then that would mean the People were nothing more than common marauders and murderers," Zephele says doubtfully. "And wouldn't that be worse than no People at all—apart from your delightful self, of course."

Malora's excitement deflates. "You are right, I suppose."

Honus says, "Your theory is possible, Malora . . . but not probable. The fact is that I have heard no tales of People on horseback, and many of wild centaurs, for as long as I can remember. Usually, where there are tales, there is some germ of truth."

Malora, thinking how true this was in the case of the Leatherwings, lets her hopes fade completely.

"Will Neal and the others have to battle the wild centaurs?" Zephele asks, looking worried.

"That remains to be seen," Honus says. "Neal carries a formal request from the Empress of the Ka. She proposes an army made up of the five nations most affected, which, in addition to us and the Ka, would be the Suideans, the Pantherians, and the Dromadi. Formal requests have gone out to the leaders of all the nations. We will see how the Apex responds."

"He'll just invoke Edicts Three and Five and Fourteen," Zephele says gloomily.

"But he has never been faced with a crisis of quite these proportions," Honus says. "In his teachings, Kheiron says that there are conditions under which some Edicts can be contravened, and I believe foreign attack is one of them."

"But we haven't been attacked," Orion points out.

"It may be just a matter of time," Honus says.

"What is so terrible about wild centaurs?" Malora asks.

"Wild centaurs are, quite simply, our father's worst nightmare," Orion says, and an uncomfortable silence falls upon the table.

Into this silence, Malora prompts, "Because . . . ?"

"Because," Orion explains patiently, "wild centaurs are a reminder of what we once were, of what it has taken us centuries to evolve away from."

Malora is about to probe further when West brushes up against her back and says, "Can I tempt you, miss?"

He is holding a gilt-edged plate. On the plate is a cake, yellow and dense and easy to eat. "Yes!" she says.

"A second pood!" Zephele says, looking impressed. "I'm sure we have you to thank for this, Malora!"

After West has cleared away the plates and bowls, Honus all but chases off Orion and Zephele and West. Once they have gone, he leans against the door and lets out a short bark of laughter that startles Malora. "Forgive me," he says. "I dearly love the Silvermanes, but they would stay and talk all night if I didn't shoo them off to bed. Now, shall we two Otherians take our tea on the terrace?"

Honus goes to the hearth and pours the fragrant wildflower tea, which West left to brew. Whole blossoms dance about in the cups, which he hands to Malora. Holding a long stick to the fire, he leads the way with a lantern in one hand and the flaming stick in the other, through a set of arched doors. Outside, there is a wide stone terrace with a low balustrade that runs along the side of the house. Along the wall is a narrow couch and a lower, deeper, cushioned one suitable for centaurs, as well as several small tables holding stacks of books. On the far end of the terrace, where the light from the lantern doesn't reach, Malora can make out small trees and leafy plants growing out of big pots.

Honus leans against the balustrade and holds the lit stick to the bowl of a clay pipe, which reminds Malora of the one her father used to light after the evening meal. She sets down his teacup within his reach and, cradling hers, leans her elbows on the balustrade and looks down at the view.

"Medon and Herself have the view to the west, of the vineyard and the rose houses. We face east into the farmlands and the Hills of Melea," Honus says, extinguishing the flaming stick with dampened fingers and puffing to get his pipe going. "From the jubilation gallery, at the very top of the house, one has a view in all directions for as far as the eye can see. It's breathtaking."

"You can see your enemies approaching from all sides," says Malora.

Honus gives her a sharply appraising look. "Yes, well, one hopes we'll never have to be doing any of *that*."

The scene below is peaceful. The rooftops of the city spill like neat, sharp stacks of stone down the mountainside toward the Flatlands. The lights from the scattered farmhouses twinkle in the darkness. Malora can see the great white road that led her here, and the Lower Neelah, like a long silver snake, slithering off toward the north. A second, narrower river glints farther to the east.

Honus says, "I'd like you to take my bedchamber."

"No, please," Malora says. She still feels bad for having displaced Orion from his tent. Not wanting to do the same thing to Honus, she points to the bench behind them. "I am happy to sleep on that."

"That is where *I* sleep. The bedchamber the Apex made for me is sumptuous, but I don't ever use it."

"Sumptuous." She rolls the new word on her tongue. "Does that mean comfortable?" she asks.

"More than comfortable. Luxurious," he says.

"Luxurious?" She echoes this second strange new word.

Honus smiles kindly. "A state of which you obviously know very little. *Luxurious* means deliciously comfortable, dazzlingly beautiful, and richly appointed, like most things in Mount Kheiron. Don't worry, you'll soon be taking it for granted like the rest of us. So I beg of you, please take my room. Otherwise, it will, sadly, go on standing empty."

"There's no sense in letting it go to waste." Malora stares at Honus's face in profile, at his sharp nose and pointy beard lit up by the flame from the pipe. Honus's horns are beautiful, so different from the horns of wild animals, which are dirty and scuffed and battle-scarred. His horns are blunt and stubby. She wonders if he buffs them to give them the rich brown luster of the combs the People made from tortoiseshells. Turning around, she stares back into the big room, where Honus's books and treasures give a rich and inviting glow.

He follows her look. "Aladdin's cave," he murmurs.

"What is Aladdin's cave?" she asks.

"A place of vast riches, from a story in one of these books."

"Like Puss in Boots," she says.

Honus smiles. "Yes, very like."

"Zephele tells me that you have read all of these books," Malora says.

"Not nearly, fortunately," Honus says. "I have much to look forward to."

"They smell musty and old to me."

"They *are* musty and old," Honus replies. "But that can't be helped. It is what is inside of the books that remains remarkably fresh."

"Why don't you have any *new* books?" Malora asks.

"An excellent question," he says. "Writing books and making books—and *reading* books, for that matter—never really caught on as Hands. We haven't the trees. We haven't the demand. We have neither the craft nor the curiosity nor the passion to acquire it."

"Then who made all these?" she asks.

"The People," he says. "But even the People, in the long years of their decline, had ceased to make books. They read from machines, so these books here were old even in the People's time."

Malora remembers what Zephele said about the centaurs stealing the People's books. "Can you tell me about the Massacre?"

Honus draws deeply on his pipe. "Not a very pleasant bedtime story, but you are entitled to know." After a short silence, he begins: "Many hundreds of years ago, this mountain was occupied by a tribe of the People known as the Kamar. The Kamar were a beacon of civilization in a brutal world comprised mostly of warring hibes. There were the Ka to the north, the Suideans to the west, the Dromadi to the east, the Pantherians and the Capricornias far, far to the south.

"Today, most of the hibes have evolved into relatively high civilizations, but in those days they were all wild and dead set against one another. The wildest of all were the centaurs. Calling themselves the Sons and Daughters of Ixion, they traveled in packs, frequently attacking the People in the outlying settlements. But after they attacked the city of Kamaria itself, during the wedding of the daughter of a high nobleman, the People declared war on the centaurs. They had sticks that shot fire and other deadly weapons of war, and many of the centaurs perished in the series of battles that followed. The People drove the centaurs across the plains to the Hills of Melea in the east. Other centaurs scattered to live in the northern Downs. In Melea, there dwelled a scholarly hermit, a centaur named Kheiron. No one knows how he came by his knowledge. Some say he was touched by the gods. Others say he had studied at the knees of the last Scienticians. Kheiron gave the centaurs sanctuary and set about civilizing them. He taught them to read, and then he taught them philosophy and medicine, mathematics and architecture, and all the arts and crafts of the Hand. He issued the Edicts, and bit by bit, the centaurs underwent the process of civilization. They stopped eating meat and forswore the drinking of spirits."

"What are spirits?" Malora asked.

"Powerful distillations of grapes or grains or yams that

addle the mind and inflame the blood," Honus said. "Medon produces spirits in the Silvermane Vineyard but only to trade with Otherian nations. Spirits are our number one export, which makes Silvermane the wealthiest house in Mount Kheiron. Anyway, the centaurs, thus reformed, began to live a life of study and reflection, but also of industry and purpose.

"Meanwhile, without the benefit of Kheiron's influence, the centaurs who had fled to the Downs maintained their lawless ways. One day, this savage band swept southward and laid waste to Kamaria, killing, raping, plundering, and then fleeing with sacks of riches. In Melea, Kheiron got word of the slaughter of the Kamars. He bade the Melean centaurs to go to Kamaria to minister to the wounded and help them rebuild their ravaged homeland. But the surviving Kamars mistook the centaurs of Melea for a raiding party from the north returning to finish them off. The centaurs, helpless to explain their purpose in being there, fought out of self-defense and with great determination and ferocity. Many innocent centaurs died in the battle, but the People, the fire of their sticks somehow having been extinguished, suffered greater losses. Your very existence, however, suggests that a small band of People must have escaped the Massacre and fled south."

"What happened to the centaurs?" Malora asks.

"The surviving centaurs buried the People down on the flats. Since the mountain was now abandoned, the centaurs moved in and made it their home. They renamed it Mount Kheiron in honor of their patron and savior, and the centaurs rebuilt a mighty nation-state on the ruins of Kamaria. The centaurs continue to abide by the Edicts of Kheiron. Up until now, they have lived in peace and prosperity."

"And the wild centaurs you spoke of at the table to-night . . . ?" Malora says. "Maybe they descend from the centaurs who fled to the northern Downs."

"It makes logical sense. But I hope not. Because if this is the case, these wild centaurs could very well destroy everything the civilized centaurs have worked so hard to create," he says. "Provided the wild ones really exist and are not some story made up by the real thieving culprits. Some of these hibes—" He wags his head, but doesn't go on.

Malora turns to face Honus. "Are you lonely here, being the only one of your kind?"

He smiles wistfully. "Lonely? Me? I am the *portarum curator.*"

"What is that?"

"I am he who stands at the gates—in this case, the gates of ancient learning," he says, gesturing to the books. "I am not so much lonely as I stand apart."

Malora wonders if she, too, is destined to stand apart.

Honus empties his pipe on the balustrade. The embers swirl off into the soft blankness like a swarm of fireflies. He sets the pipe down and turns to take her hand. His is still warm from the pipe. "You look exhausted. Let's get you to bed. Follow me and watch where you step. I wouldn't want you to get lost in this exotic potted jungle of mine."

"Why do you keep all these plants in pots?" she asks.

"I suppose it's my way of preserving a bit of nature in my own home," he says. He stops before another arched doorway and holds the lantern high.

CHAPTER 17

The Magic Canopy

It is the room Malora saw when she smelled Orion's scent Homeward Bound. There is the high vaulted ceiling with the mosaic of an orange sun in the center. The bed has a canopy of blue filmy material that the night breeze gently ruffles. Malora walks to the foot of the bed and sits down. She looks back out the arched doorway. While they are closed for the night, the buds of the flowers growing in the pots are as big as baby's fists and will, in the morning sunlight, open up into lush, oversized blooms. The tiny, colorful birds must all be asleep, but she sees that the fruits on the trees shine like gems and look ripe for the picking. She hears the sound of running water.

"Is there a stream nearby?" she asks.

"There is a fountain in the garden below us," he says. "Medon thought of every detail when he made this room for me when I first came here. He thinks I sleep in it every night, and I never had the heart to tell him otherwise. It always seemed a shame to let this lovely room go to waste, but I could never bring myself to sleep in here. How can I put it? The room never seemed meant for me. Perhaps it is meant for you instead."

Malora rises from the bed and walks out into the big room. She looks around for Jayke's rope, finds it lying on the floor near the door, and returns to the bedchamber. Going directly to the hook on the wall, she hangs the coiled rope.

Behind her, Honus lets out his bark of laughter when he sees what she has done with the rope. "Oh, that's *perfect!*" he says. "Why, it's a horse wrangler's wreath. That settles it. This room is meant for you. Now, is there anything else I can get you before I retire?"

"No," Malora whispers.

"Please avail yourself of the marble convenience. I'll leave the lantern burning in the big room and one of my sleeping shirts hanging outside your door. Lessons will begin first thing in the morning." He bows and leaves.

Malora takes refuge between the covers. The mattress molds to her body. Her heart calms as she gazes up at the canopy. The stars on the blue fabric, like golden pebbles seen through deep waters, shift with the breeze and form themselves into pictures: a running girl with flowing hair, a galloping horse, a centaur, a horse with wings, a giant raptor, a lion, a serpent, a man pulling back the string of a bow who looks just like Jayke.

Honus awakes when the sun rising over the Hills of Melea seeps beneath his eyelids. The book he was reading last night, *Lives of the Caesars,* still lies open on his chest, facedown: a terrible disservice to its already cracked binding. He sits up stiffly and finds a small feather to mark his place. Then he picks his way along the terrace, through the potted jungle, and peers into the bedchamber.

His young guest still sleeps, flat on her back with her arms and legs splayed at odd angles as if she had been dropped to earth from a great height. Continuing on to the pump on the far side of the terrace, Honus fills a bucket with water, wincing when the pump squeaks. He might have drawn the water from the convenience, but this water, which comes from the same spring that feeds the fountain below, makes for sweeter drinking. Then he goes back along the terrace to the big room.

After stirring up last night's fire, he puts water on to heat. Dough, prepared last night by West, has been rising in a covered bowl on the warm hearth. He brushes olive oil on the top and puts the dough into the oven to bake, then goes off to perform his morning ablutions.

As Honus stands before his shaving mirror, the table now strewn with brooches and ribbons and sashes, he thinks about the girl sleeping in the bedchamber. A careful listener who asks good questions, Malora has the makings of a fine pupil. She is less wild than he expected, more shy than sullen, and more curious than frightened. Honus looks forward to teaching her.

He dresses with his usual care in a pair of auburn kidskin breeches, a crisp white silk blouse, and a dark green satin vest with a pattern of small yellow butterflies. Then he shaves and combs his beard, pats on rosemary aftershave, and gives each horn a quick buff. He returns to the big room to find that the tea is steeped. He pours Malora a cup and carries it into her bedchamber, arriving just as a cloud of tiny yellow butterflies spills into the room from the terrace and flutters up over the bed. Honus looks down at his vest and feels a jolt of synchronicity. It is all he can do to hold on to the cup as he hears a rushing in his ears and dizziness overcomes him. When the reeling subsides, a thought comes to him with startling clarity: his entire life has been a preamble to this moment, standing here and staring down at the young woman with the nimbus of yellow butterflies surrounding her head. And is it any wonder? For this girl is the pure expression of the Creator, whereas all the rest of them are figments of some scientician's fevered imagination. To think that this girl, who for all anyone knows might very well be the last of her kind in the world, has been placed in his charge!

Honus's life so far has been filled with purpose: educating the Silvermanes, advising the Apex, reading. But suddenly, he feels an almost tangible elevation of his life to a higher plain. He considers himself to be a rational being. He has never been given to divination or prognostication or the reading of signs of any kind. Yet Honus knows, as surely as his feet are cloven and there are horns on his head, that this human lying before him is the reason he has come to live among the centaurs; the reason, perhaps, that he was rescued from the ice floe. A new thought occurs to him, which is that he, the *portarum curator*—the one always set apart—is finally no longer alone.

A faint breeze ripples through the canopy and sends the little yellow butterflies tumbling back out the door.

"Malora," he says softly.

She opens her eyes, blinks, and fastens her gaze on him, recognition gradually warming her face. Then she looks down the length of the bed, out the arched doorway into the garden, where the flowers have exploded into blooms of scarlet and yellow and orange and purple. A hummingbird hovers in a red bell-shaped flower as big as a teacup. Canaries are hopping in the branches of the fruit trees, twittering in the rays of the rising sun.

"Home," she whispers, and she rises from the bed to go pick fruit.

Malora eats bread hot from the oven, slathered with goat's butter and honey. This is as much of an improvement over mush and berries as mush and berries were over strips of dried kudu. In the daylight, the view from the terrace is lively. A steady line of traffic files down the great white road. "There is the road I came in on, and there is the Lower Neelah, which flows toward the Kingdom of the Ka," she says. "And those mountains there to the east . . . ?" She gestures.

"Are the Hills of Melea," Honus says.

"Home of Patron and Founder Kheiron the Wise."

"Very good," he says.

Malora watches the farmers emerging from the stone houses and spreading out across the fields, hitching horses to plows and wheeling carts this way and that. She feels the city, so quiet during the night, come to life beneath her like a great many-headed beast stirring in its lair. She hears the clatter of hooves on stone, wheels grinding, gates clattering, and voices bidding good morning. She imagines the horses, down in the Silvermane Stable, eating their morning oats and drinking water, safe behind the high stone walls of the city where no predator can get them. A feeling of contentment suffuses her.

Zephele arrives, chattering as she breezes onto the terrace, trailing the scent of wild jasmine with only a trace of the musty smell of the book she carries tucked beneath her arm. "Good morning, one and all. How did we sleep? It's a glorious morning, isn't it?" Her cap is embroidered with purple flowers and cocked at an angle so as to show off her ebony curls. Her wrap is lavender with an embroidered pattern of tiny green and purple flowers, and her boots are lavender-dyed kidskin with buttons of ivory. Malora has never seen anyone looking quite so fresh and beautiful.

"How is our dear little human being this morning? Orion sends his fondest greetings. He says to tell you he will be busy in his distillery today. He made me promise to bring you by for a visit after the midday meal."

"Did Herself see the rakish set of your cap?" Honus asks. "Or did you introduce that particular flourish after you left Her Ladyship's company?"

Zephele waves his comment away. "I think she's secretly thanking the Hills I did not wake up this morning with a driving desire to wear a leopard-skin pelt. Apparently, the leopard-skin pelt is all the talk in the house, in spite of my having expressly forbidden it. You look truly well rested, Malora. Did you find Honus's bedchamber to your liking?"

"Very much," Malora says.

Zephele inspects Malora's wrap. "That green silk is lovely against your skin. You sliced this one in half, I suppose? Of course you did. I'm sure you're quite good with a sharp blade.

Doesn't our Malora look wonderful! Like a verdant oasis in a red desert. Orion says he is going to speak to Father about your taking on a Hand. It will be great fun, bringing you around to visit all the various workshops and studios so you can decide what you will declare. It's too bad lion wrestling and leopard skinning aren't included in the List of the Hand, or I believe you'd qualify for instant recognition," she says with a broad wink.

While Zephele chatters on, Honus coaxes her over to the low bench and places a book in her hand. "You say you like the comedies. Here is *As You Like It.* Read the first act and tell me what you think."

Then Honus leads Malora into the big room to stand before the shelves. "From these books, you will learn history to make you wise, poetry to make you witty, mathematics to make you subtle, natural philosophy to make you deep, morality to make you grave, and logic and rhetoric so that you might contend. But first," he says, taking a flat book with ragged pages down from the shelf, "you must learn *how* to read." He puts the book into her hands.

Malora sneezes. Honus produces a small square of cloth from the sleeve of his coat and hands it to her. She wipes her nose and looks down at the book.

On the warped cover is a faded picture of a tall, bug-eyed creature of indeterminate species wearing a tall red-and-white-striped hat. The book falls open to a stained and yellowed page showing a small human boy and girl with pale hair chasing two other, smaller creatures with wild blue hair that look somewhat like Twani. The symbols that accompany the pictures are quite large.

Honus takes the book back, closes it, and returns it carefully to the shelf. "Don't worry. We will come back to this in
a few days' time, when you are sufficiently prepared for its
rigors. But letters must come first."

"Letters?" Malora asks.

"The symbols used in writing and reading," Honus
explains. He steers her over to the hard, straight-backed
chair and invites her to sit. He stands next to a large sheet
of smooth slate on which he has scrawled the letters in red
chalk. Honus points to each letter and says its name, then
spits out the sound the letter makes. *"A. A-a-a. B. B-b-b."*

Honus requires Malora to spit out the sounds after he
does. Together, they go through the letters, over and over
again until she can say all their names, from *A-a-a-ay* through
Z-z-z-zee. Then he points to them at random, and while she
manages the first few, she gets hopelessly mixed up after a
while. He keeps tapping the slate with the chalk until she
remembers. Her face burns with embarrassment and shame.

When Malora's head is filled with a jumble of letters,
Honus removes his gold-rimmed spectacles and lets her go
to the marble convenience to do her business and to splash
cold water on her face in preparation for the next lesson. For
this, Honus has her take a seat at what he calls his scrivening
table. He places a gray goose-feather quill in her hand and
shows her how to dip the sharp end of the quill in the ink
flask, then gently wipe off the excess ink on the wide lip of
the flask. On the slate, he has written out all the letters. Now
she finds herself copying them, scratching out the shapes of
the letters—instead of spitting out their sounds—onto a large

sheet of paper, the same stuff the books are made of, only new and clean and far less musty-smelling. Honus has incised into the paper a row of straight lines to show her where the letters must sit. Honus gets her started on the first few rows, one letter repeatedly scratched on each row, then leaves her while he goes out onto the terrace to see whether Zephele is "dreaming or reading." To the sound of their droning voices, Malora continues to dip the tip of the quill in the flask and scratch out the letters. She fills two whole sheets with letters, with Honus returning every now and then to hover and correct her.

By way of example, Honus shows her a small sheet that he has covered with his own impossibly small, exquisitely neat handwriting. His letters look to Malora like blades of grass all bowing in the same direction, whereas her own letters crawl around on the page like bugs in a panic to escape. Malora knows just how they feel. She has never sat so still for so long. It makes her shoulders and her eyeballs ache.

Malora stares down at her braid, coiled on the edge of the paper like a red snake, and thinks about what she would be doing right now if she were still in the bush. She would be galloping on Sky, rushing toward the smell of water. Or perhaps the herd would be grazing and Malora would be lying on her back in the high grass, chewing on a stalk, watching the clouds being buffeted by the wind.

Malora fills another sheet with letters. Her shoulders and hands hurt from holding the quill. Her jaw hurts from clenching it. No wonder Zephele takes such a dim view of lessons. Malora hopes the horses are not similarly cramped and miserable as they learn their lessons from Gift. Honus is a much kinder and more patient teacher than she imagines Gift to be.

"I can't do this!" she mutters to herself. She feels close to tears . . . and all because of *letters*! She wants to fling the quill across the room, and then thinks of what a mess that would make, ink spattering across the floor. Instead, she sets down the quill and flexes her sore fingers. Her father's voice speaks to her: "Tenacity, Malora. It takes tenacity to plant a lesson firmly in a horse's head. Hundreds of repetitions."

Mustering her tenacity, Malora takes up the quill and starts in on her letters again, filling a fourth sheet.

Honus returns and hovers.

"I'm no good at this," she says, her voice tight. She is ashamed of the mess she has made.

"On the contrary, you've been most diligent and have accomplished a great deal. Here, now, this is what we will do," Honus says as he reaches into a pot of quills for a gem-handled knife. It reminds Malora of the little knife she lost, except that it is much more beautiful. She watches as, with practiced efficiency, he takes the blade and scratches out all the letters she worked so hard to make. "There!" he says, when all the sheets are scratched clean. "This way you can return tomorrow and fill them all up again, as you will the day after that and the day after that, until the shapes and sounds of all the letters are imprinted up here." He taps the side of her head. "That's enough of letters for today. Tomorrow, I'll let you do the erasing. I imagine you're quite good with a blade."

Honus invites Malora to join Zephele out on the terrace. Malora unwinds the kinks in her neck, then shakes out her cramped hands and blows on her fingers. She can ride all day and all night and not feel a single aching muscle, and yet sitting and practicing her letters for half a morning has made her feel as if she is in the early stages of tick-bite fever. "Does learning lessons always make you feel so stiff and sore?" she asks Zephele.

Zephele looks up from her book and bursts out laughing. "Look at you! You're as spotted as one of Neal Featherhoof's hunting hounds." Zephele reaches into a small pouch at her waist and pulls out the tiniest mirror Malora has ever seen. It has a jeweled frame, and even in its minute surface, Malora can see that her face is covered in inky splotches. Zephele springs to her feet and trots inside. She returns moments later with a bowl of water and a cloth. She sets to rubbing at Malora's face until her skin burns.

"Ouch!" Malora says.

"Hold still while I make you presentable."

Malora feels like a lion cub being scoured by her mother's rough tongue. Holding Malora's chin, Zephele turns her face this way and that. "All clean! We can't have Orion seeing his pet all ink-stained, can we?"

"Does that mean we can go see him now?" Malora asks weakly.

"Not just yet," Honus calls out to them from the big room. "You have a numbers lesson. You may leave *following* the midday meal."

Zephele whispers to Malora, "Honus is most persistent."

"Who taught him to be a teacher?" Malora asks.

Zephele shrugs. "I don't know. He won't say. But he or she must have been frightfully wise."

Honus returns with a rack of colorful wooden beads strung on wires. Numbers, much to Malora's relief, prove far less challenging than letters. She has always been good at counting. She can count a herd of impalas while they move in a cloud of dust, or the berries on a bush, or the stars in the sky, or the freckles on her arm. Counting things and putting them into smaller groups is something she does naturally, sometimes for practical purposes, such as when she has to divide up rations into equal packets, but mostly just to pass the time. It gives Malora a surge of satisfaction that she can add numbers and divide them into groups in her head, while Zephele has to fuss with the beads and scratch away on a sheet. And even then, Malora comes up with the answers much more quickly and with greater accuracy.

"You have a high aptitude for numbers," Honus says, eyeing her keenly.

"I will just study numbers then," Malora says.

Honus shakes his head.

"Why not?" she asks.

"What good would learning be if we concentrated on what we already knew? It is only by learning those things that come to us with difficulty that we truly gain wisdom."

Grudgingly, she allows that this makes a certain amount of sense. "You sound like my father."

"I'll take that as a compliment," Honus says. "Now, let's eat. Nothing makes me hungrier than watching others labor at their studies."

They go into the big room and sit down to a meal of fruit and nuts and cheeses. All this brain work has made Malora as hungry as if she had been hunting impalas. And would that she had been hunting! What she wouldn't give now for a small steak roasted over Honus's fire.

"I thought we'd stop by Longshanks's to have her measured for footwear," Zephele says.

"Give Cylas my regards," Honus says. "And tell him I'll come by to place an order for breeches soon."

"What are breeches?" Malora asks.

Honus gestures to his legs, which are encased in dark red leather. "These," he says, "are breeches. I first came here in a state of undress and Medon ordered a pair for me, based on the traditional garb of the two-legged Pantherians. I have been quite happily sporting them ever since."

The men in the Settlement had dressed no differently from the women, in belted tunics or robes. Breeches strike her as the ideal attire for a mounted rider. Although her inner thighs are worn tough from riding, the extra protection would be welcome.

Just then, Sunshine comes through the door, looking her usual overcast self. "The Lady Hylonome says I'm to walk you and the Otherian to the distillery," she says.

Zephele throws up her hands. "Good sweet Hands! What can Herself possibly be thinking? I walk the streets all the time without an escort!"

"But never before with one of those, I think," Sunshine says, her wizened little chin jutting toward Malora.

"You make a very good point, Sunshine, thank you," Honus says kindly. "I would happily accompany all three of you, only I must wait here for Neal Featherhoof. We have an appointment to see the Apex this afternoon."

Zephele's face lights up. "Can we wait here with you for Neal?"

Honus's smile turns wicked. "What an excellent idea, Zephele! And we can pass the time by discussing Aristotle and the nature of consciousness!"

Zephele yelps. "Never mind! I'll visit with Neal another time. I'm sure Malora wants to see Orion, don't you, Malora? And I'm equally sure that Orion misses his pet."

Zephele drags Malora toward the door, but Malora digs in her heels as they pass the small scrivening table with ink flasks and the pot of quills. She points to the small, gem-handled knife sitting among the quills.

"I like this," Malora says.

"I don't doubt that you do," Honus says. "That is a pen-knife. Highly useful, as you've seen, as well as of some sentimental value because it was a gift from the Apex. It is for trimming quills as well as for scratching out errors and ink spills. But it is not for skewering your enemies, of which, may I remind you, you have none here in Mount Kheiron. Besides, I could swear I saw you slide your butter knife into your belt this morning. I'm sure you'll be able to make do with that until Armageddon descends upon us, at which time you may butter the enemy to death."

Malora intends to sharpen the blade of the dull butter knife this evening on the stone floor of the terrace. She tells herself that, while she might go without weapons, she cannot go without tools. Since the knife will be a tool, the no-weapons Edict doesn't really apply, does it?

CHAPTER 18

Cylas Longshanks

"Great, sweet, merciful Hands! I thought we'd never escape his clutches," Zephele says as she leads Malora and Sunshine down the hallway, through the receiving gallery, and down the set of broad, shallow marble steps that lead outside. Two Twani, dressed in blue and white, bow stiffly to them as they pass.

Thus they leave the house behind and step out onto a busy thoroughfare. Twani pushing handcarts loaded with goods throng the streets, along with centaurs of all colors, shapes, and sizes. Without hesitation, Zephele grabs Malora's hand and enters the stream of traffic. Bucks, elegantly wrapped and bejeweled, striding four abreast, stop and stare at Malora for a long moment before continuing on their way. They are trailed by their Twani and by dogs, long-legged and beautifully groomed, wearing gem-studded collars.

"You mustn't mind if they stare at you so," Zephele whispers in her ear. "They can't really help themselves, poor dears. Most of them are just like me. They've never left this mountaintop and have little idea of what life's like in the great wide world." Then, raising her voice a notch, she continues, "We call this the Mane Way. It is a very important street, in our little world at least, because the ten noble families of Mount Kheiron reside here, and their names all end in *mane.* We're the Silvermanes. Then there are Ironmanes, Goldmanes, Coppermanes, Fairmanes, Longmanes. Greatmanes, Shortmanes, Whitemanes, and Blackmanes. The Mane Way follows the crest of the summit and is interrupted midway by the temple of Kheiron."

"Do the Goldmanes all have gold manes?" Malora asks.

"Goodness, no. Centaurs have no manes. And as you can plainly see, Orion and I aren't even remotely silver. They are just the names of houses going way back."

They stop before the temple of Kheiron with its golden onion-shaped dome. Incense wafts from within. Malora takes a step inside. A giant golden statue of Kheiron lies smothered in a bank of flowers, among which candles burn by the hundreds. Rows of centaurs in golden wraps stand before the statue and wave things in the air that look like horse tails, except that they are tasseled with gems and richly colored. The centaurs wear long beards that glisten with oil. She hears muted chanting and the sound of bells tolling ominously.

Malora takes a step farther in. One of the centaurs puts a torch to a bowl and it flares up bright purple. An almost noxious odor billows forth. A picture forms in Malora's mind of People in white coats in white rooms with cages of rats and rabbits and monkeys. The room reeks of the animals' fear and misery. She backs out of the temple.

"Had quite enough?" Zephele asks with a grin.

"What goes on in there?" Malora asks, blinking the picture away.

"Oh, offerings are made to the spirit of Kheiron. Priests mutter and putter and sputter and oil their beards and hair. Father and Mother used to make me attend regularly, but now they don't bother, although they, of course, attend, along with the rest of the Manes. They have to. It's their obligation as the nobility."

"What makes the Manes noble?" Malora asks.

"Mostly their wealth of nubs," Zephele says airily.

"What are nubs?" Malora asks.

"Our currency. The nub." She reaches into the leather pouch at her waist and pulls out a roundish object with a picture of a centaur incised on it.

"A nub?" Malora asks.

"The richer you are, the more nubs you have. The more nubs you have, the more goods and services you can buy."

"From the Twani?" Malora asks.

"Oh, dear me, no," Zephele says. "The Twani have no use for nubs. We pay Flatlanders for services, although we don't pay them nearly as much as they'd like, which is a source of growing disgruntlement, according to my grumble-guts father. We pay other Highlanders handsomely for their services, those who have skilled Hands whose arts or crafts we covet."

Malora notices the crowd of centaurs that have stopped to stare at her while she was listening to Zephele.

"This is ridiculous!" Zephele says impatiently, barging past the gawking centaurs and hauling Malora with her. They enter a covered walkway beneath mosaic-covered colonnades.

Malora feels suddenly small. It isn't just all the eyes examining her. It is the grand scale of the city: archways soar, doorways are spacious, walkways are broad, and steps are shallow and wide. Were she on horseback, she could easily mount these steps. Doors are flung open wide to the warm air, and Malora catches glimpses into shady interiors, redolent with scent. She remembers Orion's words: "Scent sets the tone of society." What is the tone? Malora rummages in her mind for the word and latches on to it. *Luxury!* But also, she thinks, *mystery.*

They pass a bakery with tiered racks displaying cakes, decorated with designs made of fruit and colored cream. They pass a shop that sells papers fanned out like rainbows and ink in brightly colored flasks. There is a shop that sells buttons and another that sells jewelry and still another that sells little silver and gold statuettes inset with many colored gems, fashioned in the images of birds and animals and insects. Honus has similar ones sitting on the shelves in his room. Malora stops to admire a small green-and-red hummingbird perched on a red-jeweled flower. Zephele turns a key hidden in its jeweled feathers. With a start, Malora watches as the tiny bird flutters to life, its wings fanning rapidly and its sharp little beak dipping into the flower to sip nectar. It looks nearly as real as the living one she saw this morning on Honus's terrace.

"We make them for the children," Zephele explains. "Honus loves them as well. He says that he is a child at heart . . . as, clearly, are you. Allow me to purchase this one for you."

"No, please," Malora says quickly. "It must cost many

nubs, and I don't really need to have it. Besides, Honus has *real* hummingbirds on his terrace."

"Who cares how many nubs it costs!" Zephele says in a burst of impatience. Then, calming herself, she adds, "Very well. I'm sure I will have ample opportunities to spoil you."

The centaurs, shopkeepers and browsers, all stop what they are doing and stare at Malora as she passes. They aren't rude as much as openly curious, and their eyes seldom rise higher than her waist. It is as if the only parts of her that interest them are those that are different from theirs. This is just as well, for now at least, because it gives her the freedom to stare with equal openness at them. For next to the sound of human voices, it is the sight of their very human faces that quenches some deep thirst within Malora.

Of the males, some are strutting peacocks draped in elaborately woven finery. Others are more plainly dressed, as the cousins were in the bush. All of them carry themselves with a pride and grace that makes Malora fall in love with them all over again, for, surely, they are the Perfect Beings! The women are every bit as splendid, although none of them is as lovely as Zephele. Many of them hold small beribboned dogs—and are trailed by their female Twani—as they pick their way carefully along the cobbled streets, lifting high their delicately booted hooves, their wraps girded with sashes or wide belts or woven cinches, their caps offset with fresh flowers or beads or feathers or gems. Perhaps wearing a cap won't be so bad, Malora thinks as she stares after them.

"Don't even *think* about wearing a cap," Zephele says as they come to a stop before an arched doorway made of bright blue stones. Through the arch waft the mingled scents of leather and oil, which remind her briefly of her father. Cured skins hang on wooden racks, three and four deep on the walkway, big sheets of kidskin and calfskin soft as butter. What do they do to get the skin so soft? Malora wonders. And the colors! Some of the skins are natural, but others have been dyed in an array of colors that take Malora's breath away. She wants to gather this rainbow of skins in her arms and make off with them.

Zephele sighs. "I do so hate to think of the poor creatures who perished to give us their hides."

"I, for one, think of them with enormous gratitude," Malora says as she strokes a bud-green sheet of kidskin that is as soft as a horse's nose. "And I see you have no trouble wearing boots of animal skin yourself."

"Believe me," Zephele says, "if they could make attractive boots out of some other material, I'd order them in multiples. But nothing fits quite so sleekly as animal skin. I like to think the animals die quickly and without pain. Neal tells me this is so, and Neal Featherhoof would not lie to me."

"In spite of the fact that he doesn't know you exist?"

"I meant that he doesn't know I exist as a mature female centaur. For him, I am still a child," she explains. "I am also a Highlander, and therefore forbidden to him."

"What is this place?" Malora asks.

"Longshanks, the cobbler," Zephele says.

They enter the shop. Displayed on a long table are a row of wooden poles carved in the shapes of centaur legs—both forelegs and hind legs of varying sizes—modeling a wide assortment of boots, from the rustic khaki style Orion wore in

the bush to more elaborate versions made of leopard and giraffe and zebra and snake skins, with buttons of carved ivory.

"Good afternoon, Cylas!" Zephele sings out. "The People
have arrived and require your services!" She gives Malora a
grin. "I shall not soon grow weary of saying *that*!"

A pony-sized centaur with piebald flanks, ebony skin, and
a bald pate emerges from the back of the shop, blinking behind his spectacles. His own boots are fashioned from white
leather. Far from having long shanks, as his name suggests, he
strikes Malora as being somewhat deficient between the knee
and the fetlock. A wizened Twan folds sheets of leather and
arranges them on shelves according to color.

"Malora, meet Cylas Longshanks, cobbler," Zephele says.

"*Master* cobbler," Cylas corrects, nibbling on the ends
of his gray mustache. "Cobbler to the Apex and Herself and
the entire magnificent House of Silvermane." His shrewd
little eyes have not left Malora for a moment. His voice has
dropped to a hush. "And to think that in our lifetime, such a
being could still actually be walking this earth! A living fossil!
What a wonder! What an excellent choice you have made,
Zephele Silvermane, bringing her here to me. Other cobblers would not be equal to the task of outfitting the wholly
unique contours of this creature."

Zephele rolls her eyes. "My brother Orion Silvermane
would like his brand-new pet to have her feet clad in boots."

"To be sure," the cobbler says, trotting over to his desk
for string and chalk. "Have her step over here."

Malora stands with her feet on a sheet of rough leather
while Cylas kneels and makes a tracing of her feet. Longshanks

works slowly and with great care, his fingers trembling. After he has traced the bottom of each foot, he goes on to measure the tops of her feet, her ankles, and her calves. He makes notations on a small slate.

While Cylas works, Zephele paces the shop, examining the goods and returning after every lap to tap a hoof and make impatient little noises. Finally, she says, "We're expected at my brother's distillery, so a certain haste is in order."

Cylas rears back. "You won't appreciate it if I make a boot that binds her frail foot or sags or is otherwise unsightly. This is the first human boot to be produced in our time!"

Malora doesn't want to tell him that the People, young and old, all wore boots. "Could you," she ventures, addressing the shiny black bald spot on his head, "in addition to boots, possibly make me breeches, like the ones you make for Honus?"

Cylas looks up at Zephele. "With your permission . . . ?"

Zephele's expression is uncertain, then she says, "Why ever not? What is good for one pet is, I am sure, good for the next. Be sure to make it possible for her to remove them. Do you know that the skins she wore in the bush she actually sewed onto her body?"

"So I hear!" he exclaims as he holds the string up to her legs. According to Sunshine, Malora's leopard pelt drew quite a crowd when West brought it down to the furnace to be burned.

"What did she use for thread?" Longshanks asks.

Zephele looks to Malora for an answer. "Whatever sinew came to hand," Malora says, irritated that the cobbler continues to speak to her through Zephele.

"Has she any idea what such a crude material would do to delicate calfskin and kidskin?" Cylas says to Zephele. "Tell her I use silk thread, dyed to match."

Zephele says, "He says that such a crude material—"

Malora says pointedly, "I can hear him, Zephele."

Zephele claps a hand to her mouth. "Oh! Of course you do. Silly me. Dear Master Longshanks, please tell me you are finished with this excessively tedious business."

Cylas rises to stand, his hips creaking. He gestures to the racks. "Perhaps she will consent to select a color?"

"We have no time for dithering," Zephele says with an imperious wave of her hand. "Make her a pair of boots and a pair of breeches out of each and every one of these colors of kidskin. Have fun with the buttons."

Malora is startled by the enormity of the order. There are at least twenty different colors of leather. But Cylas nods amiably. "I should have a prototype made from muslin ready to fit her tomorrow."

As they leave the shop, Zephele wakes up Sunshine, who has been dozing in a pile of furs, then she calls out to Cylas, "The People extend their heartfelt thanks in advance for all your diligent and skillful labors!" Then she winks at Malora and says, "I told you I'd find a way to spoil you, didn't I? Oh, this is entirely too much fun!"

Malora, Zephele, and Sunshine are now heading down an alarmingly steep hill. Malora wonders whether it is treacherous when wet and how the centaurs, not to mention the horses they employ, manage it without slipping. Zephele, leaning back as she descends, explains that Mount Kheiron's roads circle the mountain in rings intersected by forty-eight ramplike roads that converge at the Mane Way. Three tiers down, they depart from the ramp onto the ring road, where there are more homes, less grand than those on the Mane Way but finer than anything in the Settlement. Here, too, children play games with balls and dolls and hoops, shouting back and forth. The sight of Malora inspires a new game. The object is to sneak up behind her and tug her braid before she can catch them. Zephele tries to shoo them away, but Malora is happy to play the game. Unlike Longshanks and the other strangers she has encountered, these frisky young colts and fillies are willing to risk bodily contact. Still, she lets them win for fear of catching them and turning them fearful.

The road comes to a dead end at a large gray building. At first, it reveals an unusually dull facade. But then they come around to the side, and Malora stops and stares. Three towering paintings rise up before her, separated by single columns of gray stone. They are the most beautiful paintings Malora has yet seen in a city filled with beautiful artwork.

"This is where the Hands of painting, sculpting, and draftsmanship are taught and practiced," Zephele says.

The paint glistens in the sunlight, as if it were fresh. The three centaurs pictured, shown against a background of forests and gardens, are, as Zephele explains, each performing their Hand—sketching, painting, and sculpting. They are so vividly rendered that they look alive. The subjects the artists are studying are also in the paintings: a horse, a bowl of fruit, and a centaur maiden. Their respective works of art are depicted in progress, a partially rendered drawing of the horse, a half-painted bowl of fruit, and a centaur maiden statue, from the neck down, chiseled from a large block of stone. Above the centaurs' heads, putti hover, ready to hand the centaur artists fresh tools: stubs of charcoal, pots of paint, and various chisels.

A wide stone terrace stretches out beneath the paintings, where dozens of real centaurs, male and female, stand before wooden frames that Zephele calls easels. They are sketching or painting the landscape beyond: a forest spreading out like a large pool of dark green water ruffled by the wind. Heads pop up to observe the view, then duck back to the easel. They look like a herd of grazing horses with their heads all facing in the same direction, only instead of the sound of munching, there is the harsh rasp of the chalk and charcoal and brushes against paper. What a peculiar waste of time, Malora thinks.

"Poor Orrie's distillery is hidden away in the dingy old basement of this glorious edifice. His quarters are really too shabby for words," Zephele says as she leads Malora through a wide entryway. "I tell Orion he simply must find new, more elegant quarters in which to practice his Hand, where it is light and airy, but light and airy apparently don't conduce to alchemy." They enter a high-ceilinged room, where more centaurs, with paintbrushes poised, contemplate a large bowl of fruit elevated on a draped table. As they pass through the room, one or two centaurs look up from their paintings, their eyes widening at the sight of Malora. In the next room, a centaur draped all in white stands on a platform, as still as a statue, while other centaurs stare at him raptly and trace his likeness onto paper. The centaur is ancient, with a grizzled head and a sunken chest. Malora feels sorry for the old fellow, who looks rather weary.

"Sunshine," Zephele whispers to the Twan. "Settle down

here and take a little snooze. Perhaps the artists will paint you while you sleep and give this poor old fellow a rest."

Then Zephele leads Malora down a long, shallow staircase that ends in front of a wooden door. "We must knock and make ourselves known," she whispers to Malora. "Once I went in without knocking and he was very cross, indeed." Zephele lifts her hand and raps once.

CHAPTER 19

Breath of the Bush

"Enter!" Orion calls from inside.

"You might want to hold your nose," Zephele warns as she turns the knob and pushes open the door.

The smell overwhelms Malora at first. Hundreds of scents assault her. It is as if she has entered a room containing a mob of people, each trying to elbow the others aside to make him- or herself known to her. There are loud, brash scents and pale, retiring ones, floral scents and fruity, earthy ones, and scents as salty as fresh blood. There are woody scents and spicy ones, smoky scents and moldy ones, rich, meaty scents and grassy ones. There are scents that smell delicious enough to eat, and others that make Malora want to gag. She doesn't hold her nose as Zephele has directed, because she doesn't want to hurt Orion's feelings. But she does switch to breathing through her mouth, because it is the only way she can dim the clamor in her head of the many scents.

Malora's eyes now register the narrow-shelved cases that

line the walls, teeming with glass vials of all shapes and colors, shimmering like gems in the pale light sifting down from windows set high up near the ceiling. Orion, swaddled in a black leather wrap, stands over a fire in the center of the room, over which a covered pot simmers. Running out of the top of the lid, like a twisting vine, is a long, coiling metal pipe. The pipe, sweating and dripping and wrapped in cloth, makes its winding way to yet another pot. On a tufted cushion, off in the shadows, she spies West, snoring softly.

Now that her nose is accustomed to the distillery, she picks out one scent more dominant than all the others—and as familiar to her as an old friend, although she can't quite place it. Orion dips his hand into a bucket and removes a wet cloth. He wrings it out and packs it around a section of the coiled pipe. Drying his hands on the front of his wrap, he looks over and gives her a warm and welcoming smile.

"You came!" he says.

"Of course we came," Zephele says. "Did you think we wanted to spend the entire day as prisoners of the polymath?"

Orion comes forward. "Welcome, Malora, to my distillery!"

"What goes on in this place?" Malora asks.

"Let me show you," he says eagerly, leading her over to the pot on the fire. He lifts the lid with care. Inside she sees weeds and twigs and flowers bouncing around in boiling water.

"This is where I cook up the flowers or bark or what have you," he says, replacing the lid. "The pure essence of these items evaporates out of the pot, then travels through this pipe, which is especially made for me by Brion, the blacksmith, out of copper. As the essence travels through the pipe, these wet cloths cool it, causing it to further condense. The cooled essence drips down out of the pipe into this other pot over here." He draws her over. "Are you ready?"

Malora nods. He carefully removes the lid from the smaller pot. Inside she sees a small amount of liquid with an oily scum on top. Considering his enthusiasm, she is somewhat disappointed.

"The oil floating on top is the strongest essence," he tells her. "The water below is less strong, but is nevertheless imbued with scent. I bottle them separately. Take a good whiff and tell me what you think."

Malora inhales. Instantly, she smells the bush just before a rainstorm, when every rock and bush and tree and plant and flower smells as if it were freshly made. Then she sees, galloping over a red rocky hill across a ravine, her one and only Sky. He skids to a halt and turns around, tossing his mane, beckoning her to cross over the ravine and join him.

Orion claps the lid on the pot and looks at her expectantly. "Well?" he asks, his blue eyes nearly incandescent in the dim light of the distillery.

Malora blinks as Sky's image, then the bush itself, evaporates, like the essence from the pot into the pipe. "It smells . . . like home," she says, mystified.

"Does it really?" Orion beams and hugs her. "I knew it! I call it Breath of the Bush. Are you quite all right, Malora?" His look turns from triumph to worry.

Malora does feel slightly faint and goes to lean against the one spot along the wall where there are no cases of vials. The coolness of the stone seeps into her body, and gradually she begins to revive. This must be what Orion means by scents controlling emotions and setting moods.

"The poor darling girl!" Zephele wails. "First Honus makes her slave all morning, then I drag her all over the mountaintop on errands. Surely, the final insult is bringing her down here to this gloomy old pit."

"I am fine," Malora says, and she is now, although she cannot quite get over what she has just seen. *Sky!*

"You really do like it?" Orion asks.

"Very much," Malora says.

"I made it from a selection of the plants and bark and flowers I collected on our expedition," he tells her proudly. "I made it especially for you. I know you say that scents aren't for you because they keep you from detecting predators. But since we are no longer in predator territory, won't you consent to using this scent of mine? Please say you'll accept a small vial of Breath of the Bush as a token of my great affection and admiration."

The vision of Sky has faded from her mind and she longs to call it back. "Yes," she says, "I think I would like that."

"You honor me," he says.

"You are a very good alchemist," she says.

"And you are a very good friend," he says.

"And you are both very good at boring me with all this talk," Zephele says. "Can we leave? My nose feels quite abused."

"As you wish, little sister," he says, going to rouse West.

"Oh, hello, miss," West says to Malora after he has shaken himself awake.

"Feed the fire, West, and keep adding water, one scoop

at a time, as the level goes down. If the plants start to fade, add what's in this basket here. You know what to do, good fellow."

"That I do, Your Excellence," West says.

Orion unties the black leather wrap, revealing a pure white one beneath it. He hands the black wrap to West.

Zephele, who is already on her way up the stairs, calls back to Orion, "So tell me, Brother, how did the Apex rule when you had your audience with him earlier?"

"In our favor, happily," Orion says.

"Oh, excellent!"

Since no further discussion takes place, Malora can't resist asking, "What does that mean?" as she follows Zephele's braided tail up the stairs.

"It means you will, in however belated a fashion," Zephele explains over her shoulder, "be able to declare a Hand. We may now give you a tour of the studios and ateliers so that you can begin to decide what you will choose, subject to the Apex's approval, of course. But I've never known him to veto anyone's choice of Hand, have you, Brother?" She pauses on the stairs and looks down at Orion behind Malora.

"No, I haven't," says Orion. As Malora looks back at Orion, she sees the effect of the white wrap against the deep black of his flanks is dramatic. "We can start by touring the upper floors of this very building."

"Oh, don't bother," Zephele tells him from the top of the stairs. "I don't believe Malora has any affinity for painting and drawing. Isn't that true, Malora?"

Malora wonders how Zephele can know this, but it is, in fact, the case. "It feels too much like making letters . . . only less useful," she says in a whisper, because they are back in the room where the centaurs are sketching the ancient centaur. Zephele finds Sunshine and gently shakes her awake. Sunshine shaking the sleep from her body actually makes a noise in the quiet atelier. She immediately starts licking her paw and washing herself, as if sleep has soiled the yellow scruff of her neck.

"Useful!" Zephele whispers to Orion. "Do you hear what your pet said?"

Orion doesn't answer. They are passing through the room of the fruit painters. When they are back out on the street, Orion responds in a normal tone, "I heard her very clearly, Sister. You see, Malora is accustomed to a life of hardship that is beyond anything either of us has ever experienced. It is precisely this capacity for usefulness that has helped her to survive. I'm sure most of the Hands on our list might strike her as quite frivolous." Then Orion smiles sweetly at his sister and says, "Zephie, I am most grateful to you for accompanying Malora here. But now I wonder whether you wouldn't mind running along."

Zephele looks a little hurt. Then she lifts her chin. "I quite understand, Brother," she says in a determined voice. "You wish to be alone with your pet."

"Perhaps we will see you for dinner in Honus's room tonight?" Orion says by way of compensation.

"No, Orrie, you won't," she says sulkily. "When I returned to my room last night, you see, I was both too excited and too tired to do my nightly reading assignment, and while Honus was very understanding this morning, he might not be quite so accommodating tomorrow morning." Zephele goes on, her high spirits gradually gaining momentum. "Herself says that the less the human disrupts the course of our normal lives, the more kindly the Apex will look upon her remaining with us. So! That is the way of it. You should know that she fared quite well today with her lessons. She did you proud. She practiced her letters and she scrivened, like a small child, of course, but she is as uncannily good at her numbers as I am uncannily bad. I'm trying to think what nature of Hand calls for numbers. Perhaps architecture, although it is doubtful they will ever trust an Otherian to design a building for centaurs. Maybe weaving, wherein one counts threads and warps and woofs? Perhaps Theon will enlighten us further as to warps and woofs when he gives us a tour of the Weavery."

"What are warps and woofs?" Malora asks.

"Terms pertaining to weaving, which is Theon's Hand. What peculiar words these are, really, *warp and woof*," Zephele ponders. "They sound like animal noises, don't they? I wonder who invented them, and why they chose those particular words. Oh, well! I shall run along now, as you say, and leave you two to the business of choosing a Hand for Malora. Come along, Sunshine dear, let's find you a really *ambitious* project to while away the afternoon. Let's see, what needs doing? Untangling my necklaces, perhaps? Blocking my caps? Airing out my wraps and rearranging them according to hue? I wonder if that rascal Neal Featherhoof can still be found beneath our roof. If we hurry now . . ." With Sunshine at her heels, Zephele trots off down the street, chattering all the way.

Orion takes a deep breath. "She is quite the monologist!"

"I like her very much," Malora says, staring after her in admiration. "She has a good heart."

"She does, doesn't she? And she's a good deal cleverer than she sounds. Let's go find you a Hand, shall we?" Orion holds out his arm, and they set out.

They visit the Stitchery first. "Embroidery is Zephele's hand," Orion says. "The workmanship on her caps, and my mother's as well, is all hers. Although she professes a certain indifference to her Hand, she is very good at it."

The Stitchery is smaller and more intimate than the atelier. It is a cozy round room with a hole in the ceiling, through which the afternoon sun slants, illuminating a long table covered with flowers. Over in a corner, a Twan plucks at a stringed instrument. Malora recognizes the scent Orion calls lavender. The atmosphere here is, indeed, one of serenity. Young centaurs, both male and female, kneel on cushioned benches set around the table, their heads bent intently over hoops mounted on stands across which cloth has been stretched tightly. Skeins of brightly colored thread are piled in baskets all about. As Orion leads Malora around the outside of the circle, she peers over the centaurs' shoulders and sees that they are stitching the likenesses of the flowers on the tables.

Out in the bush—as even she has begun to think of it— Malora often gazed into the hearts of flowers and marveled at their intricacy. What skill it must take to render this, Malora thinks. Could she work with needle and thread? Needles of bone and strings of rawhide, perhaps. But this kind of delicate handiwork seems beyond her.

One of the centaurs, a young male, looks up from his hoop and meets Malora's gaze, the familiar mixture of fear and wonder in his eyes. Malora smiles tentatively at him, places a hand over her heart, and then raises it in salute. The young centaur starts to cover his heart, but then checks himself. He lets his hand drop and lowers his head to his work.

"I have seen enough," Malora says.

Orion and Malora make their way downhill to the Pottery. This place bustles, smelling of damp earth. Here centaurs stand at wheels, which they turn by pumping a pedal with their front hooves. On the wheels they work wet blobs of clay into shapes with their dampened hands. Long tables along the walls bear finished work: pots and bowls and goblets and small, graceful statuary. A centaur scoops up damp pots on a flat wooden tray and sets them near a fiery furnace.

"He's drying the pots before firing them to set the glaze and harden the clay," Orion explains.

One centaur looks up from her wheel and stares so intently at Malora that her hoof slips off the pedal, the wheel falters, and the pot in her hands collapses into a formless mess.

Orion says, "I once considered taking pottery as my Hand."

"What made you decide against it?" Malora asks.

"I disliked the feel of the clay on my fingers, much the way I also disliked the sound of charcoal on paper. One has to like nearly everything about one's Hand. We spend far too much time at it between the ages of twelve and sixteen, and then afterward, of course. That's why we try out various

Hands before we make our final choice. I urge you to spend a day in each studio to get a better idea of the rudiments of each."

"We made pottery in the Settlement," Malora says.

"Ironbound red pots, I wager," Orion says.

Malora nods. "But we didn't use a wheel. We fashioned the pots with our hands. One hand inside the pot and the other outside, working our away around from the bottom to the top. Then we would set them in the sun to bake," she says. Unbidden, a picture comes into her head of red pots lying in shards everywhere, and her mother's bones. She turns away and says thickly, "No pottery for me."

Next door in the Woodworks, young centaurs wield tools to whittle and chisel wood. Malora likes the bright green smell of the wood and the way the floor is heaped with curly shavings that bring to her mind a lion's mane. She admires the sharpness and shininess of the tools, which call up a vivid image of her lost knife.

"I might like this Hand," Malora says as they leave the shop. "It seems useful. What were they making?"

"Staffs and walking sticks and decorative pieces."

"Do they also make chairs and shelves?" she asks.

"As a rule, Flatlanders pursue the practical. Highlanders pursue the decorative."

"Aren't you running out of places to decorate in Mount Kheiron?" Malora asks. "Are there any other Hands this useful?"

Orion's brow creases in thought. As they walk, Malora's ears pick up a rhythmic ringing sound. "What's that?" she asks.

CHAPTER 20

The Forge

"That sound? I believe it's coming from Brion's shop," Orion says. "It is just around the next bend. It was he who supplied my copper pipe."

"Let's go see." She grabs his hand and runs toward the increasingly loud clanging. As soon as she sees the building, she knows that it is old, ancient, built by the Grandparents. It is so simple: a big squat stone box with wooden doors and a crude chimney coming out the top. Soon she is standing before the wooden doors, which are open. She drops Orion's hand and enters. A blast of hot air hits her full on, as if the heat of the sun itself is trapped inside the shop. A smell of sweat, hot iron, and burning wood permeates her nostrils. The fine sand beneath her bare feet is as hot as the top of a mesa at midday. She digs her bare toes in and feels herself taking root here.

In the back of the shop stands a black furnace whose chimney rises up through the ceiling. To one side, a sooty-faced Twan stands in a stiff, oversized smock, his foot working a pleated leather contraption that sends air whooshing into a bed of coals. The coals flare into flame and the smoke rises from the fire and is sucked up the chimney.

A stocky centaur stands over a hulking metal block set close to the furnace. He wears heavy leather gauntlets, and his dappled hindquarters are swaddled in a stained and scorched leather wrap, beneath which his flanks are singed and his muscle-bound arms and chest are slick with sweat. In his left hand, he grasps a pair of heavy tongs, which hold a square rod of iron across the face of the block. One side of the rod glows cherry red. In a sure, steady rhythm, he brings the flat face of his hammer down onto the red-hot end of the iron.

Malora watches as the end of the iron flattens like glowing clay with each hammer blow. When the centaur is finished, he turns and immerses the flattened end in a pot of water. A hiss of steam rises up as the hot iron hits the water. The steam envelops her. She smells cold rain hitting hot rocks and has a sudden sharp aching in her bones for home. The centaur wipes off the red-hot iron with a cloth and then buries it in the pink ashes at the edge of the fire. Malora imagines one of the Grandparents, her ancestor going all those many generations back, standing at this same forge. And suddenly, she knows that *this* is the place where the little knife Thora gave her was made. She is as sure of this fact as she is of anything she has ever known, and she is equally sure that this place of iron and fire, of ashes and hissing water, of hammers and tongs and anvils is where she belongs. She looks around at the soot-covered walls, with iron hooks hung with hoops and hinges and rails and finials and screens and struts and braces.

As her grandfather did so many years ago, she will make these things—and more. She isn't sure how she is supposed to declare it.

She turns to Orion and says, "I choose this for my Hand."

Worry clouds Orion's brow. "Really? You're quite sure?"

The smith swings away from the furnace, just now noticing them. He shoves up the glass-fronted visor that protects his eyes from flying sparks, as if the act might improve his faulty hearing. He squints at her, the crinkles at the corners of his eyes white against a mask of soot. "So it's you, the Otherian everyone's been yammering about," he growls. "To what do I owe this intrusion?"

He might be rude, Malora thinks, but at least he is speaking to my face.

"Malora, this is Brion Swiftstride. Brion, this is Malora Ironbound."

"And I choose blacksmithing for my Hand," Malora adds.

"Iron*bound,* eh?" Brion asks in a loud, hoarse voice that suggests that his lungs might be as scorched as his flanks. "I think not. I haven't had a candidate for the Hand in here since the Apex took office."

"Ironwork's a bit like alchemy in that it isn't the most popular Hand these days," Orion explains.

"I don't care," Malora says. "It's what I want to do."

"I try my best to scare the youngsters off. They have no idea what this Hand demands." The blacksmith wipes the back of his hand across his forehead, leaving a long jet-black streak. "Blacksmithing is the oldest and noblest and most practical of the Hands. Without the nails and bolts and hinges and brackets and braces and handles and tools we smiths fashion at our forges, this place would fall apart at its beautiful and enlightened seams. But it is no easy Hand."

Brion whips off his gloves and comes over to stand before her. He grabs her hand roughly and holds up her arm as if it were a rod of inferior stock. "Look at you!" He drops her arm and turns back to his work. "You don't have the strength for this work, no matter how much you may want to do it. This is no work for a female—and a spindly two-legged Otherian, at that," he mutters.

Malora bristles. "I can do it," she says, setting her jaw and stepping closer to the anvil.

"Oh, can you?" he says, smiling, his eyes challenging. He sets the hammer down and picks up a much heavier version with a bigger handle and a bigger iron head. "Try lifting *this*."

"Now, wait just a moment," Orion says.

"Begging your pardon, Silvermane, but I have to know." Handle-first, he thrusts the sledge at her. She takes it and hefts it in both hands. It is heavy, but there is something immensely satisfying about its heft. She gives it an experimental swing. Orion stands back, a look of trepidation on his face. But the blacksmith seems surprised, and a little disgruntled, that Malora has not dropped the sledge right off.

"All right then," the smith says. "Try swinging it." He picks up the smaller hammer and touches it to the center of the anvil. "Lay it into the exact spot where I'm pointing," he says.

She eyes the spot on the anvil, positioning herself with one foot a half step forward of the other. Then, throwing her weight behind the hammer, she swings it up and brings it down on the anvil, hitting the spot dead on. The sledge head clangs on the anvil and bounces. She feels a metallic tingle coursing up through the anvil's dense mass, running through the sledge handle and up her arm straight to her heart.

"You did it!" the centaur says, pushing back his visor and scratching his head in bafflement.

Malora grins. "Shall I do it again?"

Brion shrugs. "Sister, if you can hit that anvil on the same spot ten times in a row without your arm falling off," he says, "I can work with you."

Malora squares her shoulders and lines up her feet, then swings the sledge up and brings it down again and again and again.

Dinner is a quiet affair without Zephele. Orion has brought a small blue glass vial containing Breath of the Bush. "I hope this will prove to be your personal scent," he says.

"Thank you." She handles the vial carefully. "Will we take my petition for the Hand to the Apex tomorrow?"

Honus and Orion exchange a look.

"Is there something wrong?" Malora asks. She can still feel the heat of the forge on her face, the tingle of the hammer hitting the anvil and rising up through her arms.

"Not *wrong*, exactly," Orion says slowly. "It's just that we centaurs generally take some time choosing our Hands."

"How much time?" Malora asks.

"Weeks . . . or sometimes months," Orion says cautiously.

"Why so long?" Malora asks.

"It's an important decision," Honus says. "Every

afternoon, you will work at it . . . and longer after you've received recognition."

"The fact of the matter," Orion says, "is that if we go to the Apex tomorrow with your petition, he will reject it."

"Why?"

"Because he will believe, and rightly so, that you have made a too-hasty decision. The Apex frowns on the fickle," Orion says gravely.

"What is *fickle*?" she asks.

"*Fickle* is the centaur who is too quick to settle upon a Hand and who then winds up flitting from one Hand to the next without fixing upon any one. My brother Athen was hopelessly fickle. He must have tried every Hand on the mountain before settling on rope making, and it was only the Apex's influence that got the craft even admitted to the List of the Hands."

Malora is discouraged. "How long must we wait, then?"

"At least three weeks, I should think," Honus says. "And in the meantime, I have a hunch we can manage to keep you busy."

Orion departs not long after dinner. Before he leaves, he says, "Try sprinkling your canopy with the scent."

After a long, hot bath, Malora dresses in one of Honus's nightshirts and retires to her bedchamber. She climbs up on the bed and, opening the flask of scent Orion gave her, sprinkles some of it on the midnight-blue canopy speckled with stars. She is surprised when no pictures come to mind. She gets beneath the covers and her thoughts drift back to the forge. Up until now, she has not realized how badly her confidence has been shaken since she came to this place. Out on the plains, with a horse beneath her and a bow in her hand, she felt a certain competence. But down on two feet, especially alongside the confident, talkative, poised Zephele, she feels earthbound and clumsy. When she took hold of the hammer this afternoon, she felt some of her old confidence surging back. She can't wait to get back in the forge. Eventually, she drifts off with the scent of the bush in her nostrils.

No sooner is she on the other side of sleep than Sky appears over the red-rock ridge, tossing his mane, his long white scars flashing in the moonlight. He turns his back and flips his tail. Malora, half running and half flying, in the way of dreams, vaults onto his back. She has just enough time to entwine her hands in his mane before Sky is off at a gallop. All night long, she lies flattened along his extended neck as he races across the plains, through places familiar and strange. Now and then, Sky stops and dips his head into a stream or a patch of high grass.

"What happened to Jayke's saddle?" she asks him.

Sky says, "I ran all that day, the day you were taken, through the storm and out the other side. Afterward, I got down on my back and rolled in the mud until I worked the saddle off. I kicked it free and left it behind."

"My little knife was in that saddlebag," Malora says. "The one that Thora gave me. The one that saved our lives."

"I'm sorry," he tells her, "but it was dangerous to keep the saddle on. Sooner or later, it would have caught on something, or a big cat might have snagged a claw in it and brought me down."

"I understand," she says to him. "I'm going to make a new knife soon. I'm learning new things among the centaurs, Sky."

"That's good," says Sky, "but never forget that you are the Daughter of the Plains."

When she wakes up in the morning, her thighs are sore from riding and her fingers smell like the wind in Sky's mane. It is the smell of Breath of the Bush.

To make the time pass more quickly, she throws herself into her lessons. She learns her letters quickly and well enough to decipher the pages of the tattered book, which, it turns out, is about a cat in a hat, although neither cat nor hat bears the slightest resemblance to Puss in Boots. It is a funny story that doesn't make a lick of sense. Still, it crackles with life, and soon she can read it faster than the powdery pages will let her turn them. She sits at the table and scrivens until her fingers stiffen into claws. To make the practice less onerous, Honus instructs her to copy down the famous sayings of his favorite thinker, a great-great-grandparent of the very Grandparents themselves by the name of Epictetus. As she writes the words over and over, learning to recognize them as she copies them down, she suspects that Honus has chosen these particular sayings as a way of teaching her a lesson quite apart from the scrivening itself.

"First say to yourself what you would be; then do what you have to do" is the first wise saying. She will be an iron-worker, a blacksmith, as soon as the Apex approves her peti-tion, and will learn to make beautiful objects from fire and iron, for she is Malora Ironbound, last of the People, and this is her fate.

Another saying Malora copies is "Practice yourself, for heaven's sake, in little things; and thence proceed to greater." To her, this means that she is practicing these letters and words so that one day she will be able to write down all the words that come into her head at will. There were times in the bush when her mind was as perfectly empty as a sheet of Honus's paper, scratched clean of letters. But here in Mount Kheiron, she finds that her mind teems almost feverishly with thoughts.

Malora also copies: "No great thing is created suddenly any more than a bunch of grapes or a fig. If you tell me that you desire a fig, I answer that there must be time, let it first blossom, then bear fruit, then ripen." It will take time, she now understands, for her relationship with the centaurs to ripen. The sight of her walking down the street can still stun a talkative centaur into silence. When she despairs of this to Honus, he gives her a book of poems. With Honus's help, she reads the poems of a Grandmother named Emily Dickinson. This is an ancient human Malora has never met, who, in fact, lived many lifetimes ago. And yet Malora has the uncanny sense that this Dickinson not only knows Malora but is writing directly to her.

I'm nobody! Who are you?
Are you nobody, too?
Then there's a pair of us—don't tell!
They'd banish us, you know.

In spite of her loneliness, Malora continues to believe centaurs to be the Perfect Beings who will one day warm to her. Every night, she sprinkles Breath of the Bush on the canopy of her bed and falls asleep, only to gallop all night across the plains on Sky's back. And in the morning, she wakes up to the hummingbirds and the butterflies and the taste of the burstingly ripe fruits she plucks from the trees in her own beautiful bower.

One night, Theon and all the cousins come over after the evening meal. The centaurs and their Twani crowd into Honus's big room and suddenly make it seem quite small. Mather and Devan and Brandle and March and Felton and the brothers Marsh and Elmon fill the room with their lively talk and their various personal scents, held to their noses in colorful cloths, all mixed up with the warm, honest smell of horse. Zephele has invited them there to discuss the theme for the Midsummer Jubilation. West, on loan for the night from Orion, slinks about, serving cake and tea from delicate cups with a pattern of pink roses.

"Our heroine!" Theon says when he spies Malora sitting at the scrivening desk, doing her homework exercises. He trots over to her, his arms full of woven goods. "We've missed you. I made these for you. They're half wraps, so you won't have to slice them in two like you did to all of Zephie's garments."

Such finery, Malora marvels. Theon introduces each of them by name. One of them, *brocade,* leaps with blue and green lightning. Another, *voile,* has thin pale stripes of purple and blue. A third, *raw silk,* has a pattern of red and orange leaves. And a fourth is a tawny color in a fabric that Theon calls *velvet*. It has a matching fringe.

"I call this the Lioness," he says with a wink.

The other cousins crowd around Malora and admire the attire Longshanks has made for her. Tonight she is wearing blue breeches with paler blue boots.

"How does Longshanks get the skins to hold such brilliant dyes, I wonder?" Theon says.

"He's not about to let you steal his secret," Mather says.

"Well, Zephie, my sweet," says Theon, "I think we've come up with our theme."

"Oh, good," says Zephele, "because I am bereft of inspiration. What is your idea?"

"We have Malora to thank again, this time for our inspiration instead of our lives. The theme is—are you ready for the absolute brilliance of it? *The bush!*"

"The bush?" Zephele says, puzzled but interested.

"The bush! We'll decorate the upper gallery with trees and rocks and logs, and each guest will come dressed as an animal of the bush. Malora can be a lioness and wear the velvet fringed wrap, along with a pair of undyed calfskin breeches and boots. Mather will make the mask."

"Mather makes masks?" Malora asks. She has taken out her honed butter knife to sharpen her quill.

"Sculpting is my Hand, but I enjoy making masks," Mather says. "I'll make yours with real lion skin and stones of topaz, and I think I'll make you a tail with a fur tassel since you don't have one of your own. I wonder if I can lay hands on a *real* lion's tail? Minus the rest of the lion, of course."

"Neal Featherhoof will probably have one," Brandle says.

"He's got all sorts of wild-animal bits and pieces down in that squalid little shack of his."

Surrounded by the cheery chatter of the centaurs, Malora suddenly feels anything but lonely.

Before they leave, Mather sidles up to Malora and says, "Does Orrie know you carry that knife?"

Malora nods. "It is a tool, not a weapon."

He eyes it thoughtfully. "But it could just as easily serve as a weapon, no?"

CHAPTER 21

Petition Denied!

From the moment Malora awakens, she does everything with special care. She takes a long, hot, fragrant bath and washes her hair. She braids it tightly, as Zephele has taught her to do, and ties the end with a velvet ribbon. She wears the green-and-blue wrap with the watery pattern and her bud-green calfskin trousers and matching green boots with silver buttons up the side. She is careful to leave the butter knife behind, just in case the Apex's powerful eyes can see through kidskin.

"I need more Breath of the Bush," Malora says, handing the flask to Orion when he comes to take her to the Apex.

He looks surprised. "Really? So soon?"

"I use it every night," she says.

"I'm glad you have taken to it," he says with a gratified smile as he tucks the empty flask into his pouch.

They pass out of the servants' quarters into the receiving

gallery, with its bunches of crystal grapes and its flock of rosy-cheeked putti.

When Ash meets them outside the big white double doors with the handles shaped like lions' paws, he nods and says, "She cleaned up very nicely, Your Excellence."

"How is his mood this morning?" Orion asks.

Ash rocks his hand. "He hasn't been what you'd call Himself lately, ever since young Featherhoof delivered the Empress's call for volunteers. The Apex turned the Empress down, as you know, but the decision isn't sitting well with him, and his digestion's been poor of late."

Malora is prepared this time for the sight of herself in the Hall of Mirrors. In contrast to the disheveled, feral creature she once saw there, she is pleased with the transformation. The Apex is pawing through his scrolls and doesn't even look up when she enters, but Herself does, and registers immediate approval of the change.

"Very nice," Herself says.

The Apex is scowling down at papers, swaddled in black, and Herself wears dove gray with a matching gray cap decorated with the speckled feather of a guinea hen.

Orion says, "She does look dashing, doesn't she, Mother?"

Herself nods. "And is that Theon's work I see in the wrap?"

Malora speaks up. "He made me several very beautiful ones."

"Theon is most accomplished at his Hand," says Herself. "He wove this wrap of mine, as it happens."

"That is very nice, too," Malora says dutifully, although to her it seems dull. "I like the guinea hen—"

"Enough!" booms the Apex, waving away the small talk. He brings his steely gaze to bear upon Malora. Malora is shocked at the difference in his face since the last time she saw him. He looks old and careworn. The skin around his eyes is loose and ashen. But his voice has lost none of its vigor.

"I am told," he says in a voice that rumbles down to the tips of Malora's toes, "that after lengthy and careful consideration, you have finally decided upon a Hand."

Orion clears his throat. "She has, sir. Malora Ironbound has, fittingly enough, declared her Hand to be iron*work*."

"What an eccentric choice!" Herself exclaims. "I like it."

The Apex shoots his mate a stormy look and turns back to Malora. "Tell me what you like about this Hand."

Malora says carefully, "Well, I like the heat of the forge and the heft of the hammer in my hand. I like the way the heated iron can be molded to make all manner of things."

His eyes narrow. "What manner of things?"

"Well . . . ," Malora says, hedging, "decorative finials and gates and hinges and—"

"Swords and spear tips and arrowheads?" the Apex finishes for her, his eyes fierce and triumphant.

Malora looks quickly away and sees her face in the mirror, blushing scarlet. She wants to say, *Actually, I just want to make a little knife,* but realizes this would amount to what Honus might call a tactical error.

She turns back to him and opens her mouth to deny his charge. Then she realizes that Veracity has taken up a firm place in her heart and won't budge. Instead, she merely closes her mouth and stares at him.

Orion whispers strenuously in her ear, "Tell him you have no intention of making weapons."

But Malora can make no such claim. And she is so angry at this moment that she wishes she could stalk down to Brion's forge and work up an entire armory of weaponry.

"I thought so," says the Apex with a satisfied nod of his great gray head. "Petition denied!"

"But, Father," Orion says, "she would no more make these implements than Brion the blacksmith would. I assure you, she has the capacity for the work. You should have seen her with the big hammer. She had no trouble swinging it."

"I have no doubt as to her *capacity*," the Apex says pointedly. "I suspect it is bred in her bones. Ironwork was my Hand, so I understand its attraction even if few other centaurs these days do."

Malora finds her voice. "If this Hand is so unpopular, isn't that all the more reason why I should take it up?"

The Apex's brows lower like twin thunderheads. "It is not!" he says.

Malora's blood simmers, and she begins to move toward the Apex. "No?" she says. "You would deny me this? You, who took away my herd, would now deny me this one thing that I want so badly?" She feels Orion's hands holding her back.

"It is precisely your driving passion to do this that prompts me to deny you your wish," Medon says with sudden weariness.

Herself puts in gently, "Honus tells us that you have many skills. You can sew, and you can count with great facility."

"There you go!" says the Apex. "Let her play to her strengths and embroider and count threads."

Malora says quietly, "Honus also says what good would learning be if we concentrated only on what we already knew? It is only by learning those things that come to us with some difficulty that we truly gain wisdom."

Herself puts in, "The human makes a good point."

The Apex slams his fist down on the table. "I have made my decision, and I will not be tripped up by slippery arguments and fancy citations. You have had your audience. I have bigger problems to deal with these days than the Hands of interloping Otherians."

Malora continues to level a hard look at the Apex.

"It's no use," Orion whispers in her ear. "It's his right. Wait for me outside. Please."

Malora turns on her heel and walks out, slamming the door behind her.

Ash's neck snaps as he wakes up and sputters, "Don't take it to heart, missy. Didn't I tell you he's been in a vile mood lately?"

"Oh, really?" Malora blows out. "How can you tell?"

"Ha! Good point. He was fine until Honus and that rascally Flatlander told him about the wild centaurs. He's been mad as a buffalo stuck in a hippo wallow ever since. Had you petitioned him three weeks ago, he might have treated your case with more favor."

Malora crosses her arms over her chest and scowls, for that is exactly when she would have petitioned the Apex had Orion and Honus listened to her.

Orion soon emerges, looking pale. He takes her elbow and steers her down the hall toward Honus's rooms. Twani on ladders, polishing the crystal grapes in the chandeliers like so many wingless putti, look down upon them as they pass.

"He is afraid," Orion explains, his voice grim. "And his fear colors all his decisions."

"Afraid of me holding a hammer?" she asks. "Or of me forging weapons of revenge?"

"He is afraid, frankly, of the unrest among the Flatlanders. Of the wild centaurs. Of the looming specter of conflict," Orion says. "He respectfully suggests you reconsider embroidery."

Malora grinds her teeth. "Never," she says.

"What about woodworking? You said you liked it."

"No!" Malora says firmly.

They enter Honus's big room. "Honus!" Orion calls out anxiously, but there is no answer. "Oh, look, he has left a note." Orion gestures to the scrivening table.

The note is addressed to Malora. Orion stands aside so she can read it, which she does out loud, haltingly: "Dear Malora, There is cheese in the crock. I have gone to the . . ." Malora doesn't recognize a word, so she points to it.

"*Salient,*" Orion says. "Oh, yes. I forgot. The monthly meeting of the Salient is this afternoon. Honus always attends. He copies down what is said. That was very good reading, by the way."

"The Salient is the lawmaking body, is it not?" Malora says. "Perhaps I should approach the Salient about granting my petition."

Orion frowns. "They would never dare to go against the Apex, especially on as trivial a matter as this."

It is not trivial to me, Malora thinks as she looks around. Where is Zephele? Perhaps she can enlist Zephele to cajole the Apex into changing his mind. Zephele could talk a rhino into flying off a cliff. Malora looks out on the terrace, but there is no Zephele sprawled on her reading couch, embroidering, or holding bread crumbs on her hand for the birds to nibble.

"Where has your sister gone?" she asks.

"Sometimes she accompanies Honus to the Salient and listens in on the discussions. Honus makes of it a lesson in civics." Orion bites his lip, looking uncannily like his sister. "Look. I'm afraid I must go down to the rose houses. The moon is full tonight and the rose petals are being harvested, and I cannot let the Twani overwater them or the harvest will be wilted and spoiled. Shall I send West to keep you company?"

Malora flares up again. "What's the matter? Afraid of leaving the distressed Otherian unmonitored?"

Orion reaches for her hand. "I know you are distraught—"

She wrenches her hand away. "I am *not* distraught! I am angry! If it weren't for the Apex, I would be down in Brion's shop, learning my Hand! And now—now I don't know what I will do." She sags, sapped by her anger.

"You had set your heart on ironwork, I understand, but you will find another Hand. I promise you that my father will put up no impediments to it," he says.

"How can you promise for your father?" she says bitterly.

"I cannot," he says. "But *he* can. And he did."

Malora lifts her shoulders and lets them fall. "It doesn't matter. I want no other Hand but ironwork."

Orion sighs. "Perhaps you should sit here and think about that. There is a whole world of Hands equally worthy of your skills and talents. When Zephele returns, you can go with her and resume your tour of the studios and ateliers."

After he leaves, quiet sifts over the place. Malora realizes that, for the first time since she has come to Mount Kheiron, she is absolutely alone. She doesn't feel truly alone, because her anger is like a simmering presence. Then hunger comes to tug at her stomach like a nagging child.

She goes to the crock and lifts out the cheese, pulls her knife from her belt, and cuts a slice. She grabs a loaf of bread from the covered basket next to the fireplace, breaks off a corner, and eats it with the cheese. She chews hard and swallows, but even after she has finished half the loaf of bread and nearly all the cheese, her stomach still complains. It seems that cheese and bread are not enough to fill her today. It is as if her anger with the Apex has made her ravenous.

Malora goes over to the shelves where Honus's toys roost among the books. There is a beautiful jeweled statuette of a lizard. She winds it up the way she has seen Zephele do it. The lizard's ruby tongue darts out and eats a jewel-work fly, then swallows it. She moves to the elephant and winds it up. It raises its trunk and gathers emerald leaves to take into its mouth. The jeweled monkey peels a yellow-jeweled fruit and eats it. The ring-tailed dove opens its mouth and sings,

"Ma-lo-ra! Ma-lo-ra!" A sapphire squirrel sits up and holds a pearly nut between its paws. The sound of the sparkling little toys fizzes around her as an idea takes form in her head. She has seen fat squirrels scampering on the walls outside the house, where they eat the stale bread crumbs Zephele leaves for them. West has said that the squirrels are too fast for the Twani to hunt, and so they have proliferated in recent years. There is a spool of silver thread sitting on the shelf. She unwinds thread from the spool and cuts off a piece. She grabs some bread, slips the knife back into her belt, and heads down the hall toward the servants' entrance.

Rain and Lemon are propped against a blue-and-white pillar, sleeping soundly as she steals past them onto the service road. The road is deserted. She crosses it to the low wall that borders the road. At the foot of the wall, Malora lays out a long trail of bread crumbs, leading to a stick that she props against the wall. At the top of the stick, against the wall, she places a big pile of crumbs. Then she ties the silver string and rigs a snare, which she arranges near the top of the stick. She goes off a ways and sinks down beneath a tree, letting herself go absolutely still. She has just begun to doze, when she hears a thrashing sound. She opens her eyes. A big, fat squirrel is struggling with its head in the snare. Grabbing the squirrel by its tail, she dashes its head against the wall, then removes the snare from its neck. She loses no time rigging another snare. It isn't long before she has caught herself a second squirrel. Skinning them both, she skewers them on green sticks and carries them past the Twani at the gate, who have slept through her small game hunt.

Back in Honus's big room, she kneels by the hearth and

stirs up the fire, then seasons the meat with salt and herbs and a little olive oil and roasts it over the open flame.

"I've never had it myself, but I'm told that it tastes a good deal like chicken."

Malora turns so quickly, she nearly dumps her meal into the fire. Standing behind her, arms folded across his chest, is a strapping, long-legged centaur with curly, ginger-colored hair whose flanks and hooves are feathered with tufts of pale golden hair. He wears a wrap of ragged impala skin that covers only his hindmost quarters, and an equally ragged buckskin vest. His arms and chest are striated with muscle and scars. From the rawhide thong around his neck dangles the claw of a lion.

Malora knows immediately whom she is looking at: Neal Featherhoof.

CHAPTER 22

Neal Featherhoof

Neal Featherhoof bursts out laughing, his incisors long and unfiled, like Malora's. "The look on your face!"

Malora scowls. "The look on my face is one of fury with the Apex for not letting me choose my Hand, and hunger at being fed a daily diet of Barley Surprise."

Neal breaks off laughing and turns suddenly serious. His eyes are the coppery color of a leopard's. "If you don't like it here, you can go back to the bush."

"I might just do that. And take my horses with me."

"Along with a trunk containing your fine new wardrobe?" he asks. "If you do, you'll have to carry it away with you on your back, because I'm afraid the Apex will be hanging on to his Furies. And if you do take your leave, poor Zephele would never recover from her disappointment. I'm told you're her pet now as much as you are Orrie's."

Malora grouses. "I don't like being called pet."

"Apologies, Pet," he says, smiling. "You have far too much dignity to be called Pet by anyone—except me."

Neal Featherhoof has a dazzling but dangerous smile. It isn't the incisors, Malora thinks, as much as the mind at work behind the smile. "And you have far too much impertinence," she replies.

Neal raises a gingery eyebrow. "Already you sound like a haughty Highlander maiden. Don't look now, but you're missing the requisite number of legs."

"And the horse's ass," Malora gripes, and then instantly regrets it. She likes horses' asses, and if she only had one, she would be allowed to pursue the Hand of her choice.

Neal cocks a hind hoof on the hearth shelf and lounges against the stone, arms folded across his chest. "I knew the moment I first saw you that I'd like you."

Malora asks, "And when was that?"

"On the road into the city. I was but one of many Flatlanders that day in the awestruck crowd. You were quite a sight, astride that big black mare. Flatlanders and Highlanders alike spoke of little else for days. I think it takes our minds off more important matters, like the thoughtless cruelty of the ruling classes, and wild marauding centaurs. And speaking of wild, don't let me interrupt. Your roasted squirrel meat must be falling off the bone by now. But take my advice, Pet, and bury the bones before sweet Zephie returns. She's rather fond of these bushy-tailed rats, you know. She sets out bowls of milk and bread for them, and even names them things like Johnnyboy and Whiskers, the way you name your horses."

Malora squats on the hearth and carves off a slice of meat. She conveys it to her mouth on the point of her knife, then chews, enjoying the solid, salty texture she has been craving. Swallowing, she opens her eyes. "Who told you I name my horses?" she asks.

"You call them your boys and girls. I know everything that goes on. I make it my business." Neal watches her chewing. "If it's meat you crave, I can take you hunting for something much more savory than Johnnyboy and Whiskers there."

Raising an eyebrow, she chews thoughtfully.

He continues, "Hunting is one of the prerogatives of the Peacekeepers. Better to practice the killing arts than to be caught short in the event of a real battle or siege."

"But the Apex thinks I must be kept far from weapons," Malora says. "I think he fears that I will rise up and avenge the Massacre of Kamaria. Single-handedly."

"With a butter knife?" Neal says with a smirk.

"You sound just like Honus," Malora says.

His smile fades. "Honus and I are not at all alike. He lives in his head, while I live in the world. Honus has exerted an unfortunate influence on Orion, for my good friend spends most of his time nowadays in his head."

"In his distillery, I think," she says.

"It amounts to the same thing. He is convinced he can change the world through olfactory means."

Malora questions Neal with a look. He taps his nose.

She swallows another mouthful of squirrel. "Scents set the tone of a society," she says in defense of her friend.

"So our boy says. One has only to look closely at this society," he says with a wave of his hand, "to grasp my point."

"Orion is smart," Malora says, feeling a spark of resentment, "and kind. And he is my friend."

Neal grunts. "He is my friend, too, but he will never become Apex being kind."

"Is he expected to?" Malora asks.

"It usually runs in families, like crooked legs or cleft palates. Athen is no longer with us, and don't tell me you think Theon is up to the task," he says.

"What about Zephele?"

Neal curls his lip.

"Why can't Zephele become Apex? Is there some Edict that forbids it? Orion says she's very good at civics." Malora, having eaten the last bite, sets aside her knife and looks around for something to wipe her hands and mouth on.

Neal says, "There was a female Apex once. I believe she died of snakebite after only two months in office."

"I'm happy to give Zephie the remedy, just in case."

"Zephele could no more be Apex than you could," Neal says.

"And why not?" Malora wipes her mouth on her hand.

"Because she's fundamentally frivolous," Neal replies, pulling loose a cloth hanging from his snakeskin belt and tossing it to her. Malora catches it and wipes her mouth and hands, then the blade of the knife.

Neal retrieves the cloth and tucks it away. "Her flightiness must be obvious to you, who are yourself anything but."

Knowing how Zephele feels about Neal, Malora is stung on Zephele's behalf. "Zephie has a sweet and knowing nature. And for all you know, *I* might be very flighty."

"Please, Pet. This Flatlander is no one's fool."

She frowns. "I have little to caper about at the moment."

"Because the Apex has thwarted your petition? That's the

way it is in Mount Kheiron! But, as I say, you are welcome to go if you are unhappy," he says. "I'm sure—provided you leave the Furies behind—that the Apex would be the first to lead everyone in the good-bye salutation."

Malora would never dream of leaving without taking the horses. But when she imagines herself leaving the centaurs, the thought causes a surprising ache in her heart. "I think I would miss Orion and Zephie and Honus. Theon and Mather and the others. And there are comforts here . . . ," she trails off wistfully.

"Say no more. There are those of us on the Flatlands who would give anything to live up here surrounded by beauty and enlightenment. I'm not one of them, mind you. Peacekeepers have better things to do."

Malora hides a smile, hearing Zephele's voice saying: "The Peacekeepers are a joke, when I really think about it, because no one ever attacks us and we attack no one. So the Peacekeepers all bash each other about in practice, and that's just about that."

She gathers the sticks and the pile of bones, and carries them out to the terrace. She buries the bones in the dirt of the large pot of a pomegranate tree, feeling a twinge of guilt for using the bower as a boneyard. The squirrel was tasty enough but far too much work considering how little meat there really was. "Are you disappointed that the Apex will not be sending you out to battle with the wild centaurs?" she asks.

Neal contemplates the tree. "I wonder if it will now sprout bright red squirrels on the ends of its branches," he muses.

Malora hides a grin.

"There is no battle to speak of," Neal says. "The Ka would like our help establishing an escort for trading parties. But apparently, this comes too close to being an act of aggression in the Apex's mind. It violates Edicts aplenty."

"The Third, the Fifth, and possibly the Fourteenth."

"They've wasted no time indoctrinating you, I see. In any case, the Apex refuses to participate in the coalition," he says. "He would rather sit on his precious mountaintop and fret like an ostrich with his head in a hole."

"When ostriches fret, they don't put their heads in holes. They lie down with their heads strung out upon the ground." Now an *ostrich,* she thinks, would make a full meal. "When might we go hunting? I have lessons in the morning, but afternoons, I'm free." She sends the sticks sailing over the rooftops.

"Good arm!" Neal says. "Afternoons, I'm told that you're supposed to be busily shopping for your alternative Hand."

Malora shrugs. "No one said I couldn't shop for my alternative Hand in the bush," she says with a smirk.

"Ah, sweet corruption!" he says, rubbing his hands together. "I am at your service any afternoon you name."

"What if the Apex finds out? Would he turn me out?"

"Now, now, Pet, you'll have to learn that part of being a rebel is tossing caution to the wind," he says. "But not to worry. The Apex won't find out. What sort of game would you like to hunt, so that I might provide the right weapons?"

Worry still nags at her. "But won't the Apex see us? When I stand here and look out, I feel like I can see everything that goes on down there on the Flatlands and even beyond."

"That's because your eyes are as sharp as your spirit of adventure is strong," Neal says.

"The Apex's eyes seem quite sharp to me," Malora says.

"Only if he bothers to look beyond the Hall of Mirrors," Neal says with a wicked gleam in his coppery eyes.

"In that case, let's hunt ostriches. Ostrich steak is my favorite meat."

"I've never tasted it. Ostriches are too fast for me."

"They are not too fast for me," Malora counters, "provided I have a fast horse beneath me. And as for weapons, all I need is my rope."

"Game hunting with *rope*? I look forward to seeing this. I think I can get my hands on a fast horse. I am sorry to say it will not be one of your beloved Furies. *That* the Apex really would notice." He pauses. "You must miss your horses."

Malora looks away. How can she possibly explain to him—or to anyone—that her longing for the boys and girls is satisfied each night when she gallops across the plains on the back of her most beloved boy, the wayward stallion, Sky? "Let's hunt tomorrow afternoon," she says.

"I live to serve," Neal says with a deep, mocking bow.

CHAPTER 23

Bolt

Before lessons begin the next morning, while Honus is in the Hall of Mirrors advising the Apex, Malora says to Zephele, "Neal Featherhoof is taking me hunting later today."

Zephele's eyes pop. "How did this come to pass?"

"He visited me here yesterday, when you were at the Salient," Malora explains. Omitting the part about Johnnyboy and Whiskers, she says, "I am to meet him in the market square directly after the midday meal."

"But how will you do that?" Zephele asks. "You cannot simply go down there, unmonitored and unsponsored. You will need my help."

Malora, who was unaware this would be so complicated, says doubtfully, "Thank you."

"Don't thank me," Zephele says. "It may be the only way I'll ever get to see that Flatlander. Orion and Honus conspire to prevent it. What poor unfortunate beast will you be stalking?" she asks, then covers her ears and says, "Never mind. Forget I asked. I don't want to know. It's too vile. But I suppose that hunting is in your nature—just as it is in Featherhoof's—and that you will fail to thrive if you do not indulge in this barbaric practice."

In haste, Zephele and Malora hatch a plan. They will say that Zephele is taking Malora on a tour of the mosaic studio, which is near the market square where Malora has agreed to meet Neal after the midday meal.

When Honus returns to his rooms, they announce their plan. Honus is full of praise for it. "Brilliant! Your mathematical acumen may serve you well in this Hand," he says to Malora. "The People have been practicing the mosaic art since ancient times."

Malora and Zephele have their separate lessons, and then, before the midday meal, Honus invites them to read aloud a poem called "The Wasteland" by Thomas Stearns Eliot. Zephele rolls her eyes. She has read the poem before and finds it impenetrable. Honus stops reading after every stanza to explain its mysteries. Malora reads aloud, "Come in under the shadow of this red rock," and then asks Honus, "Did this Thomas Stearns live in the Ironbound Mountains?"

Honus smiles with a hint of sadness. "No, he lived in a land far to the north and the west that is now completed engulfed by ice."

"Is this where you came from, too?" Malora asks.

"I have no real way of knowing," Honus says.

When they leave before the midday meal, saying they will get something to eat in the marketplace, Honus is sitting in his red-cushioned easy chair, still poring over the poem.

At the last moment, Malora dashes to her room to get

Jayke's rope. When Honus sees her with it, he removes his gold wire-rimmed spectacles. "Your plan is to rope and hog-tie the mosaicists?" he asks, one brow raised.

Malora thinks quickly. "Zephele says, if we have time, we can take this to the rope shop. It is frayed on one end and needs reweaving."

Honus, seemingly satisfied with this explanation, returns to the Eliot and wishes them both a productive afternoon.

Human and centaur are subdued as they walk swiftly down the hall and pass through the front portal of the Silvermane house. When they are on the Mane Way, Zephele explodes in astonishment. "Did you see that? He accepted your falsehood without blinking an eye! I must enlist you the next time I need to violate the Ninth Edict. You're fearfully good at it. Your color isn't even high. When I tell an untruth, my cheeks burn as if I were stricken with fever. However do you do it? You must teach me your technique."

Malora can't say how she accomplishes this, any more than she can say how she kills squirrels without guilt or remorse.

Zephele lapses into a rare silence as they make their way down the steep roads feeding into the market square. The centaurs they pass, scent cloths pressed to their noses, flick their eyes toward Malora and then flick them away coldly. After a while, the smile on Malora's face freezes, then fades. What is the use, she thinks, of trying to make friends with centaurs who go out of their way to avoid her?

Zephele leads Malora past an alley so narrow, no centaur could possibly navigate it. Pausing to peer in, Malora sees small Twani vaulting over each other and wrestling in a furry heap while a mature female Twan, her tail switching placidly, looks on.

"A Twanian nursery," Zephele explains briefly. "Aren't the little kits dear?"

They arrive in the market square to find it thronged with Twani purchasing supplies for their households. Malora and Zephele stand out above the field of milling, frizzled heads. Zephele tells Malora to keep an eye out for Ash. "We must think of a falsehood to feed him if he sees us," she says, her pretty features marred by anxiety, "for he reports everything back to Herself."

"We will say that I asked for a tour of the marketplace," Malora says, "because it was built by the People, and anything that is built by the People is fascinating to me."

Zephele says, "Malora Ironbound, you are *uncannily* gifted at this!"

They are standing before the cheese-maker's wagon, nibbling on small, delicious wedges of goat cheese topped with pieces of dried apricot, when Neal sidles up. Zephele, taken by surprise, nearly spits out her mouthful of food, then quickly composes herself, leveling a steely look at him.

"You seem very pleased with yourself today, Flatlander," she says crisply.

"No more than I usually am, Mistress Highlander," Neal answers, leaning lazily against the wagon.

"Which is far, far too pleased, if you ask me . . . which I doubt you will," Zephele says.

"The Apex's daughter is more than entitled to her opinion," he says. "But how would he feel about her aiding and abetting an Otherian in the violation of at least three Edicts?"

Zephele blushes. "Malora has asked for my assistance, and I am helpless to deny her anything," she says. "If innocent animals of the bush suffer because of my actions, then it is on my conscience, because it obviously isn't going to be on yours. Oh! That's right. I forgot. You have no conscience."

Featherhoof greets this with a chuckle.

Malora observes this exchange with a growing sense of wonder. It is not so different from the way she and Neal spoke yesterday, but Neal was a stranger of whom she was wary. Not only is Neal not a stranger to Zephele, but she has said that she likes him. Is this the way Zephele enjoys her time with the Flatlander? Malora sees that Neal shows neither surprise nor displeasure at the reception he receives from Zephele. In fact, he beams at her. "And how are you today, Mistress Zephele? You are looking unusually well. A becoming cap you're sporting."

Zephele's already-high color deepens as her eyes narrow and her hand goes to her hip. "Don't pretend to appreciate Highlander fashion, Featherhoof," she says tartly. "I know you scorn our prudish ways. Now see here—and I assure you I am not being even remotely frivolous when I say this—you must return Malora to this exact spot no later than market closing time. Honus sets down the evening meal at sunset, and if Malora fails to appear, I assure you Honus will be most upset. If Orion finds out, he will be Beyond Cross. *And* if misfortune should chance to befall her . . ."

Neal laughs. "Enough, Zephie! Nothing's going to happen to her. She's more at home in the bush than I am."

"I know," Zephele says on a note of sudden sorrow.

"Apparently, the pleasures of Highland life have not been quite sufficient to sustain her."

Malora is surprised to see that Zephele is near tears. Malora wraps her arms around her friend's neck and whispers in her ear, "Thank you for this, Zephie. I'll be fine."

"I hope so," she says, sniffing into an embroidered cloth. "I have a good mind to come with you and make sure of it."

"And warn off our kill?" Neal says. "I think not."

"I would never!" Zephele says, her cheeks aflame.

"Oh, would you ever!" Neal says, laughing, taking Malora's arm and steering her away from the market square.

"Where are your hunting dogs?" Malora asks Neal.

"I left the girls at home today," he says. "For all the training I have invested in them, they have a tendency to misbehave around ostriches."

When they pass beneath the gates of Kheiron, Neal picks up two spears that are leaning against the gatehouse. Unlike the gatekeeper's decorative spear, these are made of plain wood, the shafts discolored with the sweat of hands, the tips forged from deadly-looking metal.

"You made these yourself?" Malora asks.

"I'm no smith. I buy all my weapons in the bazaar at Kahiro," he says.

"Is there anything you can't get at the bazaar in Kahiro?" she asks.

"Not that I know of," Neal says. "You said you would need only your rope, but I make a habit never to venture into the bush unarmed. We have just one stop to make, at the Thunderheart Stable, to pick up the horse you asked for. It's on the other side of the township we will be passing through."

Human and centaur walk in companionable silence down a road that is bordered on both sides by farmland. In not much more time than it took Zephele and Malora to reach the marketplace from the Mane Way, Neal and Malora reach the township. It is a clustering of low huts with crudely painted roofs and the occasional statue fashioned from trash and pieces of sun-bleached bush wood, some representing animals and others centaurs. Centaur children with dirty faces and ragged wraps come pouring out of the huts, as if they have been lying in wait, and chase after them, plucking at Malora's clothing. They seem no more frightened of her than their Highlander counterparts, and even more curious. Finally, Neal stops and lets them have their fill of her. They swarm over Malora, tugging her braid and touching her with nervous fingers.

"Why doesn't she have round eyes like us?" they ask.

"She's different and comes from far away," Neal says.

"Where is her fur?" they ask.

"She doesn't have any," Neal says.

The children stare hard at her booted feet. "Does she have split hooves or full?" they ask.

"She has toes. Like the jungle monkeys," he tells them.

Hearing Neal's last response, their eyes nearly pop out of their heads. "Does she have a *tail* like a jungle monkey?" One child then proceeds to do a fair imitation of a monkey, making his young audience fall all over each other laughing.

"Not that she's shown me," Neal confides behind his hand.

"My father says it's a dirty deal that she lives all fancy in the Silvermane house while we got our hooves sunk in the muck down here," says a small, serious-looking lad whose cheeks are hollow and whose eyes are smudged beneath with the shadow of hunger.

"You wouldn't like the fancy House of Silvermane very much," Neal tells him. "And the food is plentiful but not very tasty."

"My mama says she's an evil omen!" another centaur child blurts.

Neal says, "She's not an omen. She's just a Person, a lonely Person, wandered in from the bush, looking for friends."

"A *Person,* that's right!" That same serious child seizes upon this. "But they said there were no more People!"

"It just goes to show you how much *they* know, doesn't it?" Neal says.

Neal goes on bantering with the young ones, answering their questions with surprising warmth and patience. He says to Malora over their shaggy heads, "I hope you don't mind. The Highlander children catch glimpses of you every day, but these little ones have only heard the tales. As you can see, you are quite a novelty."

Malora doesn't mind being a novelty, although, as with the Highlander children, she wishes they would speak to her directly. Eventually, the children scatter back into the huts, and Neal and Malora pass out the other side of the township into another patchwork swath of farmland.

"Why are they hungry if there are so many food crops?" Malora asks.

"The Highlanders own the farmlands. The Flatlanders only work them," Neal explains. "Most of the food goes to the Highlanders, leaving the Flatlanders mere scraps."

"That doesn't seem fair," Malora says.

"You believe that life is fair, do you?" Neal asks.

Malora blushes. "No," she says quietly. "There is no real fairness, is there?"

"Maybe elsewhere in the world, but not in Mount Kheiron!" Neal says with bitter cheer.

The Thunderheart Stable rises up on the crest of a barley field, an imposing gray stone edifice with no adornment except for the row of Golden Horses lined up on the rafter above the entrance. A series of training rings surrounds the stable, but there is no place where the horses can graze.

"Anders Thunderheart doesn't graze his horses," Neal says when Malora asks him about it. "He thinks they perform better when kept inside their stalls and unleashed to race."

In the training rings, female Twani are spinning horses without using ropes. It interests Malora to see how the Twani use their tails to signal direction, as well as pace, to the horse.

Human and centaur enter the stable. Malora stops and inhales deeply. How she has missed the smell of manure and hay, she thinks. Her nostrils flare. There is something else in the air here that she cannot quite place. Her eyes accustom themselves to the darkness. There are at least fifty stalls flanking a long, wide aisle stacked with bales of hay.

"Most of them," Neal explains, "are Athabanshees, from the deserts of the Sha Haro."

Malora peers into one of the stalls. The horse inside is the most beautiful, delicate creature she has ever seen: a bright bay with two white feet and a blaze. Head, eyes, ears, neck, breast, belly, haunches, legs, pasterns, and feet are all proportioned to admirable effect. On nimble hooves, she shifts and dips a nose with unusually wide nostrils into her hay. Malora walks along the stalls, and the horses inside, varying in color from white to chestnut, are every bit as exquisite as the first one. The stalls are clean and airy, but the horses look nervous and jumpy, their high spirits held in check. This, she thinks, is what she smells: their desperation to be free.

"You said you wanted fast," Neal says, "and these are the fastest. Thunderheart might be nominally a barley farmer, but it is the racing he cares about. He is determined never to let a Highlander win the Golden Horse. For this, he is considered something of a hero among the Flatlanders."

This Thunderheart is no hero to Malora, cooping up his horses like this. They pass out of the other side of the stable and back into the sunlight, where there are more training rings and a large oval enclosure with a track running around the outside. The horses on the track are harnessed to two-wheeled rigs with single seats, upon which Twani perch, leaning forward, holding the reins.

"Anders Thunderheart has taken his winnings and duplicated the Hippodrome right down to the footing and the color of the fencing. Not even the Apex has one of these."

Most of the Twani hold whips. The whips are not like those used by the hunters of the Settlement, which were thick and made from braided rhino hide. These are snakeskin, loose and many tailed, with cruel knots tied in the ends.

"Are the whips cue givers or motivators?" she asks Neal.

Neal shrugs. "I have no idea, Pet."

Malora gets her answer the next moment when a Twan unleashes the whip with a loud crack. The ends of the whip writhe and hiss over the horse's back, like a nest full of snakes. The horse leaps and surges forward around the track. Another horse prances nervously in place. The driver lets loose the whip and the horse rears, overturning the rig and spilling the Twan out onto the dirt.

"Motivator," Malora mutters. "Thunderheart authorizes the use of these whips?"

"It would seem so," Neal says.

Anders Thunderheart is a villain to her now. "Are these whips permitted in the actual races?"

Neal says, "Oh, yes. Often on the competitor's horse. But only when the Grand Provost is looking the other way, which I hear he is amply bribed to do."

Malora also notices that the horses have patches partially covering their eyes. She has seen such blinders on the horses pulling carts in Mount Kheiron. On the mountain, the blinders make sense because they distract the horses from the commotion on the streets. Here they make less sense. "Why blind the horse on the track?" she wonders aloud.

"I imagine so that they'll have no way to look but forward," Neal says.

This seems odd to Malora. A horse is generally spurred on when it spies, with its side- and-backward-seeing eyes, something coming up on its flank. The horse might overreact, but if its rider knows how to harness that nervousness, the end result will be increased speed. An uneasy thought has been churning in Malora's mind. She turns to Neal, her face heating up. "Is this how my horses are being treated?"

Neal says, "Rest easy, Pet. I'm sure the Apex coddles his horses the same way he coddles his children. It's not as if he's ever won the Golden Horse, or, in all likelihood, ever will. Ah, there's Thunderheart now."

A gray-haired, bandy-legged centaur emerges from the stable leading the horse with the blaze and the white socks, who dances at the end of the rope. He calls out gruffly to Neal, "If anything happens to my horse, Featherhoof, you will owe me a thousand nubs worth of hides and pelts."

"Agreed, Thunderheart," Neal says.

The two centaurs come together and lock hands. When they release their grip, Anders Thunderheart looks into his palm and counts out the nubs Neal has just passed to him. Satisfied, he hands off the rope to Neal. The horse shimmies and dances.

"She'll have to ride bareback. I have no riding tack, just a lead harness," Thunderheart says.

Neal looks to Malora. Malora says, "Bareback is fine."

Thunderheart says, "I'll thank you to have her walk the mare across the river and mount up in the bush. The less anyone around here knows of this, the better. No good can come of doing business with an Otherian."

"On the contrary. Your notoriety will be enhanced," Neal says.

By way of response, Anders spits in the dirt.

To Malora, Neal says, "As gossips, the Flatlanders are no better than the Highlanders. Gossip might pass for an amusement to the Highlanders, but for the Flatlanders it is more than that: it is a brightener of our bleak lives."

Neal holds the rope out to Malora. She takes it and

unhitches it from the halter, handing the rope back to Thunderheart. "I brought my own."

Anders takes the rope with an indifferent shrug.

"What's her name?" Malora asks. The horse's head is high. Her neck is stiff. The whites of her eyes flash.

Thunderheart chuckles. "Bolt, we call her. And bolt, she rightly does."

"Does she know to start and stop?" Malora asks.

"It's 'go' to start and 'ho' to stop," Thunderheart says. "Think she can manage that?"

Malora is grateful to Neal for not dignifying this question with an answer. She ties the end of Jayke's rope to the halter. "Can I exercise Bolt in one of these empty rings?" she asks Thunderheart. "There's no sense in my taking her out into the bush if she's unfit for riding."

Thunderheart says, "If she's fit for the Hippodrome, she's fit for the likes of a two-legger."

Malora decides to take this as permission to use one of the rings. She leads the horse into the ring and prepares to send the horse out for a spin. But the horse stands with her head high, eyes rolling at Malora with a look of terrified bewilderment on her face.

"You've never seen anything like me, have you, girl?" Malora asks.

An idea comes to her. She unhitches the rope from the horse's harness, and then coils the rope and holds it behind her back. Using the frayed end like a Twan's tail, she wags it at Bolt's neck to send her out. Bolt rears slightly but moves away from Malora. Keeping her eyes on the mare's hip, Malora wags the rope again and says, "Go!" Bolt goes out for a spin, one, two, three times, then Malora moves her "tail" to the other hand and, twirling it, again says, "Go!" to send the mare spinning in the opposite direction. Malora spins the rope faster and clicks her tongue to get the mare to pick up her gait. The horse lunges immediately into a canter. The three-beat rhythm of her bound is clean and well balanced, her back long and stretched. It is a lovely canter. Still, it is not precisely what Malora asked for.

"That's perfect, Bolt, but I'd like to see your trot first," Malora says, slowing down the movement of her feet and the rope. In response, the horse breaks her rolling motion and shifts her balance backward. Malora watches the transformation as the mare's back rounds, her neck rises and arches, her face moves into an almost vertical position. This is, Malora thinks, poetry even more beautiful than what Shakespeare and Thomas Stearns Eliot and Uzamo and Yeats wrote long ago. This is as beautiful a gait as Malora has ever seen on a horse. Malora stills the rope and stops turning. "Ho," she says. The horse stops and faces into her, her head low and calmer now.

"Come here, beautiful girl," Malora says.

The mare hesitates, and then takes a few steps toward Malora. Malora holds up her hand and frowns to stop the horse's forward motion. She hears Jayke's voice in her head: "Always keep a zone of safety around yourself and don't let the horse enter it. If you want to pat the horse, you are the one who steps out of the zone to approach, not the other way around."

Malora smiles when Bolt halts and remains outside the zone, and she rewards the mare by stepping forward and stroking her velvety nose, crooning in her ear, "You're a feisty little thing, aren't you? But those lady Twani have trained you well. I think we're going to get along just fine."

Then she steps away and sends Bolt out again, with a softly uttered "Go!" She tosses the frayed end of the rope as she directs the mare in a straight line toward the ring's railing. Malora walks to the side of the mare and behind her, facing forward but careful not to cross over her midline, which would cause the horse to stop and turn in.

Next to the fence, she spins Bolt again so that the mare is forced to navigate the narrow passage between Malora's body and the rail. If Bolt doesn't kick up a fuss doing this, Malora knows she will be safe to ride. The horse passes close to the fence. Malora dips her head and stares hard at Bolt's hindquarters. The mare's back legs slide sideways into a halt. Malora tries this same exercise going in the other direction, with equal success. Malora works with the mare until she is satisfied that she can move all the parts of the horse, forelegs, middle, and hind legs, from the ground using her eyes and the rope "tail." The horse will probably never be exactly calm, but Malora is reasonably confident that she will be able to ride Bolt and stay safe. She nods to Neal. Neal nods to Thunderheart.

As she and Neal are leaving, she hears Anders say something to Neal. Malora turns to Neal. "What did old Thunderheart say to you just then?" she asks.

Neal laughs. "He says if we manage to kill anything—apart from you when you are thrown on your head by his horse—he will refund my nubs."

"That seems fair to me," Malora says.

CHAPTER 24

Chasing Ostriches

"Try not to get killed," Neal Featherhoof says. "If you die, Orion will have me turned out for a certainty, and despite all its shortcomings, Mount Kheiron is my home."

"I'll do my best," Malora says. "How far from the bush are we?"

"It's right across the river, just ahead of us. There is a reliable supply of ostriches over there, probably because I've never come close to killing even one."

Malora says, "Give me a hand and I'll mount up here. Bolt and I might as well continue to get to know one another."

Neal makes a stirrup of his hands and boosts her up onto Bolt's slender back.

"*Now* you look much more like yourself," Neal says approvingly.

Malora grins down at him. She *feels* more like herself. It is good to have a horse beneath her again, even if it is a delicate and skittish one.

Neal stands back and eyes the shimmying horse uneasily. "Will she tolerate you on her back?"

"That is the idea." The skin beneath Malora's seat twitches. She senses that Bolt is itching to rid herself of this strange new burden. "Easy, now, girl. Let's give you something to do to take your mind off bucking me. Go!" She squeezes the mare with her calves.

Bolt's ears flick doubtfully, but she does go. Malora turns her body to the right and points her right toe to cue the mare to move right. When Bolt doesn't respond, Malora prods her with the heel of her left foot. She lays a hand on the left side of her neck to offer additional prompting. Finally, Bolt bends her neck and moves to the right. Malora tries this a few more times, receiving increasingly more ready responses from Bolt. Then Malora reverses the cues to get the mare to move left. As Neal attempts to stay out of their way, Malora and Bolt weave back and forth along the trail as if under the influence of monkey weed. Malora notices that Bolt moves more flexibly to the left, and thinks the horse may be urged to run around the track more often to the left than to the right. Apart from that quirk, the animal seems to have been well trained. She gets the horse to stop and go and back up on cue. Gradually, Bolt grows calmer and begins to move with something approaching willingness.

When they come to a tributary of the Neelah, a narrow ribbon of water running over a bank of smooth rocks, Neal splashes across, but the horse balks on the bank.

"We're crossing this river, Bolt, even if it takes us all afternoon," Malora says, steadily heeling Bolt's barrel.

Neal, already halfway across, turns and beckons.

"Follow the four-legger," Malora says, pointing to Neal. Bolt stays stock-still. Malora bangs her heels against the mare's rib cage until Bolt starts to move. Malora is careful to look outward, toward the bank.

"Good, brave girl," she croons to the mare.

Halfway across, the horse stops and dips her nose into the water. Malora feels the horse's forelegs begin to buckle. Bolt is about to drop into the river for a roll!

"Not with me on your back, you don't!" she says, pounding Bolt's rib cage anew with her heels.

The horse gives this some thought, then snorts and continues sloshing across the river. "Good girl, Bolt," Malora says.

On the other side of the river, there are no farmlands, no houses, no rustic towns, just tawny grassland dotted with dark green shrubbery stretching off to the hills, which rise up in the east in a low, jagged purple wall.

"We Flatlanders call these the Sisters," Neal says. "Can you see them? You ought to be able to . . . they're horses. A team of seven, the seventh being volcanic. That's the mountain that spewed on the poor Twani and sent them scurrying in our direction."

After a few moments of staring, Malora begins to see, rising up out of the mountain rock, the shapes of seven horses galloping abreast toward the north, their manes streaming behind them. "I see them. Have you ever been there?",

Neal shakes his head. "They are farther away than they look. The Hills of Melea, the Highlanders call them. They say the cave where Kheiron lived is somewhere in the middle sister. I'll visit there someday. Not to see the cave, of course—

that's all Highlander superstition. But to explore, hunt the game, see what's there."

"Look out for Leatherwings if you do," Malora says.

"For *what*?" he asks.

"The monsters that killed my People. Raptors with leathery wings and human heads. They live in the Ironbounds and, for all I know, in all mountains. They prey on People and they prey on horses, so I imagine they'd find centaurs the perfect dish."

"I'll be sure to bear that in mind," Neal says, laughing blithely. "For now, most of my travels take me north, where there are no mountains and, so far at least, no Leatherwings. Kahiro has its own surprises, however."

"Really?" Malora asks. "What kind of surprises?"

"Kahiro teems with every hibe on earth. It is a great, sprawling, brawling, rowdy city, nearly half of it given over to the market. There's a mountainous wall of sand dunes and, on the other side, the sea."

"What do you mean by *the see*?" she asks. "See *what*?"

Neal gives her a look that suggests her ignorance surprises him. "The sea is a great body of water," he explains.

"Like a river?" she asks.

"Wider and deeper than a river," he says, "stretching out beneath the sky and every bit as vast and endless-seeming. The water is salty, like blood, like tears. It's alive with fish and snakes and serpents and all manner of beasts that swim and breed and prey on each other and live out their whole lives in the watery deep. The sea is even home to some hibes."

"I'd like to go there," Malora says, trying to imagine something so immense.

Human and centaur are standing on a grassy rise, staring off into the middle distance, when Malora feels Neal nudge her. She turns to see that he is holding out a crude flask covered with the skin of a baby leopard.

"What is it?" she asks.

"It is gaffey," he says. "I usually take a nip or two before I hunt. I get it from an old Dromadi crone in the marketplace at Kahiro. She's a fortune-teller, but I am always too busy tasting her wares to listen to much of her babble."

Malora takes the flask. It is nearly empty, so she has to tip her head far back in order to shake a few drops onto her tongue. A strange, bitter but nutty taste invades her mouth. Suddenly, the air grows cooler and damp with mist. Bolt's slender body has vanished from beneath her, replaced by Sky's familiar girth. Sky springs forward from a standstill into a full gallop. Someone big is sitting behind her, making her feel as small as a little girl again, his strong arms bracing her. It is Jayke, she thinks—and yet Malora sees none of the familiar scars running up and down these arms. She cranes her neck to see who it is she is sharing the saddle with, and her breath catches.

The man mounted behind Malora is not her father. He is younger than Jayke, she can tell, even though the hair on his head, wild and wind-tossed, is silver. If such a thing is possible, this man is even bigger than Jayke, with skin the color of dark honey and eyes the gray of clouds heavy with rain. The scent of him is heady, like the way the air smells just before a thunderstorm. She opens her mouth to speak to him, but his lips close over hers and he sucks the breath right out of her. She moans far back in her throat and feels herself tumbling off Sky's back, down through layers of clouds as she hurtles toward the ground.

"A little goes a long way," Neal Featherhoof says.

Malora starts and grabs Bolt's mane to keep from falling off the mare's back. Neal snatches the flask just as she is about to drop it.

"Yes, it does," Malora says, righting herself and trying to settle the fluttering in the pit of her stomach, which is like none she has ever felt. "You should have warned me."

"It affects everyone differently," he says, tightening the lid on the flask. "I'm almost out of it. I guess it's time to return to Kahiro."

They settle back into stillness, scanning the terrain, looking for the distinctive, bottom-heavy profile of ostriches. Kudus and impalas come into their sights, as do zebras and giraffes, but not a single ostrich.

Feeling unsettled and restless, Malora says, "I might as well make good use of the time." She dismounts and unfastens the rope from Bolt's halter, then ties a loop in the frayed end. She practices tossing the loop over each of Bolt's ears, then over the mare's head.

"What in the world are you playing at *now*, Pet?" Neal asks.

"Something I should have thought of doing before. I am getting Bolt used to having this rope fly over her head."

Bolt is startled at first, but after Malora has tossed the rope several more times, the mare begins to ignore it. When Malora is sure that the horse no longer fears the rope, she coils it over her shoulder and remounts and resumes the watch.

The silence stretches out between Malora and Neal, easy

and companionable. She thinks she would like to spend time in the bush with Neal. Unlike the horses, the Twani, and the Silvermanes, he does not seem to require her protection.

Neal clears his throat and says, "It's possible the ostriches heard you were in the area and are staying away."

"That's all right," Malora says, smiling at his joke. "I like being out here, away from the crowds and the talk and the noise . . . and the Apex and the Edicts."

"I love the bush," Neal says. "I'm always happier out here. Everything is so stark and simple. Nothing in all of Mount Kheiron—no work of art or craft—is as beautiful and enlightened as those hills are at this moment."

The sun lowering in the west has bathed the Seven Sisters in an orange glow.

"When my mother first turned me out into the wild," Malora says pensively, "my mind was as empty as a cup. Gradually, it began to fill with the sky, with the animals, with the earth, with the plants, until I was brimming."

"Look!" Neal says suddenly.

Malora adjusts her eyes to follow the arrow of Neal's finger as it points to three, four, five, six ostriches dashing from north to south in a loose group. Malora nods and heels Bolt forward into a trot. "Go," she says.

"Shall I go with you?" Neal shouts after her.

"I can't think why," Malora calls back to him. "You said yourself you're not fast enough."

Neal shrugs and smiles. "In that case, I'll stay here and watch to see whether you are."

"All right, Bolt," Malora says to the horse, "let's see what you're made of. Go!" She squeezes the mare with her legs and feels the animal gather herself and surge forward. What a gallop she has! Flat and smooth as the floor of the bush. The wind whistles past Malora's ears as the horse's hooves seem to barely touch the ground.

They near the flock of ostriches. Malora can see their wide, flat black feathers stirring, the long pink stalks of their necks thrusting their tiny pink heads forward. One of them lunges comically and veers off to the left. Malora chooses this one to chase. If she chases the flock, they will scatter every which way and she will be left with nothing. She and Bolt close in on the solitary ostrich. She can see the bird's huge eyes fringed with long black eyelashes.

Hugging Bolt's slender barrel with her legs, Malora sits up straight and readies the loop at the end of Jayke's rope. When they are within ten feet of the ostrich, Malora swings the rope over her head and sends the loop sailing out toward the swerving pole of the ostrich's neck. The rope whistles as it flies through the air. The loop lands shy and spooks the ostrich sideways. The horse turns to follow the ostrich without flagging as Malora hauls back the rope and readies it. The ostrich has gained some distance but is still within reach. Malora swings the rope over her head and sends the loop out. She misses again!

Tenacity. She hears her father's voice as she gathers the rope in. When she tosses it out again, she thinks she has missed a third time, but then she sees the rope settle on the feathered shelf of the ostrich's body. She yanks on the rope, sits down hard, pulls back on the harness, and shouts, "Ho!"

Bolt's hind legs come under her as she skids to a stop in a cloud of dust. The ostrich, which has continued to run, jerks at the end of the rope and snaps its own neck. The enormous bird flies upward and then collapses in the dust.

See, Zeph? Malora thinks. Quick and painless.

Neal races over. Bolt is lathered with sweat, ribs heaving. Malora pats Bolt's flank, then leans forward to whisper thanks. As she watches Neal coming on, she realizes that this is the first time she has seen a centaur gallop. He has all the grace of a human man running and a horse galloping, in perfect harmony with one another.

"Well done, Pet!" he says, halting beside her and bending to remove the rope from the ostrich's neck. "If I hadn't seen it with my own eyes, I'd never have believed it. We'll have ostrich steaks tonight."

He returns the rope to her, expertly trusses the ostrich with his own rope, then slings the feathery bundle onto his back.

"You'll have to save my steak for tomorrow," Malora says, eyeing the sinking sun. "If I don't get home soon, Honus will have my hide."

Zephele is furious when they get to the market square. They had to stop at the Thunderheart Stable to drop off Bolt and collect Neal's refund.

"I expected you *eons* ago!" Zephele fumes, her color every bit as high as it had been earlier.

"Malora got her ostrich," Neal says proudly.

Zephele looks unimpressed. "How perfectly revolting." Then she asks, "Might I have a few feathers?" an unavoidably embarrassing afterthought.

"By all means," Neal says. "That's the least we can do to pay you for participating in our uprising against the Edicts."

"Perish the thought!" Zephele says, scanning the late-day crowd for eavesdroppers. "And I suppose you two will be wanting to repeat your little escapade on the morrow?"

"Well . . . Malora hasn't had a chance to enjoy her ostrich steak yet," Neal says, cocking an eyebrow at Malora.

"I do like ostrich steak," she says longingly.

Zephele shudders. "Very well. I'll expect my feathers tomorrow. Be sure to wash off the blood."

"It was a bloodless kill," Malora says.

"Oh, excellent," Zephele says in a flat voice. "I'm sure the ostrich appreciated your neatness to no end! Come along, Malora. Say good night to the barbarian and hello to civilization." She glances at Neal. "Wipe that satisfied smile off your face, Flatlander."

Zephele's uphill pace is surprisingly robust, and Malora, exhausted from her first real ride in weeks, finds herself huffing and puffing to stay abreast of her. "I thought you liked him," Malora says.

"I am *unbearably* infatuated," Zephele says without missing a step. "How could I not be? Have you no eyes in your head? Did you see his pectorals and his biceps? The centaur looks as if he were chiseled from marble. Flawless golden marble. And those flanks! Sheer, unadulterated bliss!" She shivers.

"If you admire him so much, why were you so rude to him?"

"Number one, he's a Flatlander, and that's all he deserves; number two, if he knew I liked him, he'd be more insufferable than he already is; and three . . . I am so nervous around him that, frankly, I don't know what I'm saying."

"Mostly very mean things," says Malora, holding back a chuckle. "Try being nicer to him next time, maybe."

"Coming from the killer of poor defenseless ostriches, that's very rich," Zephele says.

"Please try to understand," Malora says in a small voice, "that I was born to hunt just as you were born to . . ."

Zephele halts in her tracks, takes a deep breath, and raises a hand. "Don't say it," she says. "You'll only make me sound even more frivolous than I know I am. You're right. I should make a more concerted effort to understand your nature—and his, as well. And now we must compose an elaborate falsehood about our visit to the mosaic studio."

The falsehood turns out to be unnecessary because Honus waxes eloquent on the subject of mosaics during the entire meal, for which Malora arrives in the nick of time, slightly breathless and a little dusty. Malora and Honus are joined by Orion and attended by West, who takes care to serve Malora before the others. Throughout the meal, she feels him brushing up against her back. At one point, he whispers in her ear, "You have been back to the bush."

She shoots him a startled look. "How can you tell?" she mouths at him.

"Because you seem more like yourself today," he whispers.

Honus is saying, "The earliest-known examples of mosaics were found at a temple building in Ubaid, in Mesopotamia, and they are dated to the second half of the third millennium. They consist of pieces of colored stones, shells, and ivory. Some of the finest examples were in the ancient city of Ravenna, where Emperor Justinian and his wife, the Empress Theodora . . ."

Malora, hungry from the afternoon's hunt, eats all her Barley Surprise, which West replenishes without her even having to ask, while Honus discusses the mosaics in a place called Venice, where something called the tree of life was depicted in over one million pieces of colored glass.

"I'm sure Malora finds the history of mosaics as riveting as I do, but is she interested in pursuing the Hand, is what I want to know," Orion says, searching Malora's face closely.

Malora lifts her shoulders. "Who knows? But I've asked Zephele to take me back there tomorrow for a second visit."

Orion clearly finds this an encouraging sign. "Excellent!"

"Can you tell us what manner of project was laid out for the *opus regulatum*?" Honus asks.

Malora's eyes widen in desperation as she attempts to decode his question.

West comes to her rescue. "It was a tree of life," he says.

Orion and Honus blink at West in puzzlement.

"How do you know this?" Orion asks.

"Because Malora whispered it to me just now, didn't you, Malora?"

Malora nods energetically. "A tree of life, yes."

She is immensely relieved when Honus nods. "A most popular, if derivative, centaurean motif," he says. "What method were they using?"

Malora stares at Honus, at a total loss. This time, West has left her to her own devices.

Orion offers a gentle prod. "What he means is, were they using the indirect or the direct method?"

"Oh!" Malora says. "The indirect . . . I think."

Honus says, "Where will the work eventually sit?"

"I have no idea," Malora says brightly. "But I'm sure I'll find out when I return tomorrow."

Malora goes to bed that night reliving the hunt and recalling the vision that came to her with the sip of gaffey. All night in her dreams, she rides Sky across the plains, searching in vain for the mysterious man with honey-dark skin, silvery hair, and the scent of the air just before a thunderstorm. "Who is he?" she asks Sky. Sky tosses his mane and says, "He is Lume."

"This is Pel, and this is Mel," Neal says the following afternoon, indicating the two hounds that sit just outside the gatehouse, guarding the bows and quivers he has parked there. The dogs are white with brown spots. Pel has a speckled muzzle, and Mel has a brown circle around her right eye. When they see Neal, their feathery tails beat the ground. Then they catch sight of Malora and start to growl, moving stealthily forward on their haunches as if unsure whether to grovel or leap at her throat.

"Easy, girls," Neal says to them. "They're sour on two-leggers, I'm afraid, Pet."

Malora approaches the dogs slowly, holding out her cupped hands to let them sniff her. They remind her of the hunting dogs in the Settlement, except that these two are healthier-looking and better fed and they wear collars, one silver, one gold. Their cold noses graze her hands. Jayke believed in keeping hounds hungry. It sharpened their instincts. Neal obviously doesn't hold with this philosophy. Then again, dogs, like horses, are always hungry.

"To seal the new friendship," Neal says as he slips her two strips of dried bush meat.

Malora holds out her hands to the dogs, realizing that she is offering them the same food she once ate. The dogs sniff at the offering, then delicately take it from her hands and chew it. Afterward, they lick their chops, then her palms. Their tails wag in a more friendly fashion now, and Malora kneels and gives them her face to lick. The dogs' tongues tickle. They jump onto her and knock her backward into the dirt, clambering over her. She feels their feet in her ribs and their hot breath and rough tongues on her face and neck. She giggles, pushing them gently away.

Neal stamps his hoof, and the dogs pull back and hasten to settle on their haunches on either side of their master.

Malora sits up. "They are very affectionate," she says, wiping the canine saliva from her face.

"You're the first two-legger they've ever taken to. In Kahiro, I have to muzzle them. They're inclined to attack every two-legger they lay eyes on."

Neal reaches out to hoist her to her feet. He has both bows and quivers strung over his shoulder.

"I thought we were roasting ostrich today," Malora says. She skipped the midday meal to hone her appetite.

"We are, but I thought we would go to my camp via the bush and see if any tempting targets present themselves to us."

"Those are very handsome bows," Malora comments. "Did you get them at the market in Kahiro?"

"No," he says, "these I made myself. I seasoned the yew

wood for two years. The stave was made from the heartwood of an ash tree, the string from silk, and the arrows—"

"Fledged with the feather of the lilac-breasted roller," Malora says, remembering Thora's arrows.

Human and centaur walk through a stretch of deserted farmland. Up ahead, Malora hears the refreshing sound of water rushing over rocks. Neal hands her a bow and a quiver. She straps the quiver over her shoulder but holds the bow high over her head as they wade across the river. The water comes up to the middle of her thighs, soaking her breeches, and she wishes she had Bolt beneath her. They walk south along the riverbank.

"The game is nearly always plentiful here," Neal says.

Soon they spy a small herd of bachelor impalas grazing near the river. The wind carries their scent downriver, and the dogs lift their twitching noses to it.

By unspoken agreement, Neal and Malora leave the river and cross inland until they are standing between the impala and open bush. They stop. The hounds whimper.

Malora reaches back to the quiver and pulls out an arrow. She lays it across the bow stave, trapping it in her left thumb. With her right, she stretches the cord until it connects with the small nock at the arrow's fledged end. Hauling back on the cord with her forefinger, she draws the cord all the way to her right ear. As she sights an impala, she hears her mother's voice say in her ear, "Burn a hole with your eye into the target and the arrow will seek it."

Malora lets loose the arrow and hears a distant thud. The herd scatters, leaving behind a single slain impala.

"Fetch," Neal says to the dogs. The dogs hightail it through the grass, Pel returning with the arrow clenched in her teeth, followed by Mel, dragging the limp body of the impala.

Neal takes the arrow from Pel and wipes the impala blood off on a handful of leaves. "Good girl," he says.

"Thank you," Malora says.

Neal flashes a grin at her. "Not you, Pet. I was talking to Pel. She hasn't broken an arrow yet." He fits the arrow back into her quiver. Then he places the impala in a coarse net, which he slings over his shoulder. They recross a little farther upriver, where a township huddles on the opposite bank, surrounded by a fence messily woven from sticks and reeds.

"This is the farthest outlying township in the east," Neal explains. "We put up the fence last year after lions dragged off a newborn."

Once they have crossed the river, Neal unlatches a gate in the crude fence and admits her inside. He tells Malora it is one of the poorest townships on the flats. Instead of stone huts, families live in one-room hovels made of sticks and mud. Unlike the township she passed through yesterday, there is not a single statue or painted roof. Three centaur children, grubby-faced and naked, roll across the hard-packed dirt, wrestling. They stop and trot over. Malora is surprised when they ignore her in favor of Neal. They clench their hands together in a gesture of pleading. They hold up their skinny arms. They stick out their tongues hungrily. Laughing at their pantomime, Neal hands over the impala to them, and the three of them bear off their bloody prize.

"I hope you don't mind that I gave away your kill. That little impala will feed this entire township for two days," Neal says. He leads the way into a small yard bordered by bleached animal skulls, horns, and vertebrae.

"The villagers can't hunt for themselves?" Malora asks.

"Only Peacekeepers, and Twani while in the bush, are authorized to carry weapons. Why do you think I joined the Peacekeepers in the first place?" he asks, his eyes grave.

"To feed the Flatlanders?" she asks.

"And to feed myself. I sell the pelts to the cobblers for a decent nub. I'd be as rich as Anders if I hoarded my nubs, but I give them away, along with most of the meat from the kills."

Just when Malora thinks she understands Neal Featherhoof, he says something to surprise her anew.

Neal's house is a small block of stone in the center of the yard. It has a zebra skin covering the front door, which reminds her of the doors in the Settlement: skin stretched over frames hung on rope hinges. Various wild-animal hides hang on tree limbs, drying in the sun.

Malora thinks of Longshanks and his elegant rainbow of skins, and wonders if she has Neal to·thank, indirectly, for her wardrobe.

There is a big fire pit in front of his house, with a large iron cauldron resting on the rocks. "This is where I cure the skins and cook most of my meals," he says, adding, "not in the same pot, you'll be glad to know."

In the bed of the fire pit, there are bones mixed with charred wood and live coals. The ostrich meat has already been plucked and gutted and spitted. Neal stirs up the coals, feeds a few scraps of wood into the fire, and lowers the meat on the spit.

Malora sits on a rock. "Explain to me why Flatlanders can defy Edicts that Highlanders would be turned out for."

"You mean eating meat?" he asks. "We simply aren't held to the same standards," Neal says. "In many ways, Flatlanders have a great deal more freedom than the Highlanders. In other ways, we are disadvantaged. In addition to being malnourished and ill-clad, most of us are undereducated."

Malora rests her eyes thoughtfully on him. "But not you," she says. "You are different."

"Just so. That's because I was educated by Honus, the cloven-hoofed polymath, side by side with Orion. My father runs the Silvermane Vineyard, you see, and Orion and I grew up together."

"Are you still friends?" Malora asks.

"Not the way we once were. It's a long story," Neal says, pausing. "Do you really want to hear it?"

Malora nods, curious.

Neal sighs and pokes unnecessarily at the coals. "It happened shortly after Athen disappeared. We were thirteen, and I persuaded Orion to sneak out one midsummer's night and come to a carousing down on the flats. Flatlanders may not have all the privileges and luxuries the Highlanders enjoy, but we do know how to make the best of what we have and carouse in style. This incident took place in the Apex's vineyard. I had stolen the key to the cellar from my father. A few of the other bucks and I rolled out a cask of wine and cracked it open. The finest Silvermane wine flowed that night. I don't remember much of what happened. There were torches blazing and flutes playing and bucks and maidens dancing on the grass beneath the moon. Yes, we dance. We do not jubilate. The next thing poor Orrie knew, he woke up in a haystack with the twenty-one-year-old daughter of a farmhand, a crooked crown of grape leaves, and a ferocious headache.

"When the Apex got wind, he was furious but also frightened. He had just lost one son, and now there was pressure on him to turn out another for violating both the drinking and the decency Edicts."

"What happened?" Malora asks.

"The farmhand whose daughter was compromised was given a herd of cows and a tract of land about as far away from the mountain as you can go and not be in the bush. The Apex also provided a willing Flatlander husband for the daughter."

"And what about you? Did the Apex punish you?"

"By then, I was already in training to be a Peacekeeper. The captain of the Force told the Apex that I was the most promising cadet ever to come along and that it would be a loss to the state to banish me."

"So no one was punished?" Malora says.

"No one was punished," Neal says. "Scandal was averted, but my friendship with Orion suffered."

"Does Orion blame you for what happened?" Malora asks.

"Let me put it this way," Neal says. "I think Orion enjoyed himself rather *too* much that night, and ever since, he lives in fear of enjoying himself too much again. You wouldn't know it to look at him, but locked away behind that smooth

Highlander chest is the heart of a Flatlander. As a result, he is a very unhappy centaur. Unlike his sister, whose capacity for happiness and for enjoying the privileges of her class is seemingly boundless. And speaking of Miss Silvermane's happiness . . ."

Neal flips aside the zebra-skin flap and disappears into the house. He returns momentarily, toting a basket overflowing with big, lush ostrich feathers of black and pink and white. "Won't my lady be pleased?" he says.

CHAPTER 25

The Jubilation Floor

He clasps the crag with crooked hands;
Close to the sun in lonely lands,
Ringed with the azure world, he stands.

The wrinkled sea beneath him crawls;
He watches from his mountain walls,
And like a thunderbolt he falls.

"Letter perfect!" Honus declares, kicking his hooves in delight. "And a perfect little gem of a poem Lord Alfred composed for us all those many eons ago, isn't it?"

Every afternoon, Malora goes hunting with Neal Featherhoof. Every evening, when she returns she recites a short poem she has memorized the night before. She finds the recitations distract Honus from inquiring about whatever studio she claims to have visited that afternoon while she is off with Neal Featherhoof, either hunting game or roasting it over the fire in his yard. Seeking to further distract Honus, but also curious, Malora asks, "What is a *wrinkled sea*?"

Honus's head tilts back, and his eyes take on a faraway look. "The first thing you notice as you approach the sea is the air. One taste of it and you will wonder how you could have lived your entire life without its briny tonic. In the presence of the sea, one is compelled to breathe more deeply. The moisture in the air makes the light soft and hazy, as in a dream. The sound of it is like the wind sifting through the boughs of trees, deeply stirring and quickening to the heart. As for the sea itself . . . imagine the flattest of the Flatlands, extending out to the horizon in all directions. Imagine it now covered in a great watery vastness that is constantly shifting and sloshing, never at rest, for like a great pale cook with her cauldron, the moon is constantly stirring it."

"Malora, *darling*!" Zephele bursts in the door, followed by Theon and Mather and their Twani. "What do you think?"

Zephele has used the pink ostrich feathers Neal gave her to make a mask for her jubilation costume. Even more impressive, she has made a wrap with the rest, black feathers bordered by white. Malora is speechless with envy.

"Theon helped me with the cape and Mather with the mask. Is this not the most splendid jubilation costume you have ever laid eyes on?" Zephele asks. "Oh, I forget, you have never attended a jubilation, but you must take my word for it."

"You will look far more beautiful than any ostrich I have ever met," Malora says.

"I will, won't I?" she says, fluffing the feathers of the

wrap. "Mather, dearest, show Malora the brilliant mask you have made for our feisty little lioness."

Mather holds up a mask, which he has made from what looks like real lion skin. Lining the mask's upturned eyeholes are two rows of tiny sparkling onyx. "Try it on!" he says eagerly.

Malora has never worn a mask before. She fits it on over her face and peers out of the eyeholes at her friends. "Well . . . ?" she asks. It is a bit like peering out from a bush. She growls like a lioness, and the centaurs pretend to cower.

"Perfection!" says Zephele. "Theon, show her the tail. It is not authentic lion skin, but it is very lifelike."

Theon whips out a long tawny tail. "I made it from memory from velvet and stuffed it with down," he says. "Does it seem true to life, Malora the Lion Tamer?"

Malora takes the tail and examines it. It is made from the same soft tan velvet as the wrap Theon made for her. It has a dark tuft at the end made from the feathers of a guinea hen. "Perfection," she says, echoing Zephele.

Theon preens. "I opted for the more subdued black-and-white motif." He holds a striped zebra's mask before his face. "What noise do zebras make?"

"They wheeze," Malora tells him.

Theon's shoulders sag. "Well, I'll *look* handsome, even if I don't sound it. Honus the faun, where is your disguise?"

Honus cocks an eyebrow. "I will come as I am—as the cloven-hoofed polymath—or not come at all!"

"Honus, how very dreary of you!" Zephele says, lowering her mask and pouting. "The whole point of this year's jubilation is to come disguised as a wild animal of the bush."

"Nothing good ever comes of wearing disguises," Honus says.

"Honus, darling," Zephele says, "you are hopeless!"

Malora spends the following afternoon with Zephele. While she would much rather be out hunting with Neal, Zephele has begged her to stay and get ready with her.

"Wait until Neal sees me," Zephele says as she stands before the mirror in Honus's marble convenience in all her fledged splendor.

"But Flatlanders aren't invited," Malora says.

"Oh, but *he'll* be there, guarding the Apex and the Salient, who always attend the Midsummer Jubilation, even though none of them ever sets a hoof onto the floor to jubilate."

"Who or what do the Apex and the Salient need guarding against?" Malora asks.

"Against hooligans, my dear," Zephele says with a careless flip of her feathers.

"What are hooligans?" Malora asks.

"Shamefaced and thoroughly inebriated Flatlanders who sneak in. Poor things, they can't help themselves! They blunder into our midst hoping to snatch at a little of our happiness. You can't really blame them, although they will be turned out for their trouble every time. Neal himself will see to it."

"Neal turns the centaurs out?"

"He doesn't make the rule, but he does enforce it. The Apex rules, the Salient backs him up, and the Peacekeepers— like Neal Featherhoof—carry it out. That's his job," Zephele says, "and I don't imagine it is a very enjoyable job at such times, when he has to turn against his own kind and lead them out into the bush to perish, for surely that's what happens to them. Only the Peacekeepers have the skills to survive. The rest of us, Flatlander and Highlander, are as helpless as . . . as—name me the most helpless creatures in the bush."

Malora thinks for a moment. "Baby rabbits, I guess."

"There you go! We are as helpless as poor baby bush rabbits," Zephele says, adding dramatically, "with the breath of predators hot on our necks."

Orion soon arrives to escort them to the jubilation floor in the upper gallery. He is costumed as a black panther: black velveteen wrap and black velvet mask. He carries a staff that is topped with black ostrich feathers filched from his sister.

"Is the staff part of the costume?" Malora asks.

"Ah! That's right, you have never been to a jubilation before," Orion says. "We perform a traditional jubilation with staffs."

"If you have never seen a centaur jubilate," Honus says, "you have a treat in store."

Malora has been curious all along what jubilating really is, and tonight she will finally find out. It is the first time Malora has ever set foot in the upper gallery of the House of Silvermane. It is open to the air but sheltered beneath a flat roof held up by forty sleek pillars. Zephele assures her that it is quite a plain space, but with its marble fountain of Kheiron in the center and its mosaic of vine leaves running up the forty pillars, it looks anything but plain to Malora. Tonight, new elements have been introduced: boulders and potted plants and what look like entire tree trunks, rolled in from the bush and up the many flights of stairs by teams of

Beltanian draft horses, a sight Malora is sorry to have missed. The tree trunks are long dead, and Malora wonders whether she should reveal to the centaurs that there are big white grubs lurking beneath the bark.

The Twani, draped in white togas in the likeness of putti, walk among the guests carrying trays loaded with delectable treats, both sweet and savory—walnut pood and chocolate tarts, cheese and nut balls, and sweet dates stuffed with salted nuts. Malora is tempted to strip away the bark from the tree trunks, show the centaurs grubs as big as the Apex's finger, and tell them that when game was in short supply in the bush, she was reduced to eating such things. But why would she do that? To shock the centaurs? To play a prank? To make them more thankful for what they have? She concludes that she has been spending too much time with Neal Featherhoof and has begun to think dangerous Flatlander thoughts. She also thinks the Highlanders have spent too much time on the mountain, bottled up like bugs. It has not served them well.

Then she sees something that jolts her out of her thoughts. There are wild animals in the upper gallery, lurking behind the pillars. They are not costumed centaurs but real wild animals standing on pedestals. She walks up to a cheetah about to spring and waves her arms, but the cheetah remains frozen in place. "How do you arrest the animal like this? Has it been given russet bush willow?"

Orion laughs. "It is quite dead! It has been wired into this pose, stuffed, and carefully preserved."

"It is one of the oldest Hands in Mount Kheiron, the taxidermical arts," Zephele adds with a look of distaste. "And if I were Apex, I would fulminate to get the Salient to pass an Edict against it."

Malora listens, transfixed, as Orion explains how the slain animals are gutted, their bones bleached, and their innards replaced with sheep's wool, their eyes by glass orbs. Malora, who has killed more animals than she can count, finds something unaccountably sad about these once-vital creatures who are doomed to pose for the amusement of others, like the poor grizzled centaur in the drawing atelier.

"Better to let the hyenas have at them," she mutters.

But it is not the stuffed wild animals that are the focus of amusement this evening. It is the spectacle of the masked assembly costumed in wraps brightly painted to look like the skins of zebras and giraffes, of leopards and impalas, of lizards and snakes and crocodiles and birds and fish and even, in one case, a giant bright-orange scorpion. The Apex is impossible to miss in an elaborate long-trunked elephant mask and wrap of crinkled gray velvet. The rest of the Salient has followed their leader. They stand in a tight herd at one end of the room, their stuffed trunks swaying as they survey the crowd and confer from behind their masks. The Apex, Orion explains, will later award a prize to the buck and maiden with the best costumes.

"Excuse me while I have a word with Herself," Orion says.

"Good luck," Zephele calls after him. "Mother is very put out with Orion," she explains to Malora. "He is refusing to entertain an offer from the House of Fairmane."

"What sort of offer?" Malora asks.

"Why, for their daughter's hand in matrimony, what

else?" Zephele says. "When the highest-born Highlanders marry, the purpose is to unite two families, Mane to Mane. It concerns the pooling of nubs. Never love. But Orion wants nothing to do with it. Like me, he is a romantic." Zephele stops and peers through the eyeholes of her mask. "And who might *this* be?"

A centaur approaches wearing a leopard mask and draped in leopard skin. He is holding a staff topped with a melon.

"Guess who?" the centaur asks, knocking his staff against the floor in a commanding fashion.

The voice is familiar but Malora can't quite place it. The leopard pushes up his mask. It is Orion and Zephele's cousin, the mask maker himself, Mather Silvermane.

"Do you like my costume?" he asks Malora. "It reminds me very fondly of the garment you wore when we first met you."

Malora remembers with her own fondness the leopard-skin pelt that Zephele sliced off her body and ordered burned. Malora's arrival among the centaurs feels like a lifetime ago. Nowadays, it seems like Malora dons a new piece of finery every day. She bathes twice daily, washes her hair three times a week, reads and writes and does figures, and douses her canopy nightly in a scent custom-made by a highborn centaurean alchemist. Orion was right to say she was wild when she first came among them. But she is not wild now. Even when she steals away to go hunting with Neal, she is no longer a native fighting for her survival, but a visitor touring the bush for her own amusement.

"And look!" Mather says, removing the melon from the top of his staff, revealing a lethal point.

"That can't be . . . !" Malora says.

"It can, indeed! It is the very one you brandished at the lion that attacked West!" Mather says. "I couldn't resist taking it with me and smuggling it past the gatehouse as a souvenir of our bush adventure."

"You had best be careful, Mather Silvermane," Zephele says, quickly taking the melon from him and fitting it back over the point of the staff. "That does not look like a staff to me. It looks decidedly like a weapon."

"Cousin!" Mather says in a tone of mock innocence. "I assure you, it is naught but a humble fence post. It is no more a spear than Malora's sharpened butter knife is a dagger, am I right, Malora?" He winks at her.

"Right, Mather," Malora says uneasily.

"You ladies must excuse me," Mather says with a bow. "I will now employ my acute feral faculties to track down Canda Blackmane. If I succeed in unmasking her, she says she will grant me a jubilation. Wish me luck."

A group of centaur musicians disguised as green-masked bush rabbits strikes up a sprightly tune. Torches blaze from the pillar sconces. Malora and Zephele wander away from the crowd, over to the gallery railing.

Zephele heaves a put-upon sigh. "Oh, Great Hideous Hand of Kheiron, this is every bit as deadly dull as I feared, in spite of the costumes. This ought to be a good place for me to hide," she says, wedging herself between the railing and a pillar. "I warn you, I'm horrendously popular. It's just a matter of time before the bucks find me and line up for their turn. I wonder if Orion should ask you to jubilate. Do you suppose it is the done thing? A centaur jubilating with his pet? I don't imagine my father ever jubilated with Honus. Still, this seems different somehow. Orion is a very able jubilator, but my dear papa, sadly, cuts a shambling figure on the jubilation floor. And imagine if he stepped on one's hoof!"

Malora assures Zephele, "I really don't need to dance— jubilate, I mean."

Zephele breezes on. "Honus is a most courtly jubilator. Better than us centaurs. It's the split hoof, I daresay, which makes him so much lighter on his feet. Not to mention that he only has two of them to coordinate. You have no idea how busy and complicated things get when there are eight hooves vying for position in the same jubilation floor. Honus can teach you—"

"Really, Zephie. I'm fine," Malora insists. "I don't care to jubilate with Orion or Honus or anyone. I am perfectly content just to be here and watch. And Honus is right. This must be the best view in Mount Kheiron."

From where Malora is standing, she can see north, west, and east out to the flats, where big bonfires burn brightly, and even farther beyond, to where the endless pitch-blackness of the bush takes over. "Why are there so many fires out there?"

"It is Midsummer's Eve for them, too," Zephele says. "And they are probably having a good deal more fun at their jubilation than we are at ours, although I don't believe they jubilate exactly, so much as carouse. Lucky them."

A centaur done up in an elaborate kudu-horn headdress and mask peeks around the pillar. "May I have the pleasure of this jubilation, Lady Zephele?"

"You may, Milus Greatmane," Zephele says regally to

the buck. Then to Malora: "So much for hiding . . . and disguises. Are you quite sure you'll be all right?"

Malora waves her away. Zephele and Milus join the other centaur couples on the jubilation floor. The males hold staffs in their right hands. As if by unspoken agreement, they knock the bottoms of the staffs against the floor. The music begins. The bucks remain in place while the maidens dance around them. The maidens make a smart percussive sound as their hooves beat the floor. The bucks respond with a rhythmic tapping of their staffs.

Malora sees Orion being circled by a pretty green-and-red parrot. Malora wonders if the parrot is of the House of Fairmane or someone of Orion's choosing. She sees a flamingo jubilating around a hippo, a gazelle around a buffalo, and a giraffe circled by a black horse with a long black mane. Theon the zebra jubilates with a sleek white cat in a white feathered mask glinting with diamonds. Off to the side, Malora catches sight of Mather the leopard, skulking along a row of pillars.

Now the maidens stand still, and it is the bucks' turn to circle them. The bucks are as graceful in their movements as the maidens, lifting their hooves high and crossing one over the other, sidestepping with elegant ease. Zephele is right: Orion jubilates with grace, and the pretty parrot clearly cannot take her eyes off him.

In the Settlement, the grown-ups danced on warm spring nights in the Hall of the People, after the children were all bedded down. Malora wishes that she sat up and watched them so that she would now know how to dance. As it is, the only dancing she knows how to do is with horses. And since there are no horses present, and no People other than her, she is destined to stand off to the side like this, a *portarum curator,* like Honus the faun. Only, what gate is hers to guard? Then she finds herself wondering whether Lume, the silver-haired man, knows how to dance, and if she will ever dance with him—or was he a figment of the gaffey?

Suddenly, her wandering thoughts are intercepted by a loud shout and a clash of sticks. There is an explosion of violent movement on the jubilation floor. The music comes to a crashing halt. The leopard and the giraffe have crossed staves. The other centaurs pull back to give them room. Mather knocks the staff from the hands of the giraffe and rips off his mask. Even from where Malora stands, she sees that the unmasked centaur has irregular teeth, the sharp incisors nature intended him to have.

He is a Flatlander!

CHAPTER 26

The Midsummer's Brawl

"Interloper!" a male centaur on the dance floor shouts.

"Go back to the flats and dance with your filthy wenches," a maiden says.

"Turn him out!" another maiden joins in.

The rumble of protests rises. The Flatlander struggles to free himself, but Mather has pinned him to a pillar with his staff.

The Highlanders cheer Mather on: "Oust him! Oust him!"

Biceps flexing with effort, the Flatlander thrusts the staff, and Mather, away from him. Mather staggers backward. The centaur maiden costumed as a black horse lets out a shrill scream. Mather regains his footing and rips the melon from the head of his staff. Mather menaces the Flatlander with the sharpened end of the staff.

"No, Mather! Please don't!" Zephele's voice rings out.

Mather raises the staff over his shoulder and hurls it

point-first at the Flatlander's head. The Flatlander dodges, but the point makes contact. Blood blooms from the centaur's bare shoulder.

A moment later, Malora hears the loud clomping of hooves marching up the wide stairway. Neal Featherhoof emerges, carrying a real spear, with its steel point glinting in the torchlight. He is dressed in the red-and-white wrap of the Peacekeepers, with a gold band around his neck that reminds Malora of the collars around Pel and Mel. Behind him march two more centaurs, dressed the same and also holding spears.

Neal barks an order, and the two Peacekeepers spring into action. They latch on to the Flatlander's arms and drag him down the stairs, protesting.

"It's not fair!" His voice carries up the stairwell. "I came here unarmed! I made a harmless wager with my mates that I couldn't break in to the jubilation, and I did it easy!"

"He won the wager, but the price will be dearer than he bargained for," Mather says to the crowd as he retrieves his staff with its bloodied point.

Neal steps up to Mather and snatches the staff from his grip. Mather cries out in pain and staggers backward, rubbing his arm. The crowd grumbles. Neal darts a questioning look at the Apex. The Apex wags his head. Neal's jaw flexes. Malora can tell he is working to keep his anger under control. He cocks the staff over his shoulder, along with his spear, and sweeps down the stairs after the others.

Malora has trouble reconciling this cold and menacing soldier with the relaxed and charming rascal with whom she has passed so much time in the bush.

Mather stands next to the centaur maiden who must be Canda Blackmane. Who else can she be, disguised as a black horse? She peels off the mask, and the crowd gasps. Her tears have caused the dye to run all over her face and it is streaked with black, but Malora recognizes her from the vision she had so long ago in Mather's tent, after smelling from his scent vial.

Zephele approaches her and hands her a flowered cloth. It will smell of wild jasmine, Malora thinks.

"Mather Silvermane, how *could* you?" Canda sobs.

Mather replies, "Canda, how could I *not*? A Flatlander dancing with a Highlander maiden! This cannot be tolerated! Isn't that so?" he says, looking to the other centaurs.

They turn away from him, talking among themselves. The din of their gossip rises.

The Apex steps to the fountain, his heavy hooves clomping loudly. The centaurs scurry before him. The crowd falls silent. The Apex's voice, over the sound of the trickling fountain, sounds louder even than the crowd at its zenith. "This jubilation is over! There will be no prizes. You have displeased me mightily. Now leave here, all of you. Go home and speak no more of this!"

Malora finds Honus at her elbow. "Come with me," he whispers, "down the Twanian staircase."

Malora follows him down a torch-lit set of narrow, winding stairs only a two-legger could negotiate.

Honus says as he trips down the stairs, "A great philosopher and social critic once said, 'Beware of all enterprises that require new clothes.' I could not agree more."

Malora doesn't answer. She is struck dumb by what she has seen. She is also exhausted and feels a sense of having been poisoned by the ill will in the air.

When they get back to Honus's rooms, Malora begs his leave and retires to her bedchamber without a bath, leaving her lion costume in a heap on the floor and crawling naked between the covers. She doesn't even shake Breath of the Bush on the canopy, and yet the fabric must be saturated because it sends her, the way it always does, to where Sky waits for her.

She rides Sky across the dreamscape of the bush, letting the cold night air wash the evening's turmoil from her head. Suddenly, they come upon a pride of lions. A male—big and vital—and two hefty females crouch on the path just ahead. Cubs coil and whine hungrily. Sky rears. The lions roar and swipe at his legs with their claws. Malora hangs on to Sky's mane and digs her heels into the stallion's ribs.

"Jump, Sky. Jump!" she shouts in his ear. Sky circles back around and launches himself into the air, soaring over the heads of the lions, who leap and snarl in frustration. Malora wakes up with her hair sweat-damp and her heart beating wildly in her chest.

Lessons that morning are a solemn and rote affair. Zephele's face is pale and stony. "I encountered Neal this morning outside the Hall of Mirrors," she says during a study break. "He told me the Flatlanders say Gastin, the scoundrel Flatlander who interloped, is to be turned out. I blame it all on that upstart Canda Blackmane. She must have known she was dancing with a Flatlander. How could she not?"

"He wore a mask," Malora says.

"The Blackmanes always were a bad lot," Zephele says.

"But it gets worse. They say that if Gastin is turned out, then poor Mather must be turned out as well. Have you ever heard of anything so absurd?"

"Mather did violate the Edicts against squaring off and carrying weapons," Malora points out glumly.

Zephele scowls at Malora. "Whose side are you on? You sound like a Flatlander. Neal says the Flatlanders are out for Mather's blood. They say if the Salient rules in favor of Mather, the Flatlanders will most likely stage an outrage."

Malora doesn't like the sound of this. "What is an outrage?"

Zephele gnaws at her lip. "It is squaring off multiplied, Flatlander against Highlander. Not quite war, but hardly peace. It has never happened in modern times, but Papa is beside himself with worry that an outrage will break out under his rule. For years, he has worried about the unrest. I thought he was just being an old grumble guts. I didn't realize until today how deeply disgruntled the Flatlanders are."

Malora wants to say that if Zephele had even once come down off the mountain and walked among the townships, she would have gotten a very clear picture of the Flatlanders' discontent. But saying this, she knows, would only make matters worse.

"Ladies, this speculation will only add to your distress. In times such as this, it is best to keep busy." Honus issues them both their assignments. "I must attend a special assembly of the Salient. The Apex needs me. I will trust you to work independently."

"What advice will you give him?" Zephele asks as she trots behind him to the door.

"I will advise him that he turn both out," Honus says without hesitation.

Zephele cries out and claps her hands over her mouth. "No! Honus, please, tell me you won't."

"I am afraid it is the only way to keep the peace."

"Poor, poor Mather!" Zephele bursts into tears. "His doom is sealed!"

"Where does Mather live?" Malora asks as soon as Honus is gone.

"Four doors down the Mane Way to the south. Why do you ask?" Zephele says, blowing her nose hard on a lacy cloth.

"I must go to him and give him some advice on how to survive in the bush. I can tell him how to make weapons and snares, what plants are good for snakebite, which berries—"

But Zephele shakes her head vehemently. "No, no, no, no! You will not. You must not, Malora, especially if what Honus says comes to pass. No one is permitted to help a centaur who is about to be turned out. It is tantamount to treason. I won't let you risk it, because if you are turned out"—her eyes well up again—"Orion and I will be undone, so strong has our attachment to you grown."

It is as if a whole world of woe, like a great noxious cloud, has settled on top of Mount Kheiron and the surrounding Flatlands. Above the cloud, the sun might be shining, but everything Malora sees is choking in a fog of grief.

After some time has passed, Orion arrives, trailing West, bearing the news that the Flatlander has been banished but the Salient is still in conference over the fate of Mather. Orion's eyes are drained of color, nearly gray. Even West looks aggrieved. He curls up in a corner and goes immediately to sleep. Malora, Orion, and Zephele lean on the stone parapet of the terrace and stare out over the rooftops. They can hear the chanting of the Flatlanders gathered outside the walls of the city, calling for Mather's banishment. Of all the fearsome sounds Malora has ever heard in the bush—jackals barking, hyenas yelping, wildcats snarling, elephants trumpeting, even the dreaded and hateful Leatherwings humming—this is somehow more frightening. It is the sound of an angry crowd of centaurs who will settle for nothing less than the death of Mather Silvermane.

It is dark by the time Honus returns with the news that both Gastin and Mather are to be turned out this very night—Mather to the north, and Gastin to the south. Zephele throws herself into Orion's arms.

"In the dark, too. How unspeakably cruel!" she cries. "Is anything as dark as the bush at night?"

Malora wants to say that the bush is not dark. It is filled with light. There is the moon. And even when the moon is down, there are the stars twinkling like candles in the canopies of the trees. And then there are the animals' eyes: green and yellow and blue and violet, like jewels swirling in the darkness. But she keeps her thoughts to herself.

"It is harsh, Sister, no matter day or night," Orion says.

"My poor, dear, foolish, brave cousin!" Zephele sobs. "How could the Apex let this happen to his own flesh and blood?"

"It is because it is the Apex's flesh and blood that he must," Honus says quietly. "And do not think this doesn't pain him. Medon is with Mather's parents, his own brother, at this very moment, delivering the sorry news."

Orion pats his sister's back. "Kheiron give him the strength to break the news gently. This is a very sad state of affairs all around."

"If Neal is charged with turning Mather out, I shall never speak to that Flatlander ever, ever again!" Zephele says with sudden savagery, pounding her fist against Orion's chest.

"Easy now, Sister," Orion says, catching her fist and enfolding it gently in his hand. "It's not Featherhoof's judgment, nor is any of this his fault."

A heavy weight lies on Malora's chest, and she has to clear her throat to speak. "You're right, Orion. It's not Neal's fault. But it is mine."

Honus, Zephele, and Orion all turn to stare at her in surprise. Malora feels the tears begin to fall as she says in a choked voice, "It is all my fault. If I hadn't used that sharpened fence post to menace the lion, Mather would never have brought it back with him to Mount Kheiron. Because he had that post, he violated the Edicts."

Zephele puts a hand to her mouth to smother a cry. "Oh, dear Hands! Can matters get any worse?"

No one disagrees with Malora. No one thinks to remind her that she saved West's life with that post. No one stops her when she turns and goes to her bedchamber. She lies down and places the pillow over her head so no one will hear her crying. There is no Max, no horse of her heart, to lay his long head over her chest and comfort her. There are no boys and girls to surround her with their warmth. No Thora, no Jayke, no Aron, no Sky. She feels utterly alone. In all the world, there is only her. She wants to run far from this place, but wherever she goes, it will be the same. Death will follow her all her days.

Malora weeps until she is exhausted, and then she falls into a fitful sleep. Once again, she is on Sky's back galloping northward, away from Mount Kheiron. Sky keeps trying to turn around and return to the south, to Mount Kheiron, but Malora won't let him. Instead, she urges him forward.

"Go! Go! Go! Get me away from this place!" she cries.

"You must return," he tells her, tossing his mane and pawing the ground with his hooves. "You are needed."

"I am *not* needed. I bring only grief to those I love."

"If you stay, you will bring victory to one and all," he tells her.

Finally, she is too tired to go on arguing with Sky. She lies down along his neck, buries her face in his mane, and feels him shifting beneath her, turning around to take her back to Mount Kheiron.

Neal Featherhoof bursts through the door, his chest heaving, sweat darkening his golden flanks.

Malora and Honus are in the big room, reviewing her sums side by side at the scrivening table. It has been a week since the banishment, and as long since Malora has seen Neal. She has stopped stealing away to go hunting with him. Neal thinks they should suspend their routine until the mood in Mount Kheiron is less volatile. If a Flatlander happens to see her with a weapon and reports it to the Apex, who knows what would happen?

"You're needed down at the stable!" Neal says.

Malora looks to Honus, who says, "Waste no time! Go! Go! Go!"

Zephele trots in from the terrace, where she has been reading. "What now?" she asks in a voice filled with dread.

"It's one of the Furies," Neal says. "Gift, it seems, is out of his depth and has been from the very start. Come with me, Malora. I know a shortcut."

She follows Neal at a run, out the door, along the hall, and down the service-entrance stairs. They leap across the road and clamber over the wall where she once snared squirrels. Then they go charging down through the scrub and through a series of backyards and plazas and courtyards. Down and down they go, bisecting the ring roads, sending centaurs and Twani scattering before them, their expressions stunned. Running is, as Zephele says, not the *done thing*.

"What happened?" Malora asks breathlessly as they slip and slide down the mountain.

"One of the horses, Shadow, is hitched to a rig, and she ran off without a driver. She is whipping the cart this way and that behind her, and the wranglers fear she will snag it on something and hurt herself or someone else."

"What were you doing at the stable?" Malora asks.

"I was at the gate when Shadow came charging past. I saw the blue and white on the rig, so I went to the stable and learned the rest. There's more I need to tell you before we arrive on the scene."

Malora's guts churn. This scene he is talking about is where she is needed, and has been needed for a week. This is where Sky was telling her to go in the dream, and yet she did nothing about it. She didn't understand. No wonder Sky stopped coming to her in her dreams, no matter how much Breath of the Bush she lavished on the canopy.

Neal stops and grabs her arm. His copper eyes hold hers. "Gift's two oldest hands were trampled to death last week by one of the stallions," he says.

Malora sighs and shuts her eyes. "Has Gift kept the mares and the stallions separated? I just know he has," she says through gritted teeth.

"He has kept them in the stalls in the cave," Neal says grimly. "I think he's been afraid to let them loose."

"That was foolish. I told him not to keep them apart for too long. The mares have a calming effect on the stallions. I wish Gift had listened to me."

"Gift is a fraud," Neal says.

"But the Apex lured Gift away from Anders Thunderheart's racing stable. He even pays him nubs to do this job, and Twani are never paid. Do you mean Gift lied to the Apex about his skills?"

"It was a little joke Anders played on the Apex. He made sure to boast about Gift after the last race so that Medon would lure Gift away. Oh, Anders was thoroughly glad to see the last of that Twan," Neal says. "Anders told me Gift was fine with broke horses, but not so good with green. No patience. None at all."

"The boys and girls aren't green! They are broke!"

"Broke to you, perhaps, but apparently not to Gift. I think he's tried his best, but the Furies are more than he can handle. He's afraid. What's worse, he's refusing to admit his fear to anyone, least of all the Apex."

"That would only make it worse," she says, fretting.

"There's nothing that sets a horse off more surely than a lying, two-faced trainer. This is my fault. I should never have left them in the hands of fools."

Human and centaur fall silent, saving their breath for the steepest part of the descent, between the lowermost ring road and the mountain's boulder-strewn base. They pick their way over the rocks and down to the base path that follows the foot of the mountain to the stable. Dust clogs the air. Malora peers down at the ground and makes out a scrambled pattern of hoof and wheel marks in the dust. "She's been past here four times. She's looking for a way out."

"The only way out is through the main gate," Neal says. "And I've instructed the guard to bring down the gate."

The Silvermane Stable is in an uproar when they get there. Dust-covered Twani are scurrying in all directions, and horses are pounding their stalls and screaming to the mare who has cut loose and run. The screams are as intelligible to Malora as the prints in the dirt: "Run away, Shadow! Run away! Even if we can't. Run to freedom while you can!"

Malora has a picture in her mind of Shadow running, looking for a way out. It is just a matter of time before the poor distraught creature comes galloping this way, and Malora will be ready for her. She reaches back and quickly frees her horse tail from the braid. When the mare does return, Malora wants her familiar silhouette to be the first thing she sees. Inside the cave, the horses' screams rise to a higher pitch, telling Malora that the mare is closing in again.

A cloud of dust appears from around the side of the mountain, resolving itself into a horse and rig coming on at high speed. Malora steps directly into the mare's path. Legs bent slightly at the knee and arms hanging limply at her sides, she takes as deep a breath as the dusty air will allow and attempts to present the most friendly, unthreatening sight this horse has seen in weeks. Fear of being trampled courses through her, and she tries to ground that fear, sending it down through her body, out through her feet, and into the dirt beneath her. The mare is scared out of her mind. There is no guarantee that she will not run over Malora and pound her into paste. But Malora will have to take that chance.

She whispers over and over again, "Please stop. I'm sorry. Please stop. I'm sorry. Please stop."

As the horse bears down upon her, Malora smells sweat and the heat of the rig's wheels. Against every impulse, she keeps her eyes wide open and a big, warm, welcoming smile on her face.

CHAPTER 27

The Furies Are Unleashed!

Less than half a horse's length from where Malora stands, the mare digs in her hooves and grinds to a halt. The rig swings up behind her and slams down hard in the dirt, bouncing. For a long time, horse and human stand in the settling dust.

In the cave, the horses have fallen silent. The mare, her chest and stomach heaving, wheezes. Malora wheezes a little herself, from the closeness of her brush with annihilation and from the dust. As the dust begins to settle, they are breathing more calmly and breathing together. Malora experiments and takes a big breath, letting it out through her fluttering lips. The horse, seconds later, does the same. Malora stomps her feet, and the mare does the same, beginning to throw off the burden of madness. After a moment, the horse starts smacking her lips.

Malora waits a beat. "Shadow," she whispers. "Look at you."

The mare's ears twitch and swivel toward her.

"Why did you want to go and scare everybody like that? Look at me. You even scared me." Slowly, Malora raises her hand. The horse's ears flick backward, then forward again. But Malora doesn't dare touch the horse for fear of setting her off again. Instead, she smooths the air *around* the horse. "I wish you'd let me take all this gear off you. These fools don't understand that this rig is like a predator chasing after you. You're running to get away from it, aren't you? But it just keeps chasing you. Well, I'm here now. You don't have to run anymore, because I'm going to help you. Do you hear me?"

The mare grunts as if, at last, here is someone who understands her. "I can take this harness and tack off you, if you'll let me. Will you let me?" Malora asks. For a long time, she continues to stroke the air around the horse, getting an idea of where the buckles and ties are. When she has finished patiently stroking the whole horse in this way several times over, she returns to Shadow's head and says, "There, now. What do you think, girl? Can we figure out how to get this harness and rig off you?"

Shadow lets out a high whinny. Inside the stables, the other horses whinny. Back and forth, they confer. At last, the mare lowers her head and bobs it.

"You heard them, didn't you? They all think you should let me take this harness off you. You've dragged it around behind you for so long. You must be very tired of being chased by it. I promise, when I get it off you, no one's ever going to strap you into it again."

Shadow shakes out her mane with relief, and Malora sees in this gesture the permission she has been seeking. Slowly, she reaches up to the buckle beneath Shadow's chin and unfastens it. Keeping her breath even and her hands steady, she sets to work, and it doesn't take her very long to unfasten the elaborate series of buckles and straps that attaches Shadow to the rig. As she works, Malora discovers where the straps have chafed, across Shadow's chest and along her sides. Seeing these marks makes Malora simmer with anger, but she works to breathe that anger away because Shadow doesn't need to feel it right now. Shadow needs to feel relief from all stress, and nothing else.

Out of the corner of her eye, she sees Gift approaching with a lead halter and rope. "Get away from us!" Malora hisses.

"She'll only take off and run away again."

"And why shouldn't she? You and your crew have given her little reason to stay."

Shadow's ears go back at the sight of Gift. Her forelegs lift in a half rear, and she whirls around and runs off toward the city wall.

"Thanks, Gift," Malora says bitterly.

"That's all right. I should be able to catch her now without the rig," Gift says, going toward Shadow.

"You thickheaded pussemboo!" Malora says. "Haven't you had enough chasing around for one day? Let the horse be. She needs to relax and decide whether she wants to come back."

Gift throws up his hands in disgust, spooking the horse yet again. He wheels around and stalks off.

Malora returns to petting Shadow and does so for a long time, until she senses that the mare's nervousness has given way to exhaustion. Then Malora steps back and waits. Finally, Shadow folds her front legs, goes down onto the ground, and rolls on her back in the dust.

Once she is satisfied that the mare is recovering, Malora looks for Gift. She finds him mending a smashed fence rail. "Tell me what's been going on," she says in a voice of deadly calm.

"We've made some good progress. We've broken four of them to harness so far, Cloud, Raven, Ember, and Coal. But they won't run. They just stand there in the rig and don't move forward on the track. Sometimes they even move backward. But never forward, no matter how hard we whip them."

Malora grinds her teeth. "Did the Apex authorize you to whip my horses?"

Gift rubs his face. "Look, miss. They've killed two of my best wranglers and crippled a third! The Apex wants results, and the race is two months away. Then last week, we had an accident."

"What kind of an accident?"

"Fancy broke her back."

She speaks over the sudden roaring in her ears. "How did Fancy break her back?"

"She was trying to get out of this practice ring here," he says, indicating the rail he is mending. "She leapt high, tangled her forelegs, and fell backward onto the seat of a rig. You'd have thought the entire herd had broken its back from the way they all carried on. In the hubbub, Stormy, Ivory, and Thunder ran off. There's a low point in the wall farther along toward the north. Someone from the Fairmane Stable around the bend saw them leaping over it. That's the last we saw of them."

Tears sting Malora's eyes. She has been living the Highlander life up on the Mane Way, and down here her horses have been suffering at the hands of this incompetent bully.

"After we put Fancy down, the herd wouldn't do anything for us. They just screamed and battered the sides of their stalls. For three days, all we did was listen to them carry on. Last night, they finally settled down, and today was the first day we dared to pick up the training."

Malora nods slowly, absorbing this information, as painful as it is to hear. She feels herself reaching a decision. "That's it, then," she says, more to herself than to him. She looks around. Neal is nowhere in sight. She wonders where he has gone but doesn't give it more than a moment's thought. She turns and marches toward the cave.

Gift scrambles after her. "What are you going to do?" he asks nervously.

"I'm taking my horses out of this place." Malora has a good mind to take all the horses, even the ones that aren't hers, but decides against it. It will take her weeks to calm the Furies, and they will need her full attention.

She stands in the entrance to the cave and calls out, "Lightning!"

A loud whinny pierces the charged silence. Lightning lifts her head above the stalls. The rest of the horses, hearing Malora's voice, start snorting and whinnying and calling out to her. They make a racket, all speaking at once, as if to say:

"What about me?"

"Where have you been?"

"Have you missed me most of all?"

"You have some nerve!"

"I know, I know, I know all about it!" Malora says as she makes her way down the aisle to Lightning's box. She unfastens the latch and steps inside. Lightning stands with her nose buried in the back corner, her back to Malora, tail switching.

"I don't blame you for being mad at me," Malora says in a soft, low voice. "I'm furious with myself." She moves farther into the stall, positioning herself so that Lightning can, if she wishes, bash in her skull with one swift strike of her hoof.

"I know you're mad at me, and if you want to kick me simple like Aron, go ahead. I deserve it. I trusted these fools, and they betrayed me. Give me your best kick, but if you do, know that you're on your own. Spare me, and I'll help you."

Lightning swings her head around and rolls her eyes at Malora, as if to say, "Really? Do you really mean it? Or is this just another one of your two-legged tricks?"

"I know I left you here, but now I'm getting you out. This place isn't worth the fancy fresh oats and molasses, is it, girl? Give us bush grass and freedom any day, right?"

Lightning grunts and turns all the way around. Malora holds out her arms, and Lightning walks over and buries her head in Malora's embrace. Malora strokes her head and neck and mane. Lightning blows out gustily. Malora examines Lightning's hide and is relieved to see no outward signs of abuse. "They haven't put you in harness, have they, girl?"

Lightning snorts as if to say, "The cowardly fools didn't even try."

"Okay, girl, let's go and free the others." Malora turns

around, and Lightning follows her as they go to the other stalls. One by one, Max, Star, Coal, Raven, Cloud, Charcoal, and Ember come out of their stalls and follow Malora as she looks for the others. In the tradition of her clever sire, Lightning unfastens the remaining stalls with her teeth. Out come Butte, Light Rain, Posy, Flame, and Beast. She leads them out of the cave. Outside, she steps onto the rim of a stone trough, and Lightning comes trotting up alongside her. Malora swings her leg over Lightning's back and settles in.

This is what she has been missing. All this time, she has been working with only half a heart. The Breath of the Bush dreams may have tided her over, but they haven't made her complete. Now Malora is whole again. She takes a deep breath, grabs a fistful of wiry mane, and urges Lightning forward with a squeeze of her thighs. Shadow lifts her head from the grass she has been cropping and merges with the herd as it comes abreast of her. Malora leads the horses down the mountain path toward the gates of Mount Kheiron.

Malora almost doesn't recognize the Apex, standing before the Gate of Kheiron. It isn't that he looks any smaller or less formidable, for the sheer bulk of his body virtually blocks her exit. It is his expression that has changed. If Malora didn't know better, she would swear that he looked sheepish. Flanking the Apex and also looking somewhat abashed are Orion and Neal.

Malora calls down to them, "I'm taking the boys and girls and leaving, and you can't stop us."

"True enough," the Apex says, stepping forward. "We cannot stop you from leaving. But I was hoping that you might first hear me out. After you have done so, if you still want to leave, then you and the Furies may go. I will not stand in your way."

Malora sets her jaw. What can he possibly have to say to her? Four horses are gone—one dead from a broken back, and the other three, without the protection of a herd, will surely perish in the bush. Who else but the Apex is responsible?

"Give him a chance," Orion says. "Please, Malora, for my sake, if not for his."

"Come on, Pet . . . ," Neal Featherhoof says coaxingly.

Malora feels her resolve faltering. "Very well," she says, drawing a leg across Lightning's withers. "I'm listening."

The Apex smiles. "I would be much obliged if you would alight from that splendid animal long enough to speak to me face to face and in private."

Malora considers his request. For all she knows, this is a ruse to separate her from the herd. But Orion and Neal would never participate in such a trick, and she continues to read the Apex's air as being humble. "Very well," she says. She slips off Lightning's back and, lifting one finger, says, "Stay here, girl. Don't worry. I'll be right back."

Lightning snorts as if she thinks Malora a fool for tempting fate. Nevertheless, the mare stays put, like the rest of the herd.

The Apex draws Malora off to the side. "First of all," he says, and even in an undertone his voice bores into her, "I apologize for the appalling behavior of my wrangler in chief, Gift."

"He doesn't deserve the title," Malora says.

"He doesn't," the Apex agrees. "You must believe that his daily reports to me indicated nothing of the difficulties he was encountering with the Furies."

"You mean he lied to *you*?" Malora says, laughing shortly. "Couldn't you see that? What sort of leader are you if you can't even tell when one of your subjects is lying to you?"

The Apex smiles sadly. "Imperfect, at best. I chose to believe Gift, and in this respect, I am as guilty as he is. I was so intent on winning the Golden Horse—"

"That you didn't care how many of my horses you killed, maimed, or drove off to the bush in the process?" Malora finishes for him, her face burning.

The Apex pounds his breast with a clenched fist and bellows, "*Never!* Had I known what was really going on down here, I would have called you in long ago!"

"And we still would have wound up where we are right now, with me on my way out of here," Malora says defiantly.

"And so," says the Apex in a quiet voice, turning up both hands, "I am asking you to stay and help me remedy my mistake."

Malora eyes him suspiciously. "How?"

"I ask you, Malora Ironbound, leader of this herd, to train your best Fury to win the Golden Horse for the House of Silvermane."

"What?" Malora says so sharply that the horses call out to her. She hushes them with an absent wave of her arm. "Explain this plan of yours to me," she says.

"I'd like *you* to take over as wrangler in chief. Who better to fill the position?"

"You mean," she says slowly, "that I would be able to see the horses and work with them every day?"

"You would have to. With less than two months until Founders' Day, there is no time to lose," he says.

Wildly hopeful thoughts stampede through Malora's brain. She allows the dust to settle before she dares speak. "And what would I get in return, if I were to help you win this Golden Horse?"

The Apex nods, reading her easily. "You would be granted the Hand of your choosing, for a start."

"Ironwork?" Malora asks, her heart quickening.

"Certainly not *needlework*," the Apex says with a pleased chuckle.

"Blacksmithing!" Malora exclaims. "And what else? What else would I get if I were to help you?"

"For what it is worth, you would have my everlasting gratitude."

Malora suspects that to be in the Apex's debt is worth a pretty nub in the state of Kheiron. But as far as she is concerned, the other benefits far outweigh even this: to see her horses every day, to learn her Hand as a blacksmith, and to have, in addition to these privileges, the pleasure of the company of her friends. To be able to go on living here amid the comforting hubbub of horses *and* interesting, articulate, funny friends—surely, this was a favorable deal for her. Thora's voice says in her ear, "You didn't really want to return to the bush, did you?"

"All right. I will do it," she says.

CHAPTER 28

Wrangler in Chief

The Apex places his right hand over his heart, then raises it, palm out toward her. His hand is huge and calloused, and she sees for the first time that an enormous staring eye is tattooed into the palm in bold red and black ink. Malora has seen the centaurs on the mountain raise their palms to one another by way of greeting, but no centaurs, apart from Orion when they first met, have ever raised their palm to her. Hesitantly, she places her right hand over her heart, then lifts it, palm out, toward him.

"Tell me what you need, and it shall be yours," he says, lowering his hand.

Malora, having dutifully mirrored his action, gives his question some thought. "Well, first off, you must get rid of Gift. The horses hate him, and he doesn't deserve to shovel their—"

"This goes without saying." The Apex cuts short her tirade.

Malora continues, "I will speak to the other wranglers and see if any of them is worth keeping, but I doubt it. The horses will be soured on them. And so I will need a fresh batch of Twani to assist me. I know they will be thinking that it is hazardous duty, but with me around, it will be much less so. And apart from the Twanian rig driver I will be training, I will do most of the work. I would like to have West to start with."

The Apex looks surprised. "Orion's Twan?"

Malora nods. "He is a good little man. And in the bush, he treated my horses with kindness. He also owes his life to me and I think would like a chance to repay me. He will help me select a group of trustworthy Twani for my staff."

"Granted. What else?" the Apex asks.

"I will not use a whip," she says. "I will *introduce* a whip into the training, but only to accustom the horses to its sound. I will not use it on their flesh to motivate them to go faster. They will go faster because I cue them to go faster and because we have agreed that going faster is the right thing to do."

"You are the wrangler in chief," the Apex says. "I leave you fully in charge."

"And we can't stay in this cave you call a stable."

The Apex's eyebrows fly up. "But it is the most magnificent facility in all of Kheiron!"

"Terrible things happened to my horses in this magnificent facility, and I need to get them away from here to a place with no unpleasant associations."

"But—but it will take weeks to build a new stable," the Apex sputters.

Malora frowns. "We need no stable," she says. "Horses are meant to be outside. Find me some flat land with lots of green grass and we will be happy. Also, I'll need to visit the track where this race takes place."

"The Hippodrome? I will ask the Grand Provost if this is permitted," the Apex says.

Malora snorts. "The one who holds out his hand and looks the other way while whips are used? That's the least he can do, and that is all I will need."

The Apex looks bathed in relief. "Thank you, Malora Ironbound."

Malora bites back a smile and dares to say, "You are welcome, Medon Silvermane."

She watches as the Apex, flanked by Neal and Orion, clomps up a wooden ramp onto a flatbed lorry with a rail draped with the Silvermane colors. Neal pulls up the ramp and winks at Malora, then gives the signal to the driver to start the long haul up to the Mane Way. Pulling the lorry are a team of four Beltanian draft horses, looking, with their gray coats and manes, like half brothers to the Apex. The Apex, his left hand clutching the rail, places his right hand over his heart, then raises it to the crowd that has gathered at the gate. The Highlander centaurs respond in kind. The Flatlanders do not. When Neal shoots them a fierce look, they comply. Malora glances at the flag of Kheiron, flapping in the wind, with the Ever-Watchful Eye on it. She stares down at the palm of her right hand and then lifts it, along with the centaurs, and keeps it there until the lorry has disappeared into the shadows.

*　*　*

The Apex grants Malora a generous swath of land abutting the Silvermane Vineyard to the north of Mount Kheiron, where a small spring-fed lake bubbles up from the ground and makes the grass green and juicy. There is room for the boys and girls to run around and kick up their heels. Malora's change of status has a strangely buoying effect on the flagging spirits of the House of Silvermane. Despair over Mather's banishment gives way to a resurgence of hope and optimism.

The Flatlanders, on the other hand, greet the news with suspicion and gloom. It is not that they believe Malora is capable of bringing victory to the Silvermane Stable, but they dislike the fact of an Otherian trainer entering the competition. Malora is inured by now to the disdain of centaurs, whether Highland or Flat. Undaunted, she asks West and the Twanian wranglers to help her construct a big square paddock divided into fours.

Malora divides the herd into compatible groups of four and five, with the stallions separated from the mares. Mares, Malora knows, have a tendency to dominate and sometimes even terrorize the males. Let them visit over the fence line. If one of the mares should come into season, Malora will give the lucky stallion of the *mare's* choosing an opportunity to expend his passion in a private pen.

Malora chooses three horses to train for the race. Two of them, Butte and Light Rain, are merely backups because there is, as far as she is concerned, only one horse who can win the Golden Horse—the horse of her heart, Max. When

Malora tells Orion and West that Max is the chosen one, they look at her as if she has taken leave of her senses.

"You are joking!" West blurts out.

"That pitiful bag of bones?" Orion sputters.

Malora deals them both a sharp look.

"I'm sorry," Orion says, "but surely there are more fit candidates among the remaining Furies than this sad, sorry specimen of horseflesh."

True, Max is far from being a picture-perfect horse, especially by Furies standards. Whenever Max went missing out in the bush, Malora could always find him by following the trail of buzzing flies. More flies congregate on Max's mangy, scar-pocked hide than on any other horse in the herd. The poor fellow always seems too tired and dispirited to even twitch them away, much less swat at them with his sparse and graying tail. She has no idea how old Max is, but his teeth tell her he is twenty if he is a day. Raw-boned and swaybacked, with a long, narrow head and big, bloodshot brown eyes, Max doesn't give the impression of robust good health. His rib cage shows and his hip bones jut and he doesn't always smell very healthy. But all of this is an illusion.

"Max," she explains to Orion and West, "was the horse I always rode when we were passing through elephant country. If an elephant bull charged, I knew Max could outrun him without breaking a sweat."

"Is that a fact?" West says, clearly skeptical.

"Max doesn't just have the legs for running, he has the *heart* for it. Max will enjoy this," Malora insists.

Malora has the Twani construct a large circular pen. She wants the fencing high enough to create a work space, but not so high that horses who want to can't jump it without hurting themselves. She wants no more horses breaking their backs for the Golden Horse.

Years ago in the Settlement, she watched Jayke train horses to pull wagons, so she has some idea of how to go about it, even though she has never done it herself. "It's a question of easing them into it," Malora explains to West as she works with Max in the ring on the first day of training. "First, we get him used to the bit, then to the weight of the carriage harness. We will do this gradually. Not all at once. That was the mistake Gift made. Gift was impatient. You have to be patient with horses and not rush them into things. Rushing makes them feel threatened, and you might as well be a predator for all they will trust you. These horses have never had a bit in their mouths or a harness or saddle on their backs. I rode Sky with a bit and saddle, but these horses know nothing of such things. It will take time for them to get used to tack."

Malora has an audience lined up along the rail, assorted curious Flatlanders, along with Orion, Zephele, and Honus, who has suspended their lessons until after the race. Malora plans to work most days with Max, since Max is where her hopes lie. But she will also work with Butte and Light Rain, and West will always be on hand, observing and learning. West knows that whichever horse winds up running the race, he is going to be the driver. West isn't especially happy with this plan.

"Not meaning to shirk my duty, boss, but why can't *you* drive the rig?" West asks.

Honus answers for her. "Because Twani are the rig drivers.

It would cause an outrage right now for an Otherian to participate in the race. The Apex doesn't want to call any more attention to his stable."

Malora takes the bit in hand.

This time, it is Zephele who speaks up. "Excuse me, Malora, my darling dearest. I don't mean to question your methods, which I am sure are wisdom itself, but why do you need a bit at all? It seems needlessly cruel."

"The bit is not an instrument of torture. It is a means of communication, from the driver's hands through the reins to the horse's head through the bit. But the communication should be a gentle whisper and not a shout. Visit the Thunderheart Stable and you'll see the bit being used to scream at those horses. Anders's Twanian wranglers pull and saw away at those Athabanshees' mouths. The horses run fast because pain, from the bit and the whip, prompts them to. But these horses here are going to run because we have asked them nicely and because they like nothing better than running. Just the way Orion asks you nicely to do things, West, instead of thumping you hard on the head to get your attention, like I've seen some centaurs doing to their Twani."

"Orion is a prince among centaurs," West says.

"West, *really*," Orion says, blushing modestly.

Malora smiles. "Yes, well, Orion would make an excellent horse trainer. He is gentle but firm, which is the way you have to be with horses. Out in the bush, horses are prey. They travel in herds for protection, and they look to their leader to tell them when to run and where to go. When you have the reins in your hand, you become the leader of a herd of two, consisting of you and the horse. If you don't tell your horse what to do, he will take on the role of leader himself and make you follow. And believe me, you don't want to be riding in the rig when the horse is in charge."

West shivers and nods. "Got it, boss."

Max stands in the center of the ring, his nose down in the dust, flies buzzing around him, looking like the last thing in the world he wants is to be in charge.

"He's so still and lifeless," Zephele says with a moan of sympathy. "Are you sure the poor dear is up to this task?"

"Horses *like* to stand still. They do it endlessly. It's the rest of us who fuss and fiddle."

Malora approaches Max with the harness in her hand. "Try to approach a horse from the side," she advises West. "Like most prey, their eyes are set into the sides of their head. When you're this close, they can't see you head on."

Max stirs as she approaches. He rolls his eye toward the harness with bleary interest.

"If you have something in your hand, don't try to hide it from a horse. Don't try to hide anything from a horse, especially your feelings. Lying confuses horses, and sometimes it even makes them angry . . . although I don't think Max could ever be angry with me, could you, old fellow?"

Max pokes his nose into the harness, sniffing it.

"If you wear this, Maxie, old boy, you'll win the Golden Horse and everyone will adore you and shower you with yams and apples and kisses, even though you smell like the five-day-old carcass of a kudu rotting in the blazing sun."

"Don't insult the poor dear!" Zephele says. "You'll erode his self-confidence!"

Max seems as indifferent to the insult as he is to the bit.

So Malora does as her father did before her—she drops one hand between Max's ears and with the other hand reaches into the back of his mouth, to a place seemingly meant for the bit, and persuades him to open his mouth. Max swallows the bit, chewing on it thoughtfully as if it were some new exotic delicacy. Malora fastens the harness beneath his chin.

"There," she says, tidying his flyblown forelock, "don't you look handsome!"

Max snorts, as if to say, *Let other horses be handsome. I know what's important. I have character.*

Zephele applauds, and Max looks over at her and nickers.

"I think he likes me!" Zephele says.

"Of course he likes you," Malora says drily. "*Everybody* likes you."

Malora attaches reins to the harness and leads Max around the pen. He seems bored but not uncooperative. They walk in different patterns. They start; they stop. They jog and circle first one way, and then the other. When, a while later, Malora takes off the bit, she rewards him with a cold baked yam, and then turns him out in the paddock with Butte and Light Rain, who trot over to listen to him tell all about this peculiar new game Malora is playing.

The next day, which is sunny and clear, Malora goes through the same steps with Light Rain. She is less sanguine about the bit, so Malora proceeds more slowly. When Light Rain resists the bit, Malora rubs Light Rain's mouth and lips to calm her. When Light Rain doesn't resist, Malora lets her be and returns later for repeated tries. Eventually, she is able to get Light Rain to take the bit into her mouth.

In the afternoon, Malora brings Max back into the ring,

attaches long reins to the bit, and walks behind him, approximating the position of the driver in the rig. She is careful to always let Max know that she is behind him and not some stalking leopard. She gives gentle tugs to the reins to direct him left or right. She cues a start by raising both reins into the air, and a stop by hauling back gently and dropping the reins. She adds the words "Get up!" to the start cue and "Whoa now!" to the stop, and after many repetitions, he can stop and go on the words alone. He does all this without complaint, although the look on his face is one of pity that she would want to pursue such absurd amusements.

The following morning, she works with Butte and Light Rain in spite of a steadily falling rain. And in the afternoon, she puts Max into the full-body harness after rubbing him all over with it to make sure he doesn't mind the feel of it against his back and belly. Jayke had a term for this process: *sacking out*. Then, still walking behind the fully harnessed Max, she drives him around the ring, letting him get used to the weight of the harness and the jingling sound.

The following day, the rain having stopped, Malora wheels the rig itself into the ring, where Max stands in harness.

"What now?" his long-suffering eyes ask. He comes over and sniffs the seat of the rig and noses the two long staves. He looks interested but not particularly impressed. She brings him to stand between the shafts. His ears go back slightly. She waits for his nervousness to subside, and then rewards him for his bravery with a juicy apple.

The next day, beneath a brilliant sun, she has West get between the staves and pull the cart along behind the horse, following wherever Malora leads Max. "I know this looks foolish, but it will get Max used to having the cart follow him. Otherwise, he might think it's chasing him and panic the way Shadow did. But Max is smarter than she is, aren't you?"

Max blows out and bobs his head in reluctant agreement.

"Okay, West. You come up here and take my place. Hold Max's head and comfort him if necessary," she says.

"Comfort *him*?" West says, coming around. "I'm the one who needs the comforting, boss."

Malora goes behind Max and quietly hitches the staves of the cart to Max's belly harness on either side. Then Malora directs West to lead Max around the ring, pulling the cart while Malora walks alongside and watches his reaction. Max seems unexcited, so at the next halt, Malora eases herself into the seat and takes up the reins.

"Zephele," Malora says in a calm voice. "Open the gate for us, would you?"

Zephele does this. "Good luck!" she calls out softly as West escorts Max out of the ring.

"Do you need me to stay at his head, boss?" West calls back.

"I think we'll be okay. Won't we, Maxie, old boy?" Max's ears twitch, and he chews the bit.

"He looks remarkably contented to me," West says as he backs off.

"Away we go then!" Malora raises the reins slightly and says, "Get up!"

With these two simple words, Max sheds a dozen years and becomes a young horse again. His ears perk, his head lifts, his chest puffs out, and off he launches into a sprightly trot. Max is, as he has been in the ring, wonderfully responsive to the reins. Malora has only to squeeze a rein ever so lightly in one hand for him to turn in that direction. She squeezes the right rein and he heads down the path toward the Upper Neelah's western bank. Here, she has been told, a trail runs northward along the river. The trail is worn flat by the horses pulling the barges. She tests Max's stop, pulling back on the reins with a "Whoa now," and he comes down to a walk and, from there, to an easy halt. He looks back at her as if to say, "Satisfied?"

"Very good, Max. Shall we have a little run?"

Max tosses his sparse mane and paws his hoof at the dirt.

The river runs straight and the way is clear, so she snaps the reins and says, "Get up!" This time, Max lunges right into a smooth gallop. It is as if he knows that a canter will be uncomfortable for both of them. If anything, he is faster pulling the rig than he would be with her on his back. Perhaps, Malora thinks, not having the weight directly on his aging frame frees up his hips to power him forward. All she knows is that the countryside flies by in a soft, fragrant blur, green on one side, blue on the other, as they race along the riverbank.

When they have run for a good while, she decides it is time to test his stop from a gallop. "Whoa now!" she says, settling down on the rig seat and pulling back gently on the reins. Smoothly, he comes down to a trot, and from a trot to a walk, and then rocks to a halt.

"That was impressive, old man," Malora says, breathless from the ride.

Max snorts as if to say, "That? That was nothing!"

Malora climbs down from the rig, pulls up a big handful of clover, and comes around to feed it to him. While he chews with his brown crooked teeth, she checks out the fit of the halter. She doesn't like the way the leather strap rubs him across his nose. Beneath his fur, the flesh is already pink and turning red. Max's aging skin is even more sensitive than that of the younger horses. With her knife, she saws off a piece of her wrap and winds it around the leather to offer Max a buffer. She will ask Cylas Longshanks to make a lambs' wool covering for the harness.

Malora takes a deep breath and blows out. Max does the same, and adds a stomp of his hooves. The harness jingles. She feels her nervousness about the race dissipating. There is lots more work to do, of course. She will have to pace out the Hippodrome and create a mock track, as Anders Thunderheart has done. She will have to work with Max to make sure he maintains his balance on the turns. She will harness up Butte and run races between Max and Butte. Racing Max against the other horse will increase Max's speed because he will not want to lose to an arrogant young stud like Butte. She will have to remember to ask Neal to get her one of the many-tailed horse whips so she can unleash it gently and let it slither over Max's hide to get him used to the feel of it, then crack it in his ears to get him used to the sound of it. And she will have to train West to wield the mighty power of Max while keeping the reins out of the horse's mouth.

Yes, there is a great deal to do and little time in which to do it, but it is all more than possible because Max is an honest horse and a willing one. Why, even now, having run full out, he looks eager to run again.

She is just climbing back into the rig when she sees it, a short distance away from the river. It is a high, crumbling stone wall rising up in the middle of a field of wildflowers. At first, she thinks it might be the ruin of some ancient stone edifice, but then she looks closer and sees the still-vivid mural painted on one side.

"Get up!" she says to Max, and they draw closer to pay their respects to the People who fell in the Massacre of Kamaria.

The paint is faded, but the composition is still intact. Malora sees a roiling pit of centaurs and People, rendered larger than life. Mount Kheiron, a simpler, less built-up version of it, is recognizable in the background, with flames leaping from it and human bodies tumbling down its sides. On the flats, most of the People are mounted on horseback and, in the tangle of human limbs and horse limbs, it is hard to tell one side from the other, except that the People, their mouths open in terror and agony, are wounded and bleeding, some sliding off the backs of their horses, others on the ground being trampled.

Off to the side, Malora finds one human, unhorsed, standing at the center of a circle of six centaurs. His arms are raised above his head, as if he were pleading for mercy, except that it is too late. Six spears transect his body at all angles, and his wounds spurt blood, covering the centaurs' chests in gore. He is a giant of a man, with powerful arms and chest, his dark red hair tied back in a horse tail.

"Grandfather," Malora whispers, tears of grief and pity swamping her. "I'm so sorry."

CHAPTER 29

Gremlins!

There are plans in the making to build Malora a cottage near the paddocks, but in the meantime, she sleeps in a tent she has pitched between the spring and the southwest corner of the paddock. Now that they are outside the city walls, she doesn't want to leave the horses alone. It isn't predators she fears as much as Flatlanders with an interest in seeing the Silvermane bid for the Golden Horse fail yet again. While Mather's banishment has placated many of the Flatlanders, Neal Featherhoof reports that there is still plenty of grumbling among them, along with plots to mount an outrage. It is this group of dissatisfied Flatlanders that Malora doesn't trust, and neither does Neal. The Peacekeepers patrol the area to keep an eye out for troublemakers. The Twanian wranglers, whom the Apex has authorized to carry crossbows, sleep at the other three corners of the paddock.

Orion is quick to assure Malora that this is the way it

always is. "A great deal more brawling and horse thieving and prank playing goes on leading up to the race."

They are sitting together at a camp table near the tent, where West has laid out a simple evening meal: bread and cheese and nuts and fruit.

"Aren't brawling and thieving in violation of the Edicts?" Malora asks.

"Yes and no," Orion says. "Often the brawling and thieving take place between Flatlander barns, or between the wranglers of Highlander barns and Flatlander. In any case, the Apexes have turned a blind eye to it and understand that a certain generally harmless elevation of spirits comes with the Founders' Day fest."

"I wouldn't want any of my horses to get hurt during this harmless display of high spirits," Malora says.

"Which is precisely why the Apex has permitted your Twani to be armed," Orion says.

"Against predators wandered in from the bush, so he says."

Orion smiles wryly. "Haven't you always said that to a horse, almost anything is a predator?"

"True."

"Do you have everything you need?" Orion asks. "Do you need more Breath of the Bush, or have you stopped using it since you took up hunting in the bush with Featherhoof?"

Malora cries out, "You *knew* I was hunting with Neal?"

"Who do you think suggested the outings to Neal in the first place?"

"You?" Malora says, utterly surprised.

Orion nods. "I sensed, after the Apex turned you down, that you were in need of a recreational outlet."

"Did Honus know about this?"

He hides a smile, but Malora catches it. "Absolutely," he says. "He didn't approve, mind you. He seems to think you are some sort of delicate national treasure that needs to be wrapped in wool batting."

"And you two just sat smugly by and let me make up all those falsehoods about my visits to the studios? And what about all the poems I memorized to distract Honus?"

"We found your cover stories highly amusing. And Honus would never discourage the memorization of great poetry." Orion's smile widens and gradually gets the better of her irritation. "So, tell me, do you require more Breath of the Bush, or does the wrangler in chief require an uncompromised nose?" he asks.

Malora shakes her head ruefully. "Uncompromised. But I have to say that I will miss the visions."

Orion tilts his head. "I beg your pardon?"

"You know—the visions and dreams that come from inhaling the scent," she says.

The color has drained from his face. "No, I don't know. Why don't you tell me?"

Malora says hesitantly, "That is the purpose of alchemy, as I understood it from you: to alter moods, to set tones, to bring about transformations. Breath of the Bush has transformed me to a radical degree."

"Go on, please."

Malora takes a deep breath. "The first vision I had was when I crept into Mather's tent that first night. I was hungry and thirsty, and I sniffed his scent flask and saw him and Canda Blackmane standing in a field of flowers. Then, when you let me sniff your own scent cloth that day in the bush, I saw Honus's bedchamber, days before I ever set foot in it—every detail, right down to my rope hanging on a hook on the wall."

"You can't mean this." The look of utter astonishment on his face gives her momentary pause.

But Malora goes on. "Breath of the Bush has given me the most vivid nightly visions of riding Sky. It was Sky, on one of these rides, who warned me that the boys and girls were in danger, but I was too thickheaded to understand."

He stares at her, his face still ashen. "Is that all?"

"Let's see . . . not quite." She exhales. "There was a very disturbing vision I had one morning in your tent when I sniffed from the little bottle on your camp table."

"Orion's Heart," he says, his voice faint.

"I saw you and Theon . . . but you were much younger bucks, and you were playing a game with small, smooth black and white stones."

"It's called Go," he says helpfully.

"You were playing Go, when suddenly, this burly, black-haired centaur with black flanks barged in and yelled at you. I couldn't hear what he was saying, but he wrapped his big hands around your throat—"

"And strangled me until I lost consciousness," Orion says in a flat voice. "He did that whenever I had the temerity to stand up to him."

"*He?*" she asks.

He heaves a sigh. "My departed brother, Athen. He was

a ruthless bully." His eyes have taken on a vague, unfocused look. "He was most abusive to my brother and me, but my parents wouldn't hear a word against him. He was the first-born and he could do no wrong in their eyes." Orion shakes his head, his gaze returning to her face. "You saw all of this simply by inhaling Orion's Heart?"

Malora feels an odd impulse to apologize. "I thought that's how scents worked for everyone."

"Not quite," he says carefully.

"Oh."

"It would seem that I don't fully understand the power of my own Hand on the human psyche," Orion says, a smile beginning to play on his lips.

When Orion takes his leave of her not long afterward, he seems more distracted than she's ever seen him. Malora wonders why she didn't also tell him about Lume, the vision she saw under the influence of gaffey. But Orion had nothing to do with that, she thinks, and the knowledge of Lume is not something she is ready to share with anyone—even as good a friend as Orion.

Several days later, the horses droop and begin to excrete thundering cascades of brown water. At first, Malora thinks they have all been felled by the same malady. In the Settlement, when all the horses in the stable took sick at once, Jayke used to say that gremlins were in the feed bin, which meant that bird or mouse droppings or insect larvae had somehow gotten mixed in with the feed, sickening the horses. Malora combs her hands through the feed, which she is always careful to keep covered, and sees nothing to indicate any foreign objects. Just to be sure, she eats some of the feed herself. By midday, her stomach is cramping and she is showing the same symptoms as the horses.

Bent double and helpless, Malora sends Neal out to the bush to find the plant Thora recommended for binding the bowels. She is too overcome by suffering to remember the name of it, but between spasms she describes the plant as best she can. Neal returns with three different plants—roots and all. She points to the one she needs and instructs West to boil the roots and leaves and mix them with charcoal and water. She serves the healing tea to the horses first, and then herself. By nightfall, they are much improved.

Malora stays up all that night, crouched in the bushes near the feed, and early in the morning, she sees one of the wranglers sprinkling something into the bin. She pounces on him and threatens to make him eat the tainted feed himself. He confesses that he has been bribed by the manager of one of the Flatlander stables to do anything in his power to interfere with the training. She sends him back to the manager with a warning that if they interfere again, she will retaliate with the "terrible ancient power of the People."

"What is the terrible ancient power of the People?" West asks eagerly.

"I will kick their Longmane asses all the way to Kahiro," Malora says, biting back a smile.

"Terrible, indeed, boss," West agrees.

During a trial race in the mock Hippodrome that day, Butte begins to buck in the harness. West panics and starts sawing the reins. Malora calmly climbs down from the seat of Max's rig and approaches Butte's head. After some gentling, Malora finds stinging nettles under the fleece covering of the harness. Malora never finds out who the culprit is, but from then on, she puts an armed Twani on guard to watch the tack, the horses, and the feed, night and day.

From the long, low tent where the wranglers prepare their horses for the race, Malora has an excellent view of the track. The Hippodrome is a banked, oval-shaped track that is set into a natural bowl in the countryside in the southeast shadow of the mountain. Spectators are gathered on the hillsides overlooking the track's two longer stretches. The northern hillside, slightly higher than the southern, is fittingly where the Highlanders are camped out. For many of them, Malora is told, this is the one time of year when they venture down off the mountain. The Flatlanders occupy the lower hillside. They are feasting and dancing and playing catch with small disks that sail through the air like flat, spinning birds.

The Highlanders' side is more sedate and less jolly. She can see the familiar blue and white of the Apex's big tent halfway up the hill, and she can just make out Medon, resplendent in bright blue, and Herself in white with a blue cap streaming with ribbons. They are reclining in front of their tent on a great, blue-cushioned bench. Nearby, Zephele, Theon, and Honus stand side by side. Honus is scanning the scene through the antique mother-of-pearl opera glasses he purchased in Kahiro. Where is Orion?

The shorter hillside opposite the horse tent is given over to a fairground, with brightly draped stands for food vendors and hawkers of wares. Race day is Founders' Day, an annual fest in commemoration of the settlement of the centaurs on Mount Kheiron—or Mount Kamaria, as the People called it before the centaurs slaughtered them. As Malora looks out on the brightly festooned hillsides and the reveling centaurs, she tries not to think about what happened to the Grandparents on this day so long ago. Ever since she set eyes on the memorial, she has carried a picture in her mind of the man stuck all over with spears. Instead, she tries to think about the race, and about how Max is as ready as he will ever be.

And where is West? It has been some time since she sent him off to the fairgrounds to get something to eat. He was too nervous to eat anything this morning, and Malora scolded him. He can no more race on an empty stomach than Max can. She herself has eaten two bowls of mush with three kinds of berries and extra honey. Breakfast is still the best meal in Mount Kheiron.

The Grand Provost, an officious centaur with tightly curled henna locks and a braided beard, jogs along the row of stalls, five Flatlander and five Highlander, stopping to check on each team.

"Are you sure he is up to it?" he asks when he comes to the Silvermane stall. He stares dubiously at Max.

"Just you wait and see," Malora tells him.

In the next stall over, Malora hears Anders Thunderheart as he tries to keep his high-strung Athabanshee from leaping out onto the track in advance of the starting horn. Every time the mare shrieks, Max swivels his head toward Malora as if to ask, "Is this really necessary?"

She hears Anders muttering under his breath, "I have a good mind to lend her one of my own horses. She mocks us running such a forsaken creature. But does the Provost listen? I'm surprised the Apex is standing for this. He has been shamed by defeat in the past. But this old nag will drag the House of Silvermane through the dust of a more bitter defeat than ever he imagined in his worst nightmares."

Malora whispers in Max's ear, "Don't listen to him. He's just envious."

Max might get the general drift, but he doesn't look as if he cares. All around them, horses are snorting and stomping and screaming and straining against their leads, raring to race, while Max stands with his nose brushing the ground, looking as if he wants to fold up his spindly legs and have a little lie-down rather than run a nine-lap race at the speed of wind.

"Malora!"

She looks up to find Orion standing before her with West's body draped over his arms. West's head hangs down, and his tongue protrudes. "What happened?" she asks.

"He must have eaten something tainted," Orion says. "I gave him a physic. He'll be all right, but he's in no shape for driving a rig."

"What will we do now?" Malora says. Max lifts his head and twitches an ear, looking vaguely concerned.

Orion, who seems suspiciously unperturbed by the situation, says, "I've spoken to the Provost and to the other stable owners. They say they will approve your driving the rig. I think the general feeling is that there is so little likelihood of Max even placing that it is a matter of no consequence."

West stirs in Orion's arms. "I must race for the Golden Horse!" he says in a voice that quavers.

"There, there, old fellow. Rest yourself and take it easy," Orion says.

"But the race! Everyone's counting on me."

"Don't worry," Malora tells him. "I'll run it for you."

Orion lays West on a bale of hay. Malora wets a cloth in a water bucket and places it over West's forehead. She kneels beside him.

"I'm sorry, boss," he says. "Your pussemboo has let you down. It was the fruit cup. Honus always says, 'Stay away from the fruit cup,' and it's my own fault for ignoring his advice."

"Don't fret," she says soothingly. "It's only a race."

"Oh, but it's not," West protests weakly. "It's so much more than that."

"What is it, then?" Malora asks.

But West seems to have passed out.

"I have something for you," Orion says.

Malora looks up.

Orion is holding a small red crystal vial.

"What is it?" she asks.

"I call it Victory! It's a little something I have been working on in my distillery since the night we spoke."

She eyes it warily. "I don't need a scent to run a race."

Orion presses it into her hand. "Tuck it into the top of your wrap, just in case. Please," he adds, his blue eyes so intense, she has no choice. She tucks the red vial of scent into her wrap.

"Well, good luck to you both," Orion says, backing out of the stall.

"Thanks." Malora smiles. Her heart, she realizes, has already begun to race.

Max lifts his tail and lets off a huge gust of wind, followed by an avalanche of runny droppings.

CHAPTER 30

The Golden Horse

Tradition calls for all ten of the drivers and rigs to make a full circuit of the track at a trot to greet the fans and spectators on both hillsides. They are to enter the track from the tent when the Grand Provost, speaking through a big silver trumpet, announces the name of the stable and the horse. The Apex's stable and horse are, according to tradition, called last.

Malora watches as Flatlander and Highlander horses and drivers are called out in alternating order. Each time the rope is dropped, the horses spring forward as if a slingshot has released them. The overpowering roar of the crowds greeting the Flatlander teams completely drowns out the thin, reedy cheers sent up by the Highlanders.

Sitting on her rig, Malora waits for the nervous wrangler to unhitch the rope. She watches Max's ears twitch this way and that, following the crowd's roar. Her heart is pounding with excitement. Above all else, she feels a sense of wonder that there can be all this fuss and excitement about a race that will be over in less time than it takes to visit the marble convenience.

"Silvermane Stable!" The Grand Provost sends forth the call. The Twan waits to hear Max's name being called. When seconds have elapsed, Malora calls to the confused Twan, "Never mind! Who cares? Let us out of here!" The Twan releases the rope. On his hay bale, West sits up. "Run for your life!" he says, then collapses again.

Malora takes up the reins and says, "Get up!" Max rouses himself with a startled snort and trots out into the Hippodrome.

The Flatlanders, and most of the Highlanders, greet them with such a loud and rowdy booing that Malora very nearly turns the rig around and leaves the track. But then she catches sight of Zephele and Orion on the hillside. They are waving and jumping and jubilating in place. How can I let them down? Malora thinks. After that, it doesn't bother her as much as it should when objects begin to rain down upon them from both sides, mostly rotten fruit and vegetables.

Perhaps there is something about having used their own meager nubs to place wagers on today's race that drives the Flatlanders so wild. According to what Theon says, today is the only day of the year when centaurs are permitted to gamble. The odds are against Max even placing. Max will never be able to hear her over the din, so she sends a message to him through her steady hands on the reins as he trots proudly around the oval: *We will show them. We will show them all what a magnificent animal you really are.*

Someone on the Flatlander side of the track flings a large rock. It lands on the turf with an ugly thud, just missing Max's head. Max shies and pulls up short. Malora looks over to the hillside to see who has thrown the rock. She spies a commotion in the crowd and watches as Neal drags off a buck by the wrap and pounds him about the head and shoulders with his clenched fist.

Malora twitches the reins. Hesitantly, Max starts up again, this time at a more wary pace. A brigade of Twani swarms out onto the track to pick up the garbage that has been thrown. The horses assemble in a line behind the red starting ribbon. Max is in the very outside lane, which means he will run farther than the horses closer to the inside track. She has debated with herself about this and decided that they will let the other horses battle over the inside track while she and Max will dawdle on the outside. When the other contestants have exhausted each other, she and Max will move to the inside rail for the final laps.

Over the nearly deafening din, the Grand Provost's voice booms out through his trumpet, explaining the rules to drivers who already know them and spectators who do not care. There are nine laps, and using the whips on the backs of competing horses or drivers is illegal. The Grand Provost lowers his trumpet and raises the starting horn. He puts the horn to his lips. The horn blasts, and the horses burst through the tape. They are off and running!

All except Max, who stands on the turf as still as a statue of a very old and world-weary horse.

"Get up!" Malora says, lifting the reins.

Max stands there switching his tail. The other horses are barreling down the long side and rounding the first bend.

"Get up!" Malora snaps the reins smartly. Max yawns and

paws his hoof as if planting himself deeper in the turf, perhaps never to move again. The spectators start to snicker. She sees the Apex up on the hillside rise to his feet and hears him bellowing above the jeers, "You call yourself a champion? Get up and run, you useless old nag!"

Malora breaks out in a clammy sweat. It's obvious to her that the rock has discouraged Max. Max wants no part of a race where rocks fly through the air. Then she gets an idea. She takes the vial of Victory that Orion gave her from her wrap and pulls out the stopper. It smells minty, like a splash of cold water on her face. She puts it to her nostril and inhales deeply. A picture forms clearly in her mind, so compelling that she hears herself scream at the top of her voice, *"Elephants!"*

Malora looks behind her and sees a herd of elephants, their ears fanning, their tusks lowered, their feet thundering and churning up the dirt of the track. Max's ears stand on end. He springs to life and bounds off. Before she has even resettled herself in the seat, they are overtaking the hindmost runner. She replugs the vial and takes a firm hold of the reins, pinching the outer rein to keep Max balanced and upright on the two steep curves they are rounding. They overtake two rigs on the curve, both of them banking dangerously toward the fence. Ahead of her on the straight, whips crack and Twani bawl at their horses to run faster, faster. But Max, feeling the breath of elephants on his back, is running for his life and overtaking the other rigs, one after another.

The crowds on both sides leap to their feet, roaring and cheering and waving their arms. Max rounds another bend. A whip cracks in Malora's ear, and she sees the tail of the whip skim Max's back. Max doesn't even seem to feel it. She moves even with the rig and waits for the Twan to lift the whip again. When he does, she reaches out with one hand and catches it, wraps it around her forearm, and yanks it away from the driver. The Twan pitches headfirst over the front of his rig. His legs are in the air, scrambling and kicking. The unmanned chariot swerves, barely missing a collision with the next rig over. The driver rights himself and regains his stance, but he is now hopelessly far behind. Meanwhile, Malora flings the whip aside and resumes the race, as more boos and even more cheers greet her.

Round and round the track they fly, Max's hooves sending bits of turf spraying in all directions. Max runs so fast that Malora can no longer tell who is in front of them and who is behind. Up ahead, the whip of one Twan gets entangled in the wheel of another rig. Both rigs spin out of control and then right themselves, losing their momentum as Max and Malora streak past. Then Anders's Athabanshee crashes through the inside rail and into the center of the oval, where it lies down to rest. Another rig takes over the inside track, but Malora decides to stay on the outside, where the way is clear.

When Max starts to flag, Malora unstops the vial and takes another small sniff of Victory. The trumpeting elephants renew their charge! Max sprints so fast, Malora sees nothing but the blur of the track between his ears. She cannot distinguish the roaring of the crowds from the trumpeting of the elephants and the howling of the wind in her ears and the beating of her heart. She smells a looming thunderstorm and, from behind her, feels strong arms encircling her.

In a deep voice she knows belongs to him, Lume whispers in her ear: "Victory is yours, Malora! Well run."

Then a lone figure appears on the turf up ahead. It is West. He is waving the blue-and-white pennant of the Silvermane Stable. "You can stop now!" he shouts.

Malora heaves a deep breath and lets it out, willing the wall of elephants to turn around and go away. "Whoa now!"

Max slows and rocks to a halt next to West. The horse is panting and wheezing.

"Good job, Max!" West says, rubbing him ever so gently on the nose. "I've brought you a treat, but I reckon you should wait until you catch your breath and cool down before you eat this sweet radish."

Max, having other ideas, helps himself to the radish, smacks his lips, and nudges West with his nose for more.

Malora hears the crowd chanting. It is the persistent three-beat song of the ring-necked dove, only amplified many thousands of times over.

"Ma-lo-ra! Ma-lo-ra!" the crowds chant.

Malora says, "They shouldn't be cheering me! They should be cheering Max."

"I'm sure they would, but as the Provost did not announce his name, they don't know it and it wouldn't do for them to cheer 'Useless Old Nag,' would it?" West says with a wink.

Zephele trots toward them across the turf, bearing a garland of flowers that she flings over Max's neck.

"You old *darling*!" she cries, hugging Max and smothering him with kisses.

"Didn't I tell you you'd get kisses?" Malora says to Max.

Zephele turns to Malora. "Do you realize that you and Max ran *thirteen* laps to everyone else's nine and you *still* won! Max has broken every record there is!"

Malora is in the tent sponging Max down with warm spirits of spearmint when Orion finds her. "You did it, Malora! You really did it!"

"*We* did it," she says, holding up the little red vial.

His eyes widen. "You used the distillation? I wasn't sure."

"I had to. Max wouldn't move after that Flatlander pitched the rock on the track."

"Can I ask how this particular vision manifested itself?"

"As a wall of murderously angry elephants."

"Remarkable!" His eyes shine.

"Poor Max. I don't know whether he shared my vision or my fear, but it worked."

"I'm glad I was able to help."

"Did you also help with West's little attack?" she asks, arching a brow.

Orion folds his arms across his chest and recites: "The lavender fever berry's bark, when pulverized, is a stomach purgative."

"You remembered!"

"I remember everything you've ever said to me."

"But poor West. You ill-used him."

"Oh, he was always a reluctant driver. He was willing to do it to please you, but I think he was quite happy to be left on the sidelines. Are you crying, Malora?"

"It's the spirits of spearmint. See? Max is crying, too."

Max's big brown eyes are as red and watery as they ever

are. As for Malora, Orion is right. It isn't just the spearmint. She is overcome with emotion.

"I hope they are tears of joy," Orion says. "You did exactly what you set out to do. You worked hard. And you succeeded admirably, against great odds. And for your trouble, the Apex has requested your presence at the very center of everyone's attention, where I know you are least happy. But this is the price of your success."

"The Apex doesn't need me," Malora says. "He has his Golden Horse at last."

"But without you and Max, the jubilation is incomplete."

Malora looks back at Max. "Did you hear that, Max? We have been summoned."

Max continues to munch his hay and let off great gusts of gas. With a resigned sigh, Malora takes a blanket and dries off Max's coat, ties on a halter, and attaches Jayke's rope to it. "Grab some of that hay, will you?" she says to Orion. He scoops up an armload of hay and follows her out of the tent.

The crowds have spilled down from the hillsides onto the track, where they have gathered around the flatbed lorry parked in the center of the Hippodrome. Standing on the lorry are the Apex and Herself, Zephele and Theon and Honus and Ash and West and Sunshine, along with every last house Twan and Silvermane cousin. Surrounding the lorry stands the Peacekeeping Force, arms linked to keep the crowds at bay. Over the heads of the crowd, Neal Featherhoof sees Malora and Orion. He eases himself out of the chain and elbows his way toward them.

"Good work, you two!" he calls out to Malora and Max.

"Us *three*, you mean," Malora says, indicating Orion.

"I think we all had a hand in the victory today," Orion says. "Featherhoof, glad to see you giving that rock thrower his just deserts. You have my heartfelt thanks."

"At your service, Silvermane," Neal says with a grin.

"That will be the day." Orion returns the grin.

"Make way!" Neal shouts, clearing a path for them to the lorry. "Make way for the victors!"

The crowd parts before them and then resurges around them. Malora feels hands—Flatlander and Highlander—reaching out to touch her arms and tug gently at her braid. The centaurs, more reticent about touching Max, pull back to stare in a kind of horrified fascination at the wonder horse with the scarred hide and jutting bones. Up ahead, the Apex cradles the Golden Horse in one arm and beckons to Malora with the other. Malora marches up the wooden ramp, Max behind her. As she passes Honus, he reaches out and catches her arm. "You are the *one*!" he says.

Theon grins. "I placed my nubs on you, and now I am a rich buck!"

Zephele, weeping with happiness, throws her arms around Malora. "Oh! I'm so proud of you and dear, darling Max!"

The Lady Hylonome takes Malora by the shoulders and hugs her hard, then kisses her on both cheeks and the forehead. "Thank you, Daughter," she whispers in a voice choked with emotion.

Daughter of the Plains, Malora thinks. And now Daughter of the Centaurs.

Malora approaches the Apex. His right hand, with the Ever-Watchful Eye tattooed on the palm, passes over his heart and then rises. She touches her own heart and raises her hand, and a hush falls over the crowd. She looks up into his face and sees tears swimming in his fierce gray eyes. And she finds herself doing what she has wanted to do since she first saw him. She reaches up and, with her thumb, neatens his errant gray eyebrows, as if she were straightening the unruly forelock of a horse. This gesture makes his tears fall, and hers soon follow. She turns away from him and looks out through the dazzling lens of her tears to see the vast expanse of centaurs, filling the track and running up the hillsides, all of them looking up at her with proud eagerness in their eyes.

Orion kneels before Max and sets down the hay beneath his nose like an offering. Max resumes munching. The centaurs erupt in cheers of approval. Max rolls an eye toward them. *It's only hay. I'm only a horse,* his look says. *What is all this excitement about?*

"Centaurs of Kheiron, hear me!" The Apex's magisterial voice rings out, silencing the throng. "I stand before you today, like you, in awe of our victorious horse and driver."

The crowd bursts into applause.

The Apex continues, "Never, in the many years since these races have been run, has there been such an overwhelming victory won by a horse and a driver, much less by a horse as humble and unassuming as this one, and by a driver who is an Otherian and, of all things, one of the People. And that, my fellow centaurs, is what we are really celebrating today— the simple miracle of the human being among us, a miracle that I will confess, when I first beheld it, filled me with a sense of unease and fear. But I submit to you that it is no accident that she has come among us, she who is descended from the fugitives of Kamaria. No, it is no accident. It is, my fellow citizens of hill and plain, a sign. It is a sign that the time has come for us to be not two groups of centaurs, but one group united beneath the Hand. Many years ago, Kheiron preached tolerance and forgiveness and kindness. Today, I listened in wonder as you, the centaurs of Kheiron—Highlanders and Flatlanders—set aside your differences and your grudges and lifted your voices as one to cheer for Malora Ironbound and her noble steed."

Malora looks over to see if this compliment has registered on Max, only to realize that the noble steed has fallen fast asleep with his nose in the hay. Bits of straw poke out of the sides of his mouth, and a single fly, having discovered his whereabouts, buzzes around the only part of him that shows a vestige of life, his ears.

The Apex's voice rumbles on, gaining steadily like an approaching thunderstorm. "You have demonstrated today that you are not two, divided by a city wall, but one. And it is for this reason that—much as I have, perhaps weakly and vaingloriously, coveted it for so many years that I have ceased to count them—I cannot accept this Golden Horse."

The crowd moans in disbelief.

"No, this Golden Horse does not belong to me," the Apex says. "It belongs to you, the centaurs of Kheiron, Highlanders and Flatlanders. And I pledge to you that I will install this Golden Horse in a place of honor above the wide-open gates as a symbol of our oneness, as a symbol of the living spirit of Kheiron among us, as a reminder that we, the centaurs, have been forgiven our past transgressions by the spirit of the People through their lone surviving descendant,

Malora Ironbound. Let us mingle and feast this night to celebrate she who has brought us together, her fleet-footed horse, and our newly forged unity!"

Over the crescendo of cheering, he roars: *"By the Hand! We stand! Together!"* His hand rises, palm out, and everyone else brings his or hers up in the air to meet it.

Malora switches Jayke's rope to her left hand so she can join in. And then the rope slips from her grip as centaur hands reach for her and pull her onto their shoulders, passing her over the crowd as if she, and not the Golden Horse, were the trophy that they shared. And with a sudden surge of joy, Malora realizes that she is at home, at last, among the centaurs.

The Edicts of Kheiron

1. Centaurs shall live their lives in imitation of Kheiron the Wise.
2. Centaurs shall choose from amongst themselves a ruler, the Apex, the first among equals.
3. Unless authorized by the Apex, no centaur shall own, carry, or wield weapons of any kind.
4. No centaur shall eat the flesh of any living thing, be it fish, fowl, or game.
5. No centaur shall kill any living thing.
6. No centaur shall imbibe or partake of spirits or stimulants.
7. Centaurs shall be modestly clad.
8. No centaurs shall argue or brawl in a public place.
9. No centaur shall steal, tell a falsehood, or bear false witness against another centaur or Otherian.
10. No centaur shall lie with the mate of another.
11. At age twelve, all centaurs shall take up and cultivate a Hand.
12. All centaurs shall learn to read and write.

13. Any centaur who does not abide by the Edicts shall be turned out from the society of other centaurs.
14. In order to ensure domestic and universal peace, no centaur shall take up arms, or aggress in any fashion, against another centaur or an Otherian.

Cast of Characters

Denizens of the Settlement
Malora Thora-Jayke: last of the People.
Thora: Malora's mother
Jayke: Malora's father
Aron: half-wit stable boy and Malora's best friend
Felise: potter
Betts: basket weaver

Denizens of Mount Kheiron
Centaurs
Kheiron the Wise: patron and founder of Mount Kheiron
Medon Silvermane: Apex of Mount Kheiron
Lady Hylonome Silvermane: wife of Medon
Theon Silvermane: eldest living son of the Apex and Hylonome
Orion Silvermane: middle son of the Apex and Hylonome
Zephele Silvermane: only daughter of the Apex and Hylonome
Silvermane cousins: Mather, Devan, Brandle, March, Felton, Marsh, Elmon, Brea

Cylas Longshanks: master cobbler
Neal Featherhoof: captain of the Peacekeepers
Canda Blackmane: Mather's love interest
Gastin: upstart Flatlander
Brion Swiftstride: blacksmith
Anders Thunderheart: owner of the Thunderheart Stable

Otherians
Malora Ironbound: Orion's name for Malora when she comes
  among the centaurs
Honus: faun (half-goat, half-human hibe); Medon's pet and
  tutor of the Silvermane children and Malora

Twani
West: Orion's servant
Gift: Apex's wrangler in chief
Sunshine: Zephele's servant
Lemon: guardian of the back door of the House of Silver-
  mane
Rain: guardian of the back door of the House of Silvermane
Ash: Apex's servant

Ironbound Furies
Sky
Shadow
Coal
Lightning
Silky
Raven

Blacky
Posy
Charcoal
Ember
Smoke
Fancy
Streak
Stormy

Rescued Horses
Oil
Flame
Ivory
Star
Butte
Sassy
Thunder
Cloud
Light Rain
Beast
Mist
Max

Athabanshees
Bolt

Glossary of Terms and Places

Apex: chosen leader of the centaurs, first among equals

Athabanshee: small, delicate breed of horse known for its speed, originating in the deserts of the Sha Haro

Beltanian: breed of sturdy draft horse

centaur: hybrid of human and horse

Edicts: founding laws of Mount Kheiron

Flatlanders: less-privileged centaurs born on the flatlands surrounding Mount Kheiron

Grandparents: ancestors of the People

Hand: centaurean trade; entails making things that can be seen, such as alchemical potions, paintings, tapestries, sculptures; or studying things that can't be seen, such as law, religion, philosophy

hibe: hybrid of two species, usually human combined with animal

Highlanders: more-privileged centaurs, born on Mount Kheiron

Hills of Melea: mountain range to the west of Mount Kheiron, where Kheiron the Wise was once said to have lived as a hermit

Ironbound Furies: name given by the centaurs to the breed of large black horses that run wild at the foot of the Ironbound Mountains

Ironbound Mountains: mountains to the south of Mount Kheiron

jubilation: centaurean celebration, usually involving a ritual dance wherein the males wield a staff

Kahiro: the port city and capitol of the Kingdom of the Ka, north of Mount Kheiron

Kamaria: name of the People's city on the site that is now Mount Kheiron

Leatherwings: hibe of bat and human that preys upon the Settlement

nubs: currency of Mount Kheiron

Otherian: centaurean term for any race that is neither centaur nor Twani

People: last pure-bred human beings on earth

recognition: ceremony officially conferring upon a centaur his or her Hand

River Neelah: consists of upper and lower segments; runs from the Ironbound Mountains in the south to Kahiro in the north

Salient: legislative body of Mount Kheiron, consisting of twelve centaurs elected from among the Highlanders

Scienticians: group of People, half mage and half scientist, who created the first hibes

Suideans: hibe of wild boar and human

Twani: hibe of cat and human that serves the centaurs